I have lived in rural  a
story about the pec al
village called Weat a
farming community of
living without high street shops, vanishing community
amenities and no local public transport. Over the years
I have observed rich and intriguing lives; happiness and
heart-ache; warmth and humour; success and romance
as well as failure and separation. Like any narrative
about people, there are moments when the darker side
of human nature presents itself; infighting, corruption,
contaminated fields, blackmail, a suspicious death, and
narcissistic behaviour. This rural anthropology has
inspired me to write a story that is hopefully intriguing,
at times humorous, at times sad, but most of all
entertaining.

For Kerry

My inspiration and much, much more

CHAPTER 1

Brian Townsend swallowed the last of his whisky, eased himself slowly off the bar stool, and headed for the door. Having had a few too many, and swaying slightly from side to side, it took him a while to put on his tweed shooting jacket and cap.

'Good night,' he mumbled to nobody in particular, and stepped out into the late October evening. It was a mild autumn night; a gentle breeze with a thick layer of broken cloud, and a patch of hazy light giving away the hiding place of the full moon as it tried to play hide and seek amongst the clouds. On the ground lay piles of damp autumn leaves. The finale to a disappointing summer.

The farmer crunched his way across the loose pebbles to his trusty Series III Land Rover. He very seldom washed the 4x4. With the constant mud and grime of the farm, he found it tedious and a waste of time. That afternoon, he had decided for some inexplicable reason to take his vehicle down to the local superstore and get it jet washed. With the help of a gang of Poles, it took less than half an hour to discover that the vehicle did have windows and was painted blue.

He thanked the modern-day migrant labourers, and drove away wondering if he should leave the name of the farm and a telephone number with them. Why would I do that he thought to himself? I have nothing to offer them. They probably have more to offer me.

Washing the Land Rover was not the only unusual thing he had done recently. He had felt extremely bored of late, and found himself doing things around the house for no apparent reason. He hadn't woken up on any particular morning, and thought, I really should tidy my cupboards or wash all the bed-linen. He just found himself doing it. He felt disconnected from the person doing these chores. He was watching himself do it, but could not stop what was happening.

Turning right on leaving the Green Man, Brian headed back towards the village and the farm. A journey he had done more times than he could remember. At the Church, that had witnessed the life milestones of four generations of Townsends, he turned right and headed out of Weatherford.

400 yards beyond a newly completed housing development, he turned into the gate of Grey Pigeon Farm. A dark driveway with overhanging branches, leading to a thatched roof farmhouse in need of repair. He stopped his Land Rover, and sat in the dark looking at the farmhouse.

In the gloom a wave of utter despair came over him. It was like the cloud he could see out of the windscreen; grey and oppressive. There had been months of low cloud, and he couldn't remember when he had last seen the sun. Where for God's sake has the bloody sun gone, he thought.

His hopes and dreams for the farm, for his wife Sarah, for his daughter Hanna -all gone. Nothing left; except failure. In the pub tonight, he had been surrounded by successful people; successful farmers with record harvests; successful London barristers with criminals behind bars; successful engineers designing electric cars; everywhere he had looked tonight - success, success and more success. No failures - except himself.

He felt numb from the hopelessness of his situation. He watched himself get out of the Land Rover and walk back up the drive to the road. Opposite the farm gate was a large 'Hands off Weatherford' sign. He crossed over the road and stood staring at it for a moment. He then watched himself pulling and ripping the sign off its flimsy wooden frame. He frantically bent the sign and stamped on it until it was in small pieces and tossed them over the hedgerow into the field beyond.

'My life's work ruined by the people of my village,' he muttered under his breath as spit drooled out of his mouth from the exertion. Breathing heavily he walked back to the farmhouse. He kept his cap and coat on, and went into the kitchen ducking his head slightly to get through the low door. Turning on the light he poured himself a drink and swallowed it in one large gulp. The whisky was cold; there was not the familiar warmth spreading through his body. He hesitated for a moment, and looked around at his damp and cold surroundings. He started to shiver; despite the cap, the coat and the whisky.

The farmer started opening the kitchen drawers looking for a piece of paper. He found a pen, and an old invoice. It was printed on one side of the page. Sitting down at the small kitchen table, he started to write. He was not sure what he was writing, but he knew the letter was for his daughter. When he had finished, he put the letter in the middle of the table and placed a half empty bottle of ketchup on it. He sat for a moment staring at the bottle. The wave of despair came flooding back. He didn't want to cry.

He didn't want to scream either. He knew he was a failure, and all he wanted was for the misery to end.

He watched himself move the ketchup bottle, fold the letter and put it in the left inside pocket of his wax jacket. He switched off the kitchen light, pulled the front door closed behind him and walked over to the garden shed next to the house and went in. He came out with a length of rope and a ladder, loaded them into the back of his vehicle, and then climbed into the driver's seat.

He drove back into the village, passed the Church and headed out along London Road. The countryside around Weatherford is gentle, undulating farm land. Brian had lived here all his life, and knew every inch of the village and its surroundings. He drove a mile down the road, and then turned into a narrow lane just wide enough for one vehicle. He carried on up the hill, and at the first passing place pulled over and stopped.

He took the rope and ladder out of the back of his 4x4. There was a ditch running between the road and the hedgerow, with a narrow bridge made of railway sleepers. He stopped halfway across, and looked down into the trench.

Many a battle had been fought and won here. As a young boy, he and three school friends from the village had spent many happy hours during the summer holidays defending the bridge against foreign invaders - mainly the French. Equipped with wooden swords made by their fathers, they courageously defended the crossing. The imaginary castle in the field behind them, never endured the embarrassment of a siege.

Their last battle involved the only cavalry charge in the long history of summer holiday campaigns. Interest in defending the bridge started to wain as the boys grew older. It might have had something to do with the fact that no girl in the village would volunteer to stand for hours in a farm field, waiting to be saved by five imaginary battle hardy knights of the realm.

The final battle, started with French archers raining arrows down on the defenders. The boys decided to hide under the bridge and wait for the volleys to stop. Tumbling into the ditch, they sheltered under the railway sleepers. All was fine until four young stomachs needed feeding, and a cool drink was required for parched throats. One of the friends suggested a cavalry charge. All four knights agreed.

Scrambling and pulling each other out of the ditch, the knights mounted their bicycles and peddled furiously towards the enemy lines. The combination of shouting, swords and charging cavalry routed the enemy, who turned on their heels and fled. The charge ended under the apple trees at Grey Pigeon Farm with ham, cheese and pickle sandwiches, and a jug of cool lemonade.

Anyone watching Brian would not have noticed the faintest of smiles as he looked up from the ditch, crossed over and squeezed himself and the ladder through a gap in the newly trimmed hedgerow. He stepped carefully over the split and severed branches lying on the ground, and continued on up the hill towards a copse of oak trees.

He walked slowly along the edge of the newly ploughed fields; a lonely silhouette of a dishevelled man, wearing a soiled shirt with a couple of buttons missing, corduroy trousers with fraying hems and long unkempt hair sticking out from under his cap. Shoulders hunched, as if all the worries of the world, were heaped upon them.

Reaching the copse, and without hesitating or looking around, he made his way towards an oak tree that was high enough for his purpose. He placed the ladder against one of the branches, climbed up, threw the rope over and secured it as tightly as he could. Measuring the correct length he took a folding hunting knife from his jacket pocket and cut the rope.

He climbed down the ladder, and looked up at the rope tied around the branch of the oak tree. His pulse started to race. All emotion drained from him, and his entire body started to tingle and go numb. He was standing next to himself again. He watched himself climb back up the ladder as the sunrise started to paint the sky a mixture of bright orange and red, and the crows, having woken, started their morbid cries of caw, caw.

Devoid of any emotion, he saw himself place the rope around his neck and turn his head slightly in the direction of his village and his life. He could see the top of the church steeple. It was the last thing he saw.

CHAPTER 2

Jessica Burns was slightly fed-up with herself for not getting up a bit earlier. The guns were arriving in an hour and a half, and breakfast was nowhere near ready. Her husband, Alistair, was sitting at the kitchen table mulling over the shoot guest list.

'Chloe! What are you doing?'

'Watching a movie on my iPad,' came the curt reply.

'Will you please put that bloody thing down, and start laying the tables.' The 15 year old daughter shuffled into the kitchen in her pyjamas and slippers, and put the kettle on.

'Chloe, there isn't time for that,' Jessica blurted out impatiently.

'Mum, I can't start the day without my coffee.' Jessica thought my coffee, *my coffee*! When did a cup of coffee become a human right's issue? With immense self-discipline, the irritated mother ignored the comment.

'Make yourself useful. Dad and I would like a cup of tea.'

'Do you want tea, Dad?' asked Chloe hoping to prove her mother wrong.

'Um, what, yeh, ok,' he answered. 'I was slightly disappointed that we only had ten guns today, but in actual fact it makes things easier with two groups of five.' Mother and daughter were not listening, and ignored the self-appointed head of the household.

Alistair got up from the table, went over to the kitchen window, and stood looking out across the ploughed fields while sipping his tea. Looks as if it's going to be another cloudy day with no rain he thought.

He had got up as usual that morning at sunrise, and the sky had been a beautiful orange and red colour. He often wondered if many people woke up earlier enough to see such a beautiful sight. The sun, now higher in the sky, was shining through a small gap in the clouds, and the rays of sunlight looked like the beam of a giant torch pointing down at something of importance on the ground.

The Burns family have lived at Oak Tree Farm for almost twenty five years, having moved in soon after Alistair finished agricultural college. He was somewhat of a pioneer, and on graduating had taken advantage of changing farm ownership that was taking place at the time.

Farms being handed down from generation to generation had started to change years ago. Sons and daughters, with new choices and a belief that there are infinite opportunities to have it all, now exchange a life of tractors and mud for the perceived glamour and excitement of sport science and media studies. The result of this demographic shift over the past couple of decades had seen an increase in large-scale corporate farming. Alistair Burns, employed by East Anglia Farms Ltd, was proof of this changed landscape.

'Hanna Townsend has posted a message on Facebook asking if anyone has seen her father recently. She hasn't been able to get hold of him,' said Chloe looking up from her iPhone. That's strange thought Alistair turning away from the window as two crows landed on the lawn, and were promptly chased away by Ant and Dec, the family's two cocker spaniels.

There was a knock at the door, and Chloe jumped up to answer it.

'Am I pleased to see you,' confessed Jessica as Yasmin Chowdhury appeared at the kitchen door.

Jessica gave her a small hug. 'Would you like a tea or coffee? Chloe has just boiled the kettle.'

'No thanks I had one just before I left home. Hello Alistair, keeping well?' Yasmin greeted the farmer, and kissed him lightly on both cheeks.

'Yes, very well. How is Samir? He is still coming to the shoot?'

'He wouldn't miss it for anything. Ok, what would you like me to do, Jess?'

'The bacon is in, and the croissants can go into the oven at half seven. The guns are arriving at eight. I think we should start buttering the rolls. Chloe can you please start laying the tables. Where is your brother?'

'TOM, MUM WANTS YOU!' shouted Chloe.

'For heaven's sake, Chloe, was that necessary,' reprimanded her mother. Chloe shrugged her shoulders, and pretended not to notice. Yasmin raised her eyebrows. A stampede of heavy thuds coming down the stairs announced the arrival of Chloe's twin brother Tom.

'What do you want Mum? Oh, hello Yasmin.'

'Please will you arrange the tables and chairs as we had them for the first shoot,' answered his mother, 'and don't forget to put water in the bain marie and switch it on,' she added.

The Oak Tree Farmhouse is a large five bedroom home that started off with two bedrooms upstairs and a single kitchen and living area downstairs. Over a forty-five year period it was added to and updated, until the present house was completed in 1895. When East Anglia Farms became the owner, they stamped their mark on the building and extended the dining area by adding a large modern conservatory with impressive folding patio doors. This glass and pvc addition, whilst no Paxton original masterpiece, had various company functions ranging from an unofficial store room to being called 'the conference room' when head office visited.

Its main purpose was, however, as a function room for the shoot. The farming company according to the latest financial report *'had identified the shoot as an important revenue stream with great potential, and planned to invest in people and other necessary sustainable resources to develop the annual programme of shoots at Oak Tree Farm'.*

Following the delicious smell of cooking bacon, Lucas Galkeviciene and Dominic Babicas, walked from their respective farm cottages over to the main farmhouse. Both men were from Lithuania, and had originally been employed as farmhands. A semi-retired gamekeeper, Simon Partridge had, as a result of the financial report, recently joined the farm as a part-time gamekeeper. Lucas and Dominic then became, to their absolute surprise, trainee gamekeepers.

Lucas knocked on the back door and gently opened it. Jessica looked up and slowly put down the butter knife she was using, and stared wide-eyed at the two men.

'Alistair, come here.'

'What's wrong now, Jessica?' asked her short tempered husband returning to the kitchen. Standing there with silly grins on their faces was Lucas with bright pink hair, and Dominic with a mop of shiny purple hair. 'What in heaven's name have you done to your hair?' asked the astonished farmer. 'Are you guys taking the mick?'

'Boss,' began Lucas. 'We visited our Lithuanian friends last night. It was a happy time playing music and dancing.'

'Sir,' interrupted Dominic. 'I think we had a lot of vodkas. Our friend's wives placed money on the table, how do you call it, a wager, daring us to wash our hair with their coloured shampoo.'

'Boss,' continued Lucas. 'You keep telling us vodka is not good for us, but it made us some money last night.' Lucas seeing the disapproval on the farmer's face decided to stop talking.

'Heaven forbid! Today is an important day for our visitors. They have paid a lot of money, and what are they going to find? Two bloody clowns with pink and purple hair. It is going to look so unprofessional,' bemoaned the farmer.

'Alistair, we really don't have time for this,' said Jessica coming to the rescue. Ant and Dec, came trotting up to see what the excitement was all about, took one look at the two newly appointed clowns, and started barking at them.

'Mum, all done,' announced Tom as he came back into the kitchen.

'Wow, random guys! Like the hair! I want some of that. It is oh so cool.'

'Has everyone gone flipping mad in this house,' exclaimed Alistair storming out of the house, and slamming the front door.

'Ok let's all calm down,' said the real head of the household, handing Lucas and Dominic each a bacon roll wrapped in a serviette. 'Help yourselves to coffee, guys.' The trainee gamekeepers poured themselves a coffee and sat down at the kitchen table. 'Ok, is everything ready?' asked Jessica. The pink and purple heads nodded in unison. 'Lucas, you're looking after one group of pickers up and their dogs, and Dominic you're with the other group.'

'The kids haven't put out enough cutlery,' announced Yasmin coming back into the kitchen. She glanced at the trainee gamekeepers but didn't say anything despite being curious.

'Is the butter and jam out, is there enough milk and sugar?'

'I'll check everything. Don't worry, Jess, I'm on it.'

'Thanks Yasmin,' replied the farmer's wife as she bent down to look in the oven. 'Where were we?' she continued as she adjusted the temperature. 'Mr Partridge is the shoot captain today, and he will be looking after the beaters. Lucas no dogs with the beaters please.' The telephone started to ring. 'Will one of you kids answer that please,' instructed the mother.

'Mum, head office for Dad. Where is he?' asked Chloe.

'Probably sulking outside somewhere,' replied Jessica. Here we go, head office sticking their oar in as usual she thought.

'That was Carter,' announced Alistair as he came into the kitchen. 'He wanted to know how things were going.'

'Obviously doesn't have anything to do,' retorted Jessica as she looked through the oven door again at the croissants which were now finally turning crispy brown.

'Probably,' replied Alistair, glaring at Lucas and Dominic as he left the kitchen.

'Actually Lucas, if Ant and Dec are comfortable with the other dogs, let them go along as well. They missed the last shoot, and haven't had a good run lately, they need to keep sharp.'

'No problem, Mrs Jessica.'

'Nothing gets passed this woman,' observed Dominic in Lithuanian. Lucas glared at his colleague. They were in enough trouble as it was without Dominic getting smart.

'Mrs Jessica?'

'Yes, Lucas.'

'We are sorry for the trouble we have made.'

'Oh don't worry, nobody's dead. Just go and apologise to Alistair. He's had time to cool off, he'll be fine. If anyone asks, just say you did it for charity. Ok, here we go, looks like our first gun has arrived.'

CHAPTER 3

The first arrival was Simon Partridge, the semi-retired, part-time gamekeeper.

'Morning Alistair.'

'Morning Simon, looks like a nice day for it,' replied the farmer, shaking the gamekeeper's hand.

'Perfect,' agreed Simon nodding his head. He opened the back of his 4x4 and took out his gun and cartridge bag. 'Any idea how many beaters and pickers up we have?'

'If everyone who said they were coming turns up, we should have a total of about twenty. Let me give you a hand.'

'Hope we don't have too many dogs,' said the gamekeeper.

'Actually, I've spoken to the pickers up, and asked them not to bring their dogs,' replied Alistair. Both men stopped to let an approaching Volvo Estate pass. 'That's Kay Beswick, she's one of the guns. Have you met her yet?'

'No. I haven't. A lady gun, hey? Is it still pc to call them lady guns?'

'We still do. They'll soon put us right, if it changes.'

'Absolutely guaranteed, my boy,' replied Simon, and both men smiled at their little joke.

'We actually have three lady guns coming today,' continued Alistair.

'My, my, times have changed,' commented the craggy, weather-beaten keeper. 'We're but thorns among roses,' he added as he looked across at Jessica Burns and Kay Beswick taking equipment out of the back of the Volvo.

'The older chap, certainly looks the part,' commented Kay.

'Yes, that's Simon Partridge our newly appointed part-time gamekeeper. Today's shoot captain,' replied Jessica.

'Jess, leave the equipment here. I just want to go over and introduce myself to Simon and say hi to Alistair.'

Jeremy Hughes came chugging up the drive in his orange and white classic VW, waved to Alistair and Simon, and pulling up next to Kay's car, parked his campervan.

'Morning Jessica, morning Kay,' greeted Jeremy as he alighted from his 1970s artefact. 'Leave the gear, I'll take it inside.'

'Thanks Jeremy, that's very kind of you,' replied Kay, glancing down at the sandals on his feet. 'We'll catch-up later over a bacon butty,' she added.

'Don't worry about the sandals, I've brought appropriate boots along,' he reassured Kay.

Kay nodded her head in approval and walked over to Simon Partridge and Alistair Burns. The farmer introduced the gamekeeper to the lady of the manor. Jessica stood for a moment and watched the group chatting. It will be interesting to hear what Simon thinks of our laid back Lady Beswick she thought. Smiling, she picked up Kay's gun and cartridge bag and headed towards the house. Jeremy, conscience of his sandals, followed her with the rest of the equipment.

Simon Partridge had been a gamekeeper, man and boy. He had learnt his skills in a tough environment, tutored by hard outdoor men who had only one rule; do it exactly as I do it or else you'll see the back of my hand. He was a traditionalist and made no excuses for it.

Today, as the shoot captain, he was dressed for the formal shoot. A three piece tweed suit with matching trousers, waistcoat and jacket. Beneath the suit, he wore a green check shirt and matching tie. If the weather turned cold or wet he had his favourite green shooting jacket with him. A garment that had plenty of room to swing the gun, and deep pockets to keep cartridges dry. On his feet, shooting boots that gave him good ankle support and to keep his feet warm long socks, tied with garters to stop them falling down. A tweed flat cap finished off the livery. The male pheasants with their iridescent copper-coloured plumage were going to find it difficult to upstage this thorn of the shoot.

'Simon, I'll join you in the conservatory. Richard Kettering-Smythe has just arrived.
Welcome KS,' greeted Alistair as Kettering-Smythe, looking flustered and red in the face, eased his stiff back out of his luxury British car.

'Morning, Alistair. I thought I might be running a bit late. Had rather an important phone call with County Hall. Didn't realise the time.'

'You're not late at all. Plenty of time. The guests have only just started to arrive. What's happening at County Hall? Anything of interest?' enquired Alistair.

'No not really, just the same old yearly gripe from parishioners about clearing the drains before winter. What they don't seem to realise, and I spend all my time trying to explain to the village folk, is that we don't have any control nor authority over County Council. Anyway, I've done my bit. I can honestly look the people in the eye, and say I have spoken to County.' Alistair looked at the parish councillor in disbelief. You are such a self-important prat, thought the farmer.

Beaters, dogs, picker ups and shooting gear were now starting to arrive. Some on foot, some by car, teenagers dropped off by parents, others on bicycles and one or two on motorbikes. Lucas and Dominic were, not surprisingly, the focus of attention, and it was not long before the quiet countryside was filled with the sound of chatter, laughter and 'did it for charity' could be heard being repeated a number of times.

The dogs didn't take much notice of the noise. They seemed more curious about the smell of bacon, and lifting their heads, sniffed at the air in various directions. Yasmin, with Ant and Dec at her heels, came walking over from the farmhouse towards the gathering people and dogs.

'Excuse me, everyone,' she said raising her voice to be heard. 'We have hot bacon rolls, croissants, tea and coffee in the conservatory. Just follow that sign,' she said pointing.

The words 'hot', 'bacon' and 'rolls' required no further encouragement. Lucas and Dominic tied the dogs up, and followed the visitors. Ant and Dec knowing exactly where the bacon was, escorted Yasmin back to the kitchen, and the visiting dogs watched forlornly as everyone disappear behind the house.

'Tom won't you help Mr Kettering-Smythe carry his equipment to the conservatory.'

'No problem Dad. Hi Mr Kettering-Smythe.'

'Morning, Tom.'

'Any update from Hanna?' asked Alistair.

'Chloe says she's at Heathrow. Still hasn't got hold of her dad,' answered his son.

We really should be looking for Brian thought Alistair as he watched a cavalcade of two shiny black German luxury cars turn into the driveway.

'I didn't know the EU Commissioner was coming today,' he said turning to KS and Tom. Both laughed, and Alistair smiled. The two cars parked next to each other, driver's doors opened together, and out stepped two men in their mid-thirties both wearing tweed caps.

'Hi chaps,' said the thinner of the two. 'Are we at the right place, Oak Tree Farm?'

'If you are here for the shoot, you're at the right place,' said Alistair. 'Follow the sign to the conservatory.'

Belinda Thomas was the next gun to arrive, with her latest boyfriend in tow, and Charlie Pollock her stable hand; closely followed by Charlotte Broadhurst, Samir Chowdhury, and Dave Wright. A couple of breathless teenagers came running up the drive and were directed by Alistair to the now crowded conservatory.

The breakfast was well under way, when a pile of blonde hair heaped up on top of its owner's head and held together with what looked like chopsticks appeared at the conservatory door.

'Hi guys. Do you mind if I join you?' Everyone in the room looked towards the door in amusement. Under the hair was an orange tanned woman in her late twenties wearing green and gold lycra and matching trainers. Alistair jumped out of his chair as if he had been electrocuted and lunged for the door.

'I'm sorry, but who are you?' he asked.

'Lizzie Turner, Babes. You know me. I'm the wedding organiser.'

'No, I certainly don't,' Alistair assured her.

'Well Jess knows who I am.'

'Well I don't, and can't you see we are really busy,' replied Alistair who was starting to get agitated.

'I know it's the shoot, Babes. Jess told me all about it.'

'Come with me,' instructed Alistair heading off around the outside of the house, through the front door and into the kitchen. Lizzie, despite hours of powerhoops and fitsteps, struggled to keep up with the irate farmer.

'Jessica, can you explain this?' Alistair snarled as a breathless Lizzie appeared at the open kitchen door.

'Lizzie, nice to see you,' said Jessica.

'Same here, Babes.'

'We are in the middle of a shoot, Jessica.' Alistair reminded his wife.

'Alistair, calm down. Lizzie asked me some time ago if she could come along to a shoot. I didn't think it would do any harm.'

'Is this a bad time, Jess?' asked Lizzie.

'Yes,' hissed Alistair.

'No, not at all,' responded Jessica.

'She is inappropriately dressed, for God's sake.'

'Ok stop it Alistair, she can borrow my outdoor clothes. I'm sure they'll fit. Come with me Liz.' The two women disappeared upstairs. First pink and purple hair and now lycra thought the farmer gritting his teeth, and shaking his head in frustration. Taking a deep breath, he headed back to the conservatory.

'Apologies, Simon. Please carry on.'

'Thanks Alistair.' Simon Partridge stood up and loudly tapped a glass with a teaspoon. The room fell silent. 'Good morning ladies and gentlemen, boys and girls. My name is Simon Partridge, gamekeeper here at Oak Tree Farm. I would like to welcome you to the second shoot of the season, and I will be your shoot captain for the duration. May I start off by thanking our hosts, Alistair and Jessica Burns, the current custodians of the farm, for their warm welcome and delicious breakfast,' he said looking around the room at nodding heads, and smiles of approval. 'The morning programme is two, possibly three drives before lunch depending on how many birds we have. I will lead the beaters, and the pickers up and the dogs will divide into two groups. One group with Lucas, and the other with Dominic.' The trainee gamekeepers raised an arm at the mention of their names. 'With hair like that you are unlikely to lose them out there, even in the dark,' quipped Simon with a broad smile on his face. The audience laughed. 'We will start off with two groups of pegs; one group with Alistair, and the other group with Belinda.' Each raised an arm in acknowledgment. 'They are also our first aiders today. Let's be careful out there so we don't have to use them. All communication is via walkie-talkies. Please switch off your mobile phones, and only use them in an absolute emergency. I am sure that some of you know each other already, and those who don't will during the course of the day get to know each other. I would, however, like to take the liberty of asking the guns to introduce themselves. Starting on my left with Alistair and going clockwise around the table. Thanks Alistair.'

'Alistair Burns, farm manager here at Oak Tree Farm for the past twenty five years. Welcome to our home, and I hope you all enjoy the day. Thank you.'

'Richard Kettering-Smythe. Born Kettering, and for some inexplicable reason added my wife's name to mine when we got married. Please call me KS. Grew up here in Weatherford. Parish councillor, an estate agent by profession, and chairman of *Swarm International UK* a charity helping to reduce deaths from malaria.'

'Charlotte Broadhurst. Head Teacher at the Primary School. Previously ten years at a London inner city school teaching Year Sixes.'

'Belinda Thomas. I own a riding school here in Weatherford. My mother taught me to ride, and my father taught me to shoot from a very young age.'

'Dave Wright. I have a painting and decorating company. Ex-army and completed two tours in Afghanistan.'

'Dudley Baines, commercial real estate advisor with London Consultants B.A.G.; Bassett, Andrews and Goldstein. I work closely with Alexis here on my left. He's also with B.A.G. We're known at work as the bag-a-bargain boys.' The audience laughed again.

'Good morning everyone, I'm Alexis Castellanos. Dudley and I are members of the same shooting club in London, and we clay pigeon shoot as well. We're working in the area at the moment, heard about the shoot from a local resident and decided to come along. I'm married to Judith, and we have a four month old boy, Victor.'

'Samir Chowdhury. My wife Yasmin and I, both originally from East Africa, own the petrol station, shop and sub post-office in the village.'

'Jeremey Hughes, I live here in Weatherford and I'm a professional symphony orchestra saxophone player.'

'Kay Beswick. Grew up in Hong Kong and I speak mandarin fluently. I have a Chinese furniture business that I run from home.'

Jessica entered the room with Lizzie, who was now dressed in slightly ill-fitting tweed. Alistair put his head in his hands.

'Simon can I interrupt for a sec please? Lizzie is spending the day with us observing the shoot. I need someone, preferably a gun, to look after her,' asked Jessica looking around the room.

'I will,' volunteered Dudley Baines, turning to his colleague with a big grin, and looking like the proverbial cat and cream.

'Thanks. That's all Simon.'

'Thank you very much, everyone. One last thing before you head out,' shouted Simon above the noise of people getting up to leave.

'Don't forget the sweep. One pound each please. Two bottles of Prosecco for the winner. Not a bad prize for guessing how many birds we bag today. All monies will go to the County Air Ambulance. Ok, let's get started, and please take care out there.'

Kay Beswick and Dave Wright patiently followed the members of the shoot and their equipment out of the conservatory. Kay entered their names in the sweep, and Dave took the opportunity to grab two remaining croissants off the breakfast table.

'Croissant Kay?' he asked.

'No thanks. Need to watch the carbs.'

'How about a wager then? A bottle of Claret to the one who bags the most birds.'

'That's not a wager. Go mug somebody else who doesn't know that you're an ex-army sniper,' grinned the lady of the manor.

'Worth a try, my Lady,' laughed Dave taking off his cap and bowing.

'Now stop it David, I might be forced to have your head,' Kay playfully responded as he offered her his hand as they crossed a small ditch on the edge of the lawn.

'Thank you, Dave. You have a good morning. See you at lunch,'

'Laters, Kay. Be lucky,' replied the ex-marine.

Jessica and Yasmin stood watching the guns, beaters, pickers up, dogs and vehicles leaving their footprints and tyre tracks in the dew, as they headed out across the large multi-level lawn in front of the house.

'It's quite exciting to see them all going off together,' said Jessica.

'It always looks so disorganised,' commented Yasmin.

'Let's hope Lizzie doesn't let the side down.' They looked at each other and burst out laughing.

The air was crisp and smelt of wet grass and newly ploughed earth. It was a beautiful autumn day. No rain, no wind, autumn leaves sprinkled everywhere, and patches of mist lying stubbornly in the hollows at the bottom of the fields.

Everyone squinted at the horizon, as they walked towards the early morning sun. It was difficult to see the outline of the copse of trees in the mist. Soon the green and tweed coloured group started to split-up. Half of the shoot moving out to the left towards a copse of oak trees, and the other group turning slightly to their right and half walking, half stumbling they made their way across a large ploughed field towards cover that Jessica and Yasmin could not see from where they were standing. Soon the sound of talking, laughter, vehicles and barking dogs could hardly be heard.

'Come on Babes, let's crack on with lunch,' said Jessica imitating Lizzie Turner. The women, enjoying the fresh morning air, retraced the footprints across the lawn and walked slowly back towards the farmhouse. Yasmin stopped at the paved sandstone steps leading up to the top lawn, and began doing step up and step down exercises.

'Cardio, Babes?' The friends looked at each other and started to laugh.

'Can't you see we are in the middle of a shoot,' said Jessica deepening her voice to imitate her husband. 'What's more, you're inappropriately dressed,' added the farmer's wife placing her hands firmly on her hips and glaring at her friend with disapproval. The sound of raised voices cut short the laughter. The women fell silent and turned to look back across the fields. The commotion appeared to be coming from the copse of oak trees.

CHAPTER 4

The doorbell rang.

'Is that you Cassie?' Hanna Townsend's voice crackled over the intercom.

'Yes, it's me.' The door buzzed open, and Cassie Richards ignoring the lift, climbed the stairs, and stopped for a moment to look down on Regents Canal that ran past the building. Hanna was waiting on the third floor landing; delighted to see each other, the friends hugged.

'I like the new hairstyle. Very chic,' said Cassie puffing up imaginary hair on both sides of her face.

'And I see you finally decided to buy the jacket,' smiled Hanna, stepping back   slightly to admire the garment. 'Perfect. It looks gorgeous. Come in, come in.'   Cassie eased passed her friend, and stopped to look at the apartment's open plan kitchen and living area.

'Looks like you've settled in,' she commented.

'I've been here almost three weeks already. Time flies. Didn't really have a lot of stuff to bring over.'

'It's so much better than Lincoln's Field. It's much more spacious than I remember it. You happy?'

'Absolutely thrilled with it. Glass of wine?'

'Yes please. Let the evening begin,' smiled Cassie.

'How was the journey?' asked Hanna taking a bottle of white wine out of the fridge.

'The train drivers are still on strike,' sighed Cassie as she pulled out one of the breakfast bar stools. 'Luckily I arrived at the station as a train was pulling in.'

'The 1970s train strikes: the sequel. History repeating itself, and nothing appears to have been learned the first time around,' said Hanna sounding a little melancholic.

'I can't understand how a small group of people are allowed to inconvenience so many. Very selfish, but there's nothing we can really do about it. It's out of our hands,' replied Cassie.

'That's what we all say, but eventually someone with a bit of backbone comes along and sorts things out,' responded Hanna as she poured the wine.

'I suppose with robots and artificial intelligence it might one day be possible to have fully automated trains. That will sort out the problem.'

'Don't know enough about it. Goes straight over my head, I'm afraid,' replied Hanna as she sat down at the breakfast bar opposite her friend. 'A toast,' she said raising her glass. 'To Sarah and Jenny.' Two glasses clinked gently together, and the two women, fighting back the tears, sat silently looking at each other. 'Talking about artificial intelligence, any news about the new consortium?' asked Hanna.

'Early days, but it does look promising. I'm quite excited about it,' replied Cassie. 'The company is definitely joining the group, and I'm hoping there will be an opportunity to get involved in the university research side of things. Do you remember they sent me on that career development course?'

'Yes, data analysis,' replied Hanna.

'That's right. Well I've asked my boss if the company would help finance an aerial unmanned crop monitoring course for me. It's only 5 days, but I do think it's the future.'

'And?' asked Hanna.

'Well he didn't fall off his chair laughing,' answered Cassie. The doorbell rang.

'That must be the taxi. It's a bit early. Drink up. Let's go have some fun,' said Hanna.

Although it was early evening, it was already dark. The clocks had changed and Hanna enjoyed London at night; it seemed more exciting and vibrant in the dark. The orange tint of the street lighting made the buildings look much softer and cleaner than during the day. Goods displayed in brightly lit shop windows looked more enticing, and the warm light through drawn curtains welcomed home-comers in from the cold.

'Cassie, do you like London and all the people?' asked Hanna. Cassie stopped scrolling her iPhone, and looked out of the taxi window.

'Never really given it much thought. I wouldn't like to live here. I suppose it would be quite nice to be anonymous. Makes life simple. And you?'

'I like the hustle and the bustle of the city, and there's always something to do.'

'Wish it would improve the hustle and bustle in the male department,' added Cassie.

'And you've only had one glass of wine,' exclaimed Hanna. The friends giggled, and gently shoved each other.

'Who are you picking up at the airport tomorrow?' asked Cassie.

'A South African family. They're joining the Burns at Oak Tree Farm. You've met Jessica Burns.' Cassie nodded her head. 'They've got a shoot tomorrow, and didn't really have anyone available to meet the Nels at Heathrow. Jessica asked me some time ago for the favour.'

'What are they going to do here?' continued Cassie.

'Not entirely sure. It has something to do with a new generation crop seed. I think it's wheat,' answered Hanna.

'Interesting,' replied Cassie as the taxi pulled over to the curb and stopped.

'Your stop, ladies. Have a good evening,' announced the taxi driver.

The Three Sails pub overlooks the River Thames not far from Hammersmith Bridge. The wrought iron roadway crossing to Wimbledon and Richmond was lit up, and the suspension towers stood proudly in the semi-darkness. Every night, just before closing there is a toast to Sir Joseph Baguette, followed by much laughter and thumping on the bar counter, in memory of the bridge designer Sir Joseph Bazalgette.

Hanna's first visit to the pub had been with roommates from Law School, and it had become one of her favourite places to eat in London. She and Cassie had spent a number of summer afternoons sitting outside on the wide terrace, drinking Pimm's and Prosecco, while watching the boats on the river. They entered the pub, and a couple of male heads at the bar turned in their direction. Hanna, the lawyer, and Cassie, the agronomist; unlikely friends, and certainly if judged by the way they dressed.

Hanna, in her late twenties, is tall, slim with pale skin and shoulder length dark hair in a sleek bob. She likes tailored clothes that can be worn for both work and leisure. Tonight she had jazzed it up with an oversized leather handbag. Her only jewellery; small aquamarine earrings that match the colour of her eyes.

Cassie has short spiky blonde hair which looks windblown, but is actually styled. Her wardrobe is predominately rock chick. A black leather jacket, tight distressed jeans and well-worn comfortable brown leather ankle boots. Her signature chunky knit jumper, she had swapped for a soft red silk blouse.

They had first met at a London MoonWalk, a charity event to raise money for breast cancer. Hanna had just started university in London when her mother, Sarah, fell ill. Cassie's sister-in-law, Jenny, was also diagnosed with cancer the same year as Hanna's mother. They were both waiting in the big tent for the half moon walk to start, when Cassie noticed they had sequential walker numbers. They got chatting, and ended up doing the 13 mile powerwalk together. The gruelling six and a half hours turned into a lasting friendship.

'No, but it is quite early,' replied Hanna, taking her phone out of her handbag The women made themselves comfortable in two large brown leather armchairs next to the window at the far end of the wood panelled bar. The barman brought over two glasses of Prosecco, a couple of menus, and assorted nuts in a small white ramekin bowl.

'It's not very busy. Is it?' remarked Cassie.

'I'm going to text my Dad, and see if he's ok.'

'How is your Dad?' asked Cassie.

'I went home for the August bank holiday weekend. He was in the middle of the harvest, and was struggling to get it finished. There wasn't really enough sunshine to dry out the crops. He did say he was not expecting a very good yield this year. To be honest, Dad says that every year,' smiled Hanna putting the phone back in her bag. Hanna glanced across at the bar. The barman appeared to be communicating with her in sign language.

'Same again?' he mouthed, holding up two fingers of his right hand.

'Thank you,' Hanna mouthed back, giving him the thumbs up sign with both hands.

'Do you know what you have just done?' laughed Cassie.

'Oh, shut up. Let's order,' laughed Hanna, holding up a menu and signing to the barman that they were ready to order their food by tapping her finger against the menu, and mouthing 'Food'.

The pub was getting busier, and with it came the aroma of food cooking. Hanna ordered an avocado, salmon and crayfish salad starter and Cassie opted for the parma ham and melon. Both chose the same main course; chicken with creamy mushroom sauce, saute potatoes and roasted vegetables.

'I still cannot believe we walked around London in our bras,' said Hanna.

'Yeh it was a bit crazy. Would you do it again?'

'I would like to do something similar, but not that physical,' answered Hanna. Hanna's phone rang. 'Hanna Townsend,' she answered. A slight pause. 'Yes that's right.' Another pause. 'Um, when I booked it, I did ask if I could drop it off at Stansted Airport. Is there a problem?' A slightly longer pause. 'No, I understand, thanks for checking. See you in the morning. Bye.' A waitress came over to say their food was ready. 'No reply from my Dad,' said Hanna following Cassie through the throng of people at the bar. 'That was the car hire at Heathrow. They need the car later tomorrow morning, and were checking to see if I still wanted to drop it off at Stansted,' said Hanna as they sat down at a table.

'Bottle of white wine?' asked Cassie.

'Of course,' came back the reply.

After a long wait, the waitress returned with the wine, poured it into the glasses using one hand, then dragged an ice bucket and stand ignominiously across the carpet, and tossed the bottle into the ice as if it were a netball. Cassie shook her head, Hanna raised her eyebrows and both looked down at their starters without saying a word. When the waitress had gone, they both burst out laughing.

'Well the food's good,' remarked Cassie.

'Never had a bad meal here yet,' smiled Hanna.

'OK, enough talk about everyone else, let's talk about you.'

'There's not much to say really,' replied Hanna. 'The move has kept me busy. A couple of the guys at work gave me a hand moving, which was really useful.'

'Hunks from work, hey. Stripped to the waist, and lifting heavy boxes. Don't tell me, both of them drank diet coke,' teased Cassie.

'Behave yourself, Cassie,' said Hanna a little embarrassed. 'It was nothing like that. Articled clerks with glasses, who live on lettuce paninis, and have bodies to match.'

'Hanna, you are so up-tight sometimes. I'm only pulling your leg. One day, a knight in shining armour will ride into your little village back home, and sweep you off your feet. Trust me, you're a catch girl.'

'Are we going to indulge ourselves in dessert?' asked Hanna quickly changing the subject. Cassie picked up the dessert menu.

'How about a couple of vodka jelly shots? Far fewer calories than the chocolate fudge cake,' prompted Cassie. The friends carried on chatting, finished the bottle of wine, and ordered the jelly shots.

'You wouldn't want to get these mixed up with the kid's jelly at a birthday party. Can you imagine, the parents arriving to collect their kids and they're all inebriated. What a disaster,' said Cassie with a look of shock and horror on her face.

'Talking of mix ups. We've got a new articled clerk, called Rob. He's only been with us a couple of weeks. As you can imagine the Chief Clerk gives the newcomers a very hard time. Anyway, Rob was going out to buy lunch, and the Chief, not wanting to miss a menial task opportunity, gave him money to buy some roses. He was gone ages, and the Chief was fuming. Fired him at least five times by the time he walked back into the office carrying a huge bunch of red roses. He said he couldn't find a florist, and had to use his credit card because the flowers had been so expensive. Well, the Chief looked as if he was going to blow a gasket, when he suddenly stopped and realised what had happened. He had assumed that Rob was going to the supermarket for his sandwich. What he wanted was a box of Rose's chocolates. Well it was a great opportunity for the articled clerks to totally mock the Chief for the rest of the afternoon.' Hanna sat back in her chair with a rather satisfied look on her face.

'That's brilliant,' laughed Cassie drinking the last of her wine.

'I really don't want to break up the party, but I think we should order the taxis?' said Hanna.

'I'm done, you've got an early start in the morning. Thank you, it's been a lovely evening.'

The friends hugged, said goodbye, and got into their respective taxis. Cassie took out her phone, and text Hanna to thank her for the evening. She checked her Facebook, and then read her news feed for the remainder of the journey to the train station.

Hanna dialled her Dad's number. There was no reply. *Good night. Love you.* she text him.

CHAPTER 5

A uniformed police sergeant got up from his desk, and walked briskly down the corridor to the detectives' office.

'Ma'am, a caller has phoned in to say they have found a body on a farm near Weatherford.'

'Suspicious?' asked Detective Inspector Veronica James.

'Not known at this stage, ma'am. Two incident response vehicles, and an ambulance are on their way to the location,' replied the police officer.

'Name of the caller?'

'Mr Alistair Burns, ma'am.'

'DS Brown and I will take this one. Thank you Sergeant. Update us en-route,' replied the Inspector, switching off her computer and grabbing her coat.

'Chris. Let's go. Body found near Weatherford.' Detective Sergeant Chris Brown; tall, athletic and neatly dressed, pulled on his jacket as he quickly zig-zagged his way between the desks, and followed his boss out of the office.

The two police officers, each signed out a walkie-talkie, and headed downstairs to the car park. With blue lights and siren on, DI James eased the South Essex Police Volvo out into the obliging traffic, and within minutes they were on the outskirts of the city.

'Sierra 2 from Victor Tango.'

'Go ahead Victor Tango,' replied Chris Brown.

'Spoken to the caller again. It appears to be a death by suicide. The farm is called Oak Tree Farm, one mile east of Weatherford on the London Road. Apparently there was a shoot in progress at the farm when they found the deceased.'

'What about armed response?' prompted DI James, glancing quickly at her sergeant.

'With all of those shotguns at the location, are we getting any armed support?'

'Sierra 2, I'll find out, standby.'

Veronica James manoeuvred 'Sierra 2' between stationary cars on the roundabout, and accelerated down the slip road to join the northbound carriageway of the motorway. They were soon out in the countryside. The six lane motorway stretched ahead of them to the horizon, and on either side of the bitumen, the recently planted winter wheat looked as if a brand new green carpet had been neatly laid on the undulating landscape.

The motorway was busy with early morning commuters, and despite the lorries holding up the traffic in the two left hand lanes, the unmarked police car settled down in the fast lane, and started to make speedy progress.

'Ma'am, I've got a map of the Weatherford area on my phone. If I may suggest, it's probably best to stay on the motorway, off at junction 9, and the B10166 will take us right into London Road. Journey time 45 minutes,' advised the sergeant.

'Sierra 2 from Victor Tango. The caller has confirmed that no shots, I repeat no shots, have been fired at the location this morning, and every shotgun is safe. Gold Command has advised there is no requirement for armed support. The pathologist and forensics are on their way to the location.'

'Victor Tango from Sierra 2-2.'

'That's one of the response vehicles,' commented Chris Brown.

'Sierra 2-2 go ahead.'

'We are at the location. The deceased is in a copse of trees, and we have spoken to a Mr Simon Partridge, the farm's gamekeeper and a Mr Charlie Pollock, a stable hand at a riding school here in the village. Both men were the first to find the deceased. Looks like an apparent suicide. The people attending the shoot are now all at the farmhouse. Sierra 2-9 has just arrived.

We'll cordon off the area, and wait your instructions. Over.'

'Sierra 2 from Victor Tango, did you copy that?'

'Sierra 2 copied. We are approximately 30 minutes from the location.'

The two police officers sat in silence for the next few miles, watching the lorries in the left hand lanes trying desperately to race each other up the hills, while an impatient queue of motor cars were trying to overtake them using the one remaining lane.

'Ma'am. This is probably not the most appropriate time to ask, but does this job get any easier?'

'You mean having to deal with death all the time?'

'Yes,'

'I think we unfortunately get to see human nature at its worst. It is difficult sometimes to comprehend what people can do to each other or to themselves for that matter. I find the best way to deal with it, is not to think about it too much. It is after all just a job.'

'You're probably right, ma'am, but it's easier said than done.' The sergeant sat quietly watching the traffic make way for the speeding police car. After a moment's silence, the DI glanced briefly at the young man.

'What's brought this on, Chris?'

'Nothing in particular, ma'am. I'm just finding it difficult at the moment dealing with the grief and distress of the relatives. And the friends for that matter. It didn't really bother me at first. I suppose in the early days it was ignorance is bliss, but now that I know what to expect, I'm finding it arduous.'

'You will not be the first detective, nor will you be the last one to find it difficult. It will improve over time. Trust me,'

'I hope so, ma'am. Next junction is Weatherford,' advised the sergeant, switching the siren off.

The police car slowed down, changed lanes and manoeuvred between two lorries before taking the slip road off the motorway. Heading east, they were now travelling along a road that was barely wide enough for two cars to pass each other.

'Look at this road. Don't you just love the countryside, ma'am,' commented Chris Brown rather sarcastically.

'Actually, I grew up in the country. Well in Surrey. We called it the countryside, but it wasn't as rural as this.'

'Victor Tango from Sierra 2-2.'

'Go ahead.'

'We have found a blue Land Rover parked in a lane running alongside the fields, not far from the copse of trees where the deceased was found. We have checked the vehicle registration, and it belongs to a Mr Brian Townsend. Address Grey Pigeon Farm, Weatherford.'

'Sierra 2-2 from DS Brown. The lane needs to be closed immediately until forensics take a look at it. We also need a positive identification of the victim, before a name is released. DI James will deal with the deceased's identity when we get there.'

'That's all we need. A total stranger telling the next-of-kin, and we later find out it isn't the person we thought it was,' commented the DI.

'Nightmare ma'am,' commented the sergeant, looking at his phone. 'We should be just about there.'

Sierra 2 slowed down, and Chris Brown switched the blue lights off.

'Here it is. Well done sergeant.'

The police car turned into the driveway and a familiar blue and yellow battenburg patchwork greeted them; two Astra police cars, an ambulance, the pathologist's car with its green light, and two forensic vans. The only place left to park was under an old weather-beaten oak tree.

Alistair and Jessica Burns walked over to the two police officers, and introduced themselves. They all turned to watch a grey Peugeot 206, in need of a wash, turn slowly into the driveway. A grubby A4 laminated sign with **PRESS** printed in the centre of the page lay on top of the passenger's side of the dashboard.

'The press are never far behind,' remarked DI James looking down the driveway as Hanna Townsend and the Nels turned into the farm entrance. 'Not more press surely?'

'No Inspector. It's Hanna Townsend, Brian's daughter.' answered Alistair.

CHAPTER 6

Hanna Townsend arrived at Heathrow's Terminal 2 with plenty of time to spare. She checked the arrival time of the South African Airways flight from Johannesburg, and then went in search of the car hire desks. They were not difficult to find; a row of brightly lit kiosks, all in their respective loud corporate colours and oversized logos. Despite all of this marketing effort, only two desks were open. Fortunately one of them was Hanna's.

Hire car sorted, she bought a coffee and sat down at a table overlooking a row of aircraft parked on the apron. It was still very early, and there were not many people about. The sky was starting to turn a reddish orange colour. She took her phone out of her bag. I wonder why Dad hasn't phoned or text, she thought. Maybe he had a bit too much to drink last night. She opened Facebook and posted a message saying she was at Heathrow picking up the Nel family, and that she had not been able to get hold of her Dad. Did anyone know of his whereabouts? Almost immediately Chloe Burns messaged back to say she would try and find out.

Hanna finished her coffee and took the escalator down to the International Arrivals Hall. She marvelled at the sheer size of the building. High columns supporting a vast suspended ceiling decorated alternatively with white and black panels. The enormous floor made of highly polished resin tiles complimented the enormity of the ceiling. Soft white lighting and aquamarine tinted glass provided weary travellers with a calm and peaceful welcome to England.

Hanna stood at the barrier and held up a white card with NEL FAMILY written on it. The sliding doors opened and tired looking travellers, half hidden by luggage on trolleys, started to appear. The Nels stopped at the open doors, looked around, and seeing the white card, waved.

'Mr Nel. I'm Hanna Townsend.'

'Pleased to meet you Hanna. Call me Moz.' He took Hanna's outstretched hand and enthusiastically shook it. Crikey, that's a firm handshake she thought.

'This is Elsa, my wife.'

'Hello Elsa.' The women shook hands. Phew, thank goodness she's a bit gentler with the handshake.

'And these are our kids, Paul and Isabel,' smiled Moz as he proudly introduced the children.

'Nice to meet you, Mrs Townsend,' said both children politely taking it in turns to shake hands with Hanna. That's the handshakes over.

'Please call me Hanna.'

'You can call me Bella,' the daughter said shyly.

'Bella, it is. And welcome to England. I've got a hire car that we have to collect at the pound,' Hanna explained as they headed for the exit. 'Unfortunately, it involves catching a shuttle bus to the other side of the airport, and it's a bit cold outside.' Paul and Bella hesitated when they got to the travolator, and looked at Hanna. 'Keep walking, hold on to the trolley, and just step on.' With a helping hand from Moz, the two children successfully stepped off terra firma. 'You don't have to stand still, you can walk on it. Give it a go,' encouraged Hanna. The brother and sister didn't need any further encouragement, and to their delight it felt as if they were walking on air, and strode out effortlessly pushing the trolley.

'Elsa, do you have any warm clothes that you can get out of your luggage easily? It's really cold outside,' asked a slightly worried Hanna.

'No, these are our winter clothes. This is all we have brought with us,' Elsa confessed rather sheepishly.

'Hopefully we won't have to wait too long for the bus. Standing in the cold is probably the last thing you need at the end of a long journey,' said Hanna apologetically.

'We'll be ok. As long as we don't have to get back on board another aeroplane.' Moz reassured Hanna with a huge grin.

The new arrivals, shivering in the cold and surrounded by the damp concrete of the airport building, stood waiting for the bus. Hanna felt guilty in her long winter coat and cashmere scarf. She looked at the family and wondered if moving country was like going on holiday abroad. They were suntanned and neatly dressed, albeit inappropriately for the weather. She guessed Moz and Elsa were probably in their late thirties and the children were nine or ten years old. Moz had his arm around his wife's shoulders, and she seemed comfortable being close to her husband. The two children were holding on to their mother in a vain attempt to keep warm. Hanna's first impressions were of a very friendly, close knit family.

Paul and Bella dosed off in the warm bus, as it made its way around the perimeter road of the airport. Moz and Elsa sat close to each other holding hands, and looking out at England for the first time. They had been travelling for almost twenty four hours, were exhausted and at a low ebb. They had expected a green and pleasant land. What they found were dark satanic mills; a damp, heavily built-up urban area with narrow roads, and oversized road signs.

'I didn't expect it to be so dark, Hanna,' said Moz.

'The clocks went back an hour a couple of weeks ago. The sun gets up at about seven, and it is dark by four. The winter evenings are long, but then we do get nice long days during the summer when the clocks change again.'

'We don't have clock changes in SA. Possibly a good thing, we would just get confused,' laughed Moz.

The car hire office was imbedded in an enormous car park with a border of tall cypress hedges trying in vain to hold back the din of the mills; aircraft noise. The transfer of the Nel family and their luggage from the shuttle to the hire car went smoothly, and within half an hour they had joined the eastbound traffic on the M25. It was getting lighter, and the new arrivals could now see a bit more of the countryside with the last of the autumn leaves stubbornly hanging on to the trees.

'Kids, look at the autumn colours,' said Elsa.

'They look beautiful,' remarked Bella.

'We don't really get much of an autumn in SA. Actually were we live there are only two seasons; hot and bloody hot,' smiled Moz.

'Where is home, Moz?' asked Hanna.

'Kempdale. It is a small town in the North West Province next to the Vaal River.'

'Lived there long?'

'For generations,' answered Elsa.

'Hanna, it's very hot and dusty. It's on the edge of the Kalahari Desert,' Paul quietly added to the conversation and looked at his mother for approval. Elsa smiled at him and gave him a wink.

'It sounds like an interesting place, Paul,' answered Hanna looking at the young boy in the rear view mirror. 'So what brings you to England, Moz?'

'Well, where we live there is very little rain, and almost all of the crops are under irrigation. Wheat yields have been falling for a number of years, and a shortage of water also makes it difficult to grow large volumes. This means the country has to use valuable foreign exchange to import wheat to feed our people,' explained Moz. 'We have been helping with the development of a more productive seed. It is a bit complicated, but basically it's getting more out of less.'

'That's interesting. I have a very good friend Cassie, who's an agronomist in the south of England.'

'Shows you what a small world it is,' replied the visiting farmer.

'So from what you are saying, the company that owns Oak Tree Farm want your knowledge and expertise.'

'Ya. We are here on a two year contract. They want to see if they can increase the winter wheat yields,' replied Moz. They sat in silence looking at the scenery and the heavy morning traffic. Hanna heard her phone in her bag announce the arrival of a text. Ah, that must be Dad she thought.

'This freeway is huge. 5 lanes on either side,' counted Moz. 'Is there always this much traffic?'

'Pretty much. It does get much quieter at night though,' answered Hanna.

'Paul, look at all the trucks?'

'Most of them are either coming from or going to Europe via Felixstow or Harwich,' explained Hanna.

'Incredible. I've never seen so many 20 tonners in one place,' replied the awe-struck farmer.

'Do you work, Elsa, or are you tied up with the farm?' asked Hanna not wanting Moz's wife to feel she was being ignored.

'There's always something to do on the farm, but I'm a qualified bookkeeper. I've been working part-time for the local branch of a large national charity.'

'Are you taking the next couple of years off? I would, given the chance,' said Hanna looking in the rear view mirror at Elsa.

'No definitely not. I have a work permit, and once settled, I'll find some bookkeeping to do. I've also been thinking of doing a distance learning accountancy qualification,' replied the farmer's wife.

They were approaching Hobbs Cross and the M25 interchange. Hanna moved over into the left lane, and slowed down as the cars concertinaed on entering the slow section of the M11 slip road.

'Not too far now. About 20 minutes,' said Hanna as she accelerated to join the northbound motorway traffic.

'Do you live in Weatherford, Hanna?' asked Elsa.

'No I live in London. Camden.'

'Are you not afraid of living in such a big city?'

'No not at all. You do have to be careful and sensible, but London is a big pussycat really. I grew up in Weatherford on the family farm.'

'And what work do you do?'

'I'm training to be a barrister. I did a history degree at the University of Tees County, and a law degree in London, and I'm now in chambers at Lincoln's Field,' answered Hanna.

'Do you enjoy it?' asked Elsa, not quite understanding the significance of Lincoln's Field.

'Yes. I really do like being in London. And I've been treated quite well by the law fraternity. When I was growing up in Weatherford, I couldn't wait to escape the place.'

'Any particular reason?' asked Moz.

'I wasn't unhappy as a girl. I just found Weatherford too small, and the villagers are so insular,' confessed Hanna. There was silence in the car for a few minutes. Damn, thought Hanna, I shouldn't have said that.

'Moz, Elsa, I really shouldn't have said anything about Weatherford. I do apologise. Please forget I said it. You will enjoy it, I know you will, and you will be made to feel very welcome,' said Hanna angry with herself for letting her guard down in front of the newly arrived visitors.

'It's not a problem, Hanna. Don't worry about it,' replied Moz.

Hanna heard the sound of a distant siren, and looking in the rear view mirror saw what looked like an unmarked police car with flashing blue lights approaching at speed in the fast lane. She remained in the middle lane, and let the two occupants overtake and continue their journey.

'Unmarked police car,' remarked Hanna.

'Look there guys. A sign to Weatherford. 7 kilometres,' said Moz.

'7 miles, Moz,' said Hanna.

'Ya, of course, you guys still work in miles,' smiled Moz, shaking his head.

Heading away from the motorway, they were soon in the fields of the long awaited green and pleasant land. All around them was a green and brown patchwork of newly planted winter wheat and ploughed fields. The Nel family perked up a bit either because their journey was coming to an end or they thought the narrow windy roads with the oncoming traffic heralded an early termination of their journey.

Hanna accelerated and decelerated, braked hard to slow down sufficiently to swing the hire car through a series of alternating left and right hand bends. She was oblivious to the fact that Moz and Elsa were sitting on the edge of their seats watching their lives flash before them. The occasional oak tree flashed past them at 60 mph, then out of nowhere one of Moz's 20 tonners was coming towards them in the opposite direction. The Nels were experiencing a real-time sequel to *Fast and Furious* as Hanna squeezed past the lorry on the right and brushed the hedgerow on the left without slowing down.

There was momentary relief from the terror as they entered a gentle sweeping curve and a signboard indicated they were 2 miles from Weatherford. The relief was short lived. They now had a tractor in front of them. Hanna slowed down, tucked in behind it, and at the first opportunity overtook the four wheels towering above them. Moz saw a glimpse of the

Weatherford church steeple in the distance and thought it was an omen, but was relieved when it was not followed by a heavenly choir of angels.

'Phew, these roads are narrow,' gasped Moz.

'You'll get used to them. Local knowledge helps. We're almost there,' Hanna answered calmly.

'Hanna, what are the red 'Hands off Weatherford' signs?' asked Moz.

'People protesting about the building of new houses in the village. The country has a shortage of housing, and it's current government policy to build new houses across the whole of the country in an attempt to reduce the shortfall. I think every town and village has a protest group. It's become a national pastime. Probably more popular than football. You see the signs everywhere you go.'

'What do you think of the protests?' asked Moz.

'It is a very complex issue and I think as a country we are damned if we do and damned if we don't,' replied Hanna. 'People are certainly more worried about houses being built in their backyards than they are about Brexit. Ok, here we are.'

They had slowed down and were following a grey Peugeot 206. It turned into Oak Tree Farm. Hanna followed the small car, and was astonished to see a large number of police outside the farmhouse. Jessica and Alistair Burns came walking towards them, accompanied by a women dressed in a smart black suit.

'Hanna Townsend?'

'Yes.'

'I'm Detective Inspector Veronica James, South Essex Police,' said the DI holding up her warrant card. 'Let's go and sit in my car. It'll be a bit more private.'

'It's my dad, isn't it? What's happened?'

'Hanna, I am so sorry to have to break this news to you, but it looks as if your dad has committed suicide.' Hanna sat quietly with her head bowed looking down at her clasped hands in her lap.

'When did it happen?'

'The pathologist's initial estimate is between 4 and 7 o'clock this morning. It appears he hanged himself over there in the copse of trees. When did you last speak to him?'

'Must have been yesterday morning, and I last saw him four weekends ago. I live in London,' she added.

'How was he?'

'The usual grumble about a disappointing harvest, and he was slightly frustrated about the lack of progress with a planning permission application. Apart from that he seemed ok. Can I sit here for a while and gather my thoughts?' Hanna said calmly.

'Of course you can. Take your time. That's my sergeant over there, Chris Brown. If you need anything, he'll help you,' reassured the DI getting out of the car and walking over to the sergeant. 'Chris please keep an eye on her.'

'No problem, ma'am. How is she taking it?'

'Remarkably calm, no tears, very little emotion, appears to be thinking logically. It will probably catch up with her at some point.'

'Excuse me. Are you in charge?'

'And you are?'

'Hugh Flynn, reporter for *The Counties Herald*,' answered the hack showing his press card.

'Detective Inspector Veronica James, South Essex Police. How may I help you Mr Flynn?'

'Can you confirm a body was found here today, Inspector?'

'Mr Flynn, the only thing I can say is there has been an incident on the farm, and you will have to wait for the official press release.'

'Is it a murder, Inspector?'

'Enough Mr Flynn. Please will you leave the premises and allow us to get on with our job,' said the DI turning on her heel and walking over to the pathologist who was loading his medical bags into his car. I'm going to twist an ankle on these blasted pebbles she thought.

'Any news, Doctor Samuels?'

'Nothing appears to be suspicious. Open and shut I think. Obviously we need to wait for the post mortem.'

'Never take anything for granted my old governor used to say. I'd like to keep an open mind.'

'Quite right, Inspector. I'll arrange all the usual formalities. Ok, on to the next call of duty. The shops of Cambridge, with my credit card unsheathed and ready for my wife and three daughters to use when they run out of money. A man's work is never done, Inspector,' laughed the pathologist as he got into his car. He reversed a few yards, stopped, and opened the car window. 'Inspector, I've just realised there isn't a suicide note.'

CHAPTER 7

The police had finished their preliminary investigation at Oak Tree Farm, and the participants of the shoot were given permission to return to their homes. Hanna had somehow managed to maintain her composure throughout the day. Despite feeling very sad and detached from what was going on around her, she was aware of the enormity of what her father had done. Not surprisingly, DI James had more questions for her; questions that Hanna found frustrating. She was unable to give the Inspector any further useful information; no matter how hard she tried, she couldn't think of any reason why her father would kill himself.

Sergeant Chris Brown was given the unenviable task of contacting Cassie Richards to tell her what had happened, and that Hanna had asked, if it were possible, for her friend to come up to Weatherford and stay for a few days. A couple of hours later, Cassie was heading north on the M25.

'Hanna before you go, there's just one other thing.'

'What's that, Inspector?'

'We haven't found a suicide note. It might or might not be of any significance, but someone committing suicide often wants to blame someone or just asks for absolution. Forensics didn't find anything this morning. I've asked Chris to stay with you until Cassie arrives. If it's ok with you, I'll ask him to have a look around the house, the letter might be there somewhere. I need to head back to the station, so I'll leave you, but I'll keep in contact. You take care now.' The women said goodbye and shook hands.

Turning left out of the driveway, Chris stopped for a rambler who was taking a selfie with the manor house as a backdrop. Photo taken, he waited momentarily while she waved thank you and crossed over London Road.

'Not a lot of traffic,' remarked Chris as he accelerated up the hill towards the church.

'Never is. Carry on passed the church, don't turn,' replied Hanna. They both sat in silence for a while.

'Chris, what is the significance of the suicide note?'

'Nothing really. I think there is an expectation or just a hope, on the part of those left behind, that there will be some explanation. I don't know the exact figure, but from experience, probably about half of suicides have a letter. Sometimes it is just a text or voicemail message.'

'I think I can understand the need for an explanation,' said Hanna. 'Ok the farm is just passed the new houses here on the left.' Chris slowed down and turned in at the Grey Pigeon Farm gate.

'Of course, for the police, a note usually confirms that it's a suicide and not a suspicious death,' explained the sergeant as he brought the car to a halt facing the farmhouse's wooden front door. 'Forensics said the house was unlocked when they arrived this morning.'

'But there were no signs of a break-in?' asked Hanna.

'No. Apparently nothing appears to have been disturbed.' Chris opened the unlocked front door for Hanna, and she went in ahead of him.

'Let's go through to the kitchen,' said Hanna leading the way. 'Mind your head. Would you like a tea or coffee?'

'Coffee would be great. Let me get them,' replied Chris.

'That's if there's any fresh milk. I'll have tea, milk, one sugar, please,' replied the farmer's daughter opening the fridge, quickly checking the date of the milk, and handing the bottle to the sergeant. She sat down at the kitchen table, and looked around the room. 'Where do you usually find the letters?'

'Normally in full view. They're never hidden away or in a drawer or anything like that.' Hanna moved a half-empty bottle of ketchup out of the way as Chris put two steaming mugs of tea on the table. They both sat quietly sipping the hot drinks. Neither of them felt like making small talk. Chris felt it would be inappropriate and Hanna, although she did not realise it, was pleased not to be alone.

The sound of a car arriving, and the accompanying headlights sweeping across the front of the house, heralded Cassie's arrival. Hanna opened the front door and the moment she saw the agronomist, she burst into tears.

'Cassie, it's all my fault,' she sobbed.

'What do you mean it's your fault? I thought your dad killed himself?' Cassie put her arms around her friend and holding her tightly tried her best to fight back the tears herself.

'That's why he killed himself. He was all alone, and I did nothing about it. I have been so selfish. I hardly ever came home while I was at university, and since moving to London my excuse for not visiting has always been that I'm too busy. I put my happiness before his. I lost my Mum, but he lost his wife for God's sake. He had nobody to turn to for help.'

'Hanna. You have to calm down.'

'How can I calm down, I'm an orphan.'

'Cassie, I'm Detective Sergeant Chris Brown, we spoke on the phone this morning,' raising his voice slightly to be heard above Hanna's sobbing and deep intakes of breath.

'Has she been like this all day?' asked a bewildered Cassie, wiping away her own tears.

'No. She has been absolutely calm, normal, totally in control. She hasn't cried once today,' said Chris almost apologetically. 'Come on let's get inside,' he suggested. They went into the lounge, and Cassie sat down next to Hanna on the sofa, and put her arm around her distraught friend.

'Cassie. I ignored his cries for help,' sobbed Hanna, wringing her hands in desperation.

'That's not true. You're being too hard on yourself. You always said he was doing fine, and was just being a grumpy old man.'

'I didn't hear what he was trying to tell me when he was moaning about the planning permissions. I didn't take his concerns about the poor harvests seriously. I never involved him in my life in London. All those lost weekends when we could have been together, when I should have been listening to him properly. He hasn't even seen my new flat. Just a few poxy photos I took on my phone. We should have gone on holidays together after Mum died. I have totally let him down and he didn't deserve it.' The sergeant suddenly remembered he had a police duty to carry out.

'Hanna, do you mind if I take a look around the house?'

'Of', sob, 'course', sob, 'you', sob, 'can'.

'I'm going to make you a strong cup of tea with lots of sugar,' Cassie said getting up off the sofa. Despite Hanna sobbing that she had already had tea, Cassie returned a few minutes later with the hot medicinal beverage, by which time Hanna had calmed down considerably and the uncontrollable sobbing had now become an occasional sob; which was a blessing.

'Why is the sergeant looking around the house, Hanna? Didn't they have all day to do it?'

'They can't find a suicide note, and if there is one, they think it might help explain why Dad killed himself,' sniffed Hanna.

'Hanna, I'm so very sorry. What a dreadful thing to happen.' The friends sat quietly on the sofa, holding each other; sharing the grief.

'There are definitely no signs of a struggle or burglary,' commented the sergeant as he came back into the lounge. 'Possibly when you feel up to it, Hanna, you could have a look around?'

'Sure,' sniffed Hanna.

'I'll have a quick look outside.' suggested the police officer. The light was starting to fade, and the detective fetched a torch from the car. He stood for a moment and looked at the farmhouse. It was a compact thatched roof dwelling with yellow painted wattle and daub walls. Not sure in this light, thought Chris, it could be cream. The house was perfectly symmetrical with two downstairs diamond shaped leaded glass windows on either side of the wooden front door, accompanied by two matching upstairs windows. On the apex of the long straw ridge a bird finial kept a witch on a broom company. Both had, according to thatcher folklore, tirelessly kept witches and birds at bay for centuries. Chris shook his head. It was so unfamiliar. It was nothing like Lewisham or Croydon.

To the left of the house there was a large garden shed. A dark brown timber structure similar to the ones he had seen at the allotments in Croydon. It was unlocked and there was no evidence to suggest that it had ever been padlocked. His first challenge was to get passed two lawnmowers just inside the door. One was a rusty old push mower and the other a more modern looking Hayter petrol version with petrol and grass congealed around the filler cap and over the motor cover. The dusty grass collector lay on the ground behind it, half-full of grass cuttings. Having managed to negotiate the obstacle, his reward for his efforts was to find himself surrounded by clutter. There were ceramic pots, some whole and some broken; garden tools on the floor and leaning against the walls; shelves bending under the weight of half empty ant and slug poisons; tins of paint and bottles of white spirit; hand tools and dozens of glass jars filled with various sizes of nuts, bolts, nails and screws. One of the jars had fallen off the shelf, the nails spread out over the floor where it had smashed open. There's no note here he thought.

The detective closed the garden shed door, leaving behind the smell of rotting vegetation and two-stroke engine oil, and walked around to the back of the farmhouse. He was not surprised to find an untidy garden with a wooden summer house, two small ponds and a beehive. Keeping well clear of the beehive, he walked down to the bottom of the garden and through a small gap in the hedge. On the other side of the hedge were undulating farm fields stretching out to the horizon. Even though it was getting dark, he could see the green carpet of new winter wheat. There wasn't a sound. He stood in the perfect silence that surrounded him, and looked out over the land.

'Wow,' he said to himself. After a few minutes he took out his mobile and looking at the time decided he'd better get off home. Back at the house he found Hanna and Cassie still in the lounge.

'Find anything, Chris?' asked Hanna.

'No nothing I'm afraid,' he replied. 'Hanna, can I ask you a bit of a random question?'

'Sure, Chris,' replied Hanna.

'How old is the house?'

'17th Century apparently,' she replied smiling.

'Amazing,' Chris said slowly shaking his head. 'Right, if you don't mind, I'll head back to the station. Hanna, if there is anything you need to ask or talk about, please contact DI James or myself. Nice meeting you, Cassie. Look after her. Good night. Laters.'

'Come on Hanna, let's see what there is for tea,' suggested Cassie. A few minutes later, Cassie was stir frying strips of beef in a mix of worchester sauce, soy, ketchup, and chilli powder. When the meat had browned, she added a packet of part-boiled rice to the wok, and two minutes later the food was ready. Hanna poured a couple of whiskeys, and for a few moments, life was back to normal.

'Cassie, thank you so much for coming.'

'Don't be silly, it's the least I could do. We'll get you sorted. Promise.' Hanna suddenly realised that she hadn't eaten since breakfast, and was starving.

'I think we are short on dessert, would you like another drink?' asked Hanna.

'Yeh, why not.'

'I hope you don't mind me asking, but you said your Dad was worried about the harvest.'

'The last three summer harvests haven't been good. Dad was convinced that someone was tampering with the soil.'

'You mean deliberately contaminating it?' asked Cassie.

'Yes. He had no evidence, but he was convinced it had something to do with the new housing development. On the one hand, the councils are under pressure to build new houses, and on the other, there's the vocal anti-development mob trying to stop the use of green field sites.'

'So your Dad thought contaminated fields were no good for farming, but a good brown site for housing, hence the deliberate contamination.'

'Yes, pretty much.'

'But who would benefit?'

'Could be anyone, but I guess the developers and possibly the council.'

'That's quite an accusation. You mean the council are receiving some sort of back-hander if they help with acquiring land?'

'It does sound crazy, Cassie. But ask yourself this question. A new housing development next to our farm gets approval, and before the houses are even completed, a parish councillor has moved into one of the flashy new houses.'

'Said like a true barrister, but it could just be a coincidence.'

'Our farm is on the edge of the village, and adjacent to the new housing development. The farm is green field so the application gets rejected. The problem, however, has not gone away for the developers. They still need the land. If our farm becomes unusable for farming, problem solved, they have their brown site.'

'Putting it that way, it does sound possible,' agreed Cassie. 'But it would be a risky thing to do.'

'Another factor is the general feeling in the village about the councillor who just happens to be residing in the new house next door. Most people think he doesn't play with a straight bat. I can remember this being the case, years and years ago, when I was growing up.'

'You mean he is corrupt?' asked Cassie, starting to think this is better than anything on TV.

'That's the problem. He has never been caught doing anything illegal. It is very strange because no matter what he does, the villagers always think he is up to something dodgy. The rumours are rife. It's like he's using the worst PR firm on the planet.'

'Hanna, who it is?'

'Richard Kettering-Smythe. He likes to be called KS for some reason. He is also the chairman of *Swarm International UK* a charity helping to reduce malaria fatalities. In real life he is an estate agent.'

'Well that says it all,' exclaimed Cassie. The friends looked at each other and burst out laughing.

Moz waved goodnight to Alistair and Jessica Burns as they walked off in the dark towards the farmhouse. Phew, what a day he thought closing the front door to the converted barn. He stopped for a moment in the wide spacious entrance, and looked up at the cathedral-esque vaulted ceiling. At the other end of the room, there were large glass French doors leading out onto a now dark patio and lawn. The wooden floors gave the house an authentic rustic feel, but looked somewhat cold and bare despite the loose rugs and carpets. Thankfully the floorboards did hide underfloor heating. The walls were exposed beams and stud work, dating back to tutor times, and left as a reminder of the barn's original use. A severe looking iron spiral staircase corkscrewed its way to a mezzanine landing and three cosy bedrooms. Exposed red brickwork supported the roof, showing off its strength to the upstairs legacy beams and stud work. Ya, I like it, we'll be ok here thought Moz. The smell of meat cooking stopped the daydreaming about the house, and he headed back to the kitchen.

'Ok kids, I think it's an early night for all of us. Get showered. Dinner won't be long,' said Elsa.

'Smells good,' said Moz coming up behind his wife, and putting his arms around her waist. Kissing her neck, he looked over her shoulder to see what was cooking on the hob.

'Meatballs, mash potato, carrots and gravy. First proper meal in thirty six hours,' said the mother.

'What do you think of the Burns, Els?' asked Moz.

'They certainly made us feel welcome. It couldn't have been easy with the suicide thing. It probably sounds selfish, but I am quite relieved about the house.'

'Ya, me too. I didn't expect something so modern,' agreed her husband. 'We would have used the old wood for bbq, but convert it to a house, that's quite clever,' he added.

'Seeing the police here this morning was a surprise,' continued Elsa.

'Ya, who would have thought, travel all this way, and the first people we meet are the British police. The locals didn't seem bothered by the police presence. Everyone was quite calm. Did you notice how polite the police officers where?' commented Moz.

'Ya, I heard them calling people by their first names. Also there were no guns.'

'You're absolutely right, Els. Not a single gun in sight.'

DI James watched Hanna and her sergeant drive away, and it wasn't long before the remaining police vehicles followed. The reporter for *The Counties Herald*, a newspaper with a grand name and a dwindling readership, was hovering behind a couple of bushes outside the conservatory.

'Please go home, Mr Flynn. You are now bordering on trespass,' the Inspector called out to the undercover journalist as Jessica and Alistair Burns came crunching up the drive.

'Still here, Inspector?' asked Alistair.

'Just about to leave, Mr Burns.'

'Do you have time for a cup of soup and a roll? We're going to have one,' offered Jessica. DI James was too tired to refuse and took up the offer of the soup, and in the comfort of the farmhouse kitchen she brought the Burns' up to date with the day's proceedings. When DI James left, Alistair poured a couple of whiskeys, and the farmer and his wife sat at the kitchen table looking at each other in disbelief.

'What a day,' said Alistair. Suddenly the silence was broken by the sound of a speeding car, skidding to a halt on the loose driveway stones. A car door banged and Richard Kettering-Smythe came rushing into the kitchen.

'Jess, Alistair. I think I left my coat in the conservatory,' he explained as he rushed passed the surprised couple.

'It's not here,' said KS frantically searching the room.

'Possibly taken accidentally by somebody else,' suggested Alistair.

'This can't be happening,' said the estate agent, with sheer terror on his face.

'I'm sure the person who took it will bring it back in the morning,' said Jessica quite calmly.

'I sincerely hope so,' said the councillor as he disappeared into the night. My, my, I have never seen that pillar of society look so rattled thought the undercover journalist from his vantage point in the bushes.

CHAPTER 8

In 1085, Richard Delark attended a public enquiry that resulted in an entry in the Domesday Book: four beehives, one mill. It was an event that must have created much excitement in this small rural settlement that was recorded for prosperity as Weatherford. Despite the cynical view held by some of the residents that this official Norman visit was the last time anything interesting happened in the village, the royal officers involved in this monumental undertaking would be astonished, that nearly 1,000 years after their survey, almost every reference to Weatherford mentions the entry in the Book of Judgement.

It is one of a number of small farming villages that can be found in the north and west of the county. Situated between Wolburn Market and Blacktree Crossing it has a population, according to the last census, of 2,500 inhabitants. A number that has hardly changed in decades.

The cynics are partly correct about the lack of excitement in a settlement where the main activity has been ploughing and harvesting for centuries. Avoiding most civil upheavals, the farmers of this once boggy countryside transformed it into arable land, and the crops grown here helped make England a powerful and prosperous nation.

A visitor heading towards Weatherford, once having escaped the gridlocked traffic of Wolburn Market, is soon out in the countryside, and surrounded by undulating fields. The road was not always in such good condition. For years the residents complained about the potholes, and for years nothing was done. All was lost until someone in far off Leeds decided to invite the Tour de France, the most arduous athletic competition ever devised, to start up North.

The legacy of this great race has been twofold. Firstly there was a herculean effort on the part of the powers that be to resurface the roads earmarked for the race. Weatherford was on the route, and became an unexpected beneficiary of this unknown person in Leeds. The second legacy was the beautiful countryside being invaded every weekend by middle-aged pelotons of aspiring Chris Froomes, huffing and puffing their way up and down dale along the narrow country roads wearing sweaty, tight-fitting lycra.

Approaching the outskirts of the village, a recently replaced '*Hands off Weatherford*' sign welcomes the visitor. A little further on is an iconic red telephone box. No longer used for its original function; it is now a mini self-help library. A notice cello-taped to the mounting that once supported the old coin operated telephone invites residents to borrow a maximum of two books, and return them as soon as possible. Despite the polite offer, you never see anyone using this quaint recycled public service.

On the left hand side, just beyond the mini-library, there are a row of thatch roofed houses with cream walls and diamond shaped leaded glass windows; neat, closely cut grass verges and beds of colourful autumn flowers. Almost all of the houses display a bright green florescent A4 sign in a window politely demanding 'Say No to Greenfield Development'. Like the self-help library, there doesn't seem to be anyone around to read them.

On the opposite side of the road there is a remnant of the past, a large dilapidated wooden building with sliding doors that have come off their rails, and a cracked concrete forecourt over-run with weeds. Along the top of the entire length of the building, and just below the roof line the visitor can still make out the large faded yellow letters belonging to a bygone era:

COHEN'S MOTOR CAR SERVICES

A smaller rusty sign attached to a low boundary brick wall optimistically tells customers that:

SHELL WILL KEEP YOU GOING FOREVER

Passing the Alms Houses on the left, the visitor approaches the Old High Street junction with its war memorial on the corner. All Saints, a 16th century church, stands majestically on the right hand side. Wolburn Market Road becomes London Road which continues southwards out of the village past the riding school to the capital which according to google maps is 85 miles away.

The church is a large stone building, and like most English churches, it has had its fair share of renovations over the centuries. The result has been to produce a magnificent traditionally designed place of worship. Unlike the village with its air of despondency, its grandeur dominates its surroundings. There are four large beech trees, two on either side of a lych-gate, pointing 70 feet towards the heavens and were planted to commemorate Queen Victoria's coronation. The highly decorated wooden lych-gate was funded by the villagers almost eighty years later to celebrate the life of the same queen.

Sir Michael and Lady Kay Beswick are the current owners of the Manor House. According to the family's version of events, King Henry VIII granted the house and land to an ancestor Sir Randolph Beswick for his support during the dissolution of the monasteries. Sir Randolph funded the construction of the original church, and he and his Lady Beswick are buried in the south chapel.

Weatherford has not produced any famous sons or daughters since. No prime ministers, no commanders-in-chief, no thespians. There was a radically minded photographer who lived in the village in the 1970s. He specialised in taking photos of so-called police brutality and won a Weatherford Photographic Society award in 1976 for a photo of an abandoned Canary Wharf. Following this prestigious award he decided his talents were wasted on passport photos, and spurred on by mind enhancing substances escaped the lack of artistic opportunities in Weatherford to seek fame and fortune in Manchester. He was never heard of again.

Despite not having any famous residents, the village has had its fair share of brave individuals. The young men who volunteered to support the Parliamentarians during the English Civil War, numerous military exploits of the British Empire, and two World Wars. The decision of these brave individuals to go off and fight in some far off land probably had far more of an impact on the families and friends they left behind in Weatherford than the contribution to making the world a better place.

This was certainly the case of three brothers; Joseph, Thomas and Arthur Williams. A visitor to the church will discover a marble memorial plaque mounted on the wall to the left of the altar in the south chapel inscribed with the epitaph:

In loving memory of our brave sons who died
gallantly defending their country
in the South African War 1899 – 1902.
Cpl Joseph Williams killed 15 February 1900
Kimberley
L/Cpl Thomas Williams killed 18 February 1900
Paardeberg
L/Cpl Arthur Williams killed 19 February 1900
Paardeberg

They paid the supreme price for queen and country.

An army officer and his aides arrived in the village the day after Boxing Day 1899, and set up a recruitment office in the primary school hall. They were from the North Essex Imperial Yeomanry Regiment. News soon spread that they were looking for volunteers with horse- and marksmanship skills to join the Regiment, and go fight in South Africa.

When Joseph aged 22, Thomas 20, and Arthur 18, heard the news they ran down the high street to tell their father, the local ironmonger, that they were going to join the army. Their father was hardly given time to respond before the three boys disappeared down School Lane.

There was a queue of other like-minded adventurers, but it was not long before they had been interviewed by a Sergeant-Major with a huge black moustache. Name? Age? Address? Father's name? Father's Occupation? Can you ride a horse? Can you shoot with a rifle? Can you run? Pay is 5 shillings and sixpence per day, and 1 shilling and sixpence per day for forage. Any questions? This was followed by a somewhat superficial medical examination behind a white canvas screen by a tall thin disinterested man in a white coat and a stethoscope draped around his neck. Back to the Sergeant-Major.

'The doctor says you are of use to the Empire, Mr Williams. Any questions? No? Good. Please sign here so that Her Majesty knows you are happy with her offer. Please go home and bid farewell to your family, you may bring a few personal items with you and report back here at 1300 sharp. If you are late you will be considered to be absent without leave and when we find you, we will arrest you.'

The three boys decided it was best to do as they had been told, and returned home to find their mother in floods of tears. She begged them not to go, while her husband tried to calm her down by saying everything was going to be alright and the boys needed an adventure. Far better than staying in this dull boring village getting up to mischief. Let them get out there and see the world, just like Mr Rudyard Kipling.

The boys left a distraught mother and a proud father at the garden gate, and were back at the school hall at 1300 sharp. They spent most of that night travelling in an open cart to Eastbourne where their new home was a temporary tent camp. Cold and tired, Joseph the eldest brother grumbled that living in a tent was inhumane, and his brothers quickly told him to keep quiet as a Lance Corporal approached them and asked the gentlemen if there was a problem.

The next two weeks were taken up with horse- and marksmanship. Despite the long exhausting days, the three brothers found their new life exhilarating. No sooner had they adjusted to life in the tent town, they were heading off to Southampton. Two weeks later, the shipping report announced the arrival of the three brothers in South Africa.

Cape News, 30 January 1900. The St. Vincent docked in Cape Town and disembarked 40 officers, 650 men, 700 troop horses of the North Essex Imperial Yeomanry, as well as ammunition and cordite.

The first few days in Cape Town for the four Companies of the 21st Battalion involved drill and marksmanship carried out against the magnificent backdrop of Table Mountain with its cloud tablecloth. The rumour amongst the soldiers was that they were the first contingent of 10,000 soldiers on their way to South Africa.

The 500 mile train journey to the front took the soldiers through sparse, flat and desolate countryside, accompanied by a wind that created clouds of red dust. Sweat from the searing heat, caked the dust onto their skin and clothes. Tired and exhausted the three brothers were relieved to reach their stop some 25 miles south of Kimberley.

There was an opportunity to rest and see to the horses. The supply of food and fresh water was sporadic, and it soon became obvious to the newcomers that there were problems with supplies getting to the front. Two days after their arrival the Company of Yeomanry were given their battle orders to advance on, and relieve Kimberley.

The emancipation of the diamond city started at half one in the morning for the William brothers. General John French with a battalion of cavalry at his disposal set off on a diversionary route towards their objective. They reached Klipdrift and could see the mine head gear in the distance. Before them a wide plain, with high ground on either side. The General decided to attack; with the enemy firing from both flanks the battalion was given the order to chanter; two miles further on they were ordered to charge.

Soon there was an enormous dust cloud thundering across the flat ground, accompanied by the sound of enemy gunfire. As the order to charge was given, Joseph was hit by a sniper to his right. He slumped forward on his horse, and remained in that position, until he slid off his mount half a mile further on.

The relief of Kimberley was successful, and it was only later that afternoon that the two brothers were given the news about Joseph. They didn't have time to mourn the loss of their elder brother. They spent the next day, together with the rest of their regiment, trying unsuccessfully to find the enemy in the vicinity of the town. That same evening, having had no rest, they received orders to head out in pursuit of the fleeing enemy. The following morning, they caught up with them at a place called Paardeberg. They were immediately ordered to attack.

The attack was over bare, open ground with large granite boulders. The horses were unable to negotiate these obstacles and the men dismounted. They were exposed to the enemy, and despite the lack of progress, were ordered to continue the frontal attack.

The William brothers heard the command to fix bayonets and found themselves fighting hand to hand with the enemy. Arthur was killed almost immediately. Thomas found himself in a tightly-knit group of ten soldiers and miraculously kept going forward until suddenly they were told to retreat.

Thomas' fate the next day did not involve any fighting. The British received a message from the enemy and it was misinterpreted as a surrender. Although feeling unwell from drinking contaminated water, Thomas volunteered, along with 30 other soldiers, to collect the prisoners. The enemy seeing the soldiers marching towards them opened fire. No one survived.

Joseph was buried in a quiet corner of the Kimberley Cemetery. Seething heat and dry, red, dusty soil, devoid of any flowers or grass; just patches of thorns. Thomas and Arthur were buried at Paardeberg in a mass grave overlooking the battlefield. A harsh, dry and desolate place with desert scrub growing in the shade of granite rocks and trying its best to find protection from the merciless sun.

Three ordinary brothers from Weatherford paid the supreme price for queen, country, gold and diamonds in the heat and dust of a far off land at places with unpronounceable names.

The visitor leaving the church has the choice of London Road or the Old High Street. Taking the latter, the War Memorial on the right hand side of the junction is hidden by a large red '*Hands Off Weatherford*' banner which will hopefully be removed in a couple of weeks when the Remembrance Day Service takes place across the road at the church. This will be followed by the laying of wreaths by various dignitaries and organisations in memory of the 21 soldiers whose names are inscribed on the base of the memorial. It is one of the rare occasions when residents are seen out and about in Weatherford.

The visitor would be surprised to hear, ten years ago, the remembrance service became the centre of a rather bizarre controversy. A parishioner objected, in her opinion, to the disrespectful practice of a number of parish councillors attending the service in track suits and trainers. A standoff between the council and the residents ensued, and was only resolved when the wearing of track suits for all occasions went out of fashion.

With increasing car ownership, the advent of superstores, and shopping morphing into some form of entertainment, the buying habits of the residents changed almost over-night. This tectonic shift in behaviour resulted in local high street shops closing, and it was not long before community support services, such as surgeries, followed suite.

All that remains of the Weatherford high street glory days is the pub, the primary school, and the sub-post office at the garage, which always seems to be under threat of closure. The old fabric of the community that thrived on villagers stopping to talk to each other in the high street disappeared, and has been replaced by social media. Without changing out of your pyjamas, you have all the village gossip you need at your fingertips.

So while the high street is remembered with fondness, and tv murder mystery programmes portray the quintessential rural village, the reality is, this stereotype we hold so dear, has disappeared. It has gone forever. The nation voted with its feet, abandoned the high street, and now drives miles and miles to the nearest out-of-town superstore.

If the visitor looks carefully at the houses in the Old High Street, it is possible to see traces of the old shop fronts with their large display windows and slightly larger than normal front doors. A number of them have the name Pollock, and the date they were built, displayed in relief just below the eaves. The visitor will also notice that many place names include the prefix 'old'.

Half way down the high street is proof that some habits die hard; the 400 year old pub. Despite its name, the Green Man is painted a bright blue colour which was most appropriate when it was called the Blue Bell Inn. The colour doesn't seem to bother anyone. Some of the older residents still call it the Blue Bell, even though the name changed twenty-five years ago.

The old police station faces the pub from across the road. In its heyday, it provided tipsy pub customers with endless opportunities to have a laugh at the police's expense. There were two pranks that were popular. The first was a dare for a pint. Stand opposite the police station and sing *The Laughing Policeman*. The pint of beer was awarded to the prankster who could entice a police officer out of the station, and be given a warning for disturbing the peace.

The most popular prank, however, involved the arrival of new sergeants. A car would be parked opposite the police station, and a group of noisy revellers would come out of the pub, get into the car and zig-zag slowly down the high street. Egged on by the constables, the sergeant would rush out, jump on his bicycle, stop the car, and then discover it was a prank. The end result was always the same; a very grumpy sergeant.

The biggest laugh, however, had nothing to do with mischievous pub customers. Back in 1985, the bank next door to the police station was robbed. There were no firearms nor violence involved. The fully manned police station was totally unaware that a robbery was taking place. One night, a robber forced entry into the bank via the roof, broke into the safe, stole the contents, and then escaped by virtue of the same roof. The police did not hear a sound. The burglary was discovered the next morning when the manager opened the bank. The robber, despite an extensive investigation, and assisted by plenty of villagers with their own ideas as to whom it was, has never been found. For six months after the robbery, if a villager bought a new car or went off on an expensive holiday, the jury in the Green Man would discuss, as the police would say, the new person of interest.

Next to the old police station, there is another red telephone box. Like the gate-keeper library, it has also been converted to modern use, and houses the village's only defibrillator. An innocuous item that last year, made the national news.

One December morning, a villager noticed the telephone box was devoid of its piece of medical equipment. Word spread, and it was not long before a small crowd of inquisitive residents had congregated at the vandalised phone box. The police were called, and half an hour later, Hugh Flynn, the journalist from *The Counties Herald*, arrived.

The next morning, there was an article about the theft in the newspaper, and by midday the local television news had arrived. That evening Weatherford and its stolen defibrillator featured on the evening news. Villagers were interviewed and blamed the theft on the lack of police patrols; the police made a statement advising the public that they were aware of the recent spate of petty crimes in rural areas; and Richard Kettering-Smythe, a spokesperson for the parish council, expressed his disgust at a theft that placed lives in danger. The defibrillator was replaced within a day, and village life returned to normal. What went unnoticed was the fact that the police had not responded to the initial 999 call that had, quite ironically, been made from outside the old police station.

At School Lane, the visitor can leave the village and the bright green 'Say No' protest posters in the windows, and head eastwards towards Blacktree Crossing; originally a Roman encampment on the banks of the Black River. By all accounts, the Romans were initially happy with their new settlement, until tiring of the English weather, they headed back home to Rome to regroup, before setting out to conquer the world with pizza.

The Victorian primary school is, not surprisingly, in School Lane. The road is lined with large, mature pin oak trees giving sanctuary to a cluster of beautiful Victorian buildings. Coming along School Lane is Pat Pollock, one of Weatherford's oldest residents, and a member of a family that is recorded in the Domesday Book. Scratch below the surface, and you are likely to find some connection to the Pollock family.

Pat and her mobility scooter, with a walking stick and umbrella sticking out from behind her seat, have been around for so long that nobody actually knows how old she is, and doesn't dare to ask either. She always has a smile, is cheerful and affable, and the villagers always stop to chat to her. She owns a couple of properties in the village which would indicate that she probably has a life story worth asking about. Nobody ever asks and nobody ever thinks to ask about her history; Pat and her scooter are just simply part of Weatherford. She has lived in the old school house for twenty years, and mischievously tells strangers and visitors to the village that she was one of the original pupils when the Victorian School opened in 1867.

Pat does not have a 'Say No' protest poster in her window. She is fully in favour of building more houses, and objects to the double standards of the protestors. In her opinion, protesting and saying 'no' is a waste of time; the houses are needed and must be built. She believes that the villagers should concentrate on getting the best deal for improving community facilities before developers are given permission to start building houses. When she goes to *'Hands off Weatherford'* protest meetings, she frustrates the hypocrites, as she calls them, with her pro-house building stance.

'Hello dear, you look like a visitor. Do you need any help? asks Pat as she stops her scooter on reaching the Old High Street.

'Hi, I'm from Manchester. What a beautiful place,' replied the young rambler.

'It certainly is. I would suggest you carry on down the hill passed the Manor House,' suggested Pat. 'There are only a few houses and a petrol garage along Blacktree Road,' she added.

'Is there anywhere to have a bite to eat?'

'I'm afraid not. The Green Man is closed on a Monday. The garage has a little shop, but if you want to stop for a meal Wolburn Market is the nearest town. I would love to stay and chat, but I'm going to be late for book club. Enjoy the rest of your visit, my dear.' Pat bid the visitor goodbye, and drove off on her scooter.

At the Old High Street end of School Lane there is a narrow track that leads to the Manor House. An old caste-iron fingerpost confirms that the village community hall and the windmill are also in the same direction. At the entrance to the 16th Century pile, the muddy track becomes a muddy public footpath and continues down the hill.

Apart from the events that led to Sir Randolph receiving a king's grant, the manor and its inhabitants have lived quietly and peacefully for hundreds of years in Weatherford. It was, therefore, somewhat of a surprise when the manor was invaded by foreigners.

At the end of every spring, four pairs of swans arrive at the Manor, and spend the summer rearing their young on the large pond in front of the house. The swans arrived as usual at the beginning of summer 2005, and everything appeared normal with the annual visitors, until two of them disappeared.

Sir Michael and Lady Beswick, who are normally quite laidback, and level-headed people were incensed at the disappearances. The genes of Sir Randolph that had produced unflinching loyalty to past monarchs had obviously been handed down through generations of the Beswick family; they wanted revenge.

The police were called, and after a cursory look at a few swan feathers, they issued an incident number, and left. The Beswicks were so outraged that someone had taken Her Majesty's swans that they sat up for five consecutive nights in a dark house with their shotguns at the ready. Eventually, they calmed down, and sense prevailed. The shotguns were put away, and the lights were turned on. Life on the pond had returned to normal, albeit minus a pair of swans.

One evening, about six weeks after the swans disappeared, three Poles who had arrived in the country at the beginning of the summer were bragging, in the Green Man, to Lucas and Dominic about killing and eating the swans. Lucas and Dominic returned home and told Alistair Burns about the conversation. Alistair in turn passed on the information to the Beswicks without mentioning how, when and where he had received the information. Now if it had been Sir Randolph he would have put on his armour and gone out and levelled a monastery. Not quite Lady Beswick's style. She asked the police to talk to the three offenders and let them know, in no uncertain terms, that what they did was not the way we do things here. After the chat with the police, the three Poles left the Weatherford area, and Sir Randolph smiled and made himself comfortable under the floor of the south chapel.

The footpath follows the edge of the manor's 100 acres of parkland, crosses the ford just before reaching London Road, and comes out opposite the entrance to Oak Tree Farm. At which point, it would be remiss of the visitor not to take a selfie with the manor house, and the windmill at the top of the hill as a background. The selfie taken, the rambler crosses the road, and waving thank you to an unmarked police car turning out of Oak Tree Farm walks up the road towards the church.

CHAPTER 9

The sun was starting to light up the horizon as Alistair Burns and Moz Nel drove along one of the muddy farm tracks. On reaching some high ground, Alistair stopped the utility vehicle so that the farmers had an uninterrupted view of the land. It was a dry morning with a bitterly cold north-easterly wind. Moz was dressed in a thin quilted jacket, thin khaki chino trousers, and no warm head protection. He was definitely not dressed for the cold English weather. By contrast, Alistair was warmly cocooned in a long sleeved fleece shirt, a padded wax jacket, and a waterproof tweed cap.

'Moz, I think Lucas or Dominic should run you into town, and get you kitted out for the cold.'

'Ya, good idea,' said Moz shifting from one foot to the other, and rubbing his hands together. 'I really didn't expect it to be so cold. I think the whole family is going to need a new wardrobe,' laughed Moz.

'Do you want to go back?' asked Alistair.

'No, no, let's get finished,' insisted Moz.

'Ok. Obviously the fields from here back to the road belong to the farm,' said Alistair pointing back towards the farmhouse from where they had come. Turning around he pointed towards the ridge. 'And those electricity pylons run along the boundary of the farm, which we refer to as the top fence.'

'How many hectares?' asked Moz.

'500 acres in total. That's about 200 hectares?'

'Ya, sounds about right,' agreed Moz. 'It's going to take a bit of getting used to the size of the farms here. Our farm is 2,500 hectares of which 400 are wheat. Sounds big, but if you don't have irrigation you can't grow much. A lot of it is just dust.'

'I don't think we have that problem here, someone up there helps us with the irrigation,' smiled Alistair pointing up at the sky.

'So where are we doing the trial?' enquired Moz blowing into his hands, and rubbing his ears.

'That field on the right running along the copse of trees. You can see the white poles marking the four corners. It's 100 acres.'

'Was there any particular reason for selecting that field? asked Moz.

'Two reasons really. Firstly, security. It is quite inaccessible to the public, and there are no public rights of way across there, so anyone on that land will be trespassing. The other reason is it is surrounded by company land. The thinking being, if there is any cross-contamination, the company land will act as a buffer. But I must say the farmers in the immediate vicinity are very supportive about the trial. They want it to go ahead.'

'I think a priority, before we start, is to meet the researchers at the seed company, and of course, the guys at head office,' suggested Moz.

'Not a problem, we'll get head office to set up the meetings. They deal with the paperwork, and the agencies. We'll leave all of that up to them. One other thing, we're going to erect a double high steel fence around the trial area, and install cctv as a precaution against protestors.'

'Ya, we have the same thing back in SA. It's a bit irritating when you are trying to help produce more food for your country, and there are people out there, who are not hungry, trying to stop us from at least trying,' commented Moz.

'I don't disagree Moz. Still we have to be careful and responsible,' answered Alistair.

'Ya, you're right,' replied Moz nodding his head. 'I hope you don't mind me asking, but where did you find Mr Townsend?'

'Ah, yes, over there on the left in the copse of oak,' replied Alistair, his hand trembling slightly as he pointed towards the clump of trees.

'Terrible thing to happen. Let us pray he has found peace.' Alistair was surprised at the religious comment, and momentarily looked at the burly farmer standing next to him. These newcomers look like us, behave like us, he thought, but there is a restlessness about them. Some kind of anxiety.

'Coffee at the farmhouse?' asked Alistair as they got back into the utility vehicle.

'I thought you would never ask. I'm so numb I think a brandy with a dash of coffee, and a warm wife would be better.' The two men laughed, and headed back to the warm bosom of the family.

The doorbell rang, and Bella skipped through the house and opened the door. Standing there was Dominic, the owner of the purple hair.

'Miss Bella. Please call your mum, we have something to show her.' Elsa hearing the conversation came to the door.

'Mrs Elsa, wait here, we have something to show you,' said Dominic, turning and running down the driveway and disappearing around the corner. Elsa and Bella looked at each other, and giggled. A few moments later Dominic and Lucas, the owner of the pink hair, reappeared side by side, both wearing tweed caps, and strutting along with their thumbs hooked behind imaginary braces like the Artful Dodger. A few paces behind them walked Moz, wearing a waterproof tweed cap, navy blue double lined waterproof trousers, a heavy flannel red and black check shirt, all season gloves, wellington boots and a padded wax jacket.

'Mrs Elsa, please I introduce you, Mr English Gentleman Farmer,' announced Dominic. Moz was smiling from ear to ear, and pretended to be on a Parisian catwalk. By this time Paul had joined the reception party. The South Africans and the Lithuanians clapped, shrieked with laughter and wolf whistled.

Dinner was ready, and the Nel family sat down to lamb chops, roast potatoes, carrots sprinkled with sugar, rice and gravy.

'Food looks delicious, Els,' complimented Moz as he dished up for the children. 'Well you have some idea what I did today, what did you guys do?'

'We met the head teacher, Mrs Broadhurst. I liked her,' said Paul.

'She gave us a tour of the school. It's a very old building,' added Bella.

'Els what did you think of it?' asked Moz.

'Well it is very different. Mrs Broadhurst was good with the kids. Made them feel welcome. Treated them like adults. Paul is going into Year 4, and Bella Year 6. They have lunch at school which was a surprise.' Moz listened carefully, and nodded his head. 'But there was a bigger surprise. They wear uniforms,' added Elsa.

'We were told the kids didn't wear school uniforms here,' remarked an astonished Moz.

'Well apparently they do. We bumped into Jessica Burns when we got back, and she has offered to take us to Wolburn Market to sort out the uniforms, and show us around a bit. How was your day, Mozie?'

'Well, Alistair gave me a tour of the farm, and showed me the site where the trial will take place. The farms are small. This one is only 200 hectares.'

'Yeh, but I guess all of it is usable,' replied Elsa.

'Ya, you're right Els. Trouble is, everything is so unfamiliar. I'll have to learn quickly. We also set up a few meetings with the trial people, and then Dominic took me shopping,' smiled Moz. 'Phew, it was bloody freezing out there this morning. We'll have to get the kids proper warm clothes. On the way back, we stopped at the Green Man pub for lunch. It was Dominic's idea. Ag shame, I think he felt he had to be sociable.'

'I saw the Green Man on the way to the school. It's painted blue. What was it like?' asked Elsa.

'It isn't a Spur Steakhouse, that's for sure. I'll take you down there and show you. Everything is so old. Hanna Townsend was there,' continued Moz.

'Shit. How did that go?' exclaimed Elsa.

'Ya, very difficult. Not easy to think of the right things say. Just asked her how she was coping. Said she was doing fine, and introduced me to her friend Cassie who is here looking after her. She sends her love to you and the kids. We sat quite close to them, and you couldn't help but overhear their conversation. They were talking about someone called Kettering something. Hanna seemed quite uptight about it. Two guys came in, mid-thirties, a bit loud and full of themselves, started chatting them up. Talked about leads they had in the area, and that they were staying a few more nights. Dominic said they were from London, and had been at the shoot. He didn't seem to like them very much. Anyway, we finished and left.'

Hanna and Cassie were back in the kitchen at Grey Pigeon Farm. They were sitting at the kitchen table, each with a glass of wine in front of them. The friends were not getting on very well. Cassie was tired of Hanna's obsession about Kettering-Smythe.

'Hanna, as your friend, I'm telling you to either get proof about Kettering-Smythe or drop it. You've made your point about him. You need to get a grip, and stop going over and over old ground. I love you, and I understand how you feel, but this is going to get you nowhere.'

'Ok, what do you suggest I do?' snarled Hanna.

'Hanna, healthy crop production is my area of expertise. I think we must take a close look at the fields. We need to find out why the crops are failing. We need to take samples, have them analysed, and find an answer. I can help, but it will take time, and dare I say it, might cost quite a lot of money. You are the lawyer, we get the evidence, and you make a case against Kettering-Smythe. I think Dudley Baines and Alexis Castellanos could be useful.'

'They just want to get into your knickers,' was the dismissive reply.

'Hanna, that comment was unnecessary, and very hurtful. You are not listening to me. They might do the wide-boy thing, but they have a wealth of knowledge about agricultural property. They work for a large organisation in the City, not some fly-by-night outfit. We can use their experience, and work out what you are going to do with the farm in the long term. Their assistance might be invaluable. Don't reject them out of hand.'

'I'm tired and sad, Cassie. I'm so very sorry. I really shouldn't take it out on you. I don't know what to do. Please help me.'

'Of course I will. I won't let you down. I promise. Come here.' The friends stood in the kitchen, holding each other and cried.

An unmarked police car turned into Fields View, the new housing development adjacent to Grey Pigeon Farm, and stopped outside 10 View Drive. Below the house number was a grey slate nameplate with IRENE embossed in gold. DI James pressed the doorbell, and after a brief wait, the front door opened.

'Mr Kettering-Smythe?'

'Yes.'

'I don't know if you remember me, DI Veronica James, South Essex Police, and this is my colleague DS Chris Brown.' Both police officers showing their warrant cards in unison. 'We're here to ask you a few questions about the Townsend suicide. May we come in?' A rhetorical question, and they were invited in.

'Please sit. How can I help you?' asked the estate agent.

'I'll get straight to the point. We have two sets of tyre tracks, and two sets of shoe prints. One set of shoe prints we identified as belonging to Mr

Townsend, and the tyre tracks of his 4x4 start at the London Road turnoff and end at the passing place where we found his vehicle. The other set of tyre tracks were made by a vehicle that used Potts Lane, stopped at Mr Townsend's Land Rover, then drove on towards London Road.' The councillor sat very still, and looked the Inspector in the eye. 'The Potts Lane tracks match your car, Mr Kettering-Smythe,' explained DI James.

'I didn't use Potts Lane that morning, Inspector. I went from here straight to the shoot.'

'The vehicle stopped alongside the 4x4, and the second set of shoe prints we found, would suggest the owner of the shoes got out of the vehicle, opened the driver's door, then went through a gap in the hedgerow, and returned to his stationary vehicle,' continued DS Brown.

'I didn't use Potts Lane that morning,' repeated KS. The police officers looked at each other, and the sergeant raised his eyebrows at his boss.

'Mr Kettering-Smythe, we need to take a DNA sample, either here or at the station. If you don't have any objections, we would also like to take all the shoes you possess back with us for forensics,' explained the inspector. The detectives stood up, and KS remained seated looking down at the carpet.

'Inspector, I must apologise. I have misled you and your sergeant.' The inspector and the sergeant sat down again. 'I did use Potts Lane that morning, and Brian's vehicle was parked there. It was very early, and there wasn't anyone in the Land Rover. I stopped to see if there was anything untoward. I looked in the driver's side, nothing seemed out of place. There was a gap in the hedgerow, and I had a quick look across the field, but couldn't see anything. It was still quite dark. I got back in my car, and drove home.'

'So why did you lie to us earlier?' asked the DI.

'I really don't know. I'm very sorry.'

'Misleading or withholding information during a police investigation is a serious offence, Mr Kettering-Smythe.' explained the DS.

'Yes, I'm aware of that. Please accept my apology, and I can assure you, you have my full cooperation,' assured the calm councillor paddling frantically under the water.

DNA sample taken, and the bagged up shoes in the boot, the police left the chairman of *Swarm International UK* to ponder whether there were to be any repercussions for his error.

'Ma'am, do you believe him?'

'I'm not sure. The question still remains as to why he should lie in the first place.'

'Maybe we caught him off guard, he was nervous and not thinking clearly or thought it would be less complicated just to say he wasn't there,' suggested the sergeant.

'Yep, you could be right Chris, it's as simple as that,' replied the DI.

'I don't like him though. There's something smarmy about him,' commented the DS.

'Just because you don't like someone doesn't mean they are up to mischief.' The inspector's phone started to ring.

'It's the pathologist,' said the inspector, pressing the keypad. 'Doctor Samuels, good afternoon.'

'Veronica, I thought I'd give you a quick call about Mr Townsend. Nothing suspicious. Unless you have anything to the contrary, I'm very confident it was suicide.'

'Thank you Bill. Nothing suspicious our end either.'

'Any sign of a suicide note?'

'No. We don't think there is one.'

'OK, Veronica. I'll email you the report by midday tomorrow.'

'Thanks. Take care.' The DI pressed the keypad. 'We'll have to run this past the super, but I think we have a result,' she commented.

'I really feel sorry for Hanna. Without a suicide note, she will spend the rest of her life asking the question why,' commented the DS.

'Well one consolation, she can now go ahead with the funeral.' said Veronica.

CHAPTER 10

Oak Tree Farm, for the second time in two weeks, was once again a hive of catering activity. Jessica Burns had spent most of the week arranging a welcome party for the Nels. The Green Man was the venue, but it had its limitations. Sue Cooper, the landlady, was unable to provide any food due to the lack of staff.

Yasmin Chowdhury did not hesitate to offer her assistance when a rather tense and apologetic Jessica asked her for help. She enjoyed catering for parties. It was something she had done from an early age with her mother in Leicester. Over the years she had catered for many village functions, and when her two boys had played football for Weatherford Rovers, she almost single-handedly provided the burgers and drinks for the home games.

At the beginning of the week, Jessica had, as promised, taken Elsa, Paul and Bella to Wolburn Market to buy school uniforms. Shopping done, they had a bit of us-time, and in one of the town's numerous coffee shops, over a large slice of Death by Chocolate and a skinny latte to balance the calories, Jessica mentioned the problem she was having with the catering. Elsa, much to Jessica's surprise and relief, offered to help out as well.

'Hi Elsa. Sorry I'm a bit late. The traffic in the village was terrible.' Yasmin glanced at Elsa and laughed. 'Just kidding. It's a local joke. Let's have a coffee before we start. I've made us some balushahi. They're like a donut, except you add yoghurt to the flour.' Yasmin took two very bright pink floral aprons, and a couple of *Now That's What I Call Music* CDs out of a re-useable M&S carrier bag.

Jessica came into the kitchen with a mobile phone pressed to her ear, and mouthed
hi to the women.

'Latest number of guests, Jess?' asked Yasmin as the hostess finished her call.

'I've spoken to thirty people so far, but that doesn't mean they will all come. Work on twenty five. What have you decided to do?'

'We've split it up between us. I'm doing peanut chicken satay, baked onion bhajis, goat's cheese and leek tart, for the veggies, and something I've just learnt to do, parmesan cheese straws,' smiled Yasmin.

'I'm doing sweet and spicy meatballs, bacon quiche tarts, sticky garlic chicken wings and four cheeses stuffed mushrooms,' added Elsa.

'Wow, sounds fabulous, one verse of Jerusalem then crack on,' laughed Jessica, helping herself to a balushahi, and leaving the kitchen as her mobile started to ring.

Yasmin and Elsa didn't sing a verse of Jerusalem, but did crack on. They had their work cut out, if they were going to meet their early evening deadline. The women had met the day the Nels arrived at Oak Tree Farm, but had not seen each other since. It did not take long for either of them to realise that the other was a competent cook. With a common cause, and not much time to get everything done, they were soon working together as if they had done it all before.

It's Raining Men! Hallelujah!
It's Raining Men!

greeted Alistair as he came into the kitchen and threw his wellington boots down behind the door. What is going on, he thought, screeching women, loud music, pink aprons and food spread out all over the place.

What a bloody mess. Ant and Dec had sneaked in behind the farmer, and waging their tails with excitement started barking and jumping up at Yasmin and Elsa, much to Alistair's annoyance.

'Hi Alistair.' greeted Yasmin as she turned the music down.

Girls just want to have fun
Oh girls just wanna have fun

sang Jessica as she came back into the kitchen, then stopped and glared at her husband. 'Stop scowling, Alistair. We're having fun. Something you have forgotten how to do,' snarled his wife.

'Bloody cold out there. Where's my lunch?' demanded the husband, ignoring his wife's comment.

'Sorry, Alistair, we haven't had time. There's plenty in the fridge for you to make yourself a ploughman's.'

'I need hot food, I'm freezing, dammit,' cursed the irate farmer.

'I'll make some coffee,' offered Elsa, hoping to reduce the tension in the room. The farmer, behaving like a bear with a sore head, begrudgingly made his own lunch, didn't clear up after himself, and banged the door as he left the kitchen with his plate of cold food.

'Trouble in paradise,' whispered Yasmin. 'Jessica is a good friend, so it is rather sad to see it happening.'

'What's the problem?' asked Elsa.

'Not sure, but they can't seem to get on with each other at the moment.'

'Maybe it is only temporary and they will sort things out. They are nice people,' replied Elsa. 'What did Jessica mean about a verse of Jerusalem?'

'Oh that. The WI. The Woman's Institute. Groups of woman around the country get together and make jam and bake cakes for charity. It's a bit more serious than that, has a long history, and at each meeting they sing the hymn Jerusalem.'

Talk turned to the common subject of families, husbands, and children. Yasmin's family had arrived in England as refugees from East Africa in the late 1960s and settled in Leicester. Her marriage to Samir had been arranged between her family and another refugee family from East Africa, the Chowdhurys, who had settled in Weatherford.

She told Elsa how difficult it had been for them in Weatherford in the beginning. Nobody wanted them in the village. Things got a lot easier when her two boys were born and, as a family, were able to become more involved in village life.

She went on to tell Elsa how, as a young married couple, they had been befriended by Cyril Cohen, himself a Jewish refugee from Eastern Europe, and the owner of the now derelict, Cohen Motor Car Services. He had mentored Samir. Her husband realised how fortunate he was to be given the opportunity, and learnt as much as he could from Old Man Cohen. All the long hours and hard work paid off. When the village started to lose its shops and services, Samir saw an opportunity to open the garage, shop and sub-post office on the Blacktree Crossing Road. That's how I met Jessica. When she moved into the village, she came into the shop looking for a part-time job, and still does a couple of mornings and the odd late shift.

'And your sons?' asked Elsa.

'Kabir, my eldest, is training to be a plastic surgeon, and Sanjay is a very successful hairdresser in London. He has four salons, and is used by a number of London fashion labels and designers. I'm so very proud of both of them.'

'That's useful, Yasmin. One son gives your face a bit of a nip and a tuck, and the other son gives you a hairstyle to cover up the scars,' joked Elsa.

'Risky, if they decide to get their own back for my constant nagging when they were growing up,' laughed Yasmin. 'Anyway, enough of the Chowdhurys, how did you meet Moz?'

'Oh, our lives are not very exciting,' remarked Elsa. 'Our early ancestors left the Cape at the beginning of the 1840s in an attempt to escape British colonial rule. There were a number of other families that made the same journey, and they settled along the Vaal River in the Kempdale area. It was not an easy life, but eventually they managed to start growing crops. Moz and I were childhood sweethearts, and we got married in our early twenties at the local reformed church, and the kids were born at the same hospital as Moz and I. They now go to the same school as we did. Moz's father is going to retire soon, and we will take over the farm.'

'So why England? asked Yasmin.

'Moz has been growing this new generation wheat seed for a number of years. He saw an advert for research farmers here in the UK for the new trials, and he applied. It's only a two year contract. We thought it might be a bit of fun, and a good experience for the kids.'

'I read somewhere that there are a lot of murders in South Africa.' The question caught Elsa off guard. 'Aren't you afraid of the violence?'

'It is, as it is. You just remain vigilant, and get on with your life,' replied Elsa in a matter of fact way. 'I have to say it is very nice to be away from all of that. It is so safe here,' added Elsa.

The women fell silent, and busied themselves with their cooking. Yasmin had not thought about the past for a very long time. Talking to Elsa it all came flooding back. Arriving in England as a little girl, how difficult it had been for her parents to settle down, and how the people of Weatherford had initially ostracised them when they came to live in the village as a young married couple. Elsa was impressed with Yasmin and how the families had managed to overcome the difficulties they had experienced as refugees.

Yasmin liked Elsa. They were both from Africa, and in some strange way it created a bond of friendship between them. She was curious about South Africa, and there were so many questions she wanted to ask. Now's probably not the right time, she thought. I'll wait until we get to know each other a bit better. There was one question, however, that couldn't wait.

'Elsa, I hope you don't mind me asking. Why is Moz called Moz?'

'It's short for Moses,' laughed Elsa.

CHAPTER 11

Hugh Flynn, reporter for *The Counties Herald*, is a jack of all trades when it comes to journalism. He is in his mid-fifties, and a lifestyle of too much booze, excessive smoking, and no gym membership has resulted in him no longer having the body of a Greek God. The mustard coloured suit, which he bought at a Primark sale, is always creased, and his shoes could do with a polish. He has that unfortunate hair that always looks greasy, and is not helped by a large fringe that hangs down over his right eye which he constantly sweeps back away from his forehead. He walks slowly with a stoop, and from a distance he looks like the gentlemen of the elderly crossing road sign.

His newspaper, like many of its ilk, is bravely squaring up to competition from free 24 hour news, fake news and online advertising. Its survival against this onslaught is not the result of scrutinising and redefining the business model, but down to plain ordinary human nature known as local gossip. In addition to fulfilling the birth right called freedom of speech, which works quite well when everyone has the same opinion as oneself, the newspaper gives the reader the opportunity to read about uniquely local issues such as potholes and petty crime. Other community spirited articles include the presentation of obscure awards for excellence handed out to businesses and council run services, reader's letters objecting to housing development and a round-up of how the local sporting talent is doing. Circulation is also helped by the reader's almost voyeuristic need to see either their name in print or a photo of themselves or the name or photo of someone else they know. Nobody seems to notice the town mayor taking these photo opportunities to play 'where's Wally' by appearing in each and every photo.

This is how Hugh Flynn survives the ever-present threat of the dole queue. He has the ability to pick up on local non-events, and transform them into a super-scoop and never fails to get a photo of the obligatory local (or Mayor Wally, for that matter). His journalistic radar has picked up on a number of unexplained goings on in relation to Oak Tree Farm, and tonight's social event gives him an opportunity to be at the pub in Weatherford, so that he can work out, or if all else fails, make up what is happening at the farm. All that he has to do is avoid stepping on the wasps' nest called Sue Cooper.

Our journalist walks slowly up the path towards the front door of the Green Man. Built towards the end of the Renaissance, this beautiful timber framed building with blue washed external plaster and a thatched roof finished off with a peaked pinnacle upper ridge has successfully survived the demise of the village's high street. A large 1610 above the door bears testimony to this achievement. Another survivor is the current landlady, Sue Cooper, who has pulled pints in almost every town and village in the county. She and the journalist go back a long way, and both enjoy the thrust and parry of their confrontational relationship.

'Good afternoon, Landlady.'

'Mr Flynn, I hope you are not here to upset my customers.'

'Now, now, my dear Sue, banish the thought, your customers are safe. However, I have heard a rumour that there is a little get together to welcome a research farmer who has joined Oak Tree Farm.'

'Don't you go starting an argument about GM food in my pub, you old hack.'

'Madam, GM food is yesterday's news. There is something local of far more interest than GM crops. Hear me out. A research farmer, no, a foreign research farmer arrives at Oak Tree Farm from the colonies, there is an unexplained suicide at the said farm, and a well-known parish councillor is seen after the shoot, at the same farm, in a frenzied panic. I have also been reliably informed that the police have returned to Weatherford to ask this councillor a few more routine questions. So is there a gathering tonight?'

'Six o'clock. You're welcome to stay, but keep out of trouble.' Sue warned her sparring partner while noisily unpacking clean glasses from a drying rack.

'Wonderful. In that case, I'll wait quietly in your fine establishment. A pint of bitter, please.'

Hugh was the only person in the pub, and sat quietly at the bar and looked around at the familiar surroundings. It is not difficult to work out the rectangular plan of the original building with its low walls, low timber beam ceiling and crude wooden arch supports. Over time the rear of the building has been extended to make way for more tables and chairs. The transition from a chequer-board red and black ceramic tiled floor to a man-made fibre carpet separates the old from the new. The décor has not changed in all the years that I've been coming here, thought the journalist. Nothing really matches, and you get the impression that customers have either left behind items of homely bric-a-brac that were of some personal significance to them, or they just wanted to scrap it.

'How is business, Sue?' enquired the ever-inquisitive hack, sweeping back his fringe before taking a sip of his bitter.

'It would be better if I had staff.' Stupid man, thought the journalist, you have just kicked the wasps' nest. Brace yourself. Here it comes.

'Staff, don't get me started. They come asking for work, you give them a job, and at the end of the week you pay them. All they have to do is pitch-up. How difficult is it? Flipping impossible in my experience.' Mr Flynn very quickly brushed the fringe back, and took an extra long sip of his beer. 'There are the ones who, on day one, come in with a list of days they want off for the next six months. Then there are the ones who, within five minutes, are telling you how to run the business. Not to forget the ones that give you the impression that they are the best thing since sliced bread, but turn out to be plain bloody useless. I'm an experienced barman they say, ha, my dead nan, bless her soul, is of more use to me. Turns out they can't empty a dustbin or use a broom properly. No one wants to work the hours, especially Friday and Saturday nights. It's a pub for God's sake.' The journalist looked over his shoulder in the hope that there was a replacement punter coming up the path. There wasn't. Another flick of the fringe, and a large swig of beer. 'Then there are the ones that actually do pitch up on time, but are too tired, too hungover, too high, too depressed, not to mention the endless whinging about the husbands, the bit on the side, the children, the in-laws, blah, de, blah, de, blah. All of this before you even get to serve a single customer.'

Much to the journalist's relief, the pub door opened. Dudley Baines and Alexis Castellanos, wiped their shoes on the doormat, and entered the pub, accompanied by a blast of cold winter air.

'Good afternoon, gentlemen,' greeted the Landlady.

'Hello Mrs Cooper, we're here to meet Hanna Townsend,' announced Dudley looking around the room. 'Not here yet, I see. Any chance of a sandwich? Actually on second thoughts let's wait until Hanna arrives.' Sue Cooper nodded her head in agreement, and disappeared into the kitchen to carry out a quick reconnoitre of the fridges.

'Afternoon,' said Alexis turning to the journalist sitting at the bar.

'You chaps are not from around here are you? Unless I'm mistaken, you were at the Oak Tree shoot.'

'That's right. I'm Alexis and this is my colleague Dudley.'

'Hugh Flynn, journalist for *The Counties Herald*. I'm covering tonight's little gathering.' The men shook hands.

'We are commercial real estate advisors with London consultants Bassett, Andrews and Goldstein. Canary Wharf. We've been looking around the area for farmland that might be up for sale,' explained Alexis, handing Hugh his business card. It always amazes me how much information people give you if you just keep quiet thought the journalist leaning forward to take the business card.

Another blast of cold air, and Hanna and Cassie arrived.

Jessica Burns, Chloe and Tom arrived with the party food. Sue, back from her reconnaissance, helped move the chairs, and set out the evening's spread on the rearranged tables in front of the wood burner opposite the bar. Hugh Flynn ambled over to have a look at the food.

'Hello Jessica. Food looks good. I hope you don't mind me attending your function this evening, and taking a few photos for the rag. My editor is on my back to provide an interesting local story to brighten up the long hours of darkness.'

'Hugh, if you are here to pick up local tittle-tattle and report it as fact, I would suggest you leave,' replied the hostess curtly.

The journalist knew when to back off, and made himself comfortable again at the bar. He ordered another beer, and looked across the room to where Hanna, Cassie and the two Londoners were in conversation. That does not look like a social encounter thought the journalist. The body language is too serious, and there is too much writing going on to be only exchanging telephone numbers. So many questions, so few answers. Maybe I should be brash and drift over and eavesdrop for a while, he pondered.

It was approaching six o'clock and people were starting to arrive. It was not long before the quiet of the afternoon was filled with Westlife's *Uptown Girl*, the smell of food, and people talking. Alistair Burns arrived with Moz, Elsa, and their children. While the parents were being introduced to everyone in the immediate vicinity of the bar, Paul and Bella saw Hanna sitting at a table at the far end of the restaurant, and ran over to her. They were pleased to see her, and Hanna reciprocated by hugging both of them in turn. She introduced them to Cassie, and smiling and laughing they sat down at the table. After days of new faces, they were obviously happy to be with someone they knew. The brother and sister took it in turns to tell Hanna about school, their visit to Wolburn Market, and how they still had to get use to the long dark nights and the cold weather. Paul, with sheer excitement on his face, said that Mr Burns had told them it was going to snow tonight. We've never seen snow before added Bella.

Hanna was surprised how enthusiastic they were, and Cassie was pleased to see her friend happy and smiling. They were helping themselves to food, when Simon Partridge, Lucas and Dominic arrived. Once the men had their food and drink, they joined Hanna, Cassie and the children. The two bag-a-bargain boys still had a journey back to London, and wishing the group an enjoyable evening, excused themselves.

Our journalist watched Dudley and Alexis leave, then got off his bar stool and went over to Moz and

Elsa. After the introductions, he took a photo of the smiling couple, and then pounced.

'Mr Nel don't you think there is a danger that tampering with nature might unleash a monster,' he asked looking around to see if Sue Cooper was within ear shot.

'Mr Flynn, I have worked with genetically modified crops for a number of years. My motivation, which you might think is somewhat idealistic, is that I want to try and grow as much food as possible for our people back home, so that they do not have to die of starvation.'

'And make money,' added the hack.

'As you make money from misinforming people,' a slightly irritated Moz responded. With no landlady in sight, Hugh changed tack.

'Do you think President Zuma should resign?'

'He is the president of our country, and we respect the office of the president. Should he resign?' Moz glanced at Elsa. 'South Africa has inherited a first-past-the-post voting system, and the people will use the ballot box to answer your question. Whatever they decide, the wishes of the people will be respected, and that's ok even if you personally don't like the outcome,' replied Moz with a grin on his face. Calm as a cucumber or just being sarcastic mused the journalist. He saw Ms Cooper approaching, and hurriedly wished the Nels a happy stay in England.

Lady Beswick, who does not like being called 'Lady', is sitting at one of the bay windows with Jeremy Hughes and his inebriated wife Tia. Kay, despite the cold weather, looks splendid in a sapphire blue chinese cheongsam evening dress, and Sir Michael, who likes being called 'Sir', not wanting to be outdone by his lady, is dressed in an emerald coloured velvet smoking jacket. He politely declined Jeremy's offer to get a round of drinks, and is at the bar ordering his wife her first drink of the evening, and what he thinks is probably not Tia's first.

The Beswicks and the Hughes are not particularly close friends. Although Michael and Jeremy both grew up in the village, they had not spent much of their youth together. In actual fact, their paths had hardly crossed. They had very little in common, and their temperaments where quite different.

Kay and Tia had met at the primary school gate while waiting to pick up their young children. Tia had a superficial interest in chinese pottery, and this hobby was sufficient common ground for the two to become acquainted. This eventually led to their respective husbands spending more time together.

Despite this laissez-faire friendship, Kay would almost always seek out Tia's familiar face in a crowded room, and Tia would do the same. As a result, the Beswicks and Hughes had, over the years, spent a considerable amount of time socialising together.

Jeremy is a professional saxophone player. With limited orchestral pieces for the saxophone he is unemployed more than employed. He feels he is a wasted talent, and is frustrated that he cannot play the saxophone as well as Barbara Thomson.

Being a free artistic spirit he refused to listen to friends and family about his choice of musical instrument for a career. As a petulant rebellious teenager he was going to make his money as a jazz player, and 'hell would freeze over' before choosing to become a symphony orchestra member. I will not be made to feel subservient to an overpaid prima donna of a conductor beating time for me.

Unfortunately for Jeremy, his jazz contemporaries had been born with the rhythm gene in their DNA. They had a far better feel for the music than he did, and found himself having to face his demons – the conductors.

In the 1980s Tia a kind, gentle, bonny lass from Newcastle moved to the capital city to 'find herself'. She had finally escaped her dysfunctional family, and was determined not to make the same mistakes her mother had made. With no previous interest in the arts nor possessing the slightest flicker of talent, she embarked on a career as an actress. She enrolled at a drama school in Wembley, and met Jeremy, her 'free and kindred spirit', at a New Year's Eve party at the Astoria, Soho. On graduating she joined a reparatory theatre company, which resulted in her not having any idea as to which town she was in from one week to the next. A gruelling couple of years, and no nearer to finding herself, and with little hope of Hollywood, let alone the West End, she decided to marry Jeremy.

30 years on Tia is still married to Jeremy, although she has now tired of his self-pity and constant refusal to go out and get a permanent 9-5 job. Just like her mother, she has become for all intense and purposes

the family's sole earner, and works as a fulltime administrator for the charity *Swarm International UK*.

Unfortunately she does not earn enough money to make ends meet. They have no money, and they owe money. Tia's immense frustration with the unemployed musician is that she cannot understand why he refuses to help provide for his family. His only response to her pleading is to shut himself away in the back room, with his musical instruments, and sulk for days on end.

They have an unmarried daughter Jane and a grandson Noah. Ashley, a nice enough lad from Brentwood, is the father. Having met at Glastonbury, it was not until Noah was born that Ashley announced that he was gay. Jeremy did not take the news well, and locked himself away in the back room for weeks, and turned to his first musical love, the piano. During this incarceration, he tried to emulate another of his musical heroes, Andrew Lloyd Webber, and started to compose a Harry Potter musical. Just a little bit more tweaking and it will be ready for the West End became his mantra during this monastic period of his life.

Tia keeps up appearances about Jane and Ashley. What can she do except give the best performance of her life. She tells everyone it a wonderful example of a very modern relationship. How a new life has been brought into a brave, all embracing and understanding new world. Her daughter is a mother who refuses to accept the norm, and the father is not ashamed of his sexuality. I'm so proud of them, she claims.

Unfortunately, it is not the drama of a Shakespearian-like soliloquy, but enormous anger towards her reckless daughter and an irresponsible stranger from Brentwood that causes her to cry herself to sleep every night. The saddest thing of all is that this kind, gentle, bonny lass from Newcastle, like her mother, has become very partial to drink. It has not gone unnoticed by those around her, and her nickname in the village has become Tia Maria.

'Kay, I was looking at your new website the other day. It's very impressive,' remarked Tia.

'What website?' asked Jeremy.

'Kay's chinese furniture business,' replied Tia.

'Actually it was Michael's idea. The wholesale business is doing well, but he thought it might be time to go online. The danger is that if you don't keep up with current buying habits, you get left behind. Look what's happening to the big high street retailers. We discussed it at length, and decided to give it a go,' explained Kay.

'Did I hear my name being mentioned?' asked Sir Michael returning with a drink in each hand. 'A large G and T for Tia, and a pint of bitter for Jeremy. Enjoy.'

'I was telling Tia the website was your idea, Michael,' continued Kay.

'Oh that. Yes, quite an undertaking at our age. Whatsapp, viber, snapchat. It was like learning a new language,' laughed Sir Michael as he returned to the bar for the remainder of the drinks.

'Michael's right about setting up the website. It was a bit of a nightmare at first. I was at the post office, and bumped into Charlotte Broadhurst, the new head teacher, and we got chatting. I mentioned the online idea. As it turns out her son is a graphic something or other, and he has helped us set up the website.' Sir Michael returned with the two remaining drinks, and sat down.

'Good evening everyone. Mind if I join you?' asked Dave Wright.

'Pull up a chair, Dave,' responded Sir Michael.

'Thank you, Sir. Drink anyone?' Everyone declined the offer. 'Good turnout. Food looks good. Decided not to come in your overalls tonight, Kay?' teased the painter and decorator.

'Is there something we should know, Kay?' winked Tia.

'No, just pulling her leg. When I left the army, almost 15 years ago now, and moved to Weatherford, I rented a room from Michael and Kay. By sheer coincidence Michael's father and I served in the same regiment, but not at the same time. Kay was always doing maintenance around the house, and wore overalls the whole time. I didn't think she had any other clothes,' smiled the ex-soldier.

Over the years, Dave and Kay have become good friends. He's witty, reliable and ever-willing to help her. Something that proved useful when Michael was on detachment. His relationship with Michael is good, but less chummy, and tends to be a bit more formal. Probably a throwback to his army days.

'That's enough about my wardrobe, thank David. Let's talk shop. I'm redecorating the hallway and staircase, but as usual I need help with the high walls and the decorative plaster work on the ceilings. Will you come round sometime and have a look?'

'Of course I will. I'll give you a bell.'

I mustn't forget to take a photo of the Beswicks, the journalist noted to himself as the Nels stopped at their table. Moz shook hands with everyone which left five unsuspecting victims with tears in their eyes, and unsure whether they should shake Elsa's hand or not.

'South Africa what a lovely country. Had two wonderful holidays in Cape Town. You are so lucky to live there,' slurred Tia. 'Oh, those beautiful vineyards in Shhtellen, shhtellen-shhumfing. Wines to die for.' Moz and Elsa looked at each other, and struggled to hold back the laughter.

'Rugby man, Moz?' asked Sir Michael.

'Oh yes,' replied Moz.

'Six nations in a couple of weeks. Let's hope England don't disappoint. Of course, being a northern hemisphere thing, you probably don't mind who wins,' remarked Sir Michael.

'Ya, I think sometimes the rugby is more enjoyable when you don't have a preference,' said Moz politely while thinking, support England, never.

'Absolutely right, totally agree,' replied Sir Michael. 'I've got a box at Welford Road. If you have time later in the season, we can pop up to Leicester and see a Tiger's home game. Elsa and the kids must come along, the more the merrier.'

'Thank you Sir Michael, that would be fantastic,' replied the farmer smiling.

'Not at all. It will be nice to have some company. Kay's not very keen. Maybe we can persuade her to join us if Elsa's there.'

Moz indicated that he and Elsa needed to keep mingling. The Beswicks and the Hughes wished the Nels a happy stay in Weatherford, and managed to avoid the offer of shaking Moz's hand again.

Sue Cooper was pleased at the way the evening was going, and having agreed a temporary truce with Hugh Flynn, the two of them stood on either side of the bar and watched the residents of Weatherford letting their hair down. Tables had been moved to make room for an impromptu dance floor where Hanna, Cassie, Paul and Bella were jazz-handing to Elton John's *I'm Still Standing*. Lucas and Dominic were trying a vodka inspired adaptation of a malunas folk dance, by shaking their hands above their heads and intermittently shouting out 'razzle-dazzle, my friends' in Lithuanian. Elsa made her way over to the group of revellers which was our journalist's cue to follow her with his camera. Hanna stopped dancing and introduced Elsa to Cassie.

'How are you coping?' asked Elsa raising her voice to be heard over the music.

'I'm doing ok, thanks. Cassie here has been an absolute star,' replied Hanna, taking her friend's hand and holding it. 'She's dealt with everything. There is a mountain of paperwork. The funeral is on Friday the 6th, here at All Saints. You and Moz are more than welcome to attend, but no obligation, you didn't know my dad.'

'Thank you, we will be there. What are your immediate plans?'

'We're both going back to work on Monday,' answered Cassie. 'There will be plenty of time to sort out the rest of the paperwork, and it will probably do Hanna good to get back into the old work routine.'

'Who's going to look after the farm?' asked Elsa hoping she was not coming across as too nosey.

'I'm really not sure. The farmhouse is desperately in need of repair, the equipment and machinery is antiquated, but the question that really needs answering is why have the crops been failing. I keep asking myself, what was so wrong that it lead to my dad committing suicide. I wonder if I will ever know. Enough of my troubles, I'm being terribly selfish, this is supposed to be your evening.'

'No don't be silly. If there is anything Moz and I can do to help, please ask.'

'Thank you Elsa, that is very kind of you. When things have settled down, you guys must come down to London and I'll show you around.'

'I think the kids would love that,' replied Elsa.

'Evening Ladies, please can I have a couple of group photos?' smiled the old hack.

Belinda Thomas, not one for standing on ceremony, arrived on the arm of a man at least fifteen years her junior. She was wearing riding jodhpurs and boots, and looked as if she had come straight from the stables. Her trusty stable hand Charlie Pollock followed a few paces behind the couple. Charlie, in his early fifties, is a kind and gentle man with the misfortune to be slightly mentally disabled. He started working at the stables for Belinda's parents at the age of 16, and has hardly missed a day's work in almost three and a half decades.

Lizzie Turner, is the next guest to arrive, in the company of a new man wearing a t-shirt with Personal Trainer printed across the back. Jessica came over and greeted the new arrivals, and stood chatting to them. She liked Belinda and Lizzie. There was an air of innocent recklessness about them that made them fun. It was not long before they had pulled chairs closer to the wood-burner, piled food onto their plates, and with a couple of bottles of wine on the table between them, and an energy drink for the personal trainer they settled down for the evening.

Jessica called Elsa over and introduced her to Belinda and Lizzie. The former offered to give the Nel children horse riding lessons, and the latter offered to become Elsa's gym-buddy. Unfortunately, Elsa did not feel the aura of innocent recklessness, but could hear her mother saying 'they are not only ladies of the night, but of the day as well'. She was relieved to excuse herself when she saw the Chowdhurys arriving.

Samir Chowdhury was wearing a smart navy blue silk suit, and Yasmin was wrapped in an emerald green saree edged with gold thread. Richard

Kettering-Smythe seeing Hugh Flynn asking the Chowdhurys for a photo, decided it would be politically beneficial to be seen alongside the former refugees. Unfortunately he was held up by partygoers and the photo was taken without him. Undeterred, KS as he liked to be called, although the villagers called him all sorts of other names, puffed himself up with his own importance, and with a blue gin and tonic in his hand, started to mingle. His hail fellow-well-met demeanour accompanied by talking loudly so half the room could hear him did not endear him to those present. Hugh Flynn sat quietly at the bar, and watched his next potential scoop.

KS managed to collar Charlotte Broadhurst, her husband Edward, and their son Rhys, the moment they entered the pub. Hugh found it difficult to watch KS's subservient, deferential behaviour towards the head teacher, and would not have been surprised if the parish councillor had pickpocketed her. The journalist continued to watch the charade as the smiling KS tried to smarm his way into Charlotte's good books.

Hugh, not surprisingly, had a journalistic interest in the new head teacher. By all accounts, she is popular, respected, and apparently is sorting out the problems at the school. The latest village gossip is that she has got rid of a couple of married teachers who were having affairs with younger unmarried school assistants.

The journalist, having taken a few more photos, returned to his crow's nest at the end of the bar. He felt he had enough snap-shots for his article, and sat making a few notes about the evening. Who was who, who spoke to whom, potential gossip – question mark, potential scandal – question mark, Oak Tree Farm mystery – two question marks. He heard a noise in the kitchen, and looked up and leaning slightly to his left he had a good view through the open door along the length of the kitchen. He was astonished to see Jessica Burns and Rhys Broadhurst in each other's arms. Rhys was kissing Jessica up and down her neck, and she was obviously enjoying it. Hugh quickly looked around the room and saw husband Alistair talking to mother Charlotte.

For all his faults, Hugh Flynn very seldom swore. On this occasion, shit he thought, unless this is some new form of extreme sport, they must be barking mad to be fraternising in public. He excitedly turned over a new page of his journalist's notebook and wrote: Lover's tryst – Head-teacher's unmarried son and a local married woman. Yes. Thank you God!

Alistair raised his voice above the noise.

'Ladies and Gentlemen, quiet please, quiet please, thank you.' The pub fell silent, and Jessica and Rhys quietly came out of the kitchen and joined the rest of the gathering. 'First of all, a big thank you to everyone for coming tonight. As you are aware we are here to welcome Moz Nel, his wife Elsa, and their children Bella and Paul to our community. They have travelled 6,000 miles to be here tonight, which is a long way to travel for a warm pint of British beer.' Laughter rippled across the room. 'Moz has joined us at Oak Tree Farm to help with the well-publicised wheat trials. He has been trialling the new seed back in South Africa for almost five years. It is a privilege that he wants to share his expertise and knowledge with us. I'm sure our friend Mr Flynn, from *The Counties Herald*, will keep you accurately up-to-date as to our progress.'

'Throw the press out, Landlady,' someone heckled from the back of the pub, which triggered a loud round of applause and a few calls for out, out. Our journalist smiled and gesticulated go away with his hand.

'So Moz, Elsa, Bella and Paul welcome to our community, it is a pleasure to have you with us.' Alistair raised his glass. 'A toast everyone; the Nels and the trials.'

'The Nels and the trials,' the pub echoed back.

Paul Nel was bored by the speech and looked around the room at what Hugh Flynn had described as homely bric-a-brac. There were old photos of the pub, and behind Hanna was a painting of an aeroplane that said it was a B-26 Marauder of the 8th Air Force. Alongside it was a photo of a group of young men in uniform standing in front of a similar looking aeroplane. Copper pots and pans like the ones his grandmother uses hang from the walls, and the furniture is very similar to his gran's as well. Nothing matched and some of the benches looked like pews.

Chloe and Tom Burns came over to Paul and Bella and asked them if they would like to play video games. After getting permission from Elsa, the four children disappeared into the games room at the back of the pub.

Elsa was exhausted, and was sitting at one of the tables on her own sipping a diet coke. It had been an exciting day, but it had finally caught up with her. The day had started off with the cooking, which in itself was a day's work. She then had to spend the whole evening being upbeat and cheerful. Not that she was complaining. She was so surprised as to how friendly and welcoming everyone had been. It had been nice to see Hanna again, and talking to Samir Chowdhury had been interesting. The Beswicks, the Broadhurst family, the Hughes, and even Weatherford's loose women were all very nice.

'Do you mind if I join you?' asked KS slurring his words slightly.

'Not at all,' answered Elsa.

'I've been watching you all evening. I don't want to be forward, but you look like the type of girl who would appreciate a good night out. Good food, wine, excellent company, and who knows what else.'

'Mr Kettering-Smythe, I'm a happily married woman with a loving husband and two wonderful children,' replied Elsa.

'In my experience being married doesn't seem to bother most women. In actual fact, they seem to enjoy the risk. They find it exciting.'

'Mr Kettering-Smythe, I'm not interested. Please leave me alone. I'm tired, and I do not want this type of attention.'

'KS. Call me KS,' he whispered, putting his hand on Elsa's knee under the table. 'If you ever change your mind Elsa, give me a call.' Elsa pushed her chair back.

'Mr Kettering-Smythe, I'm asking you very nicely to leave me alone. Please respect me and my family. This conversation never took place,' Elsa stood up, and looked down at the seated KS. 'I made a promise to God to honour, and obey my husband. End of story.' He remained seated and looking up at Elsa realised he had totally misjudged her. The religious thing is quite scary, he thought.

'Elsa, please accept my apology,' he muttered as she turned on her heel, and walked over to her husband.

The evening was coming to an end, and most of the people had left. Suddenly at the far end of the restaurant, Hanna Townsend's raised voice could be heard. She had got up from her chair and was standing facing Kettering-Smythe.

'How dare you come over here and patronise me. Get away from me. He was not a loser. He was a kind, gentle man and you took advantage of his kind nature.'

'What are you talking about, you stupid girl,' KS replied.

'You killed him. You and your poxy parish council. For as long as I can remember, you have put every obstacle in his way. How is it possible that permission was given to build houses at Fields View, and yet my father's application to sell his farm for housing was turned down? The two pieces of land are adjacent to each other, for Christ's sake.'

'Hanna, you are talking rubbish. I'm not the only one who makes these decisions.'

'Go on hide behind that excuse, you coward. Collective responsibility, bollocks. It is all a charade. You are a cancer. You spread your blight throughout this village. You are a snake. You slither along the corridors of power at county hall spreading your venom. The whole village knows you are corrupt. Look at that swanky new house you live in. How did you get your hands on that one? Would you have given my father his permission if he had given you a backhander?'

'Hanna, I would advise you not to accuse me of things that you cannot prove.'

'What are you going to do take me to court? Well, bring it on you little prick. You think that my father was a waste of space, that his life was worthless. I am going to prove that it wasn't. I'm going to prove that you are in the pockets of Pasternak Construction, and you have been tampering with his crops for years so that the developers can get their hands on cheap land.'

'Hanna, I know you're upset. But this is not going to change anything. When you have calmed down, let's talk. You are absolutely wrong. You have got the wrong end of the stick.'

'Leave my family alone. Get out of my sight.'

'Listen mate, I think you should leave Hanna alone. Have a bit of respect. She has only just lost her father,' advised Dave Wright as he came over to see what the fracas was all about.

'I won't be told what to do by the likes of you,' replied KS.

'If you don't leave now, the likes of me who fought in Afghanistan for the likes of you, will give you a free demonstration in unarmed combat, Sir,' whispered the ex-soldier, pushing KS towards the door.

'Come on Hanna, time to go home,' said Cassie.

'Thanks Dave,' said Hanna and gave the ex-soldier a hug.

Sue Cooper looked at Hugh Flynn and raised her eyebrows as if to say, interesting.

'One unhappy young lady,' remarked the journalist walking over to the front door. He opened it, looked outside for a moment and stepping back into the pub, closed the door behind him.

'Sue, any chance of a room, the snow is quite thick out there?'

'Only the honeymoon suite available me Darlin',' she replied, winking at her old antagonist. 'Help me clear away these glasses, and I'll pour you a night cap to take to bed.'

CHAPTER 12

A text woke Elsa. Half asleep, she put her arm out and patting the bedside table with her hand, she blindly looked for her mobile.

'Moz, it's a text from the school. They're closed today because of the snow.'

'Closed?' remarked Moz swinging his legs out of bed. He sat for a moment, then got up and opened the curtains.

'Wow. Els come and look at this,' he exclaimed. Elsa joined him at the window.

'Oh my goodness. This must be how heaven looks,' she gasped.

They stood at the window, holding hands, and were awestruck by the beauty of the scene in front of them. There had been a heavy fall overnight, just as Alistair Burns had predicted. There wasn't a cloud in the sky, and the pure white of the snow sparkled in the sunlight. Condensation trails from aeroplanes flying overhead were etched across the sky. Their perfect straight lines criss-crossing the heavens; the signature of the artist who had produced this heavenly masterpiece.

'Everything is so calm, Moz, you can see the quietness, you can almost feel it.'

'It is the most beautiful thing I've ever seen,' he replied.

The parents woke the children, and having never seen snow before, were beside themselves with excitement. Pulling on clothes, they rushed outside to play. Lucas and Dominic emerged from their cottages, and soon became snowball targets. Eventually, the cold and the wet brought an end to the frolicking, and the children sought sanctuary in the warm house. It was not long before the defrosted children, Lucas and Dominic were tucking into a hot breakfast.

A text also woke up Hugh Flynn. It was from his boss, Ken Baker, asking him to pop into the office as soon as possible. Before replying, he looked out of the window on the off chance that he was snowed-in. No such luck. Sue Cooper's breakfast of burnt bacon, a runny fried egg, cold baked beans and milky coffee was not the panacea for the slightly hung-over journalist.

To make matters worse, he did not like rain or snow. It made him grumpy. His little grey car was covered in the white stuff, and by the time he had cleared enough of it away so that he could see out of the windows, his hands ached from the cold and his feet were freezing. Grumbling to himself, he eventually climbed into the car, and the windscreen immediately misted up. With the heating not working, he cracked his window, but it was not very effective. He looked around for something that might have the characteristics of a cloth. Plenty of litter, but no cloth.

As he did not expect to be returning to the Green Man in the near future, he had not been very complimentary about the breakfast when he paid the bill. He sat in the cold, misted up car, and wondered how the landlady might react to a request for a cloth or a few sheets of kitchen roller towel. He took a deep breath and plunged headlong back into the wasps' nest. Eventually he was on his way back to Wolburn Market, having learnt from Sue Cooper that it was possible to construct a whole sentence using only slang and swear words.

The media empire that is *The Counties Herald* consists of a small office above the kitchen of a tearoom. The journalist parked his car in the 'permit holders only' car park behind the tearoom, and avoiding the piles of melting snow, gingerly made his way over to the newspaper's office door. He carefully descended the few steps to the entrance, and tried to open it. It wouldn't budge. Standing in the gutter of flowing icy water, he looked through one of the small panes of glass in the door. He could see copies of this week's edition piled up on the doormat. Great he thought as the bottoms of his trousers started to behave like blotting paper. He phoned for help, and once he was on the other side of the door, took off his wet socks and shoes and climbed awkwardly up the very narrow stairs to the small office above the tearoom kitchen.

'At bloody last. Deadlines and printing presses wait for no man. Get yourself a coffee. Get in here,' shouted the Chief Editor of the success story that surrounded him.

'Ken, we really do have to stop leaving the surplus newspapers at the bottom of the stairs. Someone's going to get hurt,' Hugh suggested to his boss, as he waited for the kettle to boil.

'You sort it out. Haven't got time. Come in. Sit down. Right. What have you got for me? I've got too many empty columns. You need to fill them.' Ken Baker seldom communicated in full sentences, and Hugh never understood how anyone who spoke at an allegro tempo could possibly have become a journalist.

'And last night?' the Chief asked.

'Well, things don't appear to be as we thought, Boss,' replied Hugh, slowly drinking from the coffee mug that Sue Cooper had given him one Christmas. He placed it back on the desk. Ken, who thought the inscription on the mug was a stroke of genius, couldn't help reading it albeit for the millionth time, 'In my case, no news, is good news.'

'Explain?' he asked smiling at the mug.

'Well I don't think the story is Oak Tree Farm. The new farmer and his family are very nice people, there's nothing new about the wheat trials, and there doesn't appear to be anything suspicious about Brian Townsend's death. Everything appears to be kosher. I think Kettering-Smythe's behaviour when he went back to look for his jacket was unusual. Therein lies a story.'

'Happens all the time. Large group of people. Coats. Jackets everywhere. Someone takes the wrong one. No. Not interested,' was the editor's sharp and quick verdict.

'Brian's funeral is on the 6th,' announced the journalist.

'Kettering-Smythe and the police?' asked the Chief, ignoring Hugh's snippet of information.

'Gone quiet. The police must be happy if they have agreed for the funeral to take place,' replied Hugh.

'Keep an ear to the ground on that one,' responded the editor.

'Goes without saying,' replied the journalist. 'I do have a bit of village gossip.' Hugh paused and looked at his disinterested boss. 'Jessica Burns, wife of the farmer at Oak Tree Farm, is having an affair with the head teacher's son.'

'Dull. Unless it's under age sex. Not interested.'

'Boss, I think the story is Grey Pigeon Farm,' persisted the journalist.

'Townsend's farm?'

'Yes. At the end of the evening there was a very public spat between Hanna Townsend and Kettering-Smythe. She was spitting blood.'

'What about?'

'Here's a note I wrote last night before I went to bed. Summarises the confrontation,' said Hugh passing a piece of paper over the desk to his boss.

'I think there are three possible stories. A parish councillor taking backhanders from developers or crop contamination or both.' The editor was reading the note, and put his hand up for Hugh to stop talking. He finished reading, and looked across the desk at the journalist.

'Hugh. Not interested in planning permissions. Bent parish councillors. Not interested. Attack one. They all close ranks. Photo of Kettering-Smythe in the back of a police car. Might be interesting for a day. You agree?' asked the editor handing the note back to Hugh.

'Unfortunately, I think I came to the same conclusion last night,' responded the journalist.

'When last did we have contaminated crops?' asked Ken.

'Not in my time as a journalist in this part of the country,' answered Hugh. The editor lent back in his large brown leather chair, and looked up at the ceiling. After a couple of minutes staring at a water mark in the shape of a pumpkin, he returned the chair to the vertical.

'Any other hacks there last night?'

'No, only us,' replied Hugh.

'Ok, bang out something about last night. The usual stuff. Local interest. Locals welcoming and hospitable. Plenty of photos. On my desk by two o'clock,' instructed the chief.

'Sure, boss,' replied Hugh slowly getting out of his chair.

'Contaminated crops interest me, Hugh. Let's see where that takes us. Back to work. Deadline's looming,' said Ken ending the meeting by waving the journalist out of the office.

Hugh Flynn made himself another coffee, and looking out of the small window overlooking the 'permit holders only' car park smiled and thought, thank you boss, contaminated crops will do very nicely.

Elsa put two ivory coloured pillar candles on the dining room table and lit them. With the children in bed, the house was very quiet except for the gentle swish-swish of the dishwasher, and the purring of the central heating.

'At last, some peace and quiet,' grinned Moz as he sat down opposite his wife, and poured two glasses of red wine. 'Els, you've been very quiet tonight. Is there something wrong?'

'No. Not really.'

'Come on Koeks, I know there is something, what's the problem?' Elsa hesitated for a moment.

'Well, you know Paul and Bella are in the nativity play at school?'

'Ya, and they seem to be enjoying it,' replied Moz.

'Paul came home today all excited about the rehearsal in the church. Apparently when they started talking about the nativity play a couple of weeks ago, a Father Aldridge came to the school, and gave the children a talk about the village church's history. Well, Paul has asked if we could go to Sunday church, like we do back home.'

'I know where you're going with this, and I understand,' replied Moz. 'We discussed all the pros and cons about coming here, but church wasn't one of them,' he continued. 'Who would have guessed it would be an issue,' he added.

'Mozie, I just feel I am being disloyal to my parents if I let my children go to an English church.'

'Are you worried about this Father Aldridge and the children?'

'No not at all, Mozie. I just feel we, me, more than you, will be betraying our families.' Elsa got up and went into the kitchen to unpack the dishwasher. Husband and wife didn't speak; they were both occupied with their own thoughts.

'Why don't we skype our parents tomorrow, and see what they have to say?' suggested Moz.

After breakfast the next morning, Moz and Elsa took it in turns to skype their respective parents. Moz's parents were thrilled to have received the photos and videos of the grandchildren in the snow. His mother said she missed them all and cried a bit, but was pleased they were settling down. His father wanted to know about the trials, how they were coping with the English weather, and asked whether it was true the English only grew mud. The conversation eventually turned to the reason for the call. Moz's parents were of the opinion that as the same God was involved, and as long as the grandchildren were safe and wanted to go to church, they were happy. They said it was ultimately Moz and Elsa's responsibility and decision.

Initially the conversation went well with Elsa's parents. They were also pleased with the snow videos and photos, and asked plenty of questions about Bella and Paul. Her father became quite animated about their invitation to a Leicester Tigers home game in the New Year. However, when Elsa raised the issue about the church, her parents took umbrage and admonished her for even considering attending an English church. Although Elsa was expecting an icy response, she was quite surprised when her parents were not prepared to discuss the subject at all. She tried, but realised it was to no avail. The conversation ended a few awkward minutes later.

'Well, that was predictable,' remarked Moz.

'So what do you think we should do, Mozie?'

'Els, at the end of the day, we are here and our parents are a long way away. We have to make the decision. I don't have a problem with the kids going to church here. This is where we're living at the moment, and we cannot exclude them from participating. It's as much their adventure as it is ours. Everyone has been so welcoming and hospitable. They are good people. They have good values, and if their church teaches the same values then I don't think we need worry. Let's go to church as a family, just as we do back home.'

Alistair came into the kitchen with a newspaper under his arm, and put the kettle on.

'Tea, Jessica?'

'No, just had one,' she replied and carried on stirring a pot of steaming cabbage and broccoli soup without looking up from the hob.

'I saw Edward Broadhurst at the garage this morning, and he asked about Christmas. We are still inviting them over aren't we?' enquired Alistair.

'Um, haven't really given it much thought. Been quite busy lately,' his wife answered.

'Seeing we had Christmas with them last year, I still think we should. Edward said they're going to the funeral. Maybe we can talk to them then?' suggested the farmer. 'On second thoughts, why don't you just phone Charlotte now?'

'It's a bit early. She's probably still at work. I'll do it after dinner,' replied Jessica avoiding eye contact with Alistair.

'Well make sure you do it. Time marches on.'

'Ok, ok, I will. Stop nagging.' Alistair looked up from the newspaper he was reading.

'There's no need to snap at me. You invited them when we were there last Christmas, and if I'm not mistaken you didn't run it passed me first,' he responded.

'Forgive me for not getting your permission, your royal highness.'

'Come on Jessica. You know I didn't mean it like that,' an exasperated Alistair replied returning to his paper.

After dinner of soup and artisan bread, followed by sausage and mash, Alistair prompted Jessica to phone Charlotte. The response was for Jessica to storm out of the lounge, muttering about bloody Christmas under her breath. Alistair shook his head, and wondered why Jessica was so touchy. A few minutes later she came back into to the lounge smiling.

'Well?'

'All sorted. Charlotte says the two of them would love to join us for Christmas. She and I are going to sort out the menu next week.'

'Just Edward and Charlotte coming, what about their son, what's his name, Rick, Riley?'

'Rhys,' she snapped. 'No he is apparently going to Cornwall with some mates?' continued Jessica making herself comfortable on the sofa.

'Cornwall with a group of mates. Lots of booze, lots of totty. Ah, those were the days,' recalled Alistair, resting his head against the back of the sofa, and looking up at the ceiling. Jessica didn't reply. She grabbed the remote and started to flick through the Freeview channels. She scrolled through 1-15, without stopping at any of them. Muttering that there was never anything decent to watch on tv, she threw the remote down on the sofa, and stormed off to the kitchen. A baffled Alistair shook his head for the second time that night, and reached over for the remote.

Alistair had spent most of the day out in the freezing cold repairing fences with Lucas and Dominic. As he approached the house, he could hear Jessica and Chloe's raised voices. This is all I need he thought as he went in.

'What are you two arguing about?' he asked.

'We've got a problem, Alistair,' replied Jessica.

'You have a problem, not me,' blurted out Chloe.

'Don't talk to your mother like that. What's going on?' reprimanded the farmer.

'Chloe has just told me she wants to become a vegan,' replied Jessica.

'Where did this bloody idea come from?

'If we want to stop climate change, we have to eat plant-based food,' declared Chloe.

'Have you forgotten what happened when you went all vegetarian? This will end up the same way. No, is the answer. It won't be your climate change buddies sitting next to your hospital bed when it all goes pear-shaped, it'll be your mother and I, again,' replied the father.

'It's a free country,' responded Chloe.

'When your mother and I are no longer providing a roof over your head, you can be as free as you like. You can eat acres and acres of carrots to your heart's content.'

'I will NOT go through all of this again,' interrupted her mother. 'You will NOT disrupt this family. Your previous eating fad affected all of us. It was like having an alcoholic in the house.'

'It's my choice,' was Chloe's response.

'And it is my responsibility not to let it happen again,' replied Jessica.

'You can't stop me.'

'Oh yes I can, and I will.'

'What's for dinner, Mum?' asked Tom as he came into the kitchen. 'I'm starving. I could eat a horse.' He looked in the pot on the hob. 'Ah, Chloe's favourite, beef bourguignon.'

The next morning after the twins had left for school, their parents had a late breakfast. Jessica had a plan, and wanted Alistair's opinion. He approved of the idea, and later that morning Jessica phoned her father. She explained the Chloe situation to him, asked him for assistance, and he reluctantly agreed to help out. When the twins returned home from school, Jessica was waiting for them in the kitchen.

'Chloe, correct me if I'm wrong. Vegans object to the exploitation of animals.'

'Yes,' replied Chloe hesitantly.

'Well, I've spoken to Grandpa and he's going to stop paying for Penny's stabling.'

'Why?' replied a surprised Chloe.

'Most of your riding gear is leather, especially the saddle. You are, therefore, exploiting animals,' explained Chloe's mother.

'You've got to be joking?' screamed Chloe.

'No I'm not. I told you last night that I was not going to allow this family to be disrupted by another eating disorder. It is not going to happen again. Never.'

CHAPTER 13

Christmas Day in the Burns' household started off with Jessica getting up early to put the turkey in the oven. Tom heard his mother downstairs, and decided to get up, and keep her company.

'Merry Christmas, Mum,' greeted Tom as he came into the kitchen. 'I'm starving, can I make some toast?'

'I was just about to put the croissants in the oven,' replied his mother. 'May as well boil the kettle, and get the drinks ready. Everyone will probably have their usual.'

'Except Chloe,' Tom muttered.

'Tom, leave your sister alone. You've teased her enough.'

'Grandpa hasn't let the subject go, Mum.' Tom replied rather indignantly.

'Whatever. Let's stop it. I don't want tantrums or banging doors spoiling today. Do you understand?'

'Yes, Mum,' agreed Tom.

Chloe came into the kitchen, tapping away at her mobile.

'Merry Christmas, Mum. Merry Christmas, toe-rag,' she greeted without looking up from her phone. 'Is it ok if I go and see to Penny?'

'Let's first open the presents and have breakfast, then you can go,' replied Jessica.

'I don't have all day,' Chloe answered with a sigh. Jessica looked at Tom and raised her eyebrows. Tom smiled and kept quiet.

Alistair and Jessica's Dad eventually got up, hot drinks were made, and the family went through to the lounge to open presents. It wasn't long before everyone was knee-deep in Christmas wrapping and plastic packaging. Ant and Dec, tails wagging with excitement, behaved like puppies as they rummaged through the pile of litter. Well, spending the whole day yesterday wrapping presents was worthwhile thought Jessica as she surveyed the mini-recycling collection point. Alistair tried very hard to ignore the mess, but he eventually felt it was going to engulf him, and dashed out to fetch a couple of black bin bags. By the time he returned, everyone, including Ant and Dec, had disappeared into the dining room for breakfast, leaving him to clean up the mess.

Keeping everyone busy on Christmas Day can be a challenge. Once the presents have been opened, and breakfast is finished, there is invariably the long wait for the turkey to cook. For the person who has volunteered, or in some cases, has been press-ganged into preparing the Christmas meal, there is not enough time. For the rest of the family, it is often a period of boredom. By the time the designated cook has begun to baste the turkey, the rest of the family, have usually started to baste themselves. By the time the bird is ready, the faculties of the guests are often somewhat impaired. There is anecdotal evidence to support the fact that by the time family members sit down to Christmas dinner, many of them have no idea why they are there.

After breakfast Chloe walked over to the riding school were Penny is stabled. A present from her maternal grandparents on her 12th birthday, Penny requires a huge commitment from Chloe. She religiously attends to her horse twice a day, every day of the week, and no matter what the weather. She started riding before she was old enough to go to school. Belinda Thomas, the riding school owner, helped her find Penny, and the horse turned out to be a good all-rounder.

Jessica threatening to sell Penny had been a low blow, but another food fad and a hospitalised daughter was not an option. As a mother, she was upset that it had been necessary to be cruel almost spiteful towards Chloe, but knew as a parent that it was the correct thing to do. As she so often thought, being a mother is fun, but being a parent is arduous.

The doorbell rang. It was Charlotte and Edward Broadhurst, and their son Rhys. Charlotte Broadhurst, in her early fifties, is the newly appointed primary school head teacher. She is married to Edward, an ex-Environmental Health Inspector, who took early retirement, which in the present climate of austerity doesn't go down too well in some quarters of the village. Their son Rhys is a graphic designer, and lives in Wolburn Market where he works from home for *aceg PR*.

Charlotte had a comfortable middle class upbringing in Surrey. She studied psychology for two terms at Coventry, and then against her parents' wishes decided to do politics, economics and history at Leeds.

On the journey up to Leeds, in the car that her parents had given her for a birthday, she decided to reinvent herself. By the time she drove through the university gates she was a left-wing radical from a working class family. Her parents, both *Guardian* reading trade union members, were struggling to find work in London due to factory closures. Charlotte was anti-everything, and the university environment made it easy for her to get away with the re-invention.

When she left the safety of university and went out into the real world she found it difficult to keep up the charade. She met Edward, who from the outset saw through the left-wing façade. He wasn't too bothered about it, started buying *The Daily Mail*, and teased

Charlotte endlessly about her passionate radical views.

After a year of working in a coffee shop, she decided to seek solace in the teaching profession, and the newly qualified tutor was able to relax and carry on with the false pretences. Over a period of almost ten years, she achieved a reputation for being a competent teacher, and although there was the satisfaction of seeing the children blossom under her tuition, she wanted more. One morning on the train into work, Charlotte realised that she was becoming more and more like her real parents; ambitious and driven. She set her sights on becoming a head teacher, but soon realised her radical persona was an obstacle to her achieving her new career goal.

The financial crisis was her opportunity. After a few years of austerity, and money for education drying up, head teachers by default were required to manage their finances better. A few of Charlotte's colleagues were promoted, and she saw them abandon the worker's revolution, accept the challenge and responsibility, and change from disgruntled teachers into good administrators. A year ago a post came up in Weatherford, Charlotte applied, and was successful. By the time she arrived in Weatherford she had shrugged off the remnants of her adolescent reinvention.

Alistair, starting to relax after a couple of whiskys, heartily welcomed the Broadhursts, and lead them through to the kitchen.

'Jessica. Look what I found abandoned on our doorstep.' Jessica turned around, and seeing Rhys she thought she was going to faint. She turned back towards the sink, and held on to the edge as tightly as she could. Get a grip, you're going to make a real arse of yourself she thought.

'Jessica, are you alright? You look terrible,' asked Charlotte helping her to a chair at the kitchen table.

'I'm so sorry, I don't know what's come over me.'

'Probably the hot kitchen,' suggested Charlotte. Chloe, who had arrived back home half an hour earlier, and Jessica's father could be heard yelling at each other in the lounge.

'Oh, for pity sake. Alistair please go and see what Chloe and my Dad are arguing about. Sorry about the shouting. Chloe told us a couple of days ago that she was turning vegan, and it's been World War 3 ever since.' The raised voices subsided. Alistair returned to Jessica and the guests, closely followed by Tom carrying the presents for the Broadhursts.

'Mum, I can only find two presents. Nothing for Rhys.' Thanks for being so tactful Tom thought Jessica while waiting for the ground to open beneath her.

'Oh, that reminds me, we've left your presents in the car,' announced Edward.

'I'll go and get them,' offered Rhys.

'I'll come and help,' said Jessica offering her services. Before anyone else could volunteer for the job, the couple de liaison were halfway to the car.

'You should be in bloody Cornwall,' whispered Jessica.

'We cancelled it because they had heavy snow last night,' Rhys whispered back.

'Why didn't you warn me?' asked an annoyed Jessica.

'Jess, please keep it down,' Rhys pleaded in a whisper. 'We agreed we would never phone nor text each other. I didn't have the opportunity to warn you.'

'God, what an embarrassment,' responded Jessica looking back at the house.

'If I hadn't come over with my parents, you would probably have thought I didn't want to see you. I've obviously made the wrong decision,' concluded the boyfriend, angrily grabbing the presents off the back seat of the car.

Eventually Christmas dinner was ready, and Jessica sat down for the first time since breakfast. There was an uneasy truce in place between grandfather and granddaughter. Jessica and Rhys were keeping eye contact and conversation to a minimum. There certainly was no physical contact. Alistair, Charlotte and Edward, assisted by non-puritan refreshments, where thoroughly enjoying themselves. Tom was still starving, despite having already eaten five mince pies and a handful of pigs-in-blankets since breakfast.

Lunch had just started when there was a knock at the back door. Lucas and Dominic came into the house and followed the smell of turkey, roast potatoes and gravy into the dining room.

'Linksmų Kalėdų, my friends, Merry Christmas,' announced Lucas. The two Lithuanians made their way around the table and shook hands with everyone.

'Charlotte, you met Lucas and Dominic at the shoot,' said Alistair turning and introducing the two trainee gamekeepers to Edward. 'Ignore the hair, It's a bit of a long story,' added the farm manager.

'You haven't been able to get home for Christmas then?' asked Edward.

'No, Sir. Problem is it is so expensive to fly to Lithuania at Christmas,' replied Dominic.

'The journey is long, and all we do is get drunk with the family,' added Lucas smiling. 'So, not to worry. We stay here and get drunk with our Lithuanian friends in Wolburn Market. It is not so far to travel, and much cheaper.'

'Mrs Jessica, we have brought you present of Lithuanian amber chocolate to eat with your family and friends,' smiled Dominic handing the wrapped box to the farmer's wife.

'We must go please, Mr Alistair, our friends are waiting,' announced Lucas.

'Of course, of course, thank you for the present,' replied the farmer.

'You very welcome. We see you tomorrow for the Christmas drinks. Linksmų Kalėdų.'

'Merry Christmas,' everyone replied.

'Have the Nels gone home, Alistair?' asked Edward.

'No they're still here. We invited them over today, but I think they just wanted a bit of quiet time together, especially after the upheaval of the past few months. It's been a busy time for them. They're coming around for a drink tomorrow,' added Alistair.

'How are their children settling down at school, Charlotte?' asked Jessica.

'Very nicely. They are well behaved, don't question the rules, just get on and do as they're told. Quite refreshing really. Got involved in the nativity play, especially the youngster Paul. The parents are very serious. This will probably sound strange, but they seem to have an unusual amount of respect for authority.'

'Oh dear, your secrets out, Charlotte. Put the whip away,' laughed Edward.

'Most inappropriate, Edward, you're drunk,' responded the head teacher.

'Mum, can I have some more roast potatoes?' Tom asked without looking up from his plate.

'More in the kitchen, Tom,' answered his mother.

When Tom returned with his plate piled high with roast potatoes and pigs-in-blankets, Jessica's father asked Tom for a top up of wine, by waving his empty glass in his grandson's general direction.

'So Rhys my boy, what do you do for a living?' asked the grandpa.

'Graphic design, Mr Proctor.'

'Call me Leo or grandpa if you like. What do you think Jessica, Charlotte? You don't object to Rhys becoming an honorary grandson do you?'

'Dad, you've had too much to drink,' responded his horrified daughter.

'So what do graphic designers do?' continued Rhys' newly appointed grandparent.

'I work for a company called *aceg PR*. We deliver integrated social media campaigns across multiple platforms.'

'Lost me there, son.'

'Dad, please leave Rhys alone,' pleaded Jessica fidgeting on her chair.

'No, no Jessica. I'm interested. Rhys, give me an example of what you do.'

'At the moment we are working on a campaign for Pasternak Construction.'

'The same company building the houses here in Weatherford?' asked Alistair.

'Yes and elsewhere. They try and use local companies to do the support work associated with the construction sites,' explained Rhys.

'Right, I'm with you so far,' responded grandpa Leo holding up his empty wine glass again. 'So explain the integrated multiple platform thing?'

'The client has the contract for the expansion of the Cressinghill Hospital. There are a lot of people interested in the project, so we design information brochures, corporate publications and distribute them,' explained Rhys. 'The distribution is via the internet,' he added.

'So a bit like tv's *Mad Men* except you use computers. Instead of hand-drawing the brochures, you just 'cut and paste' from a computer programme?' probed the grandfather.

'Dad, stop it. You're being mischievous,' interjected Jessica.

'Mum, is there any turkey left over?' asked Tom.

'Plenty in the kitchen. You might have to reheat the gravy.'

''When you think about it, Rhys, although it was more than sixty years ago,' continued Leo, 'those *Mad Men* had multiple platforms as well; radio and television; the cinema; newspapers and magazines; bill boards and sides of busses. Not sure how integrated it was though.'

'Anyone for charades?' asked Jessica.

'Count me out. I think I'll go and have a little nap,' answered the grandpa slowly getting up from the table. 'Thanks for the lovely meal, my dear. I'll see you all a bit later for a sundowner.' At the door Leo stopped and looked back at the gathering. 'One thing the *Mad Men* didn't have was spellcheck. I guess that's progress.'

'Mum, when are we going to have the christmas pudding?' Tom asked from the kitchen.

'I think we'll wait until grandpa's had his rest,' replied an exhausted Jessica.

'Well, can I have a slice of this christmas cake then?'

'Yes, but offer some to everyone else.'

'My goodness, Jessica, does Tom always eat this much?' asked Charlotte.

'He is our resident locust. Doesn't stop,' she replied.

'I can't remember my little Rhys eating so much at that age. Can you Edward?'

'No,' answered Edward.

The next couple of hours were spent at the dining room table playing charades and trivial pursuit. For

Jessica, the afternoon was torture. She just wanted everyone to go home. Rhys kept manoeuvring himself so that he could sit next to her. She kept on the move. Eventually, the spurned lover gave up and sat at the end of the table with a desperately woeful expression on his face. The object of his desire totally ignoring him.

Meanwhile, Alistair, Charlotte and Edward were still thoroughly enjoying Christmas. They were definitely not attending a meeting of the temperance movement. Chloe was on her tablet, headphones in her ears, ignoring the outside world, while Tom sat in the kitchen finishing off a turkey drumstick dipped in sweet chilli sauce.

With the deteriorating behaviour of her husband and their guests, Jessica decided that it was time for christmas pudding, and wouldn't wait for her father. Dessert over, she offered to take the inebriated Broadhursts and their jilted son home. She asked Tom to accompany her, so that he could sit in the front passenger seat. When they arrived at the Broadhurst home, Jessica remained in the 4x4, and asked Tom to help everyone out. As they reversed out of the driveway, Charlotte and Edward waved them goodbye. Rhys had disappeared, he was indoors already.

Leo Proctor woke up from his nap, and came down stairs to find Jessica, Alistair and the twins tidying up.

'Oh, Charlotte and Edward gone?' asked the grandpa.

'Yes, Jessica took them home, a little too much to drink,' answered Alistair.

'There's christmas pudding and brandy cream if you would like some,' offered Jessica. Her father helped himself to dessert and sat down at the kitchen table.

'Charlotte and Edward. Nice couple,' remarked the grandpa. 'That Rhys is a bit wet though, isn't he?' Alistair laughed at his father-in-law's comment. Jessica threw the knives and forks she was drying onto the sink drainer. The sudden noise stopped the laughter.

'You two are unbelievable. Dad, how could you treat Rhys the way you did at lunchtime. Belittling him about his career. A guest in my house. As for you Alistair, you're no better. I've been on my feet all bloody day. I've had enough of this family. Everyone just takes me for granted. No more. I'm going for a drive. Get away from you lot,' fumed Jessica as she stormed out of the house.

CHAPTER 14

The Hughes' home was previously the chemist, and one of a number of shops that had once flourished in Weatherford. The demise of the village's traditional high street proved to be a double edged sword. As the shops closed, there was a decline in the use of community amenities, and as they started to disappear, it accelerated the closure of the remaining shops.

Residents who had lived in Weatherford for a long time inadvertently became part of what is now called the housing crisis. When their families grew up and left home, there were no suitable houses for the ageing residents to move to and down-size. With nowhere to go, they remained in the old family home. With a shortage of family-size homes and the lack of shops and amenities, Weatherford was no longer an attractive option for young families. The population aged, the numbers declined, and a fully functioning community disappeared.

The decreasing population prompted a review by National Health, and it was decided that the village was not large enough to have its own surgery. Despite protests from the residents, and luke-warm resistance by the Parish Council, it was closed and incorporated into a modern purpose built surgery in Wolburn Market.

The surgery closure had unintended consequences for the chemist. Its regular and almost guaranteed income from prescriptions dried up. Thrown out into the cut-and-thrust world of retail, and no longer bankrolled by the taxpayer, the proprietor was unable to retain his customers. Despite offering endless discounts and bargain buys on toiletries and gifts at prices that matched or even bettered those of the burgeoning superstores, the 'loyal' customers now headed off to Wolburn Market for their prescriptions, and on the way stopped at the superstores to buy the same toiletries.

The shop, that had for decades dispensed patented medicines, reopened as a Wine Merchant, and dispensed alternatives for medicinal purposes. This commercial venture only lasted a year, and after much resistance from the parish council, having a year previously strongly opposed the wine merchant's alcohol licence application, eventually agreed to allow the building to be added to the village's housing stock.

The Hughes, wrapped up warmly against the January cold, turned into the lane at the end of the Old High Street. It was not a long walk from the old chemist to the Manor House. They walked down the hill passed the smock mill, over the ford and a few yards further on arrived at the gate of the 16th Century manor.

The manor is set slightly back from the road, and built on level ground with the remainder of the estate sloping away from the house. Apart from the small landscaped garden and pond in front of the house, the parkland stretches down the hill as far as London Road. Over the centuries various livestock have roamed the park which has left a legacy of grassland and very few trees. Sir Michael and Lady Beswick have no interest in rearing animals, except for a few sheep that they use as mobile lawnmowers.

'It's a really beautiful house,' remarked Tia as they walked across the oval expanse of driveway.

'It certainly is. Many of these old houses have been altered so many times that they lose their basic shape. This one has had some major changes, but you can still see the basic E-shape,' remarked Jeremy.

The Hughes reached the large Tudor style oak front door with its black cast iron door handle, hinges and studs. To the right of the door, the iron bell pull has a small pvc sign below it 'Welcome. Please use the electric bell on the left. Thank you'. Most first time visitors find a Tudor manor with an electric bell quite quirky.

Sir Michael opened the door.

'Tia, Jeremy, Happy New Year, do come in.' The Hughes followed their host across the hallway with its splendid Jacobean style grand staircase. Two hand painted Chinese screens are in attendance on either side of the first flight of stairs that lead up to a large gothic window. On either side of the window hang portraits of previous male Beswicks, a second line of defence as they keep an eye on who's coming and who's going. The stairs continue their left and right symmetrical journey up to a spacious gallery which encircles the upper part of the hallway, and provides access to numerous bedrooms.

Sir Michael leading the way opens the double Jacobean oak doors of the drawing room. A rectangular room with floor to ceiling light oak panels and a single gothic window at the far end. As this is the only natural light in the room, the Victorian wall lights have to be turned on when it is in use.

Halfway down the left hand side of the room is a large wood fire. Two fireside chairs flank the ornate stonework of the fireplace and hearth. In front of the fire are two three seater sofas and between the sofas, facing the fire, two single seat armchairs.

In the far right hand corner of the room a Broadwood & Sons grand piano waits patiently for someone to come over and tickle its ivories. When the Hughes visit the Beswicks, it usually includes Jeremy and his troupe of Beethoven, Rachmaninov or Mozart, and depending on the amount of alcohol consumed, a hearty attempt at *Land of Hope and Glory*.

Almost the entire floor is covered by an enormous Persian carpet. The sheer size of it always astonishes Tia. The loud red and blue colours are in sharp contrast to the all-white Victorian plaster decorated ceiling. There are various tables and chairs filling spaces of the huge room, but despite its size, it is comfortable and warm, and the wall mounted lights reflecting off the oak panels give it a homely, soft appearance which completes this masterpiece.

'Are those new vases, Kay?' asked Tia walking over to look at a set of three Chinese blue and white porcelain vases displayed on a Tudor refectory table.

'Yes, part of the shipment I received in December. I thought it would be nice to display them in the house, enjoy them a bit, what do you think of them?'

'Very nice. How much are they?' asked Tia.

'£450 each, maybe 500 at the most,' replied Kay.

'Nice if you can afford it,' sighed Tia. There was an awkward silence in the room.

'Drinks everyone?' asked Sir Michael trying to get the conversation restarted. 'Please sit, make yourselves comfortable,' he added while guiding Jeremy and Tia towards the sofas in front of the roaring fire. 'Usual drinks?' he asked heading over to the Edwardian Art Deco drinks cabinet.

Above the cabinet hangs a portrait of Michael's father, Sir John. He joined the Army at the beginning of the Second World War, and despite being severely wounded, he remained in the military and retired in 1977. Michael's mother gave the portrait to her husband on his 40th birthday. It shows him standing in his uniform beside a mahogany table with a red velvet tablecloth with his right hand resting on a pile of four military history books. It was painted in the Victorian style of realism, and the result was an accurate portrayal of the Army Officer; even the embossed and engraved letters on the medals can be clearly seen by the viewer. Michael was born in 1958, and his only lasting memory of his father, is that of an absent parent being deployed almost every year to some or other foreign conflict.

At the insistence of his mother, Michael was shipped off to a London boarding school at a very young age, and it was a decision that had a profoundly negative effect on his relationship with her. As the years went by, he became very resentful of his philanthropic mother. He felt she had abandoned both he and his slightly younger brother. Whilst her sons had to endure a loveless existence at boarding school, Michael felt his mother was using her title to make a name for herself in the world of famine relief and other humanitarian causes.

A serious family crisis occurred one summer holiday when newspaper allegations were made that food aid that should have been distributed to starving mothers and children in war torn Africa was being diverted by charity field workers to feed rebel militia.

Michael's mother was the chairman of the charity, and although nothing was ever proved, his father returning from the conflict area in question, moved out and checked into his regiment's Officers Mess. Michael and his brother returned to school after the summer holiday, and it was not until Christmas of that year that his estranged parents buried the hatchet. It didn't snow that Christmas, but the atmosphere in the Manor House was decidedly icy.

When Michael was old enough, he joined the army, albeit not his father's regiment. His mother pleaded with him not to join up. Unfortunately the more she protested the more he dug his heels in. It was illogical behaviour, and not in keeping with Michael's true personality. In defiance of her wishes, and as a result of years of bitterness, he joined up.

Despite joining the army for all the wrong reasons, Michael never looked back.   He was involved in what is officially known as The Troubles, and saw action in the Gulf War, Bosnia, Iraq and Afghanistan. Boarding school became a distant memory, and his relationship with his mother became less volatile.

His younger brother David trained as a dentist in London. While at university he met a fellow dental student Bonnie, and a few months after qualifying they got married. Despite endless jokes about concrete cows, the newly-weds moved to the 'new city' of Milton Keynes and set-up a dental practice together.

Sir John's old war injury started to give him problems as he grew older. He was proud of Michael and David and was happy in the knowledge that with at least one married son, the Beswicks would survive a few more generations. Unfortunately, he did not live long enough to see Michael get married, and Sir John died of complications relating to his injury. He was 66 years old, and was buried alongside his ancestors at All Saints.

Major Michael Beswick, 34 years of age, was part of an army recruitment team visiting Tees County University. The university was hosting a careers fair, and Kay Holland, 20 years of age, had only one lecture that day. With nothing better to do, she decided to go over to Mount Stephen's Hall and take a look at what the exhibition had to offer.

Although Kay was in her final year, she was still not sure what to do when she graduated. She picked up a few handouts at the door and wandered into the Hall. First exhibition Daxosmith Pharmaceuticals, no; second exhibition Dubai World Airlines, no; third one Teacher Training - Department of Education, no; fourth one Foreign and Commonwealth Office - Foreign Service, I wonder, um, maybe, hello, what's this?

'Morning ma'am,' Major Beswick, North Essex Yeomanry Regiment. Can I interest you in the army?'

'I really don't think so.' Kay smiled as she looked up at over six feet of soldier standing in front of her.

'The army has a lot of interesting jobs and opportunities for women,' replied the Major. Michael didn't take his eyes off Kay, and she found herself staring back.

'Thank you, Corporal. I'm fine, thank you,' stammered the student. 'I must go, I'll be late for my lecture.' Kay turned on her heel and walked quickly out of the hall.

'Sergeant-Major, look after the stall. I'll be back in a minute,' Michael issued the order and ran after Kay. She was crossing the quad when he caught up with her.

'Excuse me.' Kay stopped and turned around. 'My name is Michael. You are probably going to think me very forward, and I will not be offended if you tell be to bugger off,' he said. 'We'll be finished here at three this afternoon, can we meet up for something to eat or a drink maybe?' he asked.

'Sure,' I'll meet you at the fountain over there at three,' replied Kay.

'Great. Yes. 3 o'clock, see you then,' answered a very surprised major. The strangers turned and walked off in opposite directions. Michael took a couple of steps and stopped, 'What's your name?' he asked.

'Kay Holland.'

'See you later Kay. By the way I'm a Major not a Corporal.' The officer smiled and gave her a wave goodbye.

Kay's father Robert, was transferred by his London-based bank to Hong Kong in the late 1960s. The move proved difficult for Kay's mother, Elizabeth. She left behind a large house and garden in Epsom, family, and friends and replaced them with a small apartment in an overcrowded city. Although the view of Hong Kong Bay was spectacular, especially at night, she didn't like the smell of the city, the constant noise, the pushing and jostling of the crowds, and not being able to speak the language.

The situation was not made any easier by the fact that ex-pats tended to gravitate towards ex-pats. Trapped in a hamster wheel of earning a lot of money, and constantly moving around the globe in search of an even larger financial package, these wealthy modern-day nomads did not get the opportunity to make long-term friendships. They were too transient, and when they got together to socialise they had nothing to talk about except to complain about the locals, whilst sipping cocktails.

The Hollands were different. Hong Kong was home. Robert's job was permanent, and they were going nowhere. Kay's mother eventually conceded defeat, stopped drinking heavily, and settled down to bring up a family. They had two daughters, Kay and Mary, each new arrival requiring a move into a larger apartment to accommodate the growing family.

Elizabeth Holland put her experience of moving to Hong Kong to use, and persuaded her husband to ask his bank to provide her with a small office in which she set-up an advice centre for ex-pats moving to and from the colony. The number of services she provided grew in number, as did her reputation.

In the blink of an eye, it was time for Kay to leave home, and head off to university in England to read Chinese Studies. The family had visited England on a number of occasions, so it was not totally unfamiliar to her. Despite these visits, she was nervous about leaving home, and was pleased her mother was travelling with her. Kay's Aunty Maggie and Uncle Peter, who she had met only once, had agreed that she could spend the holidays with them in Dorking.

Kay sat in the lecture hall with butterflies in her stomach. She couldn't believe she had just accepted a lunch invitation from a complete stranger. It was that uniform she thought. How am I going to get out of this one? I guess I could just not turn up. He is extremely handsome she conceded to herself.

In chick-lit terms, what happened next was a whirlwind romance. A prince in a snatch land rover swept Kay off her feet and carried her away. A month after meeting her, Michael telephoned Kay's father and asked him for permission to marry his daughter. The day after Kay finished her last exam, he proposed.

She agreed to a military wedding, and Michael agreed to Kay's request that the ceremony was not too formal. Initially Kay was a bit overwhelmed. She had a wedding to organise without the usual support of friends and family. However, she was not one for panic attacks and tantrums. Her small group of university friends offered to help, and over the coming months the usual wedding 'to-do' list was steadily ticked off.

Soon after the engagement, Michael took Kay back home to Weatherford to meet his mother, and his brother and sister-in-law who were visiting from Milton Keynes. To Michael's total surprise his mother and Kay got on like a house on fire. Kay was equally surprised that her future mother-in-law was nothing like Edwina Deauville as portrayed by Michael. She was energetic, calm, organised and generous with her time. She did not suffer fools gladly, but Kay discovered to her amusement that Lady Beswick was adept at mimicking accents from almost every corner of the country. It was certainly better than the less-than-ladylike jokes she could tell, after a couple of gin and tonics. She offered to help with the wedding, and despite Michael's mistrust of his mother's possible motives, she became Kay's loyal and trusty adjutant.

The wedding took place at All Saints on a surprisingly warm sunny day at the end of August. Michael's regiment provided the Guard of Honour with the regimental chaplain performing the ceremony. Father Elby, as the Priest-In-Charge at All Saints, was invited to attend as a co-officiant in recognition of the Beswick family's long association with the village church.

Kay arrived in a silver Bentley hired from A & B Stroud in Great Dunsford. It was a perfect summer's afternoon with a gentle breeze and fair weather clouds passing slowly overhead. The bride complemented the weather; she looked bright, happy and resplendent in the sunshine.

The Guard Commander was Michael's best man, and he and two members of the Guard escorted Kay from the car into the church where her father was waiting to walk his daughter down the aisle.

She wore a timeless and sophisticated wedding gown made from white embroidered lace tuille organza. Kay, as practical as ever, had decided not to have a train. The fitted flared gown was embroidered with lace applique and beading, and the ends of the sheer long sleeves had matching lace. A beaded belt showed off Kay's small waist.

Mary, Kay's sister, and Kay's best friend Sophie from uni, were the bridesmaids. Both wore off the shoulder dusty pink satin dresses with fitted and flared skirts, and matching lace bodices. All three girls had fresh flowers in their hair, and wore satin low heeled shoes.

The reception was held in the grounds of the manor house in two marquees. The formal dinner was proceeded by a cocktail hour. Held in the smaller of the two, the guests had a choice of mini bites and cocktails. There was a mini beer station for the guests who preferred beer. The children had not been forgotten; there was a wooden cocktail bar serving mock-tails, fruit juices, and frozen watermelon on sticks; an ice cream trolley with sorbet and frozen yoghurt; a popcorn trolley; and a cola fountain. As it turned out, the children's choices proved to be more popular amongst the grown-ups than the intended recipients.

The formal dinner and dance was held in the larger of the two marquees. The starters were a shrimp, calamari, mussels and octopus seafood salad or fresh figs wrapped in parma ham. The main course was a choice of salmon seasoned with garlic lemon and butter or roast leg of lamb served with seasonal vegetables. Dessert was an all-time summer favourite; lemon meringue pie and ice cream.

The DJ was one of the soldiers from the regiment who Michael had previously booked for an army function. The *Marching Band* as he called himself was quite unique in that he played the appropriate music for each phase of the evening. During the meal he played chamber music, and then changed to party music for the dancing.

The cutting of the wedding cake brought the meal to a close. The marquee fell silent when Michael drew his sword and stood behind his bride. He presented the sword to Kay over her right arm with the blade pointing outwards. You could cut the silence in the marquee with a knife. Kay placed both hands over Michael's right hand and they cut the cake together. The cheer could be heard in Wolburn Market.

Michael and Kay chose *Take My Breathe Away* for their first dance. By the time the first dance was over everyone was ready to party. It was not long before the *Marching Band* had the guests dancing, singing and having fun. The bride and groom left just before midnight, but the party carried on until the early hours of the morning. It was forty years since the Manor House had rocked to the wedding of Michael's mother and father.

When the married couple returned from their honeymoon in the Trossachs in Scotland, they stayed in married quarters until the end of the autumn. A number of discussions took place with Margaret, Lady Beswick about the manor house. She had lived in the house on her own for almost five years, and it had become a burden. With Michael and Kay married, she had someone to take over the house. The newly-weds agreed to her wishes, and with the help of her daughter-in-law she moved into a seafront apartment at Frinton-on-Sea at the end of the summer.

Michael and Kay turned into the driveway of the manor house twenty months after first meeting at the careers fair. Michael stopped the car, got out, and opened the front door. Kay was behind him and lifting her up, Sir Michael Beswick carried the new Lady Beswick over the threshold.

CHAPTER 15

For the first few months, the whirlwind continued for Kay, as she entertained a stream of visitors to Weatherford. First to arrive were her parents for Christmas. Her father announced his intentions to retire when the colony was handed back to the Chinese, and they spent most of their visit travelling around the south of England looking for potential places to live. Kay thought it a bit premature, but didn't interfere.

Kay's parents eventually left and were almost immediately replaced by Michael's brother and wife who were in the process of immigrating to Canada. The plan was to stay for two weeks while their furniture crossed the North Atlantic to Toronto. Not surprisingly things did not go according to plan. A late winter freeze on the east coast of America delayed the unloading of the container ship, and the stay in Weatherford was extended. It turned out to be a five week stay, and Kay and Michael were relieved when David and Bonnie eventually drove down the driveway and headed west.

Before Michael proposed to Kay, they had a number of serious discussions about marrying an army officer. Michael tried as gently as he could to explain to Kay that he might, no he would, be deployed at short notice, and for indefinite periods of time. Having had a father who had always been away, Michael wanted to make sure that Kay, before she made the commitment, understood that she would be left behind to look after the house and home. He wanted to impress upon her that it was not a maybe, but that it would definitely happen. He asked her to be truthful with herself before marrying him.

Luckily for the newly-weds, the hot spots around the world remained relatively peaceful for a while. Kay and Michael were able, once they had got rid of all the visitors, to settle down and enjoy some time together. If Michael had any doubts about Kay, he need not have worried.

Global peace did not last forever, and his travel itinerary during his final years in the Army included Kuwait, Bosnia, Iraq and Afghanistan. Kay did not miss a beat when Michael was away. She started a Chinese furniture business soon after arriving at the manor house, and with a lot of patience and hard work, she created a successful wholesale business. She had recently set up a website to trial the selling of her furniture online.

She took to motherhood like a duck to water when Thomas, their only son, was born. She was unable to fall pregnant again, and always regretted the fact that Thomas didn't have a brother or sister. Unlike his father and uncle, no mention was ever made of boarding school as an option. Their son attended the primary school in the village, and then the comprehensive in Wolburn Market. He went on to read law, and decided to specialise in Mergers and Acquisitions. Kay had taught Thomas to speak mandarin, and it was no surprise to either of his parents when he decided, after a couple of visits to Hong Kong, to take up a job with a law firm in the former colony.

Instead of looking after more babies, Kay looked after the upkeep of the house with the help of Dave Wright. The manor was a bit like the Sydney Bridge, in that there was a never ending cycle of fixing, replacing and redecorating. She took to wearing overalls almost all of the time which became her trademark in the village.

'Jeremy I want to ask you a favour,' said Michael, pouring another round of drinks.

'Depends what it is,' smiled Jeremy.

'Oh, don't worry nothing illegal,' replied Sir Michael.

'Tia, let's take our drinks over to the warehouse, and I'll show you the new consignment of furniture. Leave the men to chat,' suggested Kay getting up from the sofa and taking the two drinks from her husband.

'You don't mind, do you, Michael?'

'No, not at all. Have fun,' he said kissing Kay on the forehead.

'So what's the favour, Michael,' asked Jeremy as Kay and Tia left the room.

'Well, my five year procurement job ends this year, and that will be it as far the career is concerned.'

'Looking forward to stopping?' asked Jeremy.

'I think so. Not sure what I'm going to do to keep myself busy. Kay has suggested something like the British Legion,' replied Sir Michael, 'Good cause. It certainly won't be time wasted. I just don't know if I'm cut out for it.'

'Maybe help Kay with the online business?' suggested Jeremy.

'No, it's Kay's business and her project. I don't think after all these years she would want me to interfere. Anyway, back to present. I want to hold a Gatsby Themed Party here at the manor to celebrate my retirement. I haven't formally said good bye to the army and my old colleagues. The party will be an ideal opportunity to do so, and we can raise a bit of money for charity at the same time. What do you think?'

'Sounds wonderful, Michael. How do I feature in all of this?' asked Jeremy.

'Well, with your musical background, I would like you to put together a dance band for me. Is it possible?'

'Yes. Of course I can,' replied the musician.

'How many musicians do you need to make up a band?' continued Sir Michael.

'Depends, but let's say 10,' Jeremy answered after quickly counting up on his fingers.

'Grab your coat, Tia, it'll be a bit cold out there,' suggested Kay as she put on her wax jacket that was hanging up next to the front door. The women walked across the driveway towards what looks like three garages, each with a golden oak coloured roller door.

'Michael's father built this to house his car collection. The cars have long gone, and we now use them as a warehouse for the furniture. Although it looks like its three separate garages, it's actually only one.' explained Kay as she used the remote to open the middle door. The garage was full of Chinese furniture and ornaments stored on rows of long span steel shelves. 'Do you know Andrew MacGregor, owns Crockett Farm out on the Wolburn Market Road?' Tia shook her head in the negative. 'Well, he delivers the orders for me,' added Kay.

'Just in the county?' asked Tia.

'No all over the country,' replied Kay. Tia shook her head in amazement. 'Not sure how we are going to cope with the internet orders though. We'll have to hold quite a lot more stock. Space is a problem. We've started to refurbish the old barn which should go some way towards resolving the problem. Early days,' smiled Kay. 'Come on, let me show you around.'

'How is Thomas getting on in Hong Kong?' asked Tia as they stopped to look at the hand painted screens.

'He is actually doing very well. He has settled down, found himself a lovely apartment overlooking the Harbour, and enjoying work.'

'Do you talk to him often?'

'Yes, almost every day. It is so easy with the video cam, and the mobile phone. I'll be honest, it is a very surreal experience seeing and hearing my little boy in Hong Kong. It's all so familiar. I can almost smell the city.'

'Are these the new ceramics?' asked Tia as she picked up a blue and white floral vase.

'Yes. Lovely aren't they? Thomas does have girlfriend trouble though,' continued Kay.

'Oh?' Tia looked at Kay in surprise.

'No, not that sort of trouble. It's actually quite weird. You remember I told you he had met a girl called Rebecca during his second year at university?'

'The one from Hong Kong?' replied Tia.

'Yes, that's right, Rebecca Kam,' nodded Kay. 'Well, her parents were granted full British Citizenship when the colony was handed over to the Chinese, and they moved to London with her. With

Thomas in Hong Kong, she now wants to return home. Her parents don't want her to go, but more bizarrely, neither the Foreign Office nor the Chinese Authorities can decide if she is eligible to return to Hong Kong.'

'You couldn't make it up, if you tried,' laughed Tia. 'So what are they going to do?'

'Not much they can do, but wait and see what the outcome is,' answered Kay. 'Let me show you the new cabinets. I don't normally stock cabinets, they are such a slow seller, but these are a more modern design and they might create a bit of interest. How is Jane doing, Tia? Tia stopped for a moment and ran her hand over the smooth cabinet top, then stopped and looked at Kay, and burst into tears.

'Tia. What's the matter? Is she ill? Is it the baby?' asked a very surprised Kay.

'No, no, they are both well. That little coward Ashley has walked out on her. I'm so cross, I could kill him,' sobbed Tia.

'What does Jeremy say about it?'

'Jeremy doesn't live on the same planet as we do. He is so tied up with his own self-pity. The useless selfish bastard,' Tia blurted out. 'We have no money, and he refuses to get a job. I'm working full time, but it doesn't bring in enough. I would love to start pottery lessons again, but can't afford it. Now Jane has been left with a baby, and no income. We don't have enough money to live on, Kay,' cried Tia.

'Tia, I'm so sorry. If there's anything I can do to help with Jane and the baby, please ask,' said Kay putting her arms around her friend in an attempt to comfort her.

'I've been to the Council, and put Jane on the housing list. There is a twelve month wait, and if she does get somewhere to live, it's probably going to be the new housing development near the airport,' said Tia looking through her tears. Kay handed her a couple of tissues.

'Let's get together and have a chat. Phone me, and we can go through to Wolburn Market for a coffee. Talk things through. Look at the options,' suggested Kay, despite the fact that she did not have a clue as to how she would be able to help. 'Let's close up, and go back to the house, it's getting a bit cold out here,' she added.

When they got back to the warm house, Michael persuaded the guests to have one for the road.

'So what do you think of the new stuff, Tia?' asked Sir Michael.

'All lovely, Michael. I'm so jealous. I'd love to have a couple of pieces.' He was rather surprised to see Tia had been crying. 'What's wrong?' he mouthed at Kay.

'Later,' mouthed Kay shaking her head slightly and frowning.

When the Hughes's left Michael told Kay that Jeremy had agreed to form a band for the Gatsby Night, and Kay told him what had happened in amongst the chinese furniture and ornaments.

Walking home, Jeremy told Tia about the band.
'Did you talk fees, Jeremy?' she asked rather curtly.

'We can't charge the Beswicks a fee,' he replied in horror.

'How many musicians are we talking about, 8, 10?' interrogated Tia.

'Yes, 10 probably,'

'And they are going to do this gig for you for free?'

'Tia, I can't ask Michael for a fee? You're being unreasonable. They are our friends,' pleaded the would-be impresario.

'I'll tell you what, Jeremy. I'm going to stop here at the Green Man, and when I get home, you had better have come up with a better plan. Look at me; look at me, damn you. We are up to our eyes in debt. We have no money. We are bankrupt. Our daughter has a baby, nowhere to live and following in her father's footsteps, not earning any money. The Beswicks live in a bloody great house and sell pieces of Chinese tat for £500 a go, and you are telling me that you and the Chuckle Brothers are going to perform for free. God give me strength.' Jeremy stood and watched his wife storm up the path to the front door of the pub and go in.

Tia was not sober when she arrived back home, and she found Jeremy sitting at the dining room table with a half-empty bottle of scotch.

'Tia, you're right about the fee for the band. I'll speak to Michael and come up with a reasonable figure. Sorted.'

'It's not bloody sorted,' slurred his wife. 'I'll tell you what the fee is going to be, and you tell Michael. If he doesn't like it, he can get some other bunch of idiots to play for him.'

'But….'

'There is no but, Jeremy. We have been married 30 years, and you have never supported this family. For some reason you've always expected me to support everyone. You're a useless daydreamer. I go out to work all week, every week, and I still do not earn enough money to pay the bills. You cannot carry on shutting yourself away in the back room and sulking when things get tough. I'm sick and tired of you being so useless.'

'It's not my fault that nobody wants a saxophone player,' answered Jeremy.

'Jeremy, you just don't get it, do you? Read my lips. If you don't get a full time job, I want you to get out of my life, and this marriage is over.'

CHAPTER 16

Hanna emerged from London Bridge Underground Station into cold winter sunlight. Dressed up warmly against February's biting temperature, it felt good to be away from the cramped and airless chambers that imprisoned her during the week. She was looking forward to the weekend; Borough Market, the Three Sails with Cassie this evening, and with rain forecast for tomorrow, one season of *Victoria* plus duvet.

She stopped and looked up at the Shard which she had seen at various stages of its three yearlong construction. Right from the beginning it had looked fragile, and although it was an impressive building, it now looked even more precarious. Leaving the Shard, and the hotel that she thought should have been called the Shardri La, the day tripper turned right into St Thomas Street, and headed for the market.

The high street was already bustling with Saturday shoppers, and with a queue out of the door at Café Chaud, she decided a hot drink could wait. Weaving her way between the pedestrians, Hanna headed towards the bank, crossed at the traffic lights, and continued up Stoney Street to the market entrance opposite Chez Helena. She liked the market entrances in Stoney Street; they were far more impressive than the dull art deco entrance around the corner. The solicitor wasn't there for any specific reason, it was just an outing, and she slowly wandered from stall to stall. She bought a jar of honey for Cassie, and some ravioli and gnocchi pasta for herself. After an hour and a half of browsing, it was time for that postponed coffee.

On her way to the high street exit, she was passing a spice stall, and saw Chris Brown taking his change from the stallholder. She was surprised to see him, it was so unexpected, and she just carried on walking. She got to the art deco exit, turned around, and rushed back to the stall. The off-duty police officer had gone.

'Excuse me, the man you have just served, which way did he go?' The stallholder pointed towards his right without looking up. Hanna headed off in the direction of the gesture. This is ridiculous, she thought, you're behaving like a silly little schoolgirl. Jeez, there he is. The detective had stopped at a confectionary stall.

'Chris,' she called. Hearing his name, he not surprisingly turned to see who was calling. If Hanna had been surprised, Chris Brown was astonished to see her. He stood for a moment, with his mouth open.

'What are you doing here?' he asked.

'Probably for the same reason you are here,' laughed Hanna nervously.

'Yes, of course. Stupid question.' They shook hands, their eyes met, and they stood for a moment looking at each other. Hanna could feel herself starting to blush, and reluctantly let go of Chris' hand.

'It's lovely to see you again. You're looking great.'

'Thank you Chris. You're not looking too shabby yourself.'

'Wow, this is a surprise, I'm lost for words. I've a couple of days off. I'm on my way to see my parents.'

'They live in London?'

'No, Croydon. Caught the train in this morning, and thought I'd get a few spices and a nice plump chicken on my way through,' explained Chris. 'And you?'

'Just wanted to get out a bit,' smiled Hanna.

'I've still got to buy the chicken. How about something to eat? I shouldn't be too long. Do you have time?'

'I've finished my shopping. Lunch would be lovely. I'll wait here for you. Please take your time.'

Chris left Hanna at the entrance opposite The Barrow Cart pub, and with butterflies in her stomach, she watched him striding off in search of a chicken. She could hear Cassie, cheekily, calling him fit.

Low dark clouds began to replace the sunshine of earlier, and after a couple of minutes of waiting,

Hanna had to move back from the market entrance to get out of the wind. By the time Chris returned, a strong wind was driving the rain almost horizontally along the street. They could hardly hear each other above the noise of the wind and the rain on the roof.

'We're going to get soaked,' commented Chris.

'Let's go over the road to the pub,' suggested Hanna.

'OK. Take my hand. Be careful you don't slip.' Hanna didn't need persuading, and hung on tightly to the detective's arm, as they crossed the road, avoiding the puddles. Thankfully it was a very short distance. Nevertheless, by the time they got through the pub door they were both drenched.

'Oh, God. I must look terrible. I'll be back in a minute,' said Hanna as she headed off to find the Ladies. Chris chose a table next to the open wood fire, and ordered a glass of house white for Hanna, and a Peroni Beer and glass for himself.

'Thanks for the wine,' said Hanna as she sat down, 'we'll get dry next to this fire.'

'I mustn't eat too much,' remarked Chris looking at the menu. 'I'm sure there is a banquet waiting for me at home.'

'Your mum's a good cook then?'

'No, she doesn't cook at all. My dad does all the cooking. He's good,' smiled Chris.

'That's interesting. I mustn't eat too much either. Cassie and I are going to the Three Sails in Hammersmith tonight, next to the river. You're welcome to come along.' Hanna could feel herself willing him to say yes.

'Hanna, I'd love to, but my parents are expecting me. Can we take a rain check?'

'Of course we can,' replied a disappointed farmer's daughter.

'Speaking of Cassie, how is she?'

'Still the same. Her company is sending her on an aerial unmanned crop monitoring course in a couple of weeks. 5 day course at Moulsoe University. It's right up her street; she's into drones and artificial intelligence.'

'Clever stuff. Does she enjoy the job?'

'Yes, she really does. Ever since I first met her, I've always thought agronomy and Cassie were a perfect match.'

'How long have you been friends?'

'Almost nine years. We met at a London MoonWalk. Don't know if you've heard of it. Charity event for breast cancer. My mum died of breast cancer when I was at uni, and Cassie lost her sister-in-law Jenny the same year.

'Wow, that's tough. Please send her my regards.'

'Of course I will.' The barman came over to take their food order. Hanna ordered the southern fried chicken burger, and Chris chose venison and red wine sausage and mash.

'And you? How are you coping?' asked Chris.

'I think I'm doing quite well, thank you. I thought dad's funeral would give me closure. Mum's funeral was very sad, and the grief and heart-ache I felt were perfectly normal. If that makes sense?' Chris didn't quite know what to say, and just nodded his head slowly. 'But dad's funeral made me so angry. I couldn't control the outrage I felt towards those petty, narrow-minded villagers who had made him so unhappy. When I was growing up, I was aware of the in-fighting between the village residents. After mum died, dad seemed to become embroiled in petty squabbles about the farm, planning applications, and accusations of dodgy-dealings. I watched him age prematurely, and loose his drive and enthusiasm. I didn't realise how badly all of it was affecting him, and I feel so guilty for not having been there for him,' confessed Hanna with tears welling up in her eyes. Chris reached across the table, and taking her hands, gently squeezed them in an attempt to comfort her. 'On top of everything else, the farm is also a problem. The crops are failing, and the finances aren't very healthy either. Luckily, there are not too many time pressures. There's no need to make any immediate decisions about the farm. I don't know what I'd have done without Cassie. She's been an absolute star.' The pub had become a shelter from the weather, and was rapidly filling up with wet and bedraggled patrons.

'Lucky we got in here early, and claimed the fire,' remarked Chris looking around the pub. 'If they run out of food, I've got the chicken,' he joked in an attempt to lift the mood.

'Chris, I'm so sorry to be such a misery. It's poor form. You don't deserve all the doom and gloom. I'm so pleased to have bumped into you, it's made my day, and I don't want to spoil it.'

'Don't be harsh on yourself, Hanna. We certainly didn't first meet under the best of circumstances, and we've been given a second chance. It's lovely to see you again.'

'I promise I won't mention my dad nor the farm again,' Hanna smiled, and both of them leant forward, and held hands again.

'Ah, here's the food. Can we have another round of drinks please?' Chris asked the waiter while nodding his head at Hanna for her approval.

'Hot food, yummy, I'm starving,' commented Hanna. Chris helped himself to plenty of ketchup, and Hanna put a few drops of Tabasco on her chicken.

'Cheers. When I set out this morning, I didn't expect this. It's the best thing that's happened to me for ages,' smiled Chris. The waiter returned with the drinks. 'If I remember rightly you live in Camden.'

'Well remembered.'

'Isn't Camden Market a bit more local for you?'

'Yes it is, but it's very alternative. You need to be in the mood for it. I like it here. It's, what's the word, genteel, and quite relaxing. It's also an opportunity for a change of scene, a bit of an outing. Actually come to think of it, isn't Borough out of your way if you're going to Croydon?'

'I was actually born in Lewisham,' answered Chris.

'Really?'

'You sound a bit surprised. My grandparents lived there, and it's also where my brother and I were born. My parents moved out to Croydon when I was five years old. Borough Market has always been part of our lives. I can remember coming here, as a very little boy with my parents and grandparents. We have a couple of family photos of the market somewhere.'

'Did you like growing up in such a big city?'

'Didn't know any different really. Never thought about it.'

'I couldn't wait to get out of Weatherford. I think my suitcases were packed a month before I was due to start uni. I love the freedom of London.' Chris was once again unsure how he should respond, Weatherford and its inhabitants definitely irk her he thought.

'Hanna, I really don't want to break up the party, but I need to get to Croydon before the weekend's over,' smiled the policeman. 'It's a pity; I would like to have spent more time with you. Let's do this again sometime? The trains to London from home are very good. 35 minutes to Liverpool Street. I'll call you during the week. If that's ok with you?' Tears of happiness welled up in Hanna's eyes and she nodded her head.

'I would like that very much,' she replied.

'Come on, the lunch is on me,' offered Chris as he got up and walked over to the bar.

It had stopped raining, but there was still a strong blustery wind which was going to make the walk to the station very unpleasant. Chris hailed a taxi, ignored the taxi driver's comment about the short distance, and within a couple of minutes they were at the station. Hanna took Chris's arm and the two of them walked through the concourse as far as the barrier for the underground.

'Ok, I'll give you a call during the week?' said Chris.

'Looking forward to it,' replied Hanna. The steady stream of commuters were jostling past them as they stood at the barrier.

'Let's get out of everyone's way,' said Chris as he moved Hanna out of the way of the maddening crowd. 'I'm so very pleased I decided to come via the market this morning.' He bent down and kissed her, and Hanna responded by putting her arms around his neck and kissing him back.

'Me too,' she said.

Once Hanna was on the train, she texted Cassie.

You will never guess what has just happened to me.

What?

Bumped into Chris Brown at Borough Market this morning.

So?

I'll tell you all about it tonight. XX.

CHAPTER 17

Richard Kettering-Smythe climbed the wide concrete steps leading up to the glass and stainless steel revolving door of the South Essex Police Station. He waited for a mother with a pushchair and a toddler to emerge from the rotating door, and could feel his pulse starting to race. Trying to remain calm, he approached the reception desk.

'Good morning, Sir. How can I help you?'

'Kettering-Smythe to see Detective Inspector James.' The young man in his late twenties, who according to his name badge was 'Michael Roberts,

Police Administration' glanced at the computer screen in front of him.

'0900. Interview Room 3. Please take a seat, Sir, DI James won't be long,' advised the administrator looking up at the clock on the wall opposite his glass cubicle. KS sat down, and could feel the thumping in his ears. Despite taking a few deep slow breaths in an attempt to relax, he felt nervous as he followed the inspector to the interview room.

'Please take a seat, Mr Kettering-Smythe. May I call you Richard?' asked the DI as Chris Brown came into the room with the teas and coffees that they had ordered.

'Thanks for agreeing to see us today. I just want to start off by saying that you are not under caution, and you are free to leave at any time. We just want to clarify a few details in the statement you gave us the other week. Happy to proceed?'

'Ask away, Inspector.'

'When we spoke to you about the tyre tracks, and the shoe prints in Potts Lane, you initially denied being there. This was despite the fact that we identified one set of tyre tracks belonging to your car,' explained the DI summarising their previous meeting.

'It was an error of judgement, but I did own up to misleading you.'

'You certainly did, but only after we asked for a DNA sample and your shoes,' interrupted the sergeant.

'Ok, let's go through what happened that morning in Potts Lane,' continued the inspector. 'Before you answer, Richard, I must warn you that wasting police time or perverting the course of justice are very serious mistakes to make. Do you understand?'

'Yes, Inspector. And once again I apologise for misleading you the first time around,' KS replied nervously.

'What happened that morning in Potts Lane?' asked the DS, impatiently tapping his pen on the file in front of him.

'I drove down the lane, and saw Brian's vehicle parked up. There wasn't anyone in the Land Rover. I stopped to see if there was a problem. I looked in the driver's side, and nothing seemed to be out of place. There was a gap in the hedgerow, and I had a quick look across the field, but couldn't see anything. It was still quite dark, it was very early. I went back to my car and drove home.' The police officers glanced at each other.

'Will you excuse us,' requested the DI. 'Sergeant.' The detectives left the room, and stood outside in the corridor.

'What do you think, Chris?' asked the DI quietly.

'The two versions match, ma'am, and it's been what, almost four months since we spoke to him last. I still don't like him.' Veronica James looked at her sergeant, and nodded her head slowly while she made her decision.

'Intuition is not enough, sergeant. Yes, he lied, but as you said at the time it could have just been nerves. We haven't unearthed anything untoward. Tell him we have nothing further for him, thank him for his time and assistance, and that he can go home.'

'Yes, ma'am.'

KS bounced down the wide concrete steps with a smile on his face. His pulse was no longer racing. He was pleased with himself. I've managed to talk myself out of that one he thought. He took his mobile out of the left inside pocket of his jacket, and turned off the silent mode. There was a text message.

I have your jacket.

He felt he was being watched, and instinctively looked around the car park. Reading the text again, the parish councillor looked up at the police building. The two detectives were looking down at him. Breathing heavily, and conscience of the police officers, he tried to remain calm and act normally. He took off his jacket, laid it down on the back seat, and quickly got into the car. His pulse was racing again. He reread the text, and typed a reply.

Thanks ref my jacket. Send address. I'll pick it up when convenient. Rgds. KS. and pressed send. He was looking at the screen willing a reply to arrive, when the phone rang. It made him jump. It was his office manager.

'Wendy'

'Morning Richard. I've had the Hancocks on the phone, and they want to view the house in Great Dunsford this afternoon at 3. Where are you?'

'At home. 3 will be fine. I'll be back at the office in an hour.'

'Ok, see you then.'

The estate agent started the car, put it into gear, and released the hand brake. There's no reply to my text he thought as he pulled out of the parking space without looking to his left or right. There was a blast of a car hooter, and KS braked hard to avoid driving into a car passing in front of him. The other car swerved out of the way, and both cars stopped a couple of inches apart. The driver of the swerving car got out, and approached KS.

'Are you bloody blind, mate,'

'I could say the same for you,' replied KS opening his window.

'Idiot.'

'Oh, get a life,' responded the parish councillor. The driver returned to his car, and gesturing with his middle finger, drove off. KS, was a bit shaken, but managed to navigate safely out of the car park without soliciting any further unorthodox hand signals from other car park users.

The text had thrown him off balance. He was flustered, and couldn't think straight. Oblivious to everything going on around him, he was driving along the motorway by instinct, as if on auto-pilot. His head was full of questions. How did the text sender get hold of my number? How does the sender know it's my jacket? Shit, the suicide note. Please God, this is not happening to me, he pleaded with a higher authority. What happens if the sender goes to the police? As he approached the motorway exit for the services the estate agent decided he needed a coffee, and time to calm down before getting back to the office.

The services were heaving with people. It was the half-term break, and there were queues everywhere. Lorries waiting patiently at the filling station, safe in the knowledge that no-one was going to argue with them for taking up almost all of the space on the forecourt. Cars, with bicycles attached to bike carriers, were cowering in between the juggernauts. Other drivers were putting air in their tyres, buying fizzy drinks, and windscreen wash. The rubbish bins couldn't cope, and were overflowing with used packaging, and empty plastic water bottles; their contents scattered over an already fragile planet.

It took some time for KS to find a parking space. An undertaking that was greatly hampered by faded, weather-beaten signage, potholes and fellow drivers ignoring the one way system and the yellow double lines. He queued for 10 minutes at the coffee shop, repeated his name very slowly so that the puzzled barista could write Nebs on the outside of a cup, and finally after a further 10 minutes wait, Nebuchadnezzar had his cappuccino and a choc au pain, which had definitely not been baked that morning. His next challenge was to find somewhere to sit. He found a table to share, and had no sooner sat down when his phone rang.

'What?' he answered impatiently.

'Hi Richard. Sorry to bother you again. Where are you? It's terribly noisy,' replied Wendy.

'At the services. Very busy, hundreds of people, lots of bloody kids.'

'Not surprised, it's half-term.'

'Whatever. Stopped for a coffee before coming into the office, it's been a long morning.'

'The services are a bit out of your way aren't they?'

'None of your business. I don't have to justify my whereabouts. What do you want?' The person sharing the table with KS, couldn't help but overhear the ill-mannered exchange, and raised his eyebrows without looking up from his tablet.

'Henry Allerton from Pasternak Construction phoned, says it's urgent.' The estate agent felt sick to the pit of his stomach, and the noise of the crowd suddenly became unbearable.

'I'm leaving now. If he phones again, tell him I'll call as soon as I get into the office.'

Thirty minutes later KS arrived at the estate agency. The remainder of the journey had been mentally torturous for him; Pasternak, his jacket, the note, and lying to the police. He arranged for one of his staff to do his 3 o'clock viewing, and taking his post and messages from Wendy he went into his office, and closed the door.

He put his mobile down on the desk and sat there looking at it. Maybe I should text that number again, he thought. Can't do any harm. I wish I had a copy of the suicide note. See how incriminating it really is. Trouble is it does mention me by name. That's not good he thought, shaking his head. To be quite honest, am I not panicking unnecessarily? I had nothing to do with Brian Townsend's death. That stroppy daughter of his is wrong about the crops. Maybe I should come clean with the police. No, stay calm and don't panic. I've sailed close to the wind on many occasions. With my influence in the community, nobody would dare challenge me. I won't be bullied. He picked up his mobile and typed. *I'll go to the police if you do not give me your address by 6 o'clock tonight.* He read the message, was about to send it, when he hesitated. If the sender hands over the note to the police, I'm in trouble he thought. I'll sit on my hands and wait. He deleted the message.

The desk telephone rang.

'Kettering-Smythe, good afternoon,'

'KS, Henry Allerton. I left a message for you to call me.'

'I got the message, Henry. I've only just got into the office. You said it was urgent.'

'Not entirely correct. I said it was important,' replied the owner of Pasternak Construction rather abruptly.

'Does it matter who said what, Henry. I've got a lot on my plate at the moment. What do you want?' asked KS impatiently.

'Keep your hair on, matey. I've heard through the grapevine that Application 3613 is going to be rejected again.' KS didn't answer immediately. Keeping the handset against his ear, he leant forward, and resting his forehead in his left hand closed his eyes in exasperation.

'Hello, KS are you still there?'

'Yes I am. It's the first time I've heard anything about the new application's progress. Any idea why it might be rejected?'

'Not the foggiest idea, Richard. I'm very surprised you are asking me that question. I'm actually not a very happy bunny at the moment. You gave me promises and assurances about my development plans getting passed without any hassle. If I had known the hoops I would have to jump through, I would never have selected Weatherford. You're all talk and no trouser. There were so many other opportunities I could have chosen,' said the irate developer raising his voice.

'Ok, there is no need to be abusive just because we have a slight hiccup, Henry. Leave it with me. I'll go and ask some discrete questions, and get back to you.'

'Your promise to keep a close eye on my applications is the only reason I have anything to do with you, you cretan. I've kept my side of the bargain, so don't piss me off.' The telephone went dead. KS slowly put the handset back in its cradle. I really don't need this hassle at the moment he thought as he got up from his desk. He put on his jacket and went out into the front office.

'Wendy, I been watching you lot out here. Don't just sit at your desks twiddling your thumbs. It looks bad when passers-by look in and see idleness. Check the window displays are up-to-date. Vacuum the carpet or clean the toilets or something. I'm off home. I'll be back in the morning.'

KS spent the evening in his study mulling over the situation in which he found himself. He went through every possible permutation, and kept coming back to the same conclusion; do nothing for the moment. He started to relax the more Glenfiddich he consumed, and managed to convince his wife that he had a lot of paperwork to do, and she mustn't miss the last episode of *Shetland* as a result of him working. He would watch it on catch-up later.

He unlocked one of the desk drawers and took out a file marked *AWH*. He spent the best part of an hour on his laptop populating an invoice template, and having filled in the blanks, he printed off the document, placed it in the file, and returned it to the drawer which he locked.

Eve had gone to bed, and he sat at his rather large mahogany desk sipping whisky, hoping that the address text would arrive. Nothing came. When he eventually went to bed slightly inebriated, he tossed and turned, much to Eve's annoyance, until it was time to get up.

Chris Brown and his boss DI Veronica James had spent the best part of the afternoon at HMP South Essex Prison interviewing two teenagers. A mutual friend of the two young men had been found dead in the River Charmer, close to the town centre. They had not been particularly cooperative, and during one of numerous coffee breaks Chris decided to mention Hanna to his boss.

'Ma'am can I speak to you about a personal matter?' DI James put her plastic coffee cup down, and with a slight smile looked across the table at her sergeant. This is unusual she thought, he never discusses anything personal unless really pushed to do so.

'Of course you can.'

'It involves Hanna Townsend, ma'am.'

'As in the Townsend suicide case?'

'Yes ma'am.'

'What about it?'

'Hanna and I are seeing each other,' announced Chris with a huge grin on his face.

'Thank God. Is that all,' exclaimed the DI, 'I thought you were going to tell me we had made a mistake with the investigation,' laughed the inspector. 'Tell me more. I want to hear the goss.'

Chris told his boss about the chance meeting at Borough Market, and how things had developed since then. He said he thought the relationship was serious, but had to assure his boss it was far too premature to buy a hat.

'I'm so happy for you, Chris. Just one thing, and I'm sure I don't have to remind you, but you cannot discuss the case with Hanna. If anything new comes to light or we reopen the case you won't be part of the investigation.'

'I fully understand ma'am. It's the reason I wanted to tell you,' replied the sergeant.

'I appreciate it, Chris. Thanks for telling me. I think we've finished here.'

Chris declined his boss's offer of a lift, and after the stuffiness of the interview room, he enjoyed the brisk walk from the prison back into town to the railway station. He sat on the London-bound train, looking out at the uninspiring landscape rushing past the window. I cannot wait to see Hanna he thought.

Since Borough Market, Chris had travelled down to London on a number of occasions to see Hanna. When they had first met in Weatherford, he was instantly attracted to the farmer's daughter, despite the tragic circumstances. The more time they spent to together, the policeman discovered that he had met someone who was interesting, easy-going and fun. She certainly didn't do anything for show. She was not interested in appearances, and did not pretend to be somebody that she wasn't. Hanna was beautiful, and made him happy.

As the weeks went by, they both started to realise that they just wanted to be together, and what they did was of no importance. It made no difference to either of them whether they went to a fancy West End restaurant or McDonalds in Piccadilly.

If Paris is considered to be the city of love, London became Hanna and Chris's universe of love. Dressed up warmly against the cold, they walked arm-in-arm around London enjoying the spectacular views of the capital by night. The Golden Jubilee Bridge and the London Eye with its changing colours, and across the river its companion the Houses of Parliament; lit up and looking as if it was painted in gold. They stopped on Tower Bridge and kissed while the jagged Shard with its searing tip of white light looked down on the young lovers.

They didn't spend all of their time cuddling and kissing. On one of the walks, Hanna started to ask questions about Chris's family and childhood, and to his slight discomfort, she asked a lot of questions. She was particularly interested in why Chris had become a policeman.

'I've never really stopped to think about my career choice. It just happened,' he told her.

'That's such a cop-out for an answer; excuse the pun,' Hanna responded. 'You can do better than that. Try. Think about it,' she continued.

'There's not really anything to say.'

'If you want to come back to mine tonight, you'll have to think of something to say,' teased Hanna.

'That's blackmail, and it's illegal, and I'll have to arrest you,' Chris said laughing as he held both of Hanna's hands together 'You've been nicked.'

'Seriously Chris, please tell me.' He looked into Hanna's brown eyes and kissed her on the forehead.

'Well my Mum was working as a sales assistant at James and Kithering, the departmental store in Lewisham when she met my Dad. He was with the railways. Mum was from Dorset, and her father was a police inspector down there. I know from what my Mum's father told me, there was a lot of resistance to Mum and Dad getting married. Not only in Dorset, but also in Lewisham. I think it must have been a terrible time for my parents. Friends deserted them. Family members turned against them, and apparently there were many family quarrels about the marriage.

Cutting a long story short, Mum and Dad got married and over time the in-laws became very good friends. When we were old enough, my brother, Jo, and I spent the summer holidays down in Dorset. I think Grandpa Dorset influenced me a lot, and he encouraged both of us to get out there and make something of our lives. He used to say nothing is impossible. Grandpa Dorset being a police inspector fascinated me. He used to tell us stories about old cases.'

'He must have been very proud of the two of you,' commented Hanna.

'I think he was. It was still an uphill battle to jump through the hoops on the way to becoming a policeman. By the time I joined attitudes had improved, and it was a little easier than for my parents and grandparents. It was the same for Jo wanting to become a paramedic. I don't think it was as difficult because the NHS brought in nurses and doctors from all over the world. The whole environment was different. Unfortunately the resistance came from the patients. Some of them flatly refused to be treated by him. Things are much better now.'

'You have told your parents about me, haven't you?' asked Hanna.

'Of course I have, silly. I've told my parents and Jo. My Dad teases me about meeting a farmer's daughter. My Mum texts me every day asking me when am I going to bring you home to meet them.'

'Well?' asked Hanna looking at Chris and opening her eyes wide.

'It's my birthday in a couple of weeks, and I was going to ask you if you wanted to come along.'

'I wouldn't miss it for the world,' responded Hanna hugging her policeman.

Chris emerged from Camden Town Underground Station. It was dark and a light drizzle made the air slightly damp. Pulling the collar of his jacket up around his chin and neck, he headed down Camden High Street and turning into Parkway he immediately saw Hanna waiting outside the Camden Jazz Society. Pleased to see each other, they kissed and hugged before quickly getting out of the damp.

'Have you been here before,' asked Hanna.

'I haven't been here for years. It's one of my parent's favourite places. They used to bring Jo and I here. I know I should like jazz. I understand the whole genre thing and its history, but the music doesn't really do anything for me. I have never told my parents. There's too much baggage.'

'Yeh, I can fully understand that,' replied Hanna, 'You won't believe it, but there is a connection between here and Weatherford,' she continued.

'Really? What?' asked Chris.

'It's one on the villagers, Jeremy Hughes.'

'I remember him. I took his statement at Oak Tree Farm. Long hair and a beard. Scruffy. A musician, if I remember rightly.'

'Yes, that's him. Well he used to play here during the 1970s. Met his wife Tia here in London.'

'Well I never,' exclaimed Chris, 'Shows you what a small world it really is. Follow me,' he said taking Hanna's hand and lead the way up to the mezzanine floor. The restaurant had only just opened its doors, but already there were a number of tables occupied; an early indication that the jazz venue was going to have a busy evening. Too early for the live music, recorded music was playing and there was no doubt that the venue was for jazz lovers.

'The music is especially for you, Chris,' laughed Hanna.

'Watch it. I'll make you sit through an *Iron Man* movie,' he responded wagging his finger at her. 'Here ok?'.

'Perfect,' replied Hanna as they sat down at a table overlooking the empty dance floor. Not wanting to miss the start of the movie, they didn't waste any time selecting fish and chips, a glass of wine for Hanna and a Heineken for Chris. While they waited for the food they chatted about their day, and Chris told Hanna about the discussion with his boss, and explained it had been necessary to advise her of their relationship.

'You've gone a bit quiet, Hanna,' commented Chris. 'Have I upset you?'.

'No not at all. I've just thought that the investigation is the reason why we are sitting here. I have gone from being so utterly miserable to being so very happy. It will be a pity that you cannot be involved in the investigation if it is reopened. I'm sorry.'

'Don't be silly. It's purely procedural. Any further investigation cannot be jeopardised because of us.'

Woah! Woah! Woah! Chris Brown found himself tapping his feet to the opening number of *The Greatest Show*. Hanna's eyes were glued to the screen, and was nodding her head in time to the music. Seeing the smile on her face, he was pleased that he had not tried to change her mind about her choice of movie.

No sooner had the film started, when it was over.

'So did you enjoy it?' asked Hanna as they stopped in the cinema foyer to button up, and pull on gloves.

'I did actually. Much more than I thought I would. I can see you enjoyed it,' answered Chris.

'The dance routines were brilliant. There was so much energy. Not much of a story though. I think we should see it again.'

'Only if you watch an *Iron Man* movie first,' responded Chris. They were standing at the entrance to the cinema, and their eyes met.

'Thank you for the lovely evening,' said Chris putting his arms around her. Hanna liked the feel of his strong arms and nestled in closer to him. They kissed and held each other for a moment ignoring the catcalls and 'get a room' comments from the Camden passers-by.

'I love you, Hanna.'

'I love you too Chris,' came the muffled reply from somewhere in his jacket. 'My place for a night-cap?' asked Hanna.

'Lead the way, ma'am,'

CHAPTER 18

Kay Beswick and Dave Wright, each with a mug of steaming tea, were standing in the early spring sunshine, warming themselves in front of Kay's converted garages. They watched Andrew MacGregor make a wide turn in the spacious manor house driveway, and park his Ford van.

'Morning all,' he greeted as he jumped down from the cab. 'Quite a lot of work going on here by the looks of it,' he smiled removing his iPhone earphones.

'Cheeky sod,' retorted Dave. 'Would you like a brew?'

'No thanks, need to crack on. I see the old barn's getting there, Kay,'

'Yes, I'm really pleased with the way it's going. Another couple of months and it should be ready,' replied the lady of the manor.

'Nice one, Kay. Would you mind giving me a hand, Dave?'

Kay had emailed the consignee's addresses to Andrew the previous day, and he had worked out a drop off sequence. Despite the planning, it took the two men close to two hours to load the antiques destined for Birmingham and Manchester.

With Andrew MacGregor finally on his way, Kay turned her attention to the large delivery that had arrived earlier in the week, and which Dave, who was redecorating one of the bedrooms in the house, had offered to help unpack.

'Is all of this sold, Kay?' asked Dave as he started to prise open a wooden crate.

'A bit of a mixture really; some of them are orders, some on spec, and I've indulged myself a bit, and bought three pieces for myself,' replied Kay as she began marking off the items against the invoice and the packing list.

'The pottery all looks the same to me,' commented the decorator. 'Why would you buy this vase and not this one,' asked Dave pointing at the two vases he had just unpacked.

'As you would say Dave, that's an 'ard one,' smiled Kay as she teased the ex-marine. 'Many of my customers will initially buy a vase to fill an empty space in, say, the lounge or dining room. They then become interested in the history of the pottery, and as their knowledge grows, they start to collect more pieces which often reflect what they have learnt. It then becomes a question of how much they can afford. The Chinese learnt how to make this blue and white ceramic 500 years ago. It was a closely guarded secret, and became even more so when the pottery became popular in the West. It is still very popular, and the Chinese produce it for export,' explained Kay.

'Phew, I'm a bit cold. I need my jacket from the office. I'll make another brew while I'm there,' said Dave rubbing his hands together. 'Won't be a sec.' Ten minutes later, he returned wearing a paint splattered desert combat jacket, carrying mugs of tea.

'Another 'ard question, Kay?' said Dave accentuating his Essex accent. 'What about fakes?'

'Actually, not a stupid question. The Chinese do not allow the exporting of certain artefacts, for example, those from the Quing dynasty period. That's why we have a Certificate of Origin. That pink form over there,' explained Kay pointing to a pile of documents on the desk. 'These six letters on the base are known as the dynasty reign mark,' she continued, turning a blue and white porcelain shang vase over and pointing to the blue writing. If an Emperor or the Imperial Household commissioned a piece of pottery, the artisan would use the mark of the Emperor. You read it from top to bottom and from right to left. This mark is written in zhuanshu, but if it was in mandarin, it would sound like this.' Kay first read it in mandarin, and then running her finger below the letters she repeated it in english for Dave's benefit. *Made in the Great Quing Dynasty during the reign of the Emperor Yongzheng.*

'You're taking the mick, Kay. Nobody can read that. It looks like graffiti on the London Underground.'

'It's a good thing you're not the British Ambassador to China, Dave.' laughed Kay.

'That's impressive,' he replied. 'It must been brilliant to be able to speak another language.'

'So to answer your question; there are very few fakes. All of these are produced for export, and hence the certificates. If they are older than 100 years, they are considered to be antiques. As a buyer you need to be careful if something is presented as an original. Pieces do occasionally slip passed the experts, and end up being sold at an auction for silly amounts of money. I'm selling this as a dealer at £250, but the original vase would probably fetch £10,000 at auction.'

'I guess it is like everything. You are always going to get the wide-boys giving it a go,' commented Dave. 'Have you ever had an original, Kay?'

'No never. Just run of the mill stuff. I've bought these three for myself, and they are all copies.'

Both Kay and Dave looked up at the sound of a car pulling up in front of the open garage door.

'Ah, it's Eve Kettering-Smythe. Here for her vase. I won't be long Dave,' commented Kay as she went out to meet her customer.

'Morning Eve, a bit chilly this morning,' Kay greeted the parish councillor's wife.

''Tis a bit. Morning, Kay. They say we are in for a long hot spell this summer,' replied the estate agent's wife as she got out of the car.

'It would be nice to have a warm summer, but I wouldn't put any money on it. They always get it wrong. Come through to the office.' The women made their way between the rows of shelves to the back of the building.

'How's Richard. Well?' asked Kay as they entered the office. Eve paused for a moment.

'Um, he's um, yes he's well thank you,' Eve replied politely. Kay glanced at her customer, and sensed she didn't want to talk about her husband.

'Good to hear,' Kay said taking a cardboard box off a shelf marked **SOLD**.

'Actually Kay, he is so grumpy at the moment. I know he can be prickly, but it's extremely unpleasant being in the same house as him at the moment. I'm completely invisible, and he only seems to notice me when something is not to his liking. He's drinking more than normal which makes being with friends and family an absolute nightmare. He gets so argumentative.'

'Maybe he's working too hard. They all can get a little preoccupied with work,' Kay replied trying to steer the conversation towards a less embarrassing subject. She took a large porcelain blue vase with a gold and floral design out of the box.

'Ok, here it is, Eve,' announced Kay. 'This should cheer you up. It's a stunning piece. You've chosen well.'

'Actually, he forgot my birthday last month; this is a present to myself.'

Kay was embarrassed, and felt empathy for Eve being married to such a ghastly man. It was all the more poignant as she always naively thought everyone had a happy marriage like Michael and herself. She busied herself with the wrapping of the vase, making a joke as to how long it had taken her to learn how to wrap things properly. Eve just smiled and stood watching Kay in silence.

'Please may I pay by card?' asked the estate agent's wife.

'Of course you can. One advantage of buying your own present is being able to choose something that you actually like,' commented Kay as she took the card from Eve.

'You're probably right. If he had remembered my birthday, it would have been a bunch of flowers from the garage.'

'Dave and I are unpacking a delivery. Would you like to stay for a coffee, and have a peek at the new stuff?'

'Thanks Kay, that would be lovely, but I'm meeting my friend Sally for lunch, and a bit of retail therapy,' replied Eve glancing at her watch. 'Maybe some other time.'

A couple of weeks passed by, and there were no further messages from the mystery texter. As was KS's nature, he started to think that the problem had gone away. Probably someone trying to wind him up. He had been in the office all morning, and wanting a change of scene, crossed over the market square towards one of the numerous coffee shops in the town. Over the past couple of years a proliferation of coffee shops had popped up like mushrooms in every shadowy and damp part of Wolburn Market. They outnumbered the charity shops, which was an astonishing achievement, as every fourth shop was a charity shop. KS was passing the disused public drinking fountain when he received a text.

Drop off £6,000 (in various denominations) at New England Antiques on Monday morning at 10 o'clock. Place it under the first traffic cone on the left hand side of the car park. Do not wait. Leave immediately. No police.

KS's pulse started to race. He noticed the message had been sent from a different number. He changed his mind about the coffee, and decided to keep walking. He walked down to the high street, continued along the edge of the public car park until he reached the golf club. On his way back to the office, he stopped at the bank to arrange the money.

He again left the office early, and drove out to New England Antiques. With his heart pounding away he turned off the road, and drove slowly into the car park. He couldn't see any traffic cones at first, but as he drove past the building, he saw them at the far end of the car park. There were four cones placed at equal intervals along the edge of the paved surface. Not wanting to be seen nor recognised by anyone, he left and drove home.

By the time he got home, his mood had changed from panic to anger. How dare someone try and blackmail him, he thought. There is no way I'm going to capitulate. To hell with them. I'll show them. I'll report them to the police. That will wipe the smiles off their faces. By the time he went to bed, the anger had subsided, and was replaced with the sickening realisation that he had been outmanoeuvred. Years of checkmating others might have finally come to an end he thought.

He eventually fell asleep, and had been sleeping for a couple of hours, when he suddenly woke up in a sweat. He got up, and went into the kitchen to make himself a cup of tea. He sat at the kitchen table, and felt that he had tried to blag his way out of trouble just once too often. When the police had questioned him about Brian's Land Rover, he should have told the truth. They would have slapped him on the wrists, and that would have been the end of it. Do I go to the police? Do I tell Eve what has happened? No, pay the money and tell the blackmailers that there is no more where that came from. It will all go away he thought, as he climbed back into bed.

It was raining heavily as KS parked his car two doors away from his house. He got out, and looked around to see if anyone was watching him. Locking the car, he walked back to his home. By the time he opened the front door, his hair was dripping with water, and the top half of his jacket looked as if his shoulders had sprung a leak.

'Eve, I'm back,' he announced. His wife appeared in the hallway, drying her hands on a kitchen towel.

'What's happened?' she asked in surprise.

'Bloody car's gone and died on me,'

'Where?'

'Outside the Butler's house.'

'I'll give the vehicle breakdown a call,' offered his wife.

'No I don't have time for that. I'll sort it out later. I'll use your car,' he said looking at the time on his mobile.

'Sally and I are going into Wolburn this morning for a coffee. I'm picking her up at 10,' Eve replied.

'Change your plan. Get Sally to take you into town?'

'Let me phone her?'

'I don't have time, Eve. I must get going.'

'What if she can't do it?'

'Cancel, postpone, invite her here for coffee, it's not rocket science, woman. Give me your car keys, I'm late as it is.' Eve, wanting her husband out of the house, silently obeyed him.

The parish councillor had not wanted to use his car for the drop-off, and came up with the breakdown plan so that he could use Eve's car. Two miles from Wolburn Market, a gang of workmen, attired in bright orange, appeared out of the gloom of the pouring rain, and were standing in the middle of the road. He stopped and opened his window.

'Morning Sir, there's a burst water pipe, and we've had to close the road. The diversion is through Weatherford.' KS was getting drenched from the rain, and cursing quietly under his breath, quickly closed his window. What's going to happen if I don't drop the money off on time? Here I am being blackmailed, and late for the first drop-off. I'm never going to make it he thought looking at the dashboard clock.

With the grating of gears, he impatiently turned the car around and noisily accelerated back up the road towards the village. The estate agent found himself crouching down behind the steering wheel as a precaution against someone spotting him. His arms and legs started to shake as he got closer to his destination. For a brief moment, he thought he had left his briefcase at home. He quickly glanced over his shoulder, and was relieved to see it on the back seat.

A mile up the road, KS turned into the car park of the emporium of antiques, and was convinced that everyone who saw him would know why he was there. His chest was tight from the tension; he was breathing heavily, and felt as if he was sitting in a bath of sweat.

The rain made for poor visibility, and he drove slowly passed the main showroom. He was pleased to see the traffic cones had not been moved, and parked the car so that it was between the building and the left hand cone. It was 11 o'clock.

KS sat for a moment and looked around. He looked in the rear view mirror and could see an elderly couple getting into their car. While he waited for them to leave, he retrieved his briefcase from the backseat, opened it, and took out a well wrapped brown package. Getting out of the car, the rain did not offer him the opportunity to double check if anyone was watching him. He hurriedly moved around the front of the car, and placed the money under the cone.

Back in the car, with the job done and out of the rain, KS felt some of the tension subside. Should I go and have a coffee and see who collects the parcel, he thought. No don't be silly, you don't want anyone to see you. In any case you need to get back and sort the cars out. How am I going to get my car repaired without calling the breakdown service he asked himself as he headed back to town.

Two days had passed since the drop-off, and there had been no further contact from the blackmailers. KS found the waiting wearisome, and very unsettling. He tried not to think about the situation in which he found himself, and concentrated on keeping busy. He had plenty to do; the estate agency, the charity and parish council. The hardest thing for him was not being able to discuss the problem with anyone.

The estate agent was in the coffee shop having the lunch break that he had tried to take the day he received the blackmail text. What if the money has been found by someone else he thought as he took a bite of a cheese and ham toasty he had ordered with his cappuccino. He chewed a couple of times, stopped, and opened up the sandwich. The two pieces of toast looked like cardboard, and the filling was in name only. Shaking his head, he put the toasty down, and tried the coffee. At least that's hot, he thought.

Walking back to the office, curiosity got the better of him, and he decided to drive out to the antiques shop, and take a look. He popped his head around the estate agency door, and told Wendy he would be back a bit later, and was not to be disturbed.

Arriving at New England Antiques, he drove slowly towards the cones at the far end of the empty car park. They didn't look as if they had been moved. KS's pulse quickened. He parked his car, got out, walked towards the drop-off cone, and lifted it up. The parcel was still there. He was so surprised, he quickly put the cone back and looked around. There was no-one in sight. He lifted the cone again, and took the parcel.

The drive back to town was another surreal experience for the parish councillor. Why had the money not been picked up? Had the blackmailers bottled it? This is going to make me go crazy, he thought. It was school closing by the time he got back to town, and he found himself caught up in the slow moving cars and school busses. He was waiting at a traffic light in the high street when he received a text.

He pulled into a parking space, and opened the message.

Where is the money? The cone is empty. Take me seriously. I have the note.

Once again the text had been sent from a different number. That makes it three different numbers so far he thought.

Without thinking, he drove back to the drop-off point and replaced the brown package under the traffic cone. The tight chest and heavy breathing was back, as was the bath of sweat. He no sooner got back into the car when a text arrived.

Good boy.

Uncontrollable anger came over him as he read the text. It was a different telephone number. He climbed out of his car and started running down the line of parked cars, stopping briefly at each one, and bending down to look through the windows to see if the car's had any occupants. The blackmailers must be here somewhere. All the cars were empty. He stormed across to the showroom, but didn't recognise any of the people browsing around the second-hand items. He rushed over to the tearoom, and standing in the middle of the restaurant, short of breath, scanned the customers sitting at the tables. Yet again he didn't recognised anyone.

'Can I help you Sir,' asked the teenage waitress.

'No you can't. Get out of my way you silly little girl,' replied KS pushing her to one side. He stood for a moment outside the tearoom and scrutinised his surroundings. Nothing. Defeated, he returned to his car. Driving back home to Weatherford, the estate agent contemplated the significance of four texts and four different telephone numbers. By the time he turned into Fields View Drive he had come to the conclusion that the blackmailers were serious, and he was looking into the abyss.

CHAPTER 19

Cassie had been up to London on a number of occasions during the past few months to see Hanna. They had not been social visits as such. Following Hanna's father's death, Cassie did not want her friend to feel alone nor abandoned, and had kept an eye on her just in case she needed help. The agronomist was also a bit concerned about Chris Brown. She was worried that he might be taking advantage of Hanna, at a time, when she was at a very low point in her life.

Chris was part of the reason why Hanna was on a train heading for Kent. The previous weekend, he had invited her to his birthday party. Hanna knew it was just an excuse to meet his parents, and satisfy the curious aunts and uncles. Despite Cassie's reservations about the policeman, she was dying to hear the goss about Chris's family, and had nagged Hanna to meet up with her.

On reaching the river, the train entered the enclosed railway bridge running parallel to a much newer road crossing. A minute later the train slowly came to a halt at Dullsborough Station. A name famously given to the town by a genuine celebrity.

Cassie was waiting on the platform feeling a little self-conscious in a floral dress. Pleased to see each other, the friends hugged.

'I like the dress. It's lovely,' commented Hanna.

'I haven't seen that pendant before,' said Cassie feeling less awkward about the dress.

'Chris gave it to me at the weekend.'

'He did know it was his birthday?' teased Cassie. 'Let me have a closer look.' She gently held the gold piece of jewellery in the palm of her hand. 'It's gorgeous.'

The agronomist was pleased for Hanna, but looking at the object of affection, there was a momentary feeling of sadness. She paused, and took a deep breath. 'Getting a bit serious, then,' she sighed, giving her friend another hug. 'I'm so very happy for you.'

The friends walked arm in arm back across the bridge, and along the river embankment towards The Flagship Inn. The tide was out and boats of various colours, shapes and sizes were scattered ignominiously on the muddy riverbed. Across the river, the castle with its norman tower-keep, and imposing crenelated curtain wall looked impressive in the sunshine.

'So what did you give Chris for his birthday?'

'One of those activity gifts. A hot air balloon ride with champagne for two.'

'For two, hey?' Cassie felt the twinge of sadness again.

'Chris actually suggested we invite you along. I'd like it if you did.'

'I'd love to. Thank you, Hanna.'

'I'll sort it. The flight is at dawn from Blacktree Crossing. We can stay at the farm. Blacktree's only ten minutes down the road from Weatherford.'

Not surprisingly, the pub was busy. It was lunchtime, and people were sitting outside making the most of the good weather. They placed their food order, and went outdoors to look for somewhere to sit. Hanna found the heat coming off the paved patio uncomfortable. As luck would have it, a couple were getting up to leave, and they took over the table on the lawn in the shade of an oak tree.

'They're forecasting a long spell of hot weather,' commented Cassie as they sat down.

'Promises, promises. They seldom get tomorrow's forecast right, let alone long term.'

'Certainly not going to leave my wellies at home just yet. Probably have a month's rain next week,' laughed the agronomist.

'So?' asked Cassie.

'So?' teased Hanna.

'The Browns?'

'Oh, them. Not much to say really,' Hanna paused and looked at her friend and smiled, 'Apart from them being absolutely fantastic.'

'Really?'

'Absolutely super. They welcomed me as if I was a long lost relative. Chris's mum Helen is a lovely lady. The way she dresses you can see her background is in fashion. She's the store manager at James and Kithering, the departmental store, in Croydon. His Dad, Clifford, is full of craic. Always laughing. Retired from the Royal Mail. I think this might be our food.'

'Apologies for the wait,' mumbled the teenage waiter. 'Fish and Chips?'

'That's me,' answered Hanna.

'And Grilled Sea Bass,' he announced putting the plate down in front of Cassie. 'And a jug of Pimm's and ice. Enjoy.'

'What's Chris's brother like?' continued Cassie.

'Jo. He's a couple of years younger than Chris, but not as serious,' replied Hanna squeezing the slice of lemon over her fried fish, and then liberally salting the chips. 'They seem to get on. I like him.'

'Is he fit?' asked Cassie smiling mischievously.

'Cassie! Stop it. Make yourself useful and pass me the ketchup.'

'What does he do?' replied Cassie laughing at her prudish friend.

'He's a paramedic. He was called out early evening. Someone hadn't turned up for work. He says he likes the job, feels he's doing something worthwhile, but the abuse they have to put up with from the public is unbelievable.'

'Like what?' asked Cassie pushing pieces of leafy salad into her mouth.

'Smashing ambulance windscreens, throwing stones, physical abuse, that sort of thing. Occasionally they need a police escort to help them get to and from a patient. Jo says it sometimes makes things worse. He says his biggest fear is getting stabbed. He says there is new legislation coming out later this year doubling the prison sentences for offenders.'

'It's so uncivilised. It beggar's belief that people think it's ok to behave like that. It's disgusting,' fumed Cassie.' As if on cue, they heard the sound of a siren coming from across the river. 'Speak of the devil,' commented Cassie as they watched a police car speeding along the far embankment. 'Ok, so what else do you have to tell me?'

'The food was delicious. Crispy chilli squid, jerk chicken, goat curry, spicy pork belly.'

'I've never had goat curry,' interrupted Cassie.

'It was a first for me as well. It's lovely. A lot like lamb, really,' replied Hanna.

'The aunts teased Chris and I, saying they had made the passion pie especially for us.'

'Passion pie?' asked Cassie.

'It's like lemon meringue pie, but made with passion fruit.'

'Sounds yummy,' replied the agronomist. 'Tell me more about the aunts.'

'There were three aunts and an uncle, and eight cousins.'

'Wow, quite a gathering.'

'Cassie, I have to admit I was somewhat overwhelmed by it all. The noise. Everyone talking and laughing. Plus the music. It took some getting used to. Birthdays when I was growing up at home were always such sedate occasions. I've never experienced anything like it in my life. Everyone made me feel so welcome. It was wonderful.'

Hugh Flynn was returning from Wandsworth in London, in his little grey Peugeot 206, having spent the morning following up on a lead that his boss, Ken Baker, had given him the day before. His usual route into Wolburn Market was closed due to maintenance work being carried out on a water tower just east of the town. The diversion took him through Weatherford, and as he drove along the boundary of Grey Pigeon Farm, he saw a small white van parked up on the left-hand shoulder of the road. As he got nearer, the logo was that of Pasternak Construction. When he found a suitable place, he turned his car around and headed back. He pulled up behind the van, and got out. He could see a man in a suit wearing a high visibility jacket, and a yellow hard hat standing in the middle of one of the unploughed fields. It was definitely not a scarecrow.

Hugh set his mobile to 'voice recorder', placed it in the top pocket of his jacket, and started to walk towards the stranger.

'Good Afternoon, Hugh Flynn, journalist for *The Counties Herald*,' he said holding his hand out as he reached the stranger.

'What can I do for you Mr Flynn?' asked the stranger ignoring Hugh's offer of a handshake.

'You do know this is private land?' enquired the journalist.

'Well we are both trespassing then aren't we?' responded the man from Pasternak Construction with a wry smile. Cocky so-and-so thought Hugh.

'The last time I heard the name Pasternak Construction was during an altercation I overheard in the Green Man,' said Hugh returning the wry smile.

'What was said about the company?' asked the surprised stranger.

'An allegation was made that Pasternak has been contaminating the crops on this farm in an attempt to drive down the price of the land,' said the journalist as he watched his words turn the high visibility man's face ashen.

'That's absolute rubbish. Who made that allegation? That's liable,' said a now indignant stranger.

'Unless you give me your name, Sir, my lips are sealed,' replied the journalist.

'Henry Allerton. Owner of Pasternak Construction.'

'Well that wasn't too difficult was it Mr Allerton?'

'Who's making these allegations?'

'Hanna Townsend, daughter of Brian Townsend. It is not the only allegation she is making.'

'What other crap is she lying about?' asked a very uncomfortable company owner.

'That your company and certain councillors are, how should I put it, a little too cosy.'

'All bloody lies. I'll sue the backside off the bitch,' said an angry Henry Allerton kicking the ground a number of times with his right foot.

'Mr Allerton, I might be a humble journalist in some back water, but let me give you some advice. Don't under estimate the people who live here. I've been covering the news in this area for almost three decades. The landowners, particularly the farmers have been here for generations and they are a closely knit community. I have a unique relationship with the locals. I'm part of the furniture, and one thing they do not trust is strangers. You are a stranger to these parts and a property developer. You are perceived to be a danger to a way of life. That bitch, as you called her, has just lost her father, the owner of this farm. Why are you standing here in a field belonging to the Townsends?'

'I heard a rumour that this farm might be up for sale. I thought I'd just come over and take a look at it. To be quite honest matey, the reason I'm standing here has nothing to do with you,' replied a slightly less confident developer.

'And the view is totally different from here compared to the vista from Fields View?' asked the journalist.

'I have no idea what you are talking about. What are you insinuating?' replied Henry.

'Hanna's a lawyer in London and from what I have observed she is putting together quite an interesting little team to pursue her allegations. I remember when she was born. I'm certainly part of her furniture. Mr Allerton, I'm sure you will deny the allegations, and Hanna might very well find out that they are only gossip. As for me, with my journalist hat on, I have to ask the question is there a connection between Hanna's allegations and you standing in the middle of a Townsend field? My Chief Editor would say it is a question worth pursuing. Regardless of what my boss may think, my gut feeling is that there is something untoward going on. I don't know what it is, but I'll find out. If there is any hint of impropriety, I'll contact you for comment before passing it onto Hanna. By the way, 'Hands off Weatherford' are holding a meeting in the Green Man next Thursday to discuss your company's application, 3613 if memory serves me right. Good day Mr Allerton. Thank you for your time, and do enjoy the view.'

'Where is he?' shouted Henry Allerton as he burst into the estate agent. 'There he is?' he yelled, answering his own question. He weaved between the furniture in the front office, knocking over a cup of coffee on one of the desks as he brushed passed it.

'Christ are you trying to pin village gossip and bullshit on me?' he shouted as he entered KS's office.

'Keep it down, Henry. Not in front of the staff,' demanded KS as he got up from his desk and quickly closed the door. Henry Allerton flopped down heavily into the chair in front of KS's desk. 'Do you want a coffee? Wendy two coffees, now,' the estate agent called loudly through the glass wall panelling of the office. 'Ok, what's the problem?'

'I've just been accosted by some journalist. Well he said he was journalist, he looked more like a homeless beggar,' said Henry breathing heavily from the exertion of his outburst.

'That's got to be Hugh Flynn,' replied KS. 'He's a local journalist.'

'Oh Christ, that's all we need. I was at Weatherford taking a look at the Townsend land, and the next thing there he was.'

'What were you doing there, for heaven's sake? We agreed we would stay away from the Townsend property until the dust had settled,' moaned an exasperated KS.

'Why didn't you tell me that Hanna Townsend publicly accused Pasternak of contaminating her father's crops? She also accused me of being 'too cosy', her words apparently, with councillors. Who's been talking?' Wendy came into the office with the two coffees. Shaking slightly, she put them down on the desk, and tried to avoid looking at either of the men.

'Christ women, you're spilling it all over my desk. Get out, get out,' reprimanded KS impatiently using both his hands in a sweeping motion to emphasise what go away meant.

'KS have you been playing the big I-am and shouting your mouth off?' continued the developer.

'Henry, I didn't think I needed to talk to you about Hanna's accusations. They're not true. I didn't think they warranted discussion.'

'Well according to Hugh Flynn she has put together a group of people to help her prove the accusations are true. That bloody journalist has also said if he finds anything dodgy he's going to pass it on to her.'

'But, Henry, there is nothing going on.'

'Then why is it so bloody difficult, Richard? All I want to do is build a few poxy houses. Any news about 3613?'

'Not yet. I've been a bit busy. It's on my to-do list,' replied KS.

'No news? Are you for real, matey? Flynn told me that there is a protest meeting in Weatherford next Thursday about 3613? Did you know about it?'

'Ah, yes.' replied the estate agent hesitating slightly.

'And you didn't think to tell me?' The estate agent decided to ignore the question.

'Henry, there is no truth in the crop contamination allegation. Secondly, they cannot accuse you of being 'cosy' with councillors. We have followed the application procedures to the letter. You were given permission for Fields View and Townsend's application to build houses on his land was refused. We must be patient with the Townsend farm. Hanna's life is in London. Let's wait and a see what she decides to do with it.'

'What about that bloody journalist, Richard?' asked the developer.

'Actually, it might turn out to be useful. He said he would pass on anything that Hanna finds out. Let's sit back and let them tell us how they are progressing with the accusations. As I've said before let's allow the dust to settle. Agreed?' concluded KS holding out his hand. The men shook hands. KS watched the developer leave and putting his hands behind his head, leant back in his chair and closed his eyes for a moment. His mobile phone announced the arrival of a text.

Place £6,000 (in various denominations) in the salt and grit bin at the Wolburn Market and Stebden crossroads on Monday morning at 10 o'clock. Do not wait. Leave immediately. No police.

The text had been sent from yet another new number. KS read it a couple of times. Three weeks had passed since the first demand. What happens if there is a demand every three weeks. That's a lot of money. Reaching over for his calculator he divided 52 weeks by 3 and multiplied it by 6,000. 105,000 per year was the answer. I don't have that sort of money. I'll have to sell the house. The money won't last forever. Then what? Borrow?

He got up from his desk, and left the office without saying anything to Wendy or his staff, and walked down the cobbled road flanked by medieval buildings to The Cross. He entered the medieval tavern now a hotel, and ordered a double whisky on the rocks. A number of doubles later, he was still no closer to a solution. Half an hour before closing time, the landlord phoned KS's wife and she drove into town to collect her inebriated husband. It was a silent journey home. Once home, Eve struggled to put the intoxicated parish councillor to bed. She was about to turn off the bedside lamp when her husband, slurring his words, turned and looked up at her.

'Townsend has won,' he murmured.

Someone had parked in Hugh Flynn's permit parking space, and he was driving slowly around the market square in Wolburn Market looking for parking. He was about to give up his quest when a space became available. He stopped to let the vacating occupant leave, and was about to move forward when he was held up by an elderly couple crossing the road in front of him. Without looking left or right they made it safely across the road. Once out of harm's way, Hugh drove forward and stopped a little way passed the empty space so that he could reverse park. He looked in his rear view mirror, all was clear, and he put the car into reverse. He then saw Henry Allerton coming out of the estate agent. He watched him cross the market square. This is too much of a coincidence thought the journalist. The very man he was speaking to a couple of days ago about planning permissions has just visited a Weatherford Parish Councillor. I knew it, I knew it, he said to himself. There is definitely something fishy going on.

He let the clutch out and there was a sudden jolt and a crunching sound. He looked in his rear view mirror, and saw he had reversed into a car behind him.

'Shit,' he exclaimed and got out of the car. 'I'm terribly sorry,' he apologised to the driver of the other car who was a young mother with a toddler in a car seat. 'It's my fault entirely, I wasn't concentrating,' explained Hugh as they both looked at the damage. 'Are you and the baby ok?' he asked. The mother assured the shaken journalist that they were fine despite the fact that her child's screaming was drowning out the noise of the aircraft flying overhead. Fortunately the damage was minimal; a couple of scuffs on rear and front bumpers. The drivers exchanged contact details and parted on good terms. Unfortunately this minor mishap held up the traffic, and it was not long before the centre of the town was gridlocked.

It took half an hour for the gridlock to clear by which time Hugh Flynn had managed to squeeze himself through the half open door to the newspaper's office. A perspex newspaper stand was the new home for the surplus copies of the newspaper that had once occupied the same spot on the floor. Unfortunately it still prevented the door from opening fully.

'Ah, the prodigal son returns,' Hugh's boss shouted from the bowels of his office.

'Ken, have you not noticed that the entrance door cannot fully open with that newspaper stand in the way?' asked our journalist.

'Come up with a better idea old boy,' responded the chief editor. 'Sit. Tell me about your adventures.'

'I had a bit of an accident in the square.'

'Anything serious?'

'No. Reversed into a young mum with a kid in the back. Small scuff marks. Just a dented ego.'

'Good. We don't need the publicity, do we?' laughed the editor. 'What did you discover at Wandsworth?'

'Boss, it looks as if your hunch might be right. They couldn't give me any details, but offered to take a cursory look at the old files. If they find anything I might have to spend some time going through them.'

'Cross that bridge,' answered the editor.

'Boss, can I run something passed you?'

'Shoot.'

'The road into town was closed at the water tower, and the diversion was through Weatherford. As I passed Grey Pigeon Farm, I came across Henry Allerton standing in one of the fields.'

'Hugh, I've told you to drop this Weatherford conspiracy theory. There is no story there,' replied an irritated Ken Baker.

'Boss, hear me out. I stopped and asked him what he was doing there. I'll give you my notes with the conversation details. My little accident in the square was caused by me being distracted when I saw Allerton coming out of the estate agent. Boss, there has to be a connection. I rattle Allerton's cage and he pays KS a visit.'

'Pure coincidence. Hugh, how many of these dodgy councillor stories have we, you, chased after, just to find out that there is no story. Just take KS as an example. The rumours are rife that he is dodgy. Has anyone ever been able to get anything to stick. No. As for the developers, everyone's watching them like a hawk; everything they do is being scrutinised on a daily basis. I'm sorry, but we are not going to waste any time on a coincidence. Wandsworth sounds like a good lead. If we are right, we will have a tragic human story to tell and possibly we can be the catalyst for some form of compensation for the relatives. Do I have your support?'

'Of course you do, Boss. It goes without saying,' replied our journalist. On the way back to his slightly damaged car, the journalist smiled with delight at the sight of a traffic warden placing a ticket on the windscreen of the vehicle in his permit parking space.

CHAPTER 20

Five months had now passed since the death of Brian Townsend. There wasn't a day that went by that Hanna didn't think about him, and as each day passed her resolve to get to the bottom of the tragedy grew stronger. She was becoming obsessed with Kettering-Smythe, and Cassie had on a number of occasions tried to convince Hanna that her pre-occupation with the parish councillor was not healthy.

Cassie was concerned that her friend was working long hours, sleeping less and less, and when she was not at work was spending too much time obsessing about her father. Hanna's response was to assure her friend that she had everything under control.

In actual fact, she did have things under control. When the Christmas and New Year break was over, and the country had eventually returned to work, the first thing she did was to contact her father's accountant. Despite regular calls to enquire about progress, it took three months for the accounts to be finalised. Hanna was shocked at her father's financial situation, and immediately text Cassie.

I've just received the info from Dad's accountant. It's not good. Will email you later this evening. Love H. XX.

When Hanna got back home that evening she was tired and hunger, and didn't feel like sending the email to Cassie as she had promised. Revived after a hot shower, something to eat, and the obligatory glass of wine, she resisted the temptation to curl-up on the sofa in front of the television; instead she refilled her glass, and switched on her laptop.

To: Cassie Richards
From: Hanna Townsend
Subject: Dad's Finances
Hi Cassie
You ok?
Another busy day at work. Was exhausted when I got home. Feel better for a shower and something to eat. Had cannelloni and made enough for a couple of meals. Right, I will keep this brief. I don't want to bore you. In a nutshell, my Dad has run up huge debts. It looks as if the banks have been lending him money for years in an attempt to keep the farm afloat.

He bought a new tractor three years ago and the payments are in arrears. His accountant says he received only 70% of the going rate for the last four harvests due to poor yields and quality. Payment for the last harvest is still outstanding, and there are farming subsidies that have not yet been fully paid out. He saw his accountant a week before he committed suicide. They discussed applying for an Individual Voluntary Arrangement. Cassie, my Dad must have been so ashamed.

Hanna stopped typing, and tears started to stream down her cheeks. Dad must have been so alone she thought. Why didn't he talk to me about it? Why? Why? The distraught daughter angrily brought her clenched fists down on the table. The half empty glass of wine lifted slightly, and moved away from Hanna, as if startled by her sudden outburst. How could he do this to me she thought as she slammed her fists down for a second time. The glass of wine was ready for the second outburst, and held its ground. Hanna sat looking at the computer screen, and eventually the tears stopped. She sniffed a couple of times, wiped the tears away with both hands, and after fetching a tissue from the kitchen, she returned to the la
ptop.
Cassie I'll say goodnight. It's been a long day, and there is so much to talk about. We'll speak later. Love. H. XX.

After a while Hanna managed to compose herself, poured herself another glass of wine, and turned on the television. The next episode of *Madam Secretary* had just started when her phone rang.

'Hi Cassie,'

'Are you ok?' asked her friend.

'I was a bit upset earlier, but I'm fine now.'

'I thought you might be. Can I ask you a quick question or are you not up to it?'

'No, no, I'm fine. Ask,' replied Hanna.

'You still have the land or am I being stupid?'

'No, it is not a stupid question. The problem is the sale of the land might not pay off the debt. According to the accountant the price of farm land has been falling. It is about £10,000 per acre at the moment. That's 3 million pounds for the land excluding the farmhouse and outbuildings,' replied Hanna.

'The debt is more than 3 million?' exclaimed Cassie.

'Yeh. Mind boggling isn't it? I don't know much about the price of land for housing developments, but the accountant said if my Dad's planning application had been approved, the increased value of the land with the planning permission would certainly have made a difference to his situation,' replied Hanna.

'Comes back to your contamination theory. The end game is cheaper land,' responded Cassie.

'I'm still convinced that's what has happened. We need to talk to Dudley and Alexis and get more information about buying and selling farmland,' replied Hanna.

'Sounds like a good idea. Ok, Hanna. I'll stop bothering you. Are you seeing Chris this week?'

'He's coming over for dinner on Friday night.'

The salt and grit bin drop was uneventful, apart from our parish councillor shaking like a leaf, and once again feeling totally conspicuous. He arrived on time at the drop-off, and sat in his car for almost ten minutes building up courage. When the junction was eventually clear of traffic, he didn't waste any time covering the thirty yards to the yellow bin. On the way back to the getaway car he kept his head down. A car passed him, and slowed down at the yield sign. He tried to hide his face by rubbing his forehead with his right hand, and turning his head away from the direction of the slowing car. The exhausted estate agent set the air conditioning to high, and drove back to town. The cold air didn't dry his perspiration drenched shirt, but it made him feel more comfortable. By the time he pulled into his parking space behind *The Counties Herald* office his breathing was back to normal, and his pulse was no longer racing.

As the parish councillor got out of his car, he felt his right thigh start to cramp up. He tried to get his legs back into the car, but the cramp increased in severity. He had no option but to get out of the car as quickly as possible. In excruciating pain and looking as if he was being attacked by wasps, KS pulled himself out of the driver's seat as quickly as he was able, and leaning heavily on the open door pulled himself up into a standing position on one leg. He stood on his left leg for a while, and tried to relax the solid right thigh. The councillor breathed loudly in and out in an attempt to cope with the pain. He then took a few small steps, and leaning on the car hobbled along its length until he reached the rear windscreen wiper which he clung onto as if it was his mother's apron. Throughout this public display, he had tried his best to keep decorum, but unfortunately looked like the Hunchback of Notre Dame with a stone in his shoe. After a few more minutes of standing still and clinging to the wiper, the cramp subsided, and KS was able to lock his car, and walk with decisive strides to the office as if nothing had happened.

Hanna had agreed to meet Dudley and Alexis for lunch at Canary Wharf. It had not been a good morning. Her supervisor had phoned in earlier to say he was poorly, and was unable to attend court. The chief clerk instructed her to attend court to deliver the closing argument for their current case.

Although she had been in court for the duration of the trial, the change of plan threw her. Her nerves got the better of her, and her performance in court was lacklustre and unconvincing. On returning to chambers she had to endure the humiliation of a public dressing down, in front of the articled clerks, by the chief clerk for losing the case.

She was late leaving chambers for her meeting with the bag-a-bargain boys, only to arrive at Green Park to find the Jubilee Line was closed. She finished her journey by sharing a taxi with three other stranded passengers wanting to get to the wharf.

Getting out at Jubilee Park she walked the couple of blocks to South Colonnade and the restaurant. Only at

Canary Wharf she thought as she approached the restaurant. Contemporary alternative eating I think they call it. Dudley and Alexis were already seated, and both of them stood up when they saw Hanna enter the restaurant.

'Hi Hanna. Keeping well?' asked Dudley shaking Hanna's hand.

'Yes thank you. Sorry I'm late. I was in court this morning, got delayed at chambers and then the Jubilee Line was closed. Hello Alexis,' greeted Hanna shaking Alexis' hand. 'Do you mind if we sit at our own table. These communal tables are fine for a commune, but not for privacy,' smiled Hanna. The group retreated to the privacy of a smaller table for four.

'Lunch is on me, Hanna,' offered Dudley.

'Thank you very much,' replied Hanna picking up a menu. 'You guys come here often?'

'Occasionally,' replied Alexis glancing at Dudley.

'To be honest we are on the road most of the time,' added Dudley. Hanna read through the menu and suddenly didn't feel hungry. After her terrible morning, she didn't feel like deciphering a menu. Gluten-free, salt-free, 'v', 'vg', photos of anorexic food, and a dessert of berries in a small glass bowl for a meagre £8.50.

'Is there a McDonald's nearby?' asked Hanna. The bag-a-bargain boys were never short of craic, but they were now. 'What have I said?' laughed Hanna looking at both of them.

'Ok, I think we have a confession to make. When I got your text asking us to meet you, I was not quite sure were to go for lunch,' explained Dudley. 'I asked Alexis. Go on Alexis, tell Hanna what you said.'

'God this is embarrassing. I said you were probably a bloody veggie, and only ate berries and nuts. We decided to bring you here, but we actually hate the food,' confessed a red-faced Alexis.

'You plonkers,' laughed Hanna, 'I eat everything and anything. I'm a farmer's daughter.'

'Do you want to go somewhere else?' asked Dudley.

'No. Let's order something. I don't have much time, and I've got a couple of questions to ask you guys.'

'Hello, Hanna,' Cassie said answering her phone.

'Do you have a minute?'

'Of course I do. Where are you?'

'I've just had lunch with Dudley and Alexis. Walking back to work from Holburn Station,' replied Hanna.

'Did they take you somewhere nice?'

'One of those alternative restaurants in Canary Wharf. You know the type; tibetan music, kale and berries, minimalistic decor and shared tables,' laughed Hanna.

'Had kale at a restaurant once. Looked like damp green rope, tasted like damp green rope, and cost a fortune,' replied Cassie.

'It is no wonder so many restaurants are closing. They all seem too scared to simply dish up a decent plate of food that tastes good and doesn't need a mortgage. It's nutritional correctness gone mad.

Makes you appreciate the Three Sails. I've just bought a chocolate, I'm starving,' commented Hanna.

'Well, I don't have that problem. I'm sitting in my van here in Kent surrounded by winter wheat eating a coronation chicken sandwich which will be closely followed by two jam donuts,' said Cassie teasing her hungry friend. 'Ok, enough whinging. What did the guys have to say?'

'They more or less agreed with my Dad's accountant. The land will definitely fetch a higher price if it is sold with planning permission. Alexis said he would be surprised if a developer didn't use the contamination as a bargaining chip.'

'I can see the contamination being an issue if you want to continue farming. It surely can't be that important if you are just going to wack up a few houses?' interrupted Cassie.

'Well as Alexis points out, it will depend on the nature and extent of the contamination. The developer might end up having to clean up the land before the building can begin. I can understand the logic,' said Hanna.

'Yeh, I guess so,' agreed Cassie.

'He also said we should talk to the banks about rescheduling the debt, as well as chase up the harvest payments. Dudley agreed with him, but said we need to have a viable rescue plan before approaching the banks. He cautioned me about being too eager about selling. He said I must think carefully about it. Even if I can get planning permission, it's a one-off sale. It's gone forever. As he says, keeping the farm going is income for life, and for those that come after me.'

'That's all very well, Hanna. What Dudley assumes is that you want to be involved in running the farm.'

'Well that's not going to happen is it?' responded Hanna rather curtly. 'Alexis did suggest bringing in a contract farmer to run the farm until we have things sorted. I'll talk to Andrew MacGregor, you don't know him, he helps Kay Beswick with her chinese furniture business, I've known him all my life and he contracts himself out at harvest time. Goes all over the country harvesting,' explained Hanna.

'Sounds like the plan is already coming together. Well done, Hanna. It's a positive start. I'm proud of you,' replied Cassie as she looked for a tissue to mop up the jam that had dripped out of the second donut she was eating.

'Both Dudley and Alexis have offered to come up to Weatherford and value the farm for me.'

'That's kind of them. You must take up their offer.'

'I already have. Just need to arrange a date. While I was on the train coming back from seeing them, I thought it might be an idea to get Dave Wright to have a look at the farmhouse and the buildings.'

'That's being super-efficient,' replied Cassie getting out of the car and wiping a streak of jam off her trousers. 'I don't think it will really make that much difference to the price,' she added. 'Hanna can I phone you back, I've got sugar from the
se blasted donuts on my hands and it's now all over my phone.'

Cassie hung-up, and sparingly poured some bottled water over her sticky hands and wiped them on her trousers. She decided that using a damp tissue to clean her phone would probably convert the sugar into syrup and decided to brush it off instead. Getting back into her van, she discovered sugar on the driver's seat. Oh for God Sake, bloody donuts, and irritably brushed the granules off the seat onto the car mat.

'Ok where were we?' recommended Cassie when Hanna answered the phone.

'Discussing a 3 million pound debt?' replied Hanna sarcastically.

'Very funny. I've had a little crisis.'

'I'm almost at the office. I think you are correct about Dave Wright. Even if he says he'll take a look, you know what these workmen are like, you're lucky if they pitch up at all. It can wait. There's no rush.'

'I agree with you, the samples are the priority. We might have to take water samples as well. It's impossible to make a decision about the farm without knowing what is the problem,' advised Cassie.

'Ok can you find out how much it will cost to do the sampling?'

'Of course I will. I have a general idea about costs, but I'll get the prices for you. If I take the samples it might also help reduce the expense. Leave it with me,' replied the agronomist.

'I must go, I'm standing outside chambers. Thanks for listening. By the way, Dudley asked after you. I said you were doing just fine. Women's intuition tells me someone might have an admirer,' laughed Hanna.

'Don't be silly. Speak later. Love you,' replied Cassie.

'Speak later. Love you too. Bye.'

Since the second money drop, KS had spent much of his time thinking about the precarious financial situation in which he found himself. If the extortion continued, he knew he would have to somehow get his hands on more money. He kept coming back to the option of handing himself over to the police. If he did, he knew exactly how that would end. Maybe removing the uncertainty was the best option. With this in mind, he sent a text to the five mobile numbers telling the blackmailers that the second payment had been the last, and if contacted again he would go to the police. All four messages returned
Unable to send. Try again.
With his mind made up, KS drove out to the local police office that is housed in the District Council Offices. Speed limits were not uppermost in his mind as he drove along, and before he had time to slow down was speed checked on the outskirts of the town, doing 45 miles per hour in a 30 zone by a Community Speed Watch. When the nervous parish councillor arrived at the council offices there were no parking spaces available. This won't take long he thought as he parked in a drop off space in front of the ex-sanatorium. The automatic double doors opened as he walked up to them. The reception area was full of people. Dutch courage would probably have been more useful under the circumstances as he turned tail and retreated to the sanctuary of his car. The waiting was unbearable. He had second thoughts about the police, and bought a lottery ticket instead. Only three numbers came up. He gave up on that idea. Another four weeks passed; the blackmailers remained silent

and the estate agent's hope, that the extortion had ended, sprung eternal. He was definitely in need of a miracle.

CHAPTER 21

KS was sitting at his large oak desk trying to catch up with a backlog of *Swarm International UK* administration; the charity of which he is the chairman. He was expected to devote at least one day a week to the worthy cause, but found having fingers in so many pies made it difficult for him to meet this basic requirement. Truth be told, his dubious reputation should have precluded him from office, but as is always the case in these matters, nobody who was suitably qualified nor willing to offer up their time applied for the position when it became vacant. The result was an incumbent who never took any responsibility, hid behind collective decision-making, and blamed others for the mistakes.

His mobile announced the arrival of a text. Using his left hand to steady a visibly shaking right hand, he opened the message.

Place £6,000 (in various denominations) in the letter-bag of the postman scarecrow this Sunday anytime between 10 and 4 o'clock. Avoid talking to anyone, and leave as soon as you have made the drop. No police.

Yet another number observed KS. He didn't understand the message. What postman scarecrow? He quickly typed *I'm going to the police* in the hope that the blackmailers had not yet switched off the mobile. *Unable to send. Try again* came back the response. He got up from his desk, and wandered out into the open plan office.

'Does anyone know anything about a postman scarecrow?' he asked dropping two *Africa Wide Haulage* invoices into the in-tray on Tia's desk.

'In what context?' asked Tia looking up from her computer screen.

'If I knew, I wouldn't be asking, would I?' responded the chairman.

'Have you googled it?' Tia asked, typing in a search without waiting for the leader to respond. She continued to ignore KS, who by now was standing behind her chair and leaning forward. Feeling uncomfortable at the close proximity of the parish councillor, Tia scrolled through the search results. 'It hasn't given us anything.' she remarked.

'Typical,' commented the estate agent striking the back of Tia's chair with his hand. 'Find the answer, woman,' the chairman instructed. Everyone within earshot slowly shook their heads in disbelief. KS was about to return to his office, when he saw Elsa Nel standing at Reception.

'What the hell is she doing here?' asked the chairman. Tia looked up and seeing Elsa gave her a wave of acknowledgement.

'Here for an interview. My replacement,' said Tia getting up from her desk and walking over to the visitor with KS following closely behind. Elsa was dressed in a burgundy pencil skirt with a matching double breasted jacket. A crisp white linen blouse completed the business outfit. 'Hello, Elsa. Welcome to *Swarm*,' greeted Tia as she shook the interviewee's hand. 'Finish signing-in. I must say that outfit is stunning,' commented Tia.

'Thank you very much. I hope it conforms to your dress code.'

'It certainly does, Mrs Nel,' replied the parish councillor holding out his hand and slowly looking her up-and-down. Elsa ignored the outstretched hand. His hand fell slowly to his side.

'Let's crack-on. Coffee, Elsa?' interrupted Tia wanting to avoid any further awkwardness.

'Of course, don't let me hold you girls up,' continued the estate agent. 'Lovely to see you again, Mrs Nel. Good luck with the interview. As I've said in the past, if there is anything I can do for you, and I mean anything, give me a call,' smirked the chairman. 'Tia make sure you give her my contact details.'

'Bloody creep,' murmured Tia as she guided Elsa over to the coffee machine.

'Nervous,' asked the interviewer. 'What coffee would you like?'

'Yes a bit. Black, no sugar please.'

'Elsa, this is a very random question, and has nothing to do with the interview,' said Tia handing her a coffee. 'Do you know anything about a postman scarecrow by any chance?'

'Does it have something to do with the Scarecrow Trail this weekend at, is it Steadford, is that the correct pronunciation?' replied Elsa. 'They're raising money for a local hospice. You get given a map of the trail, and fill in the names of the scarecrows as you walk along. If you get them in the correct order, and name all eight of them your form goes into a prize draw. We are thinking of going there on Saturday with the kids,' she added. 'There are eight scarecrows dressed up as different occupations. One of them might be a postman.'

KS told his wife, Eve, that a show house had come up at short notice and he would not be at home on Sunday.

'Oh, that's a pity,' she replied. 'They say it is going to be lovely and sunny this weekend. I thought we could have a bbq on Sunday.'

'There will be other opportunities for a bloody bbq,' snarled the estate agent. 'Someone has to earn the money.' The long-suffering wife looked at her cantankerous husband. Living on my own would be a better option than spending any more time with this bad-tempered pig she thought.

'It's not a problem dear,' she replied.

Tia Hughes, carrying a bottle of white wine and a glass, made her way across the patio of the Green Man towards a table in the shade of a mature chestnut tree. Belinda Thomas, Charlie Pollock and Dave Wright, each with a pint of cold beer, and wearing sunglasses were sitting on the small patio wall facing the sun.

'Warm enough for you, Tia?' greeted Dave.

'What a beautiful afternoon,' Tia replied. 'Hello Belinda. Hi Charlie. How are the horses coping in the heat?'

'Just need to keep them well watered, and the stables ventilated,' replied the riding school owner. 'We're excising them just before sunset when it's cooler.'

'I don't think it's only the 'orses that need to be well watered,' remarked Dave pointing at Tia's bottle of wine.

'My only vice, Dave, my only vice. It's a small celebration to end off a successful week.'

'I guess we are having a small celebration of our own,' remarked Belinda. 'Charlie has just learnt that he has inherited a cottage and some money from an aunt.'

'That's amazing news, Charlie. Where is the cottage?' asked Tia as she sat down at the table under the large tree.

'It's on the way to Blacktree Crossing. Everyone is making such a big fuss about it. I don't want everyone to know about it, Tia. It embarrasses me,' answered a slightly distressed Charlie.

'I can quite understand that, Charlie. It is good news, but let's leave it at that. Come on, enjoy the sunshine while we've got it,' responded Tia. She kicked off her high heels, wriggled her toes in the cool grass, and poured a glass of wine. Pouring a second glass a few seconds later, she sat back and reflected on the week.

At last, she thought, things seem to be looking up. Jeremy, after years of resisting the 'world-wide corporate exploitation and prostitution of my art', had started working for a television and film production music library in Surrey. The regular money coming in had made such a difference to their lives, and their relationship.

The lack of public trust in charities had prompted *Swarm International UK* to create a public relations position in an attempt to counter the negative publicity that charities were currently experiencing. Tia had applied for the new post, and much to her surprise was successful. The new position meant a pay increase which together with Jeremy's income meant their financial worries were starting to dissipate. Tia poured herself another glass of wine.

She had also been tasked with finding her replacement. What she thought would be an easy task, turned out to be weeks of frustration. She interviewed a number of candidates, but all of them only wanted a part-time job. She couldn't find anyone willing to work more than 16 hours a week.

A chance meeting with Elsa Nel at the Chowdhury's garage solved her problem. Waiting in the queue to pay for petrol, the woman exchanged small talk, and Tia mentioned the vacancy. That evening Elsa discussed the job with Moz, and a couple of days later she was invited for an interview. Tia couldn't believe her luck. Elsa had been on her doorstep all along, and she wanted a full time job.

Tia started to feel the effect of the wine and the warm weather, and began to get busses and good news muddled up. Good news is like a bus. You wait ages for a bus, and then they all arrive at once she thought. Might be true in London, but not here in Weatherford; there is no bus service, there hasn't been one for ten years or more. Oh well, good news is good news. Should that be no news, is good news? Oh, whatever. 'Dave, be a darling and get me another bottle of wine. Have a drink on me as well,' Tia called across the lawn. The other bit of good news Tia was trying to extract from the busses was that the improvement in the family finances had meant she was finally able to enrol in pottery classes.

Dave brought over the replacement bottle of wine, and Tia did not waste any time refilling her glass. She moved her chair into the sun, rolled up the sleeves of her blouse, adjusted her skirt to just above the knees, and stretched her legs out in front of her.

The last bit of family news involved Tia's daughter Jane and grandson Noah. Jane and the baby were moving into their own home near the airport at the end of the month. Tia was a bit sad that they were moving away from Weatherford, but was sensible enough to know that it was the right thing for the young mother and the baby. They could now start making a life for themselves. Calls for another drink she thought.

CHAPTER 22

KS parked his car in the field adjoining the Steadford Church, and followed the signs to the Scarecrow Trail. In amongst the gravestones surrounding St. James the Apostle were the sad and decaying remains of daffodils that had looked so happy a few weeks earlier. As people emerged from their winter hibernation they were now greeted by early spring blossoms playing the overture for the spring extravaganza that would soon be coming to town. The sunshine and the blossoms lifted the soul. Even the parish councillor felt uplifted.

The estate agent opened a small weathered garden gate, and following the sign walked down the narrow path running alongside the sandstone vicarage. The vicar's home, is what we now call, a detached single-level bungalow, and was built out of the same stone as the church. Possibly an example of a 16th century 'buy one, get one free' although it is unlikely to have been referred to as a 'bogoff' considering its close proximity to a place of worship.

The path lead to a well-manicured garden consisting of a large circular lawn with a wide flower bed border running along three sides of the neatly mown grass. The early spring flowers were in bloom, and nature's palette of blues, purples, and violet painted out the memory of a long and dreary winter.

KS climbed the four sandstone steps, neatly framed by an archway of white clematis, to the paved patio that ran the full length of the bungalow. He brushed an arm of his jacket against the flowers, and impatiently brushing the powdery yellow stamens off his sleeve, he looked out from his vantage point to see if he recognised anyone.

There were a number of children running around the garden, and to KS's irritation making far too much noise. A couple of them ran over to the steps and having climbed them, jumped off the patio onto the lawn. Having survived this introduction to the parachute regiment, they carried on climbing, jumping and screaming, which eventually prompted our estate agent to cut short his reconnaissance.

He headed towards the line of tables and cream coloured garden parasols that had been arranged along the length of the patio for the occasion. A keen, jolly looking volunteer sat at the first table which had been christened 'Entry Forms'.

'Good morning, Sir. Nice day for it. Are you on your own?' asked the round smiling face supporting a pair of sunglasses, and a straw hat.

'Yes. Unfortunately my wife is bit poorly so she couldn't make it. She insisted I come along anyway,' replied the parish councillor. 'Tell me is there a postman scarecrow?'

'Oh you naughty boy,' laughed the round face. 'You'll know the answer to that question once you have finished the trail. Right, on to business. Please fill in this entry form. We need it for insurance purposes.' KS filled in the form, and having been wished a lovely day, and don't get lost in the wheat fields, ha, ha, ha, he moved onto the second table.

Table number two was named 'Trail Maps'. Two elderly gentlemen, both wearing green Wolburn Market Golf Club jackets were in attendance, and each with a cup of tea.

'Welcome to the Steadford Scarecrow Trail. I'm Sam. Visiting?' asked the gentleman on the right.

'Ah, yes I suppose I am,' replied KS. He was tempted to mention the fact that he was also a member of the same golf club, but decided, under the circumstances, not to divulge too much information.

'I'm Mike, by the way. On your own?' asked the gentleman on the left.

'Yes. Unfortunately my wife is a bit poorly so she couldn't make it. She insisted I come along anyway,' the estate agent replied for a second time.

'Don't blame you,' replied Sam. 'Escape the DIY list that's what I say.' Both gentlemen laughed. 'Wouldn't dare say that at home,' he continued.

'Bloomin' right you wouldn't, Sam. The missus would have you making your own coffin,' responded Mike. More gleeful laughter.

'How are we doing Mike, Sam?' asked a portly lady dressed in a very loud floral dress, sandals, a large sun hat and a stripe of sunblock on her nose.

'Having an excellent time, thank you Linda,' replied Sam as Mike gave a supporting nod of agreement.

'Good. Don't go drinking all the tea. Leave some for the visitors,' instructed the event organiser as her attention was distracted by the children having resumed jumping off the side of the patio.

'Hitler's sister,' whispered Sam when Linda was out of earshot. 'Organised the whole thing. A bit power-crazy.'

'Enough to scare off the Taliban,' laughed Mike. 'Actually, none of this would be happening if it weren't for our Linda. We love her really.'

KS exchanged £6.50 for a trail map, and Sam went through the details of the trail, where drinking tables were located, the prize draw, and finished off with health and safety considerations.

'Just between the three of us, is there a postman scarecrow?' asked KS once Sam had finished.

'Now that would be spoiling it,' replied Sam. 'Grab yourself a cup of tea and a biscuit at the next table. And enjoy the trail.'

KS was sitting alone at a table at the far end of the patio with a cup of coffee, and a blueberry muffin, when he heard a voice that he recognised. Turning around, coffee splashed out of the cup onto the map lying on the table in front of him. The voice belonged to the wife of a young couple who had recently bought a house from him. She and her husband were standing at the 'Entry Forms' table.

Not wanting to be seen, KS grabbed the soiled map, the muffin and his black leather across body bag, and quickly disappeared around the side of the house. Safely out of view, he stood in the shadows thinking he needed to get started with the trail before it got any busier. Slinging his bag over his left shoulder, and checking to see if the coast was clear he walked briskly over to the lych-gate and the start of the trail. Eating the rest of his muffin, he turned right, and set off down the road towards the first scarecrow.

It was still a cool morning despite a cloudless sky. As he passed the duck pond, the ducks paddled madly towards him in the hope of an early breakfast of bread. He didn't stop, disappointed ducks ceased paddling, and the estate agent started to feel his calves tightening as he continued on up the slight incline towards a row of alms houses nestling in amongst a clump of oak and chestnut trees. The next landmark on his map was the quarry. Being a Sunday it was closed with the tipper and articulated lorries parked in silent rows amongst cones of sand and gravel; while the line of stationary grabs looked as if they were taking a bow for a job well done.

The first scarecrow was a Second World War aviator sitting on the boundary fence of the abandoned American 8th Army Air Force airfield. He was dressed in a leather flying helmet, leather jacket and flying boots. One down, seven to go thought the parish councillor as he wrote on his map.

He crossed over the road, and followed the next trail sign which pointed down a narrow single track lane. It was starting to get warmer, and the estate agent was looking forward to reaching the first drinking table. The trail continued passed a lake belonging to the local fishing club, and little further on the house in which the poet K.J. Fines lived for twenty years.

The trail left the road at this point, and headed down a foot path running alongside a large wheat field. The ears of wheat were starting to form, and the young crop looking strong and healthy stretched up towards the sun. With the only shade being the trees around the perimeter of the field, the footpath was exposed to the full glare of the sun, and KS was starting to struggle with the heat. He perked up a bit when he saw the farmer scarecrow come into view. The effigy was dressed in a denim overall, wellington boots, a tweed flat cap and holding a pitchfork. Although 'Farmer' was pinned to his chest, KS thought he looked more like a farmhand.

Phew still six to go thought the overheating estate agent as he continued along the edge of the field. His map showed a drinking table at the end of the footpath. It couldn't come quick enough. On reaching the end of the field, there was no drinking table to be seen; only a sign pointing towards the village cricket ground. He followed the arrow, but was not quite sure in which direction he should be heading. As he got closer to the pavilion he could hear voices and laughter coming from behind the white clapperboard building. He headed for what sounded like a party. Coming around the side of the pavilion, he found a group of teenagers; two boys and two girls standing at a drinking table laughing and shoving each other. The laughter and the pushing stopped as soon as they saw the parish councillor.

'What are you kids doing?' asked KS.

'Looking after the drinking table,' answered the boy who was wearing a bright orange Rickie Fowler style cap.

'You are in the wrong bloody place. The map shows this table should be at the edge of the field back there,' responded KS. 'Why aren't you where you are supposed to be?' continued the estate agent.

'We had to move. It was too hot out there,' replied the taller of the girls, 'the only shade is here behind the pavilion,' she explained.

'Well how about changing the sign to tell people the table has been moved?' suggested KS as he helped himself to a bottle of water. 'Which way is the blasted trail?' he asked looking at his map.

'There's a public footpath behind the cricket nets,' replied the other girl, pointing towards the far corner of the field with a hand, the dark brown palm of which, was proof that it had been recently used to apply copious amounts of fake tan.

The estate agent walked towards the cricket nets, and could hear the teenagers sniggering as they mimicked him behind his back. The public footpath ran along a high ridge separating the fields. Feeling his face and balding head starting to burn, and wishing he had brought along a hat, KS took in the view.

Down in the dip, he could see the fishing lake that he had passed earlier, and adjoining it, the grounds of the football club. On the far ridge, rows of gothic chimneys belonging to Steadford Lodge poked out above the copse of trees surrounding the victorian building.

Steadford Village lay to his right and he had a google map's eye-view of the houses on either side of the road running through the settlement. He could see, as if identified by street view, familiar landmarks such as the White Hart, the row of sheltered accommodation, the rec and the seldom used village hall.

The estate agent walked on for another five minutes. Scarecrow number three had long blonde hair made from straw, wore a white medical coat with a stethoscope around her neck, a name badge Dr S Crow, and held a well-used doctor's bag. Having filled in his map, KS went over to the drinking table to restock. While he was putting a couple of bottles into his bag, he asked the custodians of the table if there was a postman scarecrow.

'It's at the end of the footpath,' came back the reply, 'next to the post box at the road junction. You can actually see him from here.' KS looked in the direction of the pointing finger, and couldn't believe his luck. Forgoing any further pleasantries, which KS didn't do very well anyway, he headed off down the path to the junction. Why didn't I think of that, he thought. Stupid man. Where are you going to find a postman? Next to a post box. It's so blooming obvious.

Approaching the postman, his heart started to thump in his chest, and he found it difficult to breath. As with the previous drops, he was bathed in sweat. Reaching the scarecrow, he looked up and down the roads at the T-junction. With nobody in sight, he quickly took the neatly wrapped package of money out of his bag and placed it in the postman's large red letter bag.

The road junction was very familiar to KS. He abandoned his map, turned towards the west, and knowing the quickest way back to the start of the trail, headed towards St James the Apostle. Tired and a bit foot weary, our pilgrim walked along knowing that there was sanctuary at the end of his journey in the form of an air conditioned car.

It is reported that previous pilgrims told tales about the burden of their sins, and their struggle to find salvation. Not KS. He walked along trying to come up with a solution to the troublesome problem of how to carry on paying the blackmailers. Since he had abandoned the idea of giving himself up to the police, he had come to the conclusion that the only way he could make the payments was to borrow money. He would have to use the house as collateral. He walked along thinking about the pros and cons of taking out a loan. He came to the conclusion that it was only a temporary fix, and was not going to solve the problem.

Half way along the road leading towards the football ground, he passed a bungalow with an overgrown garden, and a dilapidated shed. It jogged his memory. Now there's an idea, he thought. Why don't I give the gifted money trick another whirl. I've done it before. It all started with Mrs Wilson, and her bungalow. Then there was Sean Rafferty and that idiot Walter Turner who both gifted me money as a thank you for me doing a few favours for them. They were so gullible. It was so easy. I did it right under the noses of the villagers. No one suspected anything. I got away with it scot-free. The steeple of St James came into view, and KS continued the journey back to his car with a spring in his step.

CHAPTER 23

As the prolonged summer heatwave continued, people across the country were starting to get hot under the collar. Their unhappiness was not the uncertainty surrounding the impending withdrawal from the European Union, but the building of houses. Housing developments were now the number one threat to the nation. Across the land, protest groups made up of objectors who had somewhere to live, mobilised to prevent others from having the same opportunity.

Unfortunately, the Broadhursts, newcomers to the village, naively committed the sin of moving into one of the large five bedroom houses in the newly built Fields View. Eyebrows were immediately raised. Unbeknown to them, there had been strong opposition to the development, and during the first few months in Weatherford, Charlotte and Edward were subjected to abusive comments about Londoners taking farm land away from the locals to build fancy houses.

Charlotte had now been head teacher for a year. Her predecessor had opted for early retirement, and embarked on luxury travel at the taxpayer's expense, to exotic destinations such as Borneo. She had big shoes to fill, and was very conscious of the fact that her family would not be able to maintain anonymity in a small village like Weatherford as they had been able to do in the capital city. Before accepting the new post, Charlotte discussed her concerns with her husband Edward and only son Rhys. They both assured the prospective head teacher that she had their undivided support. She subsequently accepted the new post, happy in the knowledge that her husband and son, both of whom she loved dearly, were too dull to upset the apple cart. She proved to be a competent head teacher, and the primary school soon started to benefit from her sound leadership. As the months passed, the acrimony about the big house subsided.

Edward Broadhurst, an ex-Environmental Health Inspector, had also taken the early retirement option, and found he had too much time on his hands, courtesy of his neighbours working to 66 years of age to pay for his privileged indulgence. He dabbled in a bit of gardening; tried his hand at bowls; and then joined the local folk dancing group. Charlotte was not impressed with the after dancing ritual of numbing the aching body with copious amounts of beer. Once again we refer to the Old Testament; the writing was on the wall. He was advised, by the head teacher, to put away his bells and pheasant feathers; Edward's dancing days came to an abrupt end.

Unfortunately, Old Nick was waiting in the wings, and the devil found work for Edward's idle hands and recovering body. He joined the community action group *Hands off Weatherford*. Initially Charlotte took no notice of his crusade, until she started to get wind of the gossip swirling around the staffroom. Eventually, she decided she had no choice, but to confront her husband.

An opportunity presented itself a couple of weeks later in the Green Man over a ploughman's lunch, and a couple of drinks.

'Edward, I think we have a bit of a problem,' began Charlotte cutting a pickle onion in half.

'What problem?' asked the surprised ex-folk dancer.

'There are a number of staff at school who don't approve of you joining the action group,' explained the head teacher crunching her way through the half portion of pickle onion.

'Charlotte, that has got absolutely nothing to do with your staff,' exclaimed the ex-bowls player.

'What are they saying?' asked Edward angrily cutting into a wedge of Stilton.

'It's just hearsay, but there is a feeling that we made a lot of money when we sold our London home. We came up here, moved into a large new house, and now we are objecting to other new houses being built,' explained Charlotte buttering a petit pain roll.

'Charlotte, what happened to freedom of speech? When I first met you, you banged that drum the loudest. I have a right to protest about building houses on greenfield sites,' responded the ex-gardener.

'Exactly Edward, therein lies the rub. We live in a house on land that only a year ago were fields of wheat swaying gently in the breeze,' she said carefully choosing her words to create an idyllic country image. 'We are not on moral high ground here. We happen to be very privileged to have been able to move out here into a big house with a lovely garden. Something millions and millions of people in this country will never ever be able to achieve. It is unforgivable hypocrisy for us to move into a brand new house and then start denying others the opportunity to have what we have,' concluded Charlotte using carefully selected words for maximum dramatic impact.

'But what about the greenfields?' asked the ex-inspector trying to get allusive broken pieces of stilton onto his fork.

'I agree, the greenfield sites are problematic, but the country is in a crisis. It is a national crisis, and I'm not talking about Brexit. We have a housing shortage, and we must do something about it. We cannot ignore it,' explained Charlotte leaning forward and deftly scooping up her husband's scattered pieces of cheese and spreading them on his roll.

'Thank you,' mumbled Edward.

'You're welcome. I do not have the answers, but protesting for protesting's sake will not work. You can already see it is not working. Every Tom, Dick and Harry is protesting across the country about greenfield sites, and yet everywhere you go there are houses being built on greenfield. The protests are not working, and never will; we are protesting about the wrong things.'

'I'll get us another drink?' announced the attentive Edward. While he was standing at the bar watching Sue Cooper pouring the drinks, he reflected on what his wife had said. The couple had always been able to discuss things, and he appreciated Charlotte's council.

'Sue do you have any salad dressing?'

'Honey and mustard, and I think, French,' replied the landlady.

'Honey and mustard please. I like salad, but I like salad dressing even more,' he informed a totally disinterested publican.

'So what should we be doing?' Edward asked when he returned to the table.

'The whinging will not stop extra runways and HS2s from being built. Why? Because the country needs them. Protest by all means, but the best thing we can do for our children and grandchildren is make sure we protest about the right things. In this case it is not about houses on greenfield sites, but the lack of everything else a community needs. The developers must provide the infrastructure, modern community amenities, and the opportunity to create work. Just to name a few things.'

'But developers don't provide infrastructure,' pleaded Edward.

'Exactly. What we have to do is protest until the developers are forced by law to give us the amenities to support new housing, and when we have it, they can start building. Edward, as things are at the moment, the greenfield argument is not doing us any favours. It's a misguided selfish nimby argument.'

'Would you like dessert or a coffee?' asked Edward.

'No thanks. I'm done,' replied Charlotte.

'So what do you suggest we do? The houses are already being built,' exclaimed the slightly bemused husband.

'Campaign to get the laws changed. We need the houses, but we also need the support infrastructure,' repeated the head teacher. 'Name one amenity that the Fields View developers have provided for the benefit of the community. The answer is nothing.'

'You are probably right. I guess green coloured pieces of paper in house windows are not going to change anything. What you are advocating is going to take years of time-consuming, expensive and unpleasant confrontational work,' replied a slightly despondent campaigner.

'Which brings me to my next concern. You have somehow by default become the leader or chairman or whatever you want to call it of *Hands off Weatherford*. If you are brutally honest with yourself, nobody is actually giving you any real support.

You're practically running the campaign, if we really want to call it that, on your own,'

'There is a lot to be done,' responded Edward.

'You are far too capable, and people take advantage of you. I see it with the PTA at school. Lots of ideas, but it is always the same one or two people who actually do the work,' smiled Charlotte cocking her head slightly to the left and opening her eyes wide while looking at her husband in the eye. Edward was well acquainted with the 'you know I'm right' facial expression. The married couple got up from the table, and Edward smiled and gave his wife a hug.

'Thanks for lunch and the chat. Let's do it again sometime,' he said.

Yasmin Chowdhury had five customers standing in the queue waiting to pay for their petrol. It was a late Friday afternoon and it had been a long, busy day and she was looking forward to getting home; more precisely home to a long, hot bath. The day had started with one of her staff phoning in sick for the early morning shift.

'Who was that Yas?' asked Samir turning over onto his back to face his wife.

'Amber's phoned in sick.'

'Oh, not again,' moaned Samir.

'I'll go open up. You come down as soon as you can. There's a petrol delivery this morning, and the shelves need restocking urgently. It's Friday, and we're probably going to be busy,' said Yasmin wearily getting up from the bed and dragging herself to the bathroom.

Apart from the unscheduled early start the day had run smoothly, and it had been busy which was always a good feeling. Just after lunchtime, Yasmin saw Jessica Burns pull up on the forecourt. While she was putting petrol into her car, Rhys Broadhurst arrived and stopped behind her. Yasmin watched them greet, and it was obvious that they were pleased to see each another. What aroused the garage owner's curiosity was their body language. There was a familiarity between them. They were standing unusually close together, and when Jessica touched Rhys on the arm he leant forward and whispered something in her ear. Jessica laughed and lightly tapped the young man on the forearm.

'Having fun, Jessica?' asked Yasmin sarcastically when her friend came into the shop to pay for the petrol.

'Oh, same old, same old,' replied Jessica fumbling nervously in her purse, and trying to avoid eye contact with Yasmin. Yasmin gave her the change, and the friends momentarily looked at each other.

'I think we should meet up for a coffee and a natter, don't you?' Jessica could feel herself blushing, and looking at her obviously displeased friend, nodded her head in agreement. 'I'll give you a call later.'

'Yes Rhys, can I help you?'

Two days later, Jessica and Yasmin were sitting in a quiet corner of a coffee shop just off the Wolburn

Market Square. You could cut the atmosphere with a knife. Yasmin had telephoned Jessica the night of the lover's rather public tryst, and it had not gone well. Yasmin had started off by telling Jessica that she had to start thinking with her brain again. Jessica burst into tears, yelled at Yasmin that it was none of her fucking business and hung up. This was followed by 24 hours of less than friendly texting, until the exhausted friends declared a truce and agreed to coffee and an enormous wedge of chocolate cake. Nonetheless, they both refused the others offer of a lift, and ended up driving themselves to town.

They sat looking at each in silence, both waiting for the other to start talking.

'Jessica, I'm not here to judge you. After you and Rhys left the garage, I was so shocked and upset. Horrified. I went to the loo and cried my eyes out. Eventually, Samir had to come and find me,' Yasmin said breaking the ice. 'How did this all come about? How did it start?'

'I don't want to talk about it, Yasmin,' replied her tearful friend.

'Jess, we've been good friends for years. I never suspected you were having an affair. Although I have noticed, for some time, that you and Alistair have not been getting on very well. Does he know about Rhys?'

'No, of course not.'

'What do you see in him? For God's sake, he's only a little older than my boys.' Yasmin angrily tore off a piece of chocolate cake, stabbed it with the fork, and rammed it into her mouth. 'This is the sort of sordid gossip you hear in the village; who's doing what to whom. You never expect your best friend to become the subject of village gossip,' continued Yasmin with traces of chocolate in the corners of her mouth.

'I don't really know how it happened. It just did. I didn't go looking for it. Alistair just works and works on that bloody farm. He's up before dawn, and back well after sunset, and expects his meals to be on the table when he decides it's time to eat. I cannot remember when we last had a meal together. He never takes any notice of me. The only time I see him is when he comes back to the house for food. And then he is always grumpy. I just feel I'm being taken for granted, that I'm invisible,' explained Jessica indicating to her friend that she had chocolate around her mouth.

'Jess, the farm is a lot of work,' Yasmin started to respond.

'And I suppose I don't work my backside off looking after the house, my indifferent children, and ungrateful husband. He never makes any decisions. He leaves it all up to me, and then gets angry about the decisions I've made,' Jessica replied angrily. 'For Christ's sake Yasmin, who's side are you on?' The friends sat in silence.

Jessica was not going to end her affair with Rhys. No matter how risky, and inappropriate, she was determined to hang on to the little bit of happiness that the relationship gave her. Yasmin was disappointed that she was not going to be able to change Jessica's mind. This will all end in tears she thought.

'Yasmin, I'm not going to give up Rhys,' said Jessica eventually breaking the silence.

'I think you are bonkers, Jess. There is no happy end game here. What happens if his parents find out?'

'It is none of their business,' replied the farmer's wife.

'Jess, I totally disagree with what you are doing, but our friendship is very important to me. I do not want this hiccup to jeopardise it. I hope and pray that you will eventually come to your senses. No matter what happens, I don't want our friendship to be harmed,' said Yasmin taking her friends hand and squeezing it.

'Thank you, Yasmin, you are a true friend.' As the women got up to leave, Jessica put her hand on Yasmin's arm. 'Did you tell Samir about Rhys?'

'Yes I did. I'm sorry. I was in such a state when he found me that I had no choice but to tell him. Don't worry. I've sworn him to absolute silence. He won't tell anyone. I promise.'

CHAPTER 24

The Beswicks and the Pollocks were two families who had lived in Weatherford for centuries. The Beswicks, unlike the Pollocks, had not had the freedom to go forth and multiply. They had been restricted by tradition, and over the centuries their influence and power diminished, until all that remained was King Henry's gift.

The Pollocks were a different kettle of fish. Without the constraints of keeping up appearances, the family was free to marry for love. Finding a suitable bride was not limited to the borough of Weatherford, and the Pollock clan over time spread out across a large part of the county. Builders, teachers, vicars, midwives; everywhere you went there was a member of the Pollock dynasty.

Despite the family having the numbers to form a small army, the Pollocks kept themselves to themselves, and just got on with their lives. This didn't mean they never used their influence. Some ten years previously, a parish councillor received a county award *'for his outstanding contribution to the community'*. The award mystified the villagers. Who had voted for him, and when did the vote take place? The general consensus was that the recipient had some dirt on other members of the parish council, and the award was made to keep him on-side.

Pat Pollock was incensed with anger when she heard the news. The parish councillor, at the time of the mystery award, was responsible for the running of the community centre. Rumours were rife that council money was not only paying for the centre, but also subsidising the councillor's household bills.

On receiving the news of the award, Pat with the help of other family members quietly mobilised a boycott of the community centre. Attendance plummeted, the parish council did nothing, and within eight months the centre was no longer financially viable. The *coup de grace* occurred when Pat visited the award winning councillor, and out of courtesy, advised him that she intended to raise the subject of household purchases using council funds at the next parish council meeting. The councillor did some soul searching, tore up his award certificate, and resigned from the parish council a day before the meeting was scheduled to take place. The community manager vacancy was advertised, and one of Pat's granddaughters, who had primary school catering experience, took over the running of the centre.

When Charlie Pollock had been born there had been complications, and it had unfortunately left him slightly mentally disabled. He was a gentle, kind person, but vulnerable. He prided himself in the fact that he had worked every day since he had left school, saved his money, and had never relied on welfare.

He had been Belinda Thomas' stable hand for years and was intensely loyal. He would not hear a bad word about her, always arrived for work on time, worked the long hours in all kinds of weather, and often put the interests of the riding school ahead of his own. He was not shy to come forward and chat to new visitors to the centre often taking them on a tour of the stables and proudly showing off the horses. People quickly warmed to him, and Belinda was very aware of the fact that despite his limitations, he was an important part of the school's success.

Charlie climbed the steps leading up to the open front door of the Green Man. He looked up at the building, and noticed that something was different about it. All the windows were wide open. He felt a little uneasy; he didn't like change. He gingerly stepped through the open door, and saw a familiar face. KS was standing alone at the bar. Seeing a familiar face, his anxiety subsided.

'Good afternoon, Charlie,' greeted KS as he turned to see who had entered the pub.

'Good afternoon, Richard,' replied the newcomer politely.

'Come and join me. What can I get you?' invited the estate agent. Sue Cooper hearing voices appeared behind the bar.

'Alright, Charlie,' greeted the landlady while she skilfully pulled him a pint of beer.

'Sue why are all of the windows open?' asked Charlie placing the beer on a coaster.

'It's the bloody heat, Charlie. Place is so hot. The punters who stay overnight are all complaining that they cannot sleep. What am I supposed to do about it? I can't help the heatwave, can I?' The two men at the bar were not going to argue with the formidable Sue, and just nodded their heads in agreement.

'Give me a call if you need anything,' instructed the landlady as she disappeared from behind the bar.

KS the estate agent, chairman of a charity, and parish councillor and Charlie Pollock, stable hand sat in silence and stared at the arrangement of bottles behind the bar. It was an awkward silence and KS tried to make conversation, but Charlie was not particularly responsive.

'Charlie, you're very quiet. Is there a problem?' asked KS with his usual display of irritation.

'I'm too embarrassed to discuss it, Richard,' replied the stable hand.

'You can talk to me, Charlie. We've known each other all our lives. Your secret is safe with me,' encouraged KS. 'I'm a parish councillor after all,' he added.

Richard Kettering-Smythe had not always been a confidence trickster. His father had been a bank manager and his mother was, at the time, one of only a handful of women who ran their own architectural businesses. They were not rich, but he and his brother had never wanted for anything.

After finishing school, Richard went on to obtain a second in geography and much to his parent's horror started working for a local estate agent. Ten years later he was able to mitigate his parents' displeasure by starting his own business. Unfortunately his father had passed away by then, and much to his irritation, his mother became the custodian of the parental disappointment. She never missed an opportunity to voice her disillusionment. Behaviour that KS resented, especially as his brother had discovered marijuana at an early age, dropped out of university, lived on a kibbutz until he was thrown out for displaying Palestinian sympathies, and finally set off on a fateful Cairo to Cape Town cycle-ride which ended with him being killed by a gang of militia near Victoria Falls for his bicycle.

KS did not have the suave, slick personality to be a natural confidence trickster. He was rude, bad-tempered and impatient. His default setting was to be confrontational and condescending. The bizarre thing about the cons was that he actually didn't need the money. So what happened?

Opportunity.

One day he received a phone call from an elderly widow wanting to put her bungalow on the market. He had gone out to see the property, and during the course of the visit learnt that Mrs Wilson had no relatives who lived in the area, and hadn't seen her children nor grandchildren for years. The house was put on the market, but unfortunately shortly thereafter Mrs Wilson was diagnosed with cancer, and had to move out of the bungalow prematurely. KS visited her on a regular basis during her remaining nine months of her life. He arranged, with Mrs Wilson's consent, for the empty property to be kept in good repair, and the garden to be kept neat and tidy.

Initially, he insisted that he didn't want to be paid for his kindness. After a brief period of charity, he intimated to Mrs Wilson that the upkeep of the property was more expensive than he had expected, and needed to recoup the costs. Terminally-ill and vulnerable, the old lady offered to gift some money to the estate agent. Mrs Wilson left her bungalow to KS, and to his surprise not a single family member came forward to contest it.

He was hooked. The money still didn't motivate him; it was now the thrill of the chase. After Mrs Wilson, he went out hunting, and found more vulnerable people; all living on their own and separated from family. He would gain their confidence, and wait. He was not doing anything illegal, and being immoral was hardly a crime.

He was aware that there were rumours in the village about his dodgy dealings, but bizarrely nobody ever challenged him. He deliberately used his position as a parish councillor to hide any suggestions of impropriety. He created an aura of honesty and openness by making sure that his name appeared under Disclosure of Interests in as many minutes of the parish council as possible. Not every month; that would have aroused suspicions.

He also volunteered to do various community-minded activities which meant his name was regularly associated with words of thanks from the council chairman. His name would keep appearing in the minutes, like a subliminal insertion, to convince the reader of his squeaky-clean community image.

His chairmanship of *Swarm International UK* completed the illusion. He knew it did. He would get close to his target, and when within range he used the kudos of his position like heavy artillery to pummel his hapless victim into submission.

'Have another beer on me, and tell me all about it, Charlie,' encouraged KS. Nursing another pint of beer Charlie told his listener about the cottage and money he had recently inherited from an aunt. He told KS how he didn't like the attention, and it made him feel embarrassed. He just wanted to be left alone. A bigger problem, he explained, was he didn't know what to do with two cottages. He was happy living in the little cottage he had, and didn't have a use for two houses.

'Where is your aunt's cottage,' asked KS.

'It's in Guster Lane, Cock's Cottage,' replied Charlie.

'Well Charlie. I would suggest you rent it out. While we are looking for a tenant, I'll make sure the maintenance is done, and the garden is kept neat and tidy. It won't cost you a penny. I'll do it as a favour. You won't have to do a thing. Trust me. It'll all be ok.'

'Are you sure, Richard,' asked Charlie. 'I don't want to be a nuisance.'

'It'll be my pleasure. Just out of interest, how much money did your aunt leave you?'

'150 grand,' replied the newly snared Charlie. KS looked at his victim and smiled. I have found money he thought. What he didn't realise was that in his desperation to find the money to pay the blackmailers, he had made a fundamental error of judgement by choosing a Pollock for his next scam, and it would change his life forever.

CHAPTER 25

Alistair Burns was sitting in his small untidy office when Moz Nel knocked, and popped his head around the door.

'Morning Moz, come in, come in. Good weekend?'

'Yes thanks Alistair. Bella's doing the Second World War at school, so we drove over to Coventry to see the cathedral. Elsa and I were quite moved by it. Standing there in the quiet sanctity of God, you can only imagine how the people must have felt when it was bombed. They were unable to do anything but watch the desecration of their community. It must have been terrible.'

'Indeed Moz. All nations and peoples of the world experience the evil that men do at some time or other,' mumbled Alistair putting on his reading glasses. Moz felt Alistair was preoccupied, and decided to drop the subject.

'I'll go on ahead and get started, if you like,' offered Moz.

'Um, sit Moz. I should have offered you a coffee. Very rude of me. Not a great start to the week.'

'Oh. What's the problem?'

'It never rains, but it pours,' remarked Alistair. Moz looked out of the window and was going to comment that it had not actually rained for three months when the farmer interrupted him. 'Results here from the last crop visit,' continued Alistair as he passed a letter over the desk to Moz. 'The boffins think we might have to start the harvest early if we don't get any rain. The Chief Agronomist, Paul Lancaster, is planning another visit in a few weeks. He'll make a final recommendation then.'

'They suggest we start harvesting at the end of this month. That's almost a month early isn't it?' asked Moz looking up from reading the letter.

'At least,' answered Alistair.

'This yield forecast is not good either.'

'No, it's not good. Crap actually. There's always some bloody thing,' Alistair blurted out in frustration.

'What about irrigating?'

'Head Office don't want to irrigate. They don't think it would improve the yield at this late stage,' answered Alistair shrugging his shoulders. 'There was another bolt out of the blue yesterday. Lucas and Dominic are returning to Lithuania at the end of the month.'

'Why?' asked a surprised Moz.

'Brexit. They are concerned that they may not be able to stay in the UK.'

'But that's crazy. They're employed, and the work is not going to disappear,' commented Moz.

'Totally agree. You cannot get the Brits to work on a farm. It's impossible. They just won't do it. Timing couldn't be worse, what with this harvest business as well. You switch on the tv, and all you see are those morons in parliament, bickering and squabbling like children in a playground. I'd like to round them all up, and make them work on the farm for a week. Show them what real work is all about. Overpaid spoilt twits. ' Moz was a bit taken aback by Alistair's outburst, and was not quite sure how to respond. He agreed with Alistair that the pictures on television were not doing Britain's image any good. He was, however, a visitor to England and didn't think it was his place to pass comment about the Brexit circus.

'Alistair don't worry about the harvest. I'll help you day and night until it's all done. It's not going to be easy, but we can do it. We get ourselves organised, and just get stuck in and work at it.'

'Thanks Moz. That's very kind of you. Let's wait and see how things pan out. The other thing I need to talk to you about are the trials.' Alistair took his glasses off and handed Moz an A4 blue plastic folder. 'The trials are not producing the expected results either.' Moz opened the report, and sat quietly reading the executive summary on the first page.

Every stage of the trial had been below expectations. The unusually hot weather, and the lack of rain were cited as the most probable cause. Moz's heart sank as he read the summary. He felt personally responsible for what had happened. Had he not worked hard enough? Had he done something wrong? He looked at Alistair over the piles of paper on the desk.

'I'm sorry Alistair. It must be my fault. I've let you down.'

'Nonsense, Moz. You can't help the weather. It's a natural product, and unless you have a 5G hotline to that God you keep talking about, there is nothing anyone can do about it.'

'So what happens now?' asked a dejected Moz.

'I've just spoken to John Carter at Head Office, and we've set up a lunch meeting here next Monday at 11 o'clock to discuss the situation. Don't worry about it Moz, we'll probably put it down to experience, and give it another go next summer. What are the chances of having another dry summer like this one, eh?'

'Not very likely,' replied Moz. 'Thanks for bringing me up to speed Alistair. If you don't mind, I'd better get out there, and do some work.'

'I'll join you chaps in a bit. Thank you for your support, Moz.'

Lucas and Dominic had already started to dismantle the section of fence that needed repairing when Moz arrived on his utility vehicle. The three men were unusually quiet, and the customary banter that normally went on between them was missing.

Nobody even mentioned the England Football Team's semi-final.

Moz was preoccupied with the news about the trials. He wondered if his contract would be affected. It could be cancelled he thought. That would be a pity. Elsa and the kids had settled down nicely. They like living in England. It would be a great shame if they had to return to South Africa early. How am I going to break the news to them? I hope Elsa doesn't think I've let them down. I think I'll wait until next week's meeting before telling them.

Ironically, both Lucas and Dominic had similar thoughts. Both men had lived in England for eighteen years, and both wanted to stay. They had always worked, paid their taxes, and apart from drinking too much vodka, and occasionally dying their hair they considered themselves to be model citizens. Being separated from their extended families for so many years had been difficult, but given the chance they would do it all over again. They felt let down by their adopted country. Nobody could tell them if they would be allowed to stay after Brexit. The scare stories in the media did not help. Fake news made the situation worse, and without any leadership from the authorities the two men had been spooked into making the decision to return to Lithuania. They had a lot of farming experience, and wanted to return home early in order to find jobs before any of their compatriots swelled the ranks of unemployed Lithuanians.

It was another hot day, and perspiration poured off the men. They had removed the section of fence that needed repairing, dug the holes for the new fence posts, mixed the cement, and were manhandling the posts into position when Alistair arrived on his utility vehicle with a plastic jerry can of ice cold water. The men sat on a nearby concrete anti-aircraft emplacement, thankful for the break, and the cold water.

They took it in turns to pour some of the remaining water over themselves, and were about to resume working when they heard an engine noise. Looking up, they saw a yellow coloured ultralight flying towards them. As it flew passed, the ultralight pilot waved at them. 'It's pulling something along behind it,' remarked Alistair.

'Looks like a banner of some sort,' replied Moz. Before reaching the power lines at the edge of the field, the small aircraft turned, and flew back towards the group on the ground.

'NO MORE GM,' read Alistair as it flew passed them for the second time. 'A bloody protestor,' remarked the farmer. The ultralight flew over London Road towards the Manor House, and descending to tree level turned back towards the watching men. It flew passed them for the third time, and the pilot showed them his middle finger.

'He's very low,' commented Moz.

'Christ, if he doesn't pull up soon he's going to hit the power lines,' commented Alistair. The ultralight crossed the edge of the field, and the pilot applied more power. The aircraft started to climb.

'He's not going to get over the lines,' said Lucas in horror. The ultralight was lower than it had been on the first pass, and the pilot had not taken into account the fact that the hot temperature would reduce the aircraft's climb performance. The bystanders watched in horror as the flying machine struggled to reach the top of the power lines, loose speed, and stall. The right wing dropped violently, and caught one of the thick cables. It cartwheeled over the power lines, and plummeting the remaining 150 feet slammed into the ground. The sudden deceleration caused the pilot's seat harness to come away from its fittings, catapulted through the air, and ending up some fifty feet from the wreckage of his aircraft.

'Lucas, quick as you can, go back to the house, and get the large first aid kit. The one in the office. Moz call 999, and get an ambulance. Dominic you come with me,' instructed Alistair without any hint of emotion. Alistair and Dominic scrambled onto the utility vehicle, and headed off in the direction of the accident. They couldn't get close enough, and leaving the vehicle on the path ran across the field towards the injured pilot.

'Ok, Dominic. Don't touch him. He might have a neck or back injury. Let's see if he's alive,' said Alistair kneeling down, and placing two fingers on the pilot's neck. He listened for breathing.

'Is he alive, Mr Alistair?' asked Dominic.

'Yes.' replied the farmer. 'His body is lying at a strange angle to his head, and I'm not sure if his legs are ok. There's no sign of bleeding. Might have internal bleeding though. He is lying very still. I don't think we should do anything until the ambulance arrives. We could do more damage if we try and move him.'

Lucas and Jessica arrived with the first aid bag. When she saw the injured pilot lying on the ground, she started to panic.

'Alistair, you've got to help the poor man.'

'Jessica, it's all under control. There is nothing we can do at the moment. We need professional medical assistance,' replied her husband calmly. Moz came running up.

'Ok, ambulance and the police are on the way,' he panted. 'How is he? Looks pretty bad,' he added looking at the pilot's crumpled body.

'Lucas take the UV, and wait at the farm gate for the ambulance. Do you have your mobile on you?' asked Alistair. Lucas showed Alistair his phone, and headed off.

'Alistair, we can't just let him lie there. We must do something,' pleaded his wife.

'Jessica, trust me. We mustn't move him. If he starts to move, we will have to keep him still. Any movement could be fatal. It's going to be ok,' he said looking up at his wife.

The ambulance arrived, and the paramedics, like Alistair, were concerned that the pilot might have a head or spinal injury, and that he should be taken to the spinal unit at Peterborough Hospital. The County Air Ambulance was requested. Alistair, Moz and the Lithuanians started to move the farm equipment off the concrete hardstand in front of the sheds so that the helicopter could land as close as possible to the injured pilot.

A few miles away, the telephone rang in the flight office of the County Air Ambulance. Critical Care Paramedic Kamal Khan spun around on the swivel chair he was sitting on, and pulling himself closer to the desk, lifted the telephone off its cradle.

'Helimed nine, seven,' he answered swopping the phone over to his left ear, and holding it in position with his left shoulder. Moving the incident log closer, he started to write. 'Yes, go ahead.'

Pre-hospital Care Doctor Emily Jones stood up, and lifted her heavy paramedic backpack onto an office desk before putting her arms through the shoulder straps and fastening the quick release buckles. Pilot James Walsh had just made bacon sandwiches and a coffee for the helimed crew, and without any expression on his face tipped the sandwiches into the dustbin, and poured the coffees down the sink.

'Affirmative, Helimed nine, seven responding at time one, one, zero, nine.' Kamal signed the log, and replaced the phone in its cradle. Grabbing his red medical bag, he followed Dr Jones and James Walsh out of the flight office. 'Ultralight accident at Weatherford. Hit a pylon. Pilot badly injured. Possible head or back injuries,' briefed Kamal as the three jogged across the concrete apron towards the waiting helicopter.

Within a couple of minutes the noise of the helicopter starting up drowned out all other sounds at the rural airfield. The noise grew louder as the rotating blades changed pitch, and the brightly painted red and yellow helicopter lifted off the ground. It started to move forward, tilting slightly nose down as the speed built up. Once clear of the ground, Pilot James Walsh flew the rescue medical helicopter parallel to the runway and making a gentle turn away from the aircraft hangars on his left he climbed the helicopter and set heading for Weatherford. He pressed his radio transmission button,

'VFR traffic this is Helimed nine, seven lifting at Earlsfield, destination Weatherford.' James stopped the climb at 500 feet above the ground, and levelled off. The HEMS helicopter quickly accelerated to its cruising speed, and two minutes later they were passing Blacktree Crossing. 'VFR traffic Helimed nine, seven passing abeam Blacktree Crossing to the north at five zero, zero feet. Destination Weatherford. ETA at time one, one, two, nine.'

'Any update on the patient,' asked the pilot.

'Only that assets are attending,' replied Kamal.

'Electricity pylons here on the left at ten o'clock,' commented Dr Jones pointing towards the ground.

'Probably take us straight to the accident. The visibility isn't very good today, must be the heat,' remarked the pilot. A couple of minutes later Weatherford came into sight, and the helicopter was now rapidly converging with the power lines. 'Let's keep the lines on our left until we have a positive sighting of the accident,' instructed the pilot. The Weatherford Church came into view. 'Distance and time please, Emily,' requested James.

'GPS gives us 2 minutes to run. The grid reference places the accident slightly to our left at 5 miles,' replied the doctor reading the information off the screen of the hand held navigation computer.

'Thanks,' responded James as he looked out to the left over the instrument panel console.

'Ok, I've got the assets. And there's the ultralight in the field on the other side of the power lines,' said Emily pointing.

'Slowing down, let's find a place to land,' responded James. The pilot hovered the helicopter at 300 feet above the ground, and turning the stationery machine to his left he had a clear view of the activity on the ground. 'People waving down there. Looks like they've cleared that concrete area for us. It's well clear of the pylons,' James commented.

'Those sheds on the left might be a bit close,' added Kamal.

'Ok, keep an eye on them, Kamal. Here we go let's ease her in, nice and gently,' said the pilot. James slowly descended the helicopter towards the square of concrete.

'Probably use it for farm equipment. Should be strong enough to take us,' he added as they moved slowly towards the improvised helipad. As the helicopter got close to the ground a dust cloud started to rise, and the onlookers and vehicles disappeared in the haze.

'Ah, dust, not good,' commented James. 'I'll hold it here. It might clear it away.' Hovering above the concrete slab, the dust cloud dissipated and the onlookers reappeared. With the ground in sight, James completed the landing. When the blades had stopped rotating, the two paramedics quickly egressed the helicopter leaving James on his own to complete the shutdown checks, and let Base know that they were safely on the ground at Weatherford.

Once the helicopter had disappeared over the horizon on its way to Peterborough and the ambulances had left, the police, for the second time in eight months, took statements at Oak Tree Farm. The police notified the Air Accident Investigation Branch of the incident, who in turn contacted Alistair.

Jessica went back to the house and made scones for everyone. They all deserved cream and scones after what they had gone through. Alone in her kitchen her thoughts turned to Alistair. She had seen a completely different Alistair today; not the grumpy, impatient, and irritable husband she despised, but someone working calmly under pressure, and making life-changing decisions. His actions today have probably saved a man's life she thought. Her thoughts were interrupted by knocking at the front door. She wiped the flour off her hands, and when she opened the door, the smiling face of Hugh Flynn greeted her.

CHAPTER 26

'Still sulking?' asked Chris nudging Hanna gently with his elbow and smiling.

'I'm not sulking,' replied Hanna looking over the top of her sunglasses at her policeman.

'Isn't this much better than being in chambers? You don't have this view from your tiny little office window.'

'Very true,' answered the lawyer looking down at the enormous expanse of the River Thames below them as they drove across the Queen Elizabeth Bridge.

'All that work will still be there when you get back on Monday. I promise you, we're going to have an amazing time this weekend.'

'I hate surprises,' replied Hanna leaning over and squeezing Chris's arm. 'Tell me where we're going, and I'll stop nagging.' Chris just shook his head and smiled while concentrating on the fast moving motorway traffic. 'It would be useful to have a blue light,' commented Hanna.

'A siren would be better,' laughed Chris.

'Give me a clue,' asked Hanna as she looked out at the uninspiring scenery on either side of the motorway.

'It's a place that I visited a couple of times as a boy. Once with my parents and brother, and the second time it was a school trip,' replied Chris.

'How far is it?'

'About twenty minutes.'

'I'm very tempted to say Croydon, but I think it's Hever Castle.'

'How did you work that one out?'

'Read it on a road sign a couple of miles back.'

Leaving the dreariness of the M25 they drove the next ten miles along a country road bordered by hedgerow, oak and chestnut trees.

'You wouldn't think that there is such a lovely country road just off the motorway,' commented Chris.

'The sunshine helps,' replied Hanna. 'You're right. It's lovely to be away from work.'

The closer they got to the castle the more prolific became the signs to their destination. The entrance was opposite a large car park; a gatehouse guarded by four enormous ancient oak trees. Following the signboards to the accommodation, they caught a glimpse of the 13th century castle surrounded by its moat.

'There's a restaurant over there,' Hanna said pointing in the direction of a row of low modern buildings clustered together with outside seating.

They checked in to their bed and breakfast accommodation with its low oak beam ceiling, four poster bed, and large fireplace.

'It's weird to think that King Henry VIII might have stood here, and looked out of these windows,' commented Chris.

'Not to mention using this,' added Hanna as she sat down on the edge of the four poster bed. Chris looked at her, and shaking his head, laughed. 'Later Miss Boleyn. Let's go and get a bite to eat.'

Walking hand in hand the couple made their way back towards the restaurant that Hanna had spotted earlier. The sun was shining and a gentle breeze added to the pleasure of being outdoors. Chris ordered a coronation chicken sandwich, a slice of chocolate cake, and a coffee. Hanna decided on a blt, lemon drizzle cake, and an orange juice. They sat down at one of the outdoor tables which gave them an unhindered view of the castle.

'So what's the latest news about the farm, Han,' asked Chris.

'The contamination issue has opened up a can of worms,' answered Hanna. 'I thought withdrawing the building application would make life a bit easier. It seems to have made things more complicated. Both the Environmental Agency and the Council have got involved. Emails are flying to and fro arguing about who's responsible, who's legally required to clean it up, etcetera, etcetera.'

'Don't tell me. Slopey shoulders,' commented Chris.

'Exactly. All I want is for one of them to tell me what I must do to sort it out.'

'And Pasternak Construction?'

'Haven't heard anything since they went into administration,' replied the lawyer.

'So putting the contamination problem to one side, what are your options?'

'Alex and Dudley are looking at the two obvious solutions; sell it or get a tenant farmer in. However, their latest idea is a solar farm,' replied Hanna.

'I have a confession to make, Han,' Chris reached across the table and held Hanna's hands.

'Oh yes,' replied a slightly puzzled Hanna.

'The more time I've spent at the farm, the more I've got to like it.'

'I know you have, and it hasn't gone unnoticed. I've actually started to see the farm through fresh eyes because of it,' answered Hanna squeezing his hands.

'Come on, I want to show you something,' announced Chris. He took Hanna by the hand, and headed off along the path leading away from the restaurant towards the castle. Hanna was a bit surprised when Chris walked them straight passed the towering fortress, and continued along the path.

'Aren't we going into the castle?' she asked.

'Later,' Chris replied. At the end of the path there was a maze with eight feet high hedge walls. 'Come on, we're giving it a go. I told you this morning we were going to have an amazing time,' he laughed. They entered the maze, and like many before them, found it was not as easy to navigate as one might think. Eventually they found the sundial in the centre of the puzzle.

'You do know that we have to find our way out of here,' laughed Hanna.

'Plenty of time, Hanna,' Chris said going down on one knee.

'Chris, what are you doing?'

'Hanna Townsend will you marry me?' he asked opening a ring box. Hanna took the solitaire diamond rose gold ring out of the little box, and looked at it. She looked at her policeman.

'Why wouldn't I, DI Brown,' she answered with tears streaming down her cheeks.

The newly engaged couple stood in the middle of the maze hugging, kissing and laughing. Unbeknown to the happy couple, a group of visitors were standing quietly watching the proceedings. They clapped and cheered when Hanna agreed to the offer of marriage.

'Hey mate, I've taken a photo. Would you like me to send it to you?' called out one of the onlookers. A couple of minutes later Chris had a photo of himself kneeling in front of Hanna and proposing.

It was a warm morning as Alistair, Moz and Paul Lancaster, the Company's Chief Agronomist walked down the dirt track towards the winter wheat trial. On reaching the security fence surrounding the field, Alistair unlocked the gate using the keypad, and the men entered the enclosure under the watchful eye of an array of cctv cameras.

'Paul, we've actually been very fortunate in that we haven't had any large-scale disruption from protestors,' remarked Alistair closing the heavy gate behind them.

'There were initially a few in Hertfordshire, but as far as I know, except for your ultralight crash, all the sites have been quiet,' replied the agronomist. 'Do you get many anti-GM demonstrations back home Moz?' asked Paul looking up at the tall research farmer.

'Ya, there have been a few demonstrations over the years. I think the arguments for and against growing

GM crops in South Africa are very similar to here in the UK. There's plenty of mudslinging between the pros and the antis. Those against the science say using GM seed does not increase the amount grown, and will in actual fact increase wheat prices. Of course, the two biggest reasons why they are against GM is the belief that the modified food is harmful to humans, and the second objection is that the seeds are controlled by a few multi-nationals. I know I earn money from the GM trials, but I have worked with genetically modified crops for a number of years, and I honestly believe they are safe for people to eat. All I want to do is what every farmer has done since Adam tilled the soil in the Garden of Eden; try and grow as much food as possible. You'll never get to Mars if you don't try.'

The group had reached the edge of the field when a voice called out.

'Mr Burns, excuse me Sir.'

'That's Dai James from *PowerEnergy Network*,' remarked Alistair recognising the Team Leader in his orange hi-vis jacket and trousers. 'You two carry on. I'll go and see what he wants.'

The Team Leader had driven his small white van up to the gate, and half-sat, half leant against the bonnet waiting for Alistair to reach him. The men shook hands, and exchanged pleasantries about the warm weather, their health, and the well-being of their respective families.

'Mr Burns, Sir, I've dropped in to let you know that we will be carrying out maintenance on the farm in four weeks time. Here are the details,' advised the Team Leader handing the farmer a printed notice.

'Pylons ES495 to ES506,' Alistair read out aloud, 'So that's all of the pylons on the farm. Is that correct?'

'Yes Sir,' replied the Team Leader.

'Ok, thanks for letting me know. Same team?'

'Pretty much. There are a couple of new boys,' replied Dai in his heavy welsh accent.

'If you have an early start on our pylons, I'll get Jessica to rustle up a full monty for you and the boys. Give me a call a couple of days before you are due to start.'

'Thank you very much, Alistair. Greatly appreciated. At least that will be one less breakfast that we have to endure at the Green Man,' smiled the Team Leader. Alistair laughed, and nodded his head in agreement.

'See you in a few weeks, Dai. Please excuse me. I need to get back to the crops,' smiled the farmer, turning towards the gate, and entering the door code. Moz and the agronomist were in the middle of the 100 acre field. When Alistair reached them, Paul was squatting down on his haunches inspecting the wheat.

'Problem, Alistair,' asked Moz.

'No, no. Pylon people just letting me know they are here in a couple of weeks to carry out maintenance. It's the same team who were here the last time. All from Wales. Nice bunch of lads. How are we doing here, Paul?' asked the farmer.

'The stems and leaves seem to be coping with the heat, but they could do with a bit more rain. I've taken a few soil samples so we can cross-check against the ones we took before planting,' replied the agronomist standing up rather stiffly from his crouched position.

'There's no rain forecast for the foreseeable future. The lack of rain has certainly effected the trial,' commented Moz.

'And the rest of the crop,' remarked Alistair. 'If the forecast is correct, we could lose the entire lot,' added the farmer rather glumly.

'Alistair I know I've already asked the question, but should we not irrigate? I never thought I'd be standing in the middle of a field in England asking the question,' smiled Moz.

'It's not a silly question. No one can recall a long term forecast like this one. The media keep quoting 1976 and standpipes in the streets,' replied Alistair.

'Bloody press, always scaremongering. The long term forecasts hardly ever happen anyway,' commented the agronomist.

'To answer your question Moz, we do have a water permit. Getting permission from the authorities to recharge the irrigation system from ground or river water is not always straightforward. Having said that, if we get to that stage the Environment Secretary has usually intervened anyway. But it is a good point. Paul can you talk to someone at head office about the water issue. We need to keep it in mind.'

'Of course I will.'

'If the forecast is correct, we also need to monitor how much water this trial gets, and compare it with the amount of water used in the tunnel trials,' added Moz. 'It could produce a different result.'

'I would go one step further and say we should check the results, not only against the tunnels, but also other open air trials,' concluded the agronomist.

'Never a dull moment, hey,' commented Alistair. 'Let's go back to the house. I told Jessica to prepare lunch for us,' he added.

As usual Jessica Burns had excelled herself. She had laid out, on the kitchen table, a summer spread of chicken and ham cutting pie, quiche, thinly sliced ham, old vintage cheddar, coleslaw, potato salad and a huge bowl of green salad.

'Jessica, this looks absolutely delicious,' remarked Moz as the men entered the kitchen. 'I think I've died and gone to heaven,' he added.

'Don't be silly, Moz. It's my pleasure,' replied the farmer's wife, looking up from the sink, and taking off her pink washing up gloves. 'Enjoy it. I'm going to watch *Bargain Hunt*. I'll eat my lunch in front of the telly. Leave you guys to talk shop.'

'Do we not have any salad dressing, Jessica?' asked her husband rather curtly.

'It's in the fridge, Alistair.' Jessica angrily opened the fridge door, causing the jams and condiments to clunk against each other. She took out the salad dressing, thumped it down on the table in front of her husband, and banged the fridge door closed. Once the clunking jams and condiments had quietened down, an awkward silence descended on the kitchen as the farmer's wife left the room.

'Tuck in, gentlemen, bon appetit,' announced a seemingly un-phased husband.

'Jess, sorry to disturb you.' Jessica looked up and muted the tv. 'Just wanted to say thank you for the lovely lunch,' said Moz.

'It is a great pleasure, Moz,' replied the farmer's wife.

'Alistair tells me the two of you are taking a few days off next week,' continued the research farmer.

'Yes. Samir and Yasmin have kindly offered us their holiday lodge at Walton-on-the-Naze for a week. The twins are going to fend for themselves. Actually would you and Elsa mind keeping an eye on them? How are Elsa and the kids? I haven't seen them for a few weeks.'

'Ya, of course we will keep an eye on Chloe and Tom. Elsa is as beautiful as ever, and the kids are healthy. I think they are all looking forward to the school holiday. It's a bit strange having the summer holiday in the middle of the year,' commented Moz. Jessica wasn't quite sure she understood what Moz was talking about, but decided not to ask. 'Both Paul and Bella were so excited this morning. Hanna and Chris Brown have taken them to London for the day. They are very fond of Hanna.'

'Who, our Hanna?' asked a surprised Jessica.

'Yes. Hanna Townsend,' replied Moz.

'Chris Brown. Should I know him? Name's familiar,' responded Jessica.

'Chris Brown was one of the police detectives investigating Mr Townsend's death. They've been seeing each other for a number of months now, and have just got engaged,' replied Moz.

'That didn't take long, did it? Actually, I'm really pleased for her,' said a visibly delighted Jessica. 'Poor girl, she deserves a bit of luck and happiness.'

'Totally agree. Well, if you will excuse me, I need to get back to Elsa. She's preparing Hanna and Chris a little thank you meal for when they drop the kids off. I must say it feels very strange that my kids are visiting London with a policeman.'

When Moz had gone, Jessica stared at the muted tv, and for the second time was not quite sure what Moz was talking about. Summertime in the middle of the year, and visiting London with a policeman. Must be a South African thing she thought, switching the tv sound back on again.

Moz had only crunched his way a few yards along the drive towards his house, when Paul Lancaster passed him in his car. The men waved farewell.

'Excuse me Moz,' called Alistair from the open front door of the farmhouse. 'I meant to ask you earlier. There is a charity golf game at the golf club in July. It's in support of The County Air Ambulance. I was wondering if you would like me to put your name down? The whole family's invited.'

'I haven't really played much golf, I'm more of a rugby bloke. I've played tennis quite a bit, and tug of war for my province. Sure, put my name down. July you say, no problem, gives me plenty of time to practice,' smiled Moz.

A familiar grey Peugeot 206, still in need of a wash, turned into the drive and approached the farmers, and stopped alongside them.

'Afternoon, gentlemen,' greeted a perspiring Hugh Flynn. 'Hot enough for you? I see there is not much rain forecast for the foreseeable future, Alistair. You farmers must be starting to get worried about this year's crop,' added the sweaty hack.

'Hugh, what do you want? We are months off the harvest. Stop trying to make up a disaster story when there isn't one to be told. If you cannot make a useful contribution, I would suggest you get off the property,' responded an irritated farm manager.

'Keep your hair on. Do you have Hanna Townsend's telephone number?' asked the journalist.

'Hugh, leave Hanna alone. She has had enough crap recently to last a lifetime. She doesn't need the press hounding her. Get off the property before I call the police.'

'Alistair, I'm not harassing Hanna. I have some very useful information about Grey Pigeon Farm. All I want, is for you to give her a call on my behalf, and ask her to please contact me when she has a moment. Here's my number. Please Alistair, you'll be doing her a big favour,' said the journalist handing his business card to the farm manager. Alistair looked at the card, and stood staring at the journalist whilst he made up his mind.

'OK Hugh, I'll give her a call, but don't you dare heap any more misery on her.'

'Thank you Alistair. You have my word.' The farmers watched the grubby Peugeot do a three point turn, and head off down the drive bellowing a thick cloud of black smoke from the exhaust.

'Bloody press,' muttered Alistair under his breath.

CHAPTER 27

'The problem is we don't have sufficient funds to keep challenging the constant stream of planning applications, the latest one being the re-submission of Application 3613, the Townsend land,' said Edward Broadhurst the leader-by-default of the community protest group *Hands off Weatherford*.

'Well we must keep organising fund raising events then,' added Tia Hughes. Everyone sitting around the table nodded their heads in agreement.

'Easier said than done,' commented Edward. 'Firstly, there are plenty of ideas, but there are very few people in this group who actually come forward, and offer to organise anything. Secondly, we are a bunch of amateurs pitted against a formidable adversary.'

'I think that's being a bit disingenuous, Edward,' commented Jeremy Hughes.

'Jeremy, if we're to be successful, we need the help of a brief who is knowledgeable about the construction industry. Do you think for one minute that the developers haven't got lawyers looking for loop-holes that can be used to reverse a decision rejecting a planning application. We're on a hiding to nothing.'

'Edward I think you are being over dramatic. We must protest, we cannot give up, otherwise we will be overrun with houses,' responded Tia.

'It is your right to protest, Tia. Unfortunately, the reality is, we do not have the funds, and are unlikely to ever raise sufficient money to pay for a top-flight lawyer.'

'Oh well, then let's just throw in the towel, shall we?' Jeremy blurted out, angrily thumping his empty beer glass down on the table. Edward was angered by the outburst, and was about to respond, when he decided to keep his own counsel.

'In the final analysis, we have not stopped a single house from being built. The planning permission for Fields View was rejected twice, until a sharp-eyed lawyer working on behalf of Pasternak Construction discovered that the council had not met its 5 year house building target. The Inspector ruled that houses were needed, the council had not provided them, and he granted permission for the development to go ahead. The same thing will happen with 3613. It will be another round of ping-pong between Pasternak and the council until a lawyer on either side finds a loophole. Personally, I think permission will be granted on the same grounds as Fields View.'

'So what is it you want us to do, Edward?' asked Jeremy.

'To start with, Jeremy, I am tired of being taken for granted. Your outburst earlier has made my decision easier.' The musician was surprised that he had been singled-out because he had voiced his opinion. 'I seem to be running this campaign on my own,' the soon-to-be ex-leader continued. 'If members of this group think they are contributing to the cause by posting comments and selective newspaper articles on Facebook to prop up their own personal agendas, they are mistaken. I spend two weeks a month putting together the newsletter. Where are all of you when I'm sitting alone at night toiling on your behalf? In addition, someone must give up their time to deal with the lawyers, go to the council meetings and spend days listening to inspectors deliberating over appeals,' lamented the almost ex-leader. Everyone around the table sat in silence. 'Organising a walk around the village with your dogs and carrying a couple of silly placards is not going to make a blind bit of difference.' The comment about the dogs touched a nerve, and the table erupted into a chorus of how dare you, and it's our right to protest.

'Ay-up. Trouble at t'mill,' whispered Pat Pollock as she gave her grandson Michael a gentle nudge.

'Ladies and Gentlemen, you might think you are the only people frequenting my establishment, but you are not. Please keep the voices down. Let my other punters enjoy themselves without having to listen to your squabbling,' commanded Sue Cooper. 'And don't you encourage them Mr Flynn,' she added wagging her finger at the journalist.

'But I .....,' exclaimed a surprised Hugh Flynn.

'Enough,' the landlady demanded holding up her hand for him to be silent, 'or you can leave right this minute.' Everyone at the table mouthed 'sorry' and looked at each other rather sheepishly, except for

Hugh Flynn who glared at the landlady, and wished the second plague of Egypt upon her pub.

Edward Broadhurst, unaware that a plague might be about to descend on the public house, slowly closed his feint and margin A4 refill pad, placed his pen neatly in the middle of it, and looked at the faces around the table.

'It has come to my attention that my membership of this protest group is frowned upon by a number of villagers. The reason? We have moved into a newly built house in Fields View, and I'm now trying to stop others from doing the same. On reflection, the dissenters are correct, and for that reason I no longer wish to be a member of this group,' announced the ex-almost of everything. Edward could hear his wife's voice spurring him on. 'If I'm guilty of stopping others from having a home to live in, then everyone sitting around this table are also guilty of the same thing.' Gasps of surprise around the table replaced the ensemble from *Les Miserable*. 'Yes, we live in a house on land that only a year ago were fields of wheat swaying gently in the breeze. We are privileged, just like all of you are,' said Edward sweeping his hand around the table, 'to have been able to move into a family home with a lovely garden. Something millions and millions of people in this country will never be able to achieve. I am not going to apologise, but it is unforgivable hypocrisy for us to deny others the opportunity to have somewhere decent to live.' *Go Edward, Go, the voice cheered him on*. Hugh Flynn sat up in his chair and started to pay attention.

'Hear, hear,' shouted Pat Pollock prodding the air with her walking stick. Her grandson was enjoying his nan's misbehaviour, and he punched the air a couple of times, shouting 'boom' at the top of his voice.

'Edward, we will never allow houses to be built on greenfield sites,' Jeremy blurted out. Hugh Flynn took out his notebook, and started to write.

'The greenfield sites are problematic, but I am sure a solution can be found. We have a housing crisis that this country has not seen for generations. We cannot ignore it, but protesting for protesting's sake will never work. You can already see it is not working. Every Tom, Dick and Harry is protesting across the country about greenfield sites, and yet houses are being built on those very sites. The protests are not working, and never will because we are protesting about the wrong things.' *My words exactly said the voice*. The protest table sat in silence, the rest of the pub sat in silence, and listened, and our journalist's pen ran out of ink.

'Sue, a pen, quick,' demanded the hack.

'The best thing that we can do for our children and grandchildren,' continued Edward standing up to address the pub, 'is to protest about the right things. It is not about houses on greenfield sites, but the lack of everything else a community needs. We have to protest until the developers are forced by law to give us the infrastructure to support the new housing, and close the loop-holes that allow them to abdicate their responsibility to provide affordable housing. And another thing. We also need age-friendly housing that is appropriate for the area in which they want to build the new houses.' Everyone in the pub nodded their heads vigorously in agreement. *Ok Edward don't overdo it. Less is more, advised his council.* Our journalist was struggling to keep up.

'Sue, quick, another beer,' pleaded Mr Flynn.

'Green fluorescent coloured pieces of paper in windows are not going to change anything. What I am advocating is years of hard, and at times confrontational campaigning. Get out there and get the laws changed.' *Don't mention the war, we don't have to fight them on the beaches cautioned the voice.* 'We need lots of houses, but we also need the infrastructure. As I mentioned earlier, due to the criticism, I no longer want to be a member of this protest group. I would like to wish my successor the best of luck, and will follow your progress with interest. Thank you for listening, and good luck.' Edward sat down and everyone in the pub gave him a round of applause. A few of the punters started to sing *For He's a Jolly Good Fella* and for some unknown reason followed it with *Auld Lang Sayne.*

Pat Pollock, leaning on her grandson's arm, walked slowly over to Edward.

'Well done Edward. You spoke out for the silent majority. Unfortunately, your wise words have probably fallen on deaf ears. Too much self-interest. Not surprising considering the example being set by the members of parliament. Anyway, you did well. For what it is worth we are fortunate to have someone like Charlotte running our school. Please don't take any notice of the gossip. You and your family are very welcome in our village.'

Edward thanked Pat for her kind words, and spent the remainder of the evening accepting the offer of a drink from well-wishers and ex-comrades-in-arms. After a few beers, he gave Hugh Flynn permission to print a story about the meeting in the next issue of *The Counties Herald.* As closing time approached, Sue Cooper arranged for Charlotte to come and collect her husband. She was rather disappointed at Edward's condition when she arrived at the pub. Her displeasure soon changed to pride when the landlady told her about Edward's speech, and the response he had received from the audience.

The Green Man meeting was duly reported in *The Counties Herald,* and two days later Edward received three phone calls; the first one was from a national newspaper, the second one was the regional television news and the third one was an invitation to a chat show hosted by a London based commercial radio station. Possibly this newcomer was about to put the village on the map, and become the long awaited famous son.

Moz and Chris Brown were standing at the edge of the patio looking out across the lawn towards the fields. It was an unusually warm evening for the time of year. The sun was low on the horizon, and the light filtered through the crops, illuminating the dust particles floating in the air. The valley was a haze of shimmering gold.

They watched a sparrowhawk, hovering above the hedgerow, and holding its position above the earth, as if it were a geostationary satellite. Spotting its prey, it dived at high speed into the undergrowth. A split second later, it lifted off from the target area with a small bird in its talons.

'That's impressive,' commented the policeman.

'Survival of the fittest,' replied Moz rather nonchalantly. The men stood in silence; the breathtaking view in front of them doing the talking.

'You know, Chris, our farm back home is flat and dusty, and there are no trees, just scrawny little thorn bushes. It is a hostile and harsh place to live. I suppose it has a beauty of its own, but it is so different to this.'

'Before I met Hanna, I had a somewhat townie attitude towards the countryside; you know, large mansions, weird people, and fox hunting. When we were called out for Hanna's Dad, I couldn't wait to get back to the city, and the bright lights,' remarked Chris. 'Hanna absolutely hates the place. She doesn't have a good word to say about it. The problem for me is, the more time I spend here, the less I want to go back to the city.'

'Does Hanna know how you feel?'

'Yes, but it doesn't seem to have changed her views.'

'To be quite honest, her life is in London, and it must be a real pain in the backside to have the burden of the farm. It'll sort itself out. Let's go inside, it's getting a bit chilly,' replied Moz.

'Kids, come to the table please,' called Elsa as she heard the patio door closing.

'Food, yummy,' said Paul as he ran into the dining room. He pulled a chair out next to his mother, and Bella sat down next to Hanna.

'Elsa, I hope kids includes Moz and I?' smiled Chris as he sat down, and took Hanna's hand.

'How about an honorary kid?' laughed Elsa. 'Help yourselves everyone.'

'Chris, Hanna, before we start eating, Els and I, and the kids, would like to congratulate you on your engagement, and wish you the very best for the future.' Moz raised his glass. 'To Chris and Hanna.' They clinked their glasses together, and the children boisterously emulated the grown-ups without breaking any glasses.

'Hanna, can I see your ring again, please,' asked Bella as she sat down.

'Of course you can,' laughed Hanna stretching out her left hand.

'It's beautiful. Why did Chris give it to you?'

'Because he loves me.'

'I hope someone gives me a ring one day.'

'Yugh,' intervened Paul.

'They will. Don't you worry,' replied Hanna giving Bella a hug. Moz and Elsa gave each other a parental great-we-still-have-that-to-look-forward-to look. 'While we're on the subject, Chris and I would like Paul and Bella to be our page boy and flower girl.'

'It's so kind of you to ask. I don't see why not. Moz?' The farmer nodded his head in agreement and smiled.

'Have you set a date yet?'

'We're looking at September, here in Weatherford,' replied the bride-to-be.

'That's lovely, Hanna. I can't wait,' replied Elsa. 'It's so exciting.'

'Hey kids, how was London?' asked Moz. Paul said the city was very 'streety'. Which made everyone laugh. He enjoyed the Changing of the Guard, and Bella said the ride on the London Eye was amazing. Chris started to tell the story of the horse at Horse Guard Arch who had nibbled a tourist, but was interrupted by an excited Paul who wanted to re-enact it. He mimed the part of the guard on the horse, and got his sister to stand in front of him as the tourist having the photo taken. Paul came quietly up behind Bella, who started to squeal in anticipation. Being shorter than his sister, he used his hands to reach up and pinch the back of her neck. Bella ran off screaming with pretend fright. The grown-ups clapped, and laughed.

'At least we didn't catch any wrong trains today,' said Hanna looking at Chris and starting to laugh. 'Tell them Chris.'

'I don't think I'm ever going to live this down. Hanna and I went to Paris a few weeks ago for the weekend. On the Monday there was a taxi driver strike in Paris, and we stupidly caught a bus to the station. It was late evening, and the city was completely gridlocked. Cutting a long story short, we were late, and I saw a train at one of the platforms and in the rush mistakenly thought it was for London. There was a guy standing on the platform dressed in a railway uniform. I pointed to the train and said

Londre, but he didn't reply, probably because we were English. We jumped on the train just as the doors closed,'

'It was the wrong train, wasn't it,' laughed Moz.

'Brussels,' laughed Chris. 'We got back to Paris four and a half hours later. The guys at work have put up two photos on the notice board; one of London with a great big tick and a cross through a photo of Brussels.'

'Great story, I like it,' laughed Moz.

'The scones are lovely, Elsa. Can I try the …melk…?' struggled Hanna.

'Melktart. It's baked custard with a cinnamon topping,' explained Elsa as she passed a slice over to the lawyer.

Paul and Bella started to get restless, and eventually Elsa despatched them upstairs to shower and get ready for bed. They gave Chris and Hanna a good night hug, and did as their mother had asked.

'I don't have any experience with young kids, but you guys can be proud of Paul and Bella,' commented Hanna when the children were out of earshot. 'Paul seems very mature for his age, and Bella is so girlie. Their enthusiasm is contagious,' she added.

'Ya, they have both been like that from day one,' commented an obviously pleased mother.

'While you guys were bonding out on the patio earlier, Elsa told me about the crime in South Africa,' said Hanna changing the subject and the mood.

'What sort of crime,' asked Chris.

'You name it. We've got it. Murder, armed robbery, carjackings, rape. It does depend on where you live, and sometimes it's just plain bad luck; wrong place, wrong time,' said Moz. 'The farming community, and that includes the workers, are an easy target,' he added.

'What about the police,' asked Chris.

'I think we have one of the largest police forces in the world, but the problem is the area that has to be protected is vast. I don't think they can really cope. The direct distance between the farm dwellings is probably about 15-20 kilometres. That's more than 10 miles. Living here in Weatherford, it's hard to imagine the distances involved. Most of the farms here are, what, a mile apart? Our greatest concern at the moment is for our elderly parents. They are very isolated, and exposed to danger all the time,' explained the research farmer.

'You know, Chris, it took us a few weeks to realise how safe England is compared to back home. The daily worry that something might happen has disappeared completely. You can go anywhere, at any time, day or night and not have to worry about a gun being shoved in your face. You guys are so lucky. You must appreciate what you have here,' commented a slightly emotional Elsa.

'It is something we noticed when Michael Beswick took us to the varsity rugby game at Twickenham in December. There was a good atmosphere between the police and the supporters. Plenty of joking and laughter. A couple of mounted policewoman were on duty. The spectators were stopping to stroke the horses and talk to the police officers. I don't know who were enjoying themselves more, the police or the horses. It was amazing, and not a gun in sight,' said Moz.

'It's a bit quiet upstairs, I wonder what the kids are up to,' Elsa said wanting to change the subject. Not surprisingly, brother and sister were fast asleep. When Elsa returned to the dining room, Moz and Chris were clearing the table.

'Chris and Hanna are heading home, Els,' announced Moz.

'Of course, you've had a long day. Thank you for giving the children such a wonderful time, and thank you for asking them to be your page boy and flower girl,' said the farmer's wife.

Moz stood at the front door with his arm around Elsa's shoulders and watched Chris and Hanna walk hand in hand towards their car.

'You know, Chris and Hanna probably have a much brighter future than our little Bella and Paul will have when they reach their age,' Elsa said quietly.

'Els, we are destined to walk through the valley of the shadow of death. All we have to do is maintain our faith; God will show us mercy,' said Moz looking into his wife's sad eyes.

'Moz, what are you talking about. Just for once stop the ecclesiastical drivel,' Elsa replied angrily, pushing her husband away from her. 'Show us mercy. When, Moz, when? God has certainly done a poor job of it up till now. How can we have faith, when all He has done is dish out the dirt when it comes to our people.'

CHAPTER 28

It is difficult to describe the sheer beauty of the English countryside in May. Almost overnight an invisible hand silently orchestrates the magical transformation of the damp grey winter trees and hedgerow into an interlude of blossoms and buds. The newly engaged couple were on their way to Weatherford, and sat silently enjoying the undulating countryside showing off its spring pageant.

'We've been talking about this weekend for ages,' commented Hanna.

'I'm really looking forward to it. I hope everyone gets on with each other,' replied Chris.

'No reason why they shouldn't. Have you noticed all the different hues of green? Everything always looks so fresh and clean at this time of year.' Chris glanced at Hanna and smiled. 'Talking of which, I'm very pleased that Andrew MacGregor has agreed to help manage the farm. It gives me a bit more time to think about what I'm going to do with it. I guess the wedding is at the top of the to do list.'

'How many rsvps have we got so far.'

'35,' replied Hanna.

'And we sent out,....?' asked Chris trying to remember the exact number of invitations.

'40,' replied Hanna, slightly impatiently.

'God, these roads are so narrow.'

'They're more than adequate. Stop being a ninny,' replied Hanna laughing.

'What are these white flowers growing along the roadside?' asked Chris wincing as an oncoming car flashed by.

'Cow Parsley,' replied Hanna. 'It's beautiful isn't it? It grows every year next to the roads, but I cannot ever remember seeing so much of it. Maybe it's enjoying the warm weather.'

'It all looks so different to when I was here in October,' commented the policeman. 'The leaves coming out, the green fields, sunshine, blue skies.'

'I have to say it is a lovely time of year. Prince Harry and Meghan certainly chose a lovely day didn't they?' commented Hanna.

'I suppose you girls are going to watch it on the telly.'

'Oh, yes,' came back the quick reply.

'Can't see what all the excitement is about.'

'It's a lovely thing to watch. The clothes, the pageantry, the crowds going crazy, and of course the romance,' replied Hanna.

'Yeh, my Mum has been going mental about it for weeks. She says it's not pretend like Disneyland, and we are the only country in the world that knows how to put on a real parade,' said Chris smiling. 'She'll buy a copy of *Hello Magazine*, and look at the photos for months. Trouble is she will want us all to look at the photos as well.'

'God, you men are such Neanderthals,' teased Hanna. The policeman smiled, and shook his head.

'35 rsvps. That's actually not a bad response. There's still almost 5 months to go,' said Chris restarting the conversion about the wedding. 'What do you think Han?'

'I'm very pleased. 75 people is enough,' replied the solicitor. 'Are you still ok for us to stop here at the church?'

'You don't have to ask,' replied Chris looking across at his fiancée and squeezing her hand.

Chris pulled up outside the church, and parked in the shade of the enormous beech trees. Hanna looked up at the church tower, and remembered how angry she had been at her father's funeral. Standing in the sunshine next to Chris, she felt much calmer, although the determination to find out why he had killed himself was as strong as ever. Chris held the lych-gate open for her, and the two of them walked hand-in-hand passed the church entrance, and avoiding the clumps of bluebells, made their way towards the far corner of the church yard.

Hanna's parents are buried next to each other, and without saying anything their daughter placed a bunch of brightly coloured flowers on each grave. She stood looking down at the gravestones, and tears started to roll down her cheeks. Chris put his arms around her, and struggling to keep back the tears, held Hanna against him. They stood for a few minutes in the silent churchyard, holding each other tightly.

'I'm ok Chris. Let's go. Thank you for coming with me.'

'How does it feel to be back?' asked Chris, as they stopped outside the Grey Pigeon farmhouse.

'My whole life has changed, but none of this is any different. It's still the same. So familiar,' replied Hanna getting out of the car. 'It's as if time has stood still,' she commented as she looked around at her childhood home. Hanna unlocked the front door, and Chris put their overnight bags down just inside the entrance, and went back outside to where Hanna was standing looking at the house.

'I'm pleased I changed my mind about Dave Wright painting the outside. It looks so much better,' said Hanna nodding her head in approval. 'He phoned me one day to say the window frames were in need of some urgent tlc. He arranged for one of his carpenter mates to come and repair the frames before he painted them. They look brand new.'

'This is the first house with a thatched roof that I have seen from close up,' commented Chris. 'It's amazing to think its waterproof.'

'Unfortunately, it's in need of repair. I cannot really remember when it was last done. I've had a thatcher come and look at it for me. The problem is I'm out of my depth. I know nothing about thatch roofs. Apparently the ridging and cement flashings need redoing, and the thatch has be dressed and brushed,' said Hanna.

'I guess it's expensive,' commented Chris.

'Yeh, I'll have to wait until the harvest is in,' replied the farmer's daughter. 'I also need some time to brush up on my thatching knowledge. I'm sure there is something on Y*ouTube* that will be of help. The other problem is there are not many master thatchers around anymore. It's hard physical work, and the youngsters are not interested.'

With Hanna tucked in under Chris's arm, they walked around the outside of the house, passed the garden shed, to what Chris remembered was an unkempt garden.

'Andrew has done a great job, here,' said a delighted Hanna. 'He's painted the summer house, and tidied up the garden. I hope we get some rain.'

'The whole property look's much better than when I first saw it,' commented Chris. 'I don't think the dark, damp, winter weather helped much; it looked like a haunted house.'

'We have a witch living next door.'

'How do you know?' Chris stopped and looked at Hanna who was shaking her head and laughing. 'Pisstaker,' said Chris as he put his arms around her waist, and lifting her off her feet, kissed her. Hanna didn't object.

'Let's take a look at the view.' suggested Chris, as he put Hanna back down on the ground. He recalled the first time he had looked out over the fields, and how the view had mesmerized him. They stood in the gap in the hedge, holding hands and looking out over the fields.

'This view is like you, Hanna. Beautiful,' said Chris.

'Wow, someone's getting soppy,' replied Hanna as she hugged her policeman.

'Why is there no wheat growing in that field over there,' asked Chris pointing to his right.

'That's the so-called contaminated field. It's just over 200 acres, and the curved boundary on the far side is the line of the old railway line from Blacktree Crossing.'

'Ok, so that's the field your dad stopped cultivating.'

'Yes. He appears to have given up trying to grow anything in that field. It's the field that he was convinced was being sabotaged by Kettering-Smythe, the developers or both,' explained Hanna.

'It would be a major exercise to contaminate such a large area without someone noticing,' commented Chris.

'Absolutely. That's why there are so many unanswered questions. I'm still convinced my dad was right about KS. The question is how did he do it? I just wish we had a suicide note.'

'That Dudley is being a right old pain.'

'Why what's he doing?' asked Hanna smiling. The friends were in the kitchen and Hanna was making a green salad, while Cassie was sorting out the tortillas and dips.

'He's following me around like a puppy,' replied Cassie picking up a carrot and loudly snapping the end off with her teeth. 'He keeps on trying to chat me up.'

'Cassie, I told you months ago that he fancies you,' laughed Hanna.

'Cas, are you enjoying yourself? Can I refresh your drink?' Cassie mimicked as she unsuccessfully tried to impersonate her unwanted suitor.

'For heaven sake, Cassie. Relax girl. Enjoy yourself. You're always moaning that you don't have a man in your life. He's fit, though not as fit as my Chris; handsome….'

'But not as handsome as *your* Chris,' sneered Cassie.

'I've been watching you, Miss butter-wouldn't-melt-in-your-mouth. You've been making a play for him from the minute he arrived.' Cassie could feel herself blushing.

'No I haven't,' she replied indignantly. Dudley and Alexis' wife Judith came into the kitchen with Victor, her son, taking up the rear with some high speed crawling. Cassie started to blush again.

'Cassie bring your drink, I want to show you the sunset,' invited Dudley.

'That's a lovely idea. Off you two go. I'll finish up here,' encouraged Hanna. Cassie glared at her friend. 'Thanks Dudley, I'll have a refill,' said Hanna looking at her friend, and mouthing the instruction 'Go'.

With drinks topped-up, Dudley and Cassie went out into the garden. Chris had lit the barbeque and it was producing more smoke than flame. Alexis was enthusiastically fanning the column of smoke with a newspaper which only seemed to make matters worse.

'Chris, I don't think Alexis has barbequed before. Good luck, mate,' laughed Dudley. Dudley's colleague responded by hitting him on the back with the rolled up newspaper. 'Just want to show Cassie the sunset, then I'll come over and give you chaps a hand.'

The two barbequers watched Dudley and Cassie walk towards the bottom of the garden.

'Get your coat Cassie, you've been pulled,' murmured Alexis.

'Looks like it,' responded Chris.

'She's lucky. Dudley's a good person to have on your side,' remarked Alexis.

Dudley and Cassie went through the gap in the hedge and stopped at the edge of the fields. The huge red disc of a sun was balancing on the horizon, and the thin wispy high cirrus cloud had taken on the burning red colour of the setting sun.

'Now that's something you don't see living in the city,' commented Dudley.

'I'm outside almost every day, but seldom at this time of the evening. It is an amazing sight,' added Cassie looking up at two aircraft silently etched out pink coloured condensation trails as they sped northwards towards the darkness. 'I would imagine you get some spectacular views of the full moon out here,' added Cassie moving closer to Dudley and linking arms with him.

'Not to mention the stars,' he added.

'Dudley, I've been thinking. I'm heading out after breakfast tomorrow to collect Hanna's soil and water samples. Would you like to keep me company?'

'Would I just,' replied Dudley. 'I've always been interested in agronomy.'

'So that's a yes then,' Cassie replied and gave him a light kiss on the cheek.

'Sealed with a kiss. Let's get back to those two alpha-males before they burn the house down,' laughed a very happy young man.

The early sunrise woke Victor, who promptly announced to the rest of the household that it was time to get out of bed. When the human cockerel started to cry, Alexis was already sitting in the lounge, with a mug of tea, watching a cooking programme hosted by a minor celebrity with major botox. His two over-excited guests were overdoing the enthusiasm as they tried their hand at a poached egg on a bed of spinach.

'Judging by how thin that guest is, it looks as if it's the first time she's been in a kitchen,' remarked Cassie as she momentarily stopped to look at the tv.

'Not very pc Cassie,' said Alexis smiling.

'Well there are a lot of people who will disagree with you, Alexis,' responded Cassie. 'There are a number of countries that have banned the fashion houses from using skinny models. The advertising industry will be next. It's about reducing eating disorders, and I think it is the right thing to do.'

'It's the first time I've heard about banning the models,' replied Alexis slightly taken aback at Cassie's forthrightness. Hanna and Chris came into the lounge, and sat down on the two seater sofa.

'You guys ok?' asked Hanna sensing tension in the air. 'It was a bit muggy last night. Took me ages to go to sleep,' she continued.

'Chris's snoring?' asked Dudley having caught the end of the conversation as he entered the room.

'Speak for yourself, Dudley,' replied Chris. Judith, carrying a grouchy Victor on her hip, joined the group.

'I really must feed this little monster,' said the mother. Chris looked up and waved at Victor who totally ignored the greeting.

'Judith are you ok? Your eyes have puffed up,' asked Dudley.

'It's hayfever. It started during the night. It's making me feel dreadful,' replied a miserable Judith.

'I don't think we have any anti-histamine in the house. We'll have to go over to Great Dunsford after breakfast. There's a chemist there that opens for a few hours on a Sunday, explained Hanna. I'll check on my phone what time it opens.'

'Ok chaps, who's ready for breakfast. A fry-up?' asked Dudley.

Hanna and Cassie assisted Chef Dudley by putting out the cereals, milk and sugar on the kitchen table, and Dudley having taken everyone's orders started to cook breakfast of fried eggs, bacon, sausage, black pudding, mushrooms and tomato. Victor was strapped into his high chair, and was enthusiastically eating porridge and honey.

'Very domesticated,' remarked Cassie as Dudley gave everyone their requested breakfasts.

'Cas, don't get too excited. I'm a one trick pony when it comes to cooking. The full monty, and boiling the kettle is about it,' replied Dudley gently roughing up Cassie's hair. While Cassie irritatingly re-arranged her hair with her fingers, Hanna and Judith brought in the hot drinks.

'Question for Dudley and Alexis,' said Hanna as she sat down at the table. 'How do you think Brexit is going to affect farming?' Victor started laughing and banging a spoon on his chair tray.

'Well my son thinks it's a bit of a joke,' laughed Alexis. Victor looked at the laughing grown-ups, and unsure as to whether or not it was safe to continue, stopped banging on the furniture.

'Dudley and I have slightly differing views on it,' continued Alexis. 'I voted to stay. It didn't turn out that way, and it is as it is. The thing that worries me is the lack of progress with the negotiations. The Europeans seem to think we'll change our minds. They appear to be stalling in the hope that either the withdrawal is too difficult, and we lose interest or they are hoping that there's going to be a change of Prime Minister, government or the referendum result will somehow just disappear. In my opinion, it is imperative that we secure a long-term agricultural deal with the EU, but at the moment I don't think it's going to happen,' said Alexis shaking his head. Everyone turned and looked at Dudley in anticipation.

'I also voted to remain. What frustrates me is so many of the remain politicians haven't accepted the fact that the people voted to leave. Someone needs to explain the first-past-the post concept to them. We are a great country and have only been in the common market a short while. Before that we traded successfully for thousands of years with the rest of the world, and we will do it again. Despite all the scare stories and misinformation in the media, and Radio 4 who, in the run-up to the referendum, treated it all as one big joke, I am confident that there will be a settlement. Having said that, I think we should stay, but the people have voted, and leaving the EU will not change the fact that farming will continue, farms will still be bought and sold, food will be grown, and people will continue to eat.'

'Well if we leave, I hope they start making light bulbs that when you switch the lights on, you can actually read and write after dark,' commented Judith.

'Second that,' added Alexis.

'What I want to know, is what are they going to do with all those curved cucumbers,' smiled Dudley. The group laughed, and then voted in favour of Dudley doing the washing up as a penance for being a plonker.

'Are we going to walk?' asked Dudley as he trotted along behind Cassie. He was wearing a well-worn panama hat that Hanna had found in one of the bedroom cupboards.

'You can if you like. I'm taking the van,' replied the agronomist turning to the   love-struck puppy following her. She looked up at Dudley and trying her best not to laugh, burst out laughing. He tipped his hat, and started to sing *'under the broadwalk, we will be falling in love, under the broad walk, broadwalk'*.

'You'll be so lucky,' replied Cassie. 'Are you walking or coming with me?' she asked getting into her van and starting it. Not wanting to miss the opportunity to sit in a confined space with the agronomist, Dudley quickly folded his tall frame into the passenger seat. He knocked off his hat against the doorframe, and was left trying to put it back on and close the door as Cassie impatiently reversed the van.

'Christ, it's like taking part in a bloody rodeo,' exclaimed Dudley hurriedly putting on his seatbelt.

The little van headed out of Weatherford towards Wolburn Market.

'Have you ever taken samples from this farm before,' asked a breathless Dudley.

'No. I don't actually do any work in this area. My patch is mainly the south east of England,' replied Cassie looking across at a rather flustered Dudley. 'Ok, this should be far enough, we'll park here.' Cassie opened the back of the van and took out a small folding table on which she placed a map. 'Find me a couple of stones to help hold down the map.' Dudley eagerly collected four pieces of flint and placed them at each corner of the map. He looked up and caught Cassie's eye.

'Cassie, you do fancy me just a little bit, don't you?'

'Dudley, it's not a question of like or dislike. You are a lot of fun, and you obviously have feelings for me. I get it. It's just me, really. I've been on my own for so long, and the thought of sharing my life with someone else is a bit frightening.'

'I guess it is not really what I wanted to hear, but I understand.'

'Hanna told me last night that Chris had said that Alexis had told him that you were a good person to have on side. Let's get to know each other better. Let's not force the issue.'

'I'm more than happy to give it a try,' replied Dudley. 'Give us a hug.' The two stood on the edge of the wheat fields, in the blazing sun, and hugged. Dudley kissed Cassie on the forehead, and squeezed her tightly.

'Ok, enough of this. Let's get to work,' announced the agronomist turning back to the map. 'This is Grey Pigeon Farm, and here is the field that is causing the problems,' explained Cassie marking out an area on the map with a felt tipped pen. 'When you compare the fields that look normal, and compare them with the lack of growth in our problem field, it's obvious that there's something wrong,' she continued turning away from the map and pointing at the fields. 'From now until the harvest, the plants will be working pretty hard. They capture solar energy, water and carbon dioxide and convert it into an edible form of energy. The better the capture, the greater the yield,' explained Cassie.

'And I guess this is what you do. Monitor the crops' progress,' remarked Dudley with a smile.

'Exactly. May is the start of an important last few months. We monitor for diseases, pests, and the condition of the soil,' continued Cassie. 'The plants draw nitrogen, phosphorus and potassium from the soil in order to grow properly. So part of the job is to decide if the plants need any extra nutrients added to the soil,' concluded Cassie.

'Surely Hanna's dad must have known something was wrong?' remarked Dudley.

'He knew there was something wrong about three years ago, but from what Hanna has told me, he lost interest and gave up on the farm after her mum died.

'Quite understandable,' remarked Dudley.

'Things were made worse when the house building started. Hanna says her dad started having this conspiracy theory about his fields being deliberately contaminated,' continued Cassie.

'The value of the land for farming goes down, but makes the land cheaper to acquire for house-building,' smiled Dudley nodding his head.

'What we have to do is get a representative sample of the field. It's a big field so it's going to take a while to complete. Let's drive over and take a look,' suggested Cassie.

'You must do a far bit of walking, Cassie,' said Dudley as they bumped over the uneven ground.

'Well there's certainly no need to go to a gym,' replied the agronomist. 'When I first started I kept a tally of the miles I walked. At the height of the season, it was about 3 miles per farm.'

'That's a fair old distance. If I'm not sitting at my desk, I'm sitting in my car travelling to clients,' commented Dudley. 'You don't realise that there are people out there with very physical jobs. I suppose it's ok when you're young, but I wonder if folk with those types of jobs will make the state retirement age of 66,' he added. 'If they don't, the scheme will land up with a contributions shortfall.'

'Funny you should say that, we were discussing the very same thing in the office a couple of weeks ago. The general consensus was it is highly unlikely that a field agronomist would work 'til 66 because it's so physical. It's also outdoors which makes it even more difficult. Technology might help. I recently did a course about using drones to monitor the crops. A drone could be used to scan the crops on a daily basis, and that information can be enhanced using artificial intelligence to select specific areas for field walking. There are a few issues that need to be sorted out; the drone can only fly line-of-sight which means it cannot go up and down dale, and the other problem is how do you make sure it doesn't fly into people and buildings and the like.'

'How do you know an agronomist has visited your farm?' asked Dudley.

'When do you know?' replied Cassie looking at her passenger and smiling.

'Remains of a drone dangling from the electricity pylons.'

'Cheeky sod,' laughed Cassie. 'Ok, this will do. Let's stop here.'

Victor was playing in a galvanised bath that Chris had found in the garden shed. He had filled it with a couple of inches of water, and Alexis' young son, armed with a couple of plastic cups and a saucepan was happily playing in the cool shade of the unusually large goat willow in the front garden. He poured water into the saucepan using one of the mugs; poured water over the side of the bath and leant over to look at his handy work; poured water over his head, coughed and spluttered, and looked surprised. He stopped for a moment and watched Cassie and Dudley walking across the lawn towards the group.

'The two of you look as if you've run a marathon,' commented Hanna.

'It's a bit warm out there,' puffed a red faced Dudley. There was a jug of ice cold orange squash on the table; he poured two glasses, and gave one to Cassie who had flopped down in a deckchair in the shade. Dudley downed his drink in one go. 'Aaahh, that hit the spot. OK chaps, I'm off to have a cold shower. See you in a mo.'

'Well, Cas what do you think?' asked Hanna.

'It really doesn't take an expert to see that there is definitely something wrong with that field. The strange thing is the damage is confined to a specific area,' commented the agronomist. 'It's fairly uniform and consistent, so we took samples from about one quarter of the area. We also took a few water samples from the stream on the northern boundary. It's some distance from the damaged land, and there isn't much water in it due to the dry weather, but it will tell us if there has been any runoff from the contaminated field,' explained Cassie as she poured herself another glass of squash.

'So the damage being confined to a specific area could indicate someone has deliberately targeted that piece of land?' asked Hanna.

'The two are not necessarily mutually inclusive,' replied Cassie. 'Let's wait for the test results. I'm sure we will get a definitive answer from the samples.'

'Hi chaps, what's occurin',' asked Dudley as he re-joined the group and sat down at the garden table. 'How're you feeling Judith? It looks like the puffiness has gone down a bit.'

'Much better thanks, Dudley. Chris and Alexis went to the chemist and got me anti-histamine. I've managed to make us lunch, so I must be feeling better,' she replied.

'A 14 mile drive; 7 there and 7 back,' exclaimed Chris. 'And those ridiculously narrow roads the whole way,' he protested for Hanna's benefit.

'Shopping must be a nightmare if you live out here in the country,' commented Judith. 'Travelling those long distances on such windy roads just to buy groceries must be a right pain. What happens if you forget something or just need one item? I'm really surprised the village doesn't have a few basic shops. How do people cope with the day-to-day stuff?'

'It is difficult, and there isn't a bus either. When my dad was a boy, the village did have a fully functioning high street, but it has all disappeared and will never return. There is a little shop at the garage if you need a tin of beans or a loaf of bread,' explained Hanna. 'And another thing is, we get cut off from the rest of the country when it snows. They grit the major roads, but the ones around here are a low priority, and by the time they get around to gritting us the sun's shining again and the snow's melted.'

'If I may change the subject. Alexis have you and Hanna discussed the farm?' asked Dudley.

'Yes, we did my friend. While you were out courting amongst the fields and impressing Cassie with your stunning panama hat, Hanna and I had a serious chat about the farm,' replied the bag-a-bargain partner. Hanna glanced at Cassie, who was scowling at Alexis, and smiled.

'And?' asked the other bag-a-bargain partner.

'Well it is a good size tract of land. 300 acres. It has a substantial farmhouse and outbuildings. Both could do with a bit of tlc. Very similar to that farm we sold in Hertfordshire a few months back.' Dudley nodded his head in agreement. 'Without seeing the farm's agricultural performance, I'd say it is worth £3 million before taking into account the contamination issue.' Chris looked at Hanna with wide-eyed surprise.

'Sorry to interrupt. Chris would you give me a hand with the food please,' asked Judith.

'If the bean counters are correct, the sale of the farm pays off the debt. But, and there's always a but,' continued Alexis. 'How much is left over after settling the debt will depend on the Lord Chancellor's two henchmen Inheritance Tax and Capital Gains Tax.'

'Can the contaminated land be sorted,' asked Chris returning with bowls of food.

'Normally it can,' answered Cassie. 'It does depend on the type of contamination, how deep it goes and if there has been any seepage into the underground watercourses. The clean-up is possible, but it will be expensive,' explained the agronomist.

'The trouble is this raises more questions than answers,' commented Hanna.

'I agree with you, Hanna,' replied Dudley. 'I think keeping the farm going in the short-term whilst you make a decision, is a good call. If you decide to sell, you should have some change over after settling the bills. The more difficult decision is if you decide not to sell. Keeping it means you'll still have to find the money to pay off the debt. Not impossible, but not ideal,' concluded Dudley.

'Ok, everyone, let's eat,' announced Judith as she put a jug of orange squash on the large garden table. 'There's also fizzy drink in the fridge,' she added. Victor, seeing his dad bring out the high-chair, knew it was time to end his spa treatment and hurriedly half staggered, half crawled towards the grown-ups.

Judith had prepared bowl food for everyone. Using thinly sliced meat from the bbq, she had added olive oil, garlic, pepper, chilli and stir-fried everything in a jerk sauce. It was served up on a bed of basmati rice, and decorated with slices of raw sweet red and yellow peppers. The group fell silent as they tucked into Judith's creation.

'You could always start a glamping business,' said Dudley suddenly breaking the cuisine silence.

'What?' spluttered Hanna as the table burst out laughing.

'Glamping,' repeated Dudley.

'Dudley, you cannot be serious. How can you trivialise Hanna's situation by being so flippant. I suppose your next idea will be a themed Harry Potter Hotel,' said Cassie chastising her would like-to-be-her boyfriend.

'What is glamping?' asked Chris rather sheepishly.

'Camping but with all the luxuries of home,' replied Cassie.

'I can understand wanting to get out into the country if you live in a big city, but why would you want the luxuries of home?' asked the bemused detective.

'It's just camping by another name. It's all the rage at the moment,' remarked Judith.

'So what's the attraction?' continued a bemused Chris.

'If you go glamping, you don't take your own tent along,' continued Judith.

'And?' asked Chris.

'There is no and. It's just camping. You still end up being surrounded by mud. You still have to take a shower in a less than glamourous communal lean-to. And why do these eco-warriors, who run these places, insist on toilets without any running water. The Romans who visited these shores 2,000 years ago had toilets with running water, for God's sake. And another thing, what is so glamorous about carrying your plates, cutlery and food, quarter of a mile in the rain, down a muddy path, that has been half-heartedly cleared by the owners, to a communal eating tent. When you get there you have to start a fire before you can even have a cup of tea. And they think providing a fire pit makes up for the total inconvenience. I can't understand why people are so stupid. Some of these glamping sites charge hundreds and hundreds of pounds a night, and you get absolutely nothing for your money. It is a total rip-off,' ranted Judith. It was the most Judith had said the whole weekend, and everyone sat in stunned silence; completely surprised at the outburst.

'So you're not a fan then,' joked Dudley.

'I think it's a case of *The Emperor's New Clothes*,' said Alexis.

'How do you mean,' asked Cassie.

'I think there are a lot of people who do things just for show. There's this desperation to show off how cool and on-trend they are to friends and colleagues. They go glamping, pay an extortionate amount of money to do it, and discover it is dreadful. Unfortunately their egos prevent them from breaking away from the herd or is it lemmings, and simply tell the truth. There's no glamour, it is just very expensive camping with below standard facilities,' explained Alexis.

'It's like the recent cycling craze,' continued Dudley. 'Everyone suddenly started cycling to work, stinking of sweat, and walking around the office in lycra and sunglasses with a John Wayne bow-legged gait. Cycling was the only topic of conversation, particularly how much had been spent on equipment. And now, four years later, and despite the BBC proclaiming that cycling was the latest and greatest family past-time, most of the pelotons have disappeared. Tackling the Alps is not mentioned anymore, and all those absent dad's on their bicycles at weekends have been reunited with their families.'

'There's nowt so queer as folk,' concluded Alexis with a smile.

'We'll all drink to that, Alexis,' said Chris raising his glass of squash.

'Changing the subject totally, how are the wedding preparations coming along, Hanna?' asked Judith.

'Quite well, thanks. Chris and I were talking about the rsvps on the way up here yesterday. Looks like we'll have about 75 people. Kay Beswick has offered us her newly refurbished barn for the reception, and Lizzie Turner is doing the catering. We've had to change the time of the wedding ceremony. Bit of a nuisance seeing the invitations went out two weeks ago.'

'Sounds like a typical wedding, hardly ever goes according to plan,' remarked Judith in her usual up-beat manner.

Victor had, for a toddler strapped in a chair, been remarkably quiet and content throughout the grown-ups' fascinating discussion about the nuances of group psychology. He had however, made a terrible mess of himself and his lunch. Some of the food had found his mouth, some of it was a badly applied face-mask, and the remainder had either been spread around the chair-tray or dropped over the side onto the grass below. He eventually tired of trying to master the life skill of eating with a spoon, and started to wriggle and shriek.

'He's probably a bit tired, he needs a nap,' remarked Judith unstrapping her son.

'I guess it's time to head off home, guys,' added Alexis.

Within half an hour the weekend gathering had dissipated. Victor could be heard wailing as Judith and Alexis headed off down the drive in their newly acquired white SUV. Dudley and Cassie helped clean up the kitchen and, with a parting hug and a kiss on each cheek, the couple went their separate ways. Chris and Hanna put the remaining garden furniture away in the shed, and securing the farmhouse, loaded Hanna's overnight bag and Chris's backpack into the boot of Chris' car. They were just about to get into the car, when a white brilliantly white overall, a white wide brimmed hat and veil, and in each hand a stainless steel canister blowing out plumes of smoke came walking up the drive.

'That's Rob Beresford, the beekeeper,' said Hanna heading off down the drive to meet the visitor. She was pleased to see the long-standing family friend, and from where Chris was standing he could see the feeling was mutual. They stood for a while exchanging pleasantries, and Hanna managed to embarrass Chris by introducing him as my handsome police detective, the police services' finest.'

Rob had come to ask Hanna if she objected to him moving his beehives into the echium fields in the neighbouring farm. With the promise of a jar of echium honey for her kindness, she agreed.

'The family's eaten Rob's honey since time began,' remarked Hanna as they headed off home along London Road. 'Do you know what's the correct name for a beekeeper?

'No idea,' replied Hanna's handsome police detective.

'An apiarist,' smiled Hanna.

CHAPTER 29

Due to the nature of his work, Hugh Flynn did not spend much time at *The Counties Herald* office. Today however, he had been placed under office arrest by his boss, Ken Baker. It took a lot to rile the journalist, but today the old hack was hacked off.

A week previously he had received a tipoff that there had been an aircraft accident at Oak Tree Farm. With only five hours to the printing deadline, he had dashed over to Weatherford, written the copy, and sent it to his boss all within three hours of receiving the call. The newspaper editor was thrilled with the scoop, and cancelled the front page article about a council meeting. An aircraft crash was far more of a lead story than the council's recent discussion about the effectiveness of double yellow lines in the town.

Hugh's newly won brownie points did not last long. His next job was to investigate the theft of outdoor gym equipment at Bistlebury. He was not impressed.

'Boss, can't one of the juniors take this one. It's such a trivial story?' he remonstrated.

'All busy, Hugh. In any chase I'll decide what's trivial and what isn't, old boy,' replied the boss.

'I give him a scoop, and this is the how he rewards me,' muttered the journalist as he stomped down the stairs. He opened the door as far as it would go. Bloody newspapers.

Bistlebury is five miles out of town on the Cambridge road. The journey through the gentle countryside gave Hugh the opportunity to calm down, and by the time he arrived at the crime scene, he was his old self again.

The village green was deserted, and the area next to the community centre, where the equipment had once stood, was cordoned off with black and yellow hazard tape. He took a photograph of the cricket pitch, and another of the cordoned off crime scene. Where's Wally the Mayor when you need a statement of indignant condemnation. He's missed this photo opportunity thought the journalist smiling to himself. With nobody to interview, Hugh left his suit jacket in the car, and walked back to the road in the blazing sun. He knocked on a couple of doors.

'What gym equipment?' was the response from the first resident.

'Don't surprise me. Bloody Londoners. Moving into the brand new houses,' was the community spirited reply from the neighbour.

'It's to be expected. You never see the police around here,' was the upbeat contribution from the third resident as a passing 20 tonne lorry almost blew the journalist through the open front door into the house. 'And that's another thing. What's the point of speed limits, when nobody takes any notice of them.'

He tried a couple more doors, but there was no reply at either. The overheating journalist lost interest, and returned to his car. With the air conditioning on full cold, he opened his laptop. This is a complete waste of time thought the perspiring journalist.

Hugh Flynn very seldom experienced writer's block. He sat in the cooling car, looking at the laptop screen with his hands resting lightly on the keyboard. His mind was a complete blank. He had no idea how to start the article nor what to write. He ignored the telephone calls and the texts from his boss. They were a distraction. After a lengthy standoff, a text which included the word P45 brought him to his senses.

Having returned to the office, at the eloquent request of Ken Baker, the dejected hack sat at his desk desperately trying to clear his writer's blockage. He had managed to type a couple of sentences containing a string of clichés and sound bites that had some relevance to the stealing of outdoor gym equipment. His mobile rang.

'Hugh Flynn,'

'Good morning Hugh, it's Hanna Townsend. Alistair Burns contacted me and said you wanted to talk to me.'

'Yes, yes. Thanks for calling back. I'm at my desk. I need to find somewhere a bit more private. Hang on a sec,' replied the journalist as he made his way over to the empty meeting room, and closed the door. 'Still there, Hanna?'

'Yes, I'm here Hugh.'

'A few months ago, my boss and I were discussing your dad's unfortunate death.'

'Hugh, if I may stop you right there,' interrupted Hanna. 'There are still many questions about my father's death that have not yet been answered. There is, however, one thing I do not want, and that's your one penny rag meddling in my family's tragedy,' responded Hanna.

'Hanna I totally understand, and I can assure you that we're not meddling in your family's business. It involves the contaminated fields on your farm,' replied the hack.

'Carry on,' replied Hanna after a brief moment of silence.

'My boss grew up in this area, and he couldn't recall there being any crop contamination incidents. We looked into it, and we found one occurrence back in the 1960s. It was caused by aviation fuel. He asked me to investigate the story.'

'Ok Hugh. That's very interesting, but what has it got to do with my father's death?' asked a bewildered Hanna.

'My boss had a hunch, and he sent me down to Wandsworth to visit the US Embassy.'

'So what did you find?' asked Hanna impatiently.

'The embassy was very helpful. They gave me limited access to documents and information, and more importantly, there were a number of people I spoke to who were of the opinion that Ken's hunch could be right,' continued the journalist.

'Well, what was the hunch,' asked Hanna curtly.

'As you know, during the Second World War, the Americans built aerodromes all over our county. They had a logistics bridgehead at Blacktree Crossing, and ran an aviation pipeline from Blacktree along the route of the railway line to Weatherford, and further west to other USAAF bases,' explained Hugh.

'The old railway that ran along the boundary of the farm,' Hanna said quietly.

'The very same,' replied Hugh. 'Storage tanks were also placed at intervals along the pipeline so that the aerodromes could manage their own supply and demand,' added the journalist.

'So the Americans are saying that there is still aviation fuel in those pipes and tanks?' asked a surprised Hanna.

'Hanna, for obvious reasons they would not admit to anything. The official line is that all equipment was dealt with appropriately when they pulled out of England, and headed for Europe,' explained Hugh.

'So you're saying there is an American cover-up,' Hanna said raising her voice slightly.

'No, not at all. The officials I spoke to were extremely helpful. They said in principal they are willing to investigate this further, and assured me that they would try and assist you. Obviously they have a chain of command, and appropriate authority will have to be obtained,' continued the journalist.

'I cannot believe this.' Hugh could hear Hanna was crying. 'My dad was convinced there was deliberate tampering going on. He gave up living, he gave up trying, it destroyed him. If this American thing is true, he killed himself for no reason,' sobbed Hanna.

Give me a call when you have a mo. I have the soil sample results. Cas. XX.
I already know. It's aviation fuel. Hanna. XX.

Hanna had no sooner sent the text when the phone rang.

'How the hell do you know that?' asked the surprised agronomist. Hanna told her friend about the conversation with Hugh Flynn, and how devastated she was at hearing the news about the aviation fuel. She told Cassie how, since hearing the news, she had been tormented by the thought that her father had killed himself for nothing. All she wanted to do was bring him back, and tell him that everything was going to be ok. She was crying and sobbing so much that Cassie could hardly hear what her friend was saying. 'Hanna, I don't think you should be on your own,' said Cassie between sobs.

'I'll be fine, Cassie. Chris will be here just after tea,' replied Hanna sniffing loudly. 'I'm so sorry. I'm being so selfish. Tell me about the results.'

Cassie explained to her friend that they had found that the majority of the samples showed traces of aviation gasoline, commonly known as avgas. She went on to say that they had identified the fuel as being 100/150 octane. It was the type of fuel that was used during the first half of the Second World War, and from what Hanna had told her, Hugh Flynn was probably correct.

'The white coats at the lab were a bit baffled as to how this old type of fuel could have got there,' said Cassie. 'What are the chances that we would find the answer so quickly. It is so random.'

'The trouble is I'm not sure where I go with this,' commented Hanna. 'I've made such a spectacle of myself. Ranting and raving at KS; accusing him of wrongdoing towards dad. It is so embarrassing. I keep on asking myself the same question over and over again. Did my father just make a terrible mistake?'

Hanna was so nervous that she felt she was going to be sick. The swaying of the newly refurbished northbound train to Wolburn Market was not helping the situation, and she tried to take her mind off the nausea by concentrating on the view rushing past the window.

Hanna's absolute conviction that KS and the developers had deliberately sabotaged the crops made the truth even more difficult to comprehend. Chris had in his usual calm and measured way tried to convince her that she was not responsible for her father's death. Yes, she had carried a torch for him, but that was to be expected.

He had suggested that she go and see KS and apologise. At first, she was absolutely adamant that she was not going to do it. Hell will have to freeze over first. Never, never, never, she raged. Chris held her in his arms and comforted her. It is what she needed; reassurance that she did not have to cope with this unexpected setback alone.

Her fiancé gently persevered about the apology. He pointed out to her, that the source of the problem was the lack of cooperation, and the level of mistrust between the Weatherford residents. He couldn't understand how so few people living in such an idyllic place could be so suspicious of each other. It's the behaviour you would expect in a big city.

'I saw the same behaviour in our neighbourhood when I was growing up. So much mistrust against ordinary people just trying to make a life for themselves. My mother and father went out of their way not to make the same mistake. It's a case of do unto others as you would have others do unto you. Please consider an apology. It's not going to change anything in the great scheme of things, but that doesn't mean it's not the right thing to do.'

As she listened to Chris, Hanna realised that she appreciated his sensible, no-nonsense council. As a police detective he saw the harm people do to each other, and probably felt that there had to be a better way. She kissed him, and agreed to go and see KS.

The train pulled into Wolburn Market Station, and Hanna walked up the high street towards the market square. Her nerves had settled down, and she felt more confident about the meeting. She didn't notice Jessica and Yasmin in the coffee shop waving to her. The friends watched her head towards KS's office.

'I wonder why she's paying KS a visit?' asked Jessica.

'Possibly something to do with the farm,' replied Yasmin.

'I don't think he buys and sells farms, does he?'

'Not sure,' answered Yasmin. 'Anyhoo, I think you're doing the right thing giving Rhys the heave-ho,' she continued.

'I know I am. Watching Alistair deal with that ultralight crash made me so proud of him. Below that grumpy exterior is a good, dependable husband, and Yasmin don't laugh, but when he is in control like that he's seriously gorgeous.' The friends looked at each other, and both laughed.

'Good on you girl. Changing the subject, how is the injured pilot doing?'

'Apparently he is doing well. He's got a back injury, but by all accounts it could have been a lot worse. He has asked the helicopter charity if, as soon as he is well enough, he could meet everyone who helped save him,' replied Jessica.

'Wow, that's a lovely gesture,' remarked Yasmin looking across the square towards the estate agent.

KS was printing off an *Africa Wide Haulage* invoice, when he looked up from his desk, and saw Hanna approaching the shop. He quickly put the invoice into a yellow manilla document holder, and watching Wendy, the office manager, greet his visitor, he put the folder into one of the desk drawers and locked it, placed the key in the breast pocket of his jacket, and straightening his desk nameplate stood up to greet Hanna.

'Hanna, welcome. You are looking so well. My, London certainly agrees with you. Please sit, make yourself comfortable,' schmoozed the estate agent. Hanna sat down and put her handbag on the floor next to the chair. She declined a hot drink, but accepted a glass of water.

With the pleasantries over, Hanna, with her voice trembling slightly, told KS about the developments of the past few days. Feeling more confident, she admitted that she had been wrong to accuse him of any wrong doing with regards to the farm. She wanted to apologise, and draw a line under the saga.

KS showed no emotion as he listened. When Hanna had finished he thanked her for her courage and honesty, and accepted her apology unreservedly. With nothing else to say, Hanna thanked KS for being so understanding and shaking hands, the councillor suggested that Hanna join Eve and himself for dinner in the not too distant future. The meeting had taken less than five minutes.

KS sat down at his desk. He could not believe how his luck had changed in only a few days. First, there was Charlie Pollock and the money, and now Hanna was no longer an adversary. She had been a thorn in his side since her father's death. Although he had told the truth about the contaminated fields, she was tenacious like her mother. He had always considered her a threat, and certainly did not need a determined lawyer snapping at his heels.

CHAPTER 30

At the beginning of the year, Sir Michael came up with the idea of holding a Great Gatsby Charity Party to celebrate his retirement from the Army. Apart from tentatively asking Jeremy Hughes back in January if he would put together a band for the occasion, very little preparation had taken place during the summer. Kay had thought it was a great idea, and had agreed to organise the event. She had been blissfully unaware of the time pressures that establishing the new online business were going to have on her, in particular, the refurbishment of the old barn. As a result, the autumn approached and very little party planning had taken place. Jessica Burns suggested Kay approach Lizzie Turner, the wedding organiser, for help.

'Wow Babes, that's mental,' was the response from Lizzie. 'Nice change from bridezillas and mothers-of-the-bride. I've actually done a Gatsby function before. Yes, yes, I can do it. The catering's no different to a wedding, and the 1920s theme is awesome.'

With only four weeks to go and the danger that she would pick up the habit of calling everyone Babes, Kay was relieved to have Lizzie on board. Her enthusiasm was contagious. Michael was not quite sure how to handle Lizzie, but was pleased to see Kay and the Essex Catherine Wheel getting on well together. There was a lot of laughter at the manor.

A week before the party, Sir Michael received a letter from the Cabinet Office informing him that he had been shortlisted for the position of Lord-Lieutenant. That was the first surprise. The second one was the Head of Honours and Appointments Secretariat wanted to spend a couple of days with the nominee. The suggested dates were the Thursday and Friday before the party. Michael and Kay read through the information pack that had accompanied the letter. Kay was very excited at the news, and wanted her husband to accept the invitation. Michael's response was his usual 'let me sleep on it'. After dinner, Kay with a glass of red wine, and Michael with a whisky and ice, spent time researching 'Lord-Lieutenant, England' on Google.

'What are you going to do, Michael?' asked Kay as she climbed into bed and cuddled up to her husband.

'It's only an interview really. Can't do any harm can it?'

'I agree. Go for it. Good night, my Lord-Lieutenant.'

THE COUNTIES HERALD
LORD-LIEUTENANT NOMINEE BIDS
FAREWELL TO THE ARMY

The normally sleepy village of Weatherford came alive at the weekend with the sound of jazz and a return to the 1920s. The venue was the 16th Century Manor House belonging to the Beswick family; the occasion a Great Gatsby Party to mark Sir Michael's retirement from the Army, and an opportunity to raise money for various service charities.

Two Rolls-Royce Twenty, not dissimilar in shape to modern SUVs, were parked on either side of the large Tudor oak front door, and set the scene for the occasion.

Sir Michael and Lady Kay greeted my wife Barbara and I on arrival. Kay showed us were we would be sitting, and emphasised that the table places had been selected at random. The Great Hall was divided into two groups of tables, West Egg and East Egg, with the dance floor in the middle. We were seated at the West Egg end of the hall; an irony that, despite Kay's assurances, didn't escape Barbara and I.

Liz Turner, the owner of Weatherford Brides, came over and chatted to us. She looked the part in a gold flapper dress covered in sequins and wearing a gold lace skull cap. As bubbly as ever, she enthusiastically pointed out her art deco handy work, and giggled at the party favours; a lace garter for the ladies and a hip flask of gin for the gentlemen. Sir Michael had asked for a candlestick telephone as the centre piece for each table, and my masterpiece, her words not mine, the bar, a library look-alike with shelves of books reaching up to the ceiling.

The Beswicks must have been pleased with the turnout. Every table was full, and the Great Hall echoed with the sound of talking and laughter against

*a background of jazz being played by local musician
Jeremy Hughes and his band The Jazzers.*

*The guests excelled themselves and, despite the
warm summer evening, had certainly come dressed
for the occasion. The men in either black or white
ties, and the woman wore fringed sequin dresses,
some wearing long black satin gloves, and an
assortment of headbands; feathers, jewels, pearls,
sequins, beads and lace.*

*Liz Turner's food did not disappoint. Platters of
bite-sized caprese skewers and bruschetta were doing
the rounds as the guests arrived. The starter was
caesar salad, the main course roast turkey with sage
and onion stuffing and roast vegetables, followed by
dessert of either tiramisu or a fruit platter.*

*Sir Michael, a seemingly quiet and modest man
when you first meet him, entertained his guests with a
speech which was both humorous and at times sad.
His potted history included his hatred of boarding
school, joining the army in 1978 against his mother's
wishes, meeting his wife Kay at Tees County
University, and their son Thomas who lives in Hong
Kong.*

*He paid tribute to his army comrades with a couple
of funny incidents, and thanked them all for their
loyal support and camaraderie during the Troubles,
in Kuwait, Bosnia, Iraq and Afghanistan. He also
reflected on those who had been killed whilst serving
for their country.*

*Lady Kay prompted him to tell the guests about his
nomination for Lord-Lieutenant. News which
prompted a standing ovation. When calm had been
restored, Sir Michael thanked everyone for making*

the evening a success, and ended his speech with a toast to Her Majesty the Queen.

Formalities out of the way, a green light at the back of the bandstand signalled that the dancing was about to begin. As the evening wore on, thirsty dancers were tempted with blackboards at the bar advertising cocktails; gin rickey, sidecar, bee's knees, hanky-panky and grasshopper. For the hungry, platters of cold fried chicken were circulated amongst the party-goers, and then placed on tables.

There were enthusiastic versions of the charleston and the fox-trot. Nobody seemed to quite know what they were doing, but they were certainly enjoying themselves. The waltz allowed for periods of calm when the flinging around of arms and legs were replaced with confused versions of one, two, three, one, two, three.

In the spirt of good neighbourliness the live music ended at midnight, and the green light was turned off. Guests slowly melted away into the night, and a few stragglers, including yours truly, sat in the muggy, dimly lit Great Hall surrounded by the remnants of a wild and carefree evening, drinking cocktails, chatting, and eating what remained of the hors d'oeuvres and cold chicken. Spotify provided quiet background of jazz until traces of a new day started to appear.

Just prior to going to print Sir Michael let us know that a total of £8,800 had been raised, and would be divided amongst the various service charities nominated by the guests. hughflynn@countiesherald.co.uk

----

Kay Beswick and Jeremy Hughes were sitting at the large table in the kitchen of the manor house. If you were expecting the kitchen to be stereotypical of those found in large 16th century manor houses, you would be wrong. Disappointed, probably; surprised, probably not; especially if you knew it had been modernised by Kay.

She had cleverly modified the vast 'space', as modern-day estate agents are prone to call 'a room', into a modern kitchen worthy of being showcased in *Kevin McCloud's Grand Designs*.

When the old kitchen was stripped out, what remained was a large rectangular room with a high ceiling and four original Tudor windows overlooking the rear garden. Kay wanted a kitchen that was more homely and practicable. She reduced the height by using a false ceiling incorporating oak beams and industrial dome lighting. An AGA was put into the recess of the original open fire, with a row of copper cooking utensils displayed above it as a reminder of the past. The old stone floor was raised to provide space for plumbing and electricity. The main attraction of the kitchen turned out to be the island with storage on all sides, and made from recycled oak. Grey coloured cupboards with glass fronts, recessed lighting, and German engineered self-closing drawers had replaced the old wooden shelves and wobbly standalone cupboards that had been press ganged into service over the centuries. The uninterrupted natural light provided by the four Tudor windows subtly changed the grey decor of the kitchen into a soft cool blue hue.

The lady of the manor and Dave Wright were busy covering and moving furniture in   what is referred to as the nursery, when Jeremy Hughes arrived unannounced to see Kay. Leaving Dave to start the decorating, Kay took the visitor through to the kitchen.

'How's Tia? Feeling better?' asked Kay sitting down opposite Jeremy at the table. 'It was such a shame she couldn't make the dance, she would have loved it.'

'You're probably wondering why I'm here, Kay,' said Jeremy ignoring Kay's questions about his wife's health. Although she and Tia had known each other for a long time, Kay had never really liked Jeremy. She had always thought he was away with the fairies. Knowing the way he treated Tia did not help either. The sun was streaming through the windows, and the room was starting to become unbearably hot.

'I have to say, I'm a little intrigued by your visit,' replied Kay getting up and opening the large oak backdoor. Jeremy took his phone out of his pocket, tapped it and scrolled the screen with his right thumb. When he had found what he was looking for, he placed the phone down on the table in front of Kay. She noticed he was trembling slightly.

'I showed Tia these photos of the party. She was very interested in the chinese pottery,' he said looking across the table at Kay.

'What about them?' asked the lady of the manor.

'Well, Tia said she thought they might be rare vases. She showed the photos to her pottery class teacher who thought they were Quing artefacts.'

'The point being?'

'If they are rare artefacts, Tia's of the opinion you must have brought them into the country illegally.'

'Jeremy, you must be joking. Why in heaven's name would I do that? I have a successful business. Why would I risk everything by getting involved in smuggling ancient artefacts?' Kay asked the visitor.

'For the money,' replied Jeremy.

'What utter nonsense, Jeremy. Have you taken leave of your senses? Does Tia know you're here?'

'No, she doesn't,' replied the musician. 'I'll get straight to the point. I'm sick and tired of seeing people like you use their titles, grand houses, and money to get even richer. Not only that, you have the bare faced cheek to think that you'll get away with it.'

'Jeremy, just listen to yourself. You and Tia have been our friends for as long as I can remember,' replied Kay.

'Ha, what friendship? You pretend to be Tia's friend, and yet I've watched you for years and years paying lip-service to her when she has needed help. Enough. You are now going to help her. I want £50,000 or else I'll go to the police about the vases.' Kay looked him in the eye and wished she had a vase at hand to hit him.

'Jeremy, you are making such an idiot of yourself. Those vases ARE Quing, but they are replicas. Read my lips rep-li-cas, They are produced as replicas, they are marked as replicas, and they are sold, no EXPORTED as replicas. Tia and that pottery teacher have got it all wrong. As for you. You're an imbecile. You come into my house demanding money without checking your facts. What were you thinking? I was just going to pay up without a fight. You are a complete loser, Jeremy. You cannot even blackmail someone properly. Now get out of my house,' she shouted at her visitor. Kay got up from her chair, and grabbing the seated Jeremy by his collar, half dragged, half bundled him out of the kitchen.

Dave Wright heard Kay shouting and rushed out of the nursery to see what was going on. He was standing at the top of the staircase when the kitchen door flung open, and saw Kay man-handling Jeremy across the hallway by his shirt collar. She opened the front door and pushed him out.

'Get off my property, you bastard,' Kay screamed after him. She slammed the door, and turning saw Dave at the top of the stairs. 'Who the fuck does he think he is?' she shouted at the top of her voice. She paced up and down the entrance hall, cursing under her breath. 'Leave me. Just leave me alone. Get back to work,' was her response when Dave attempted to find out what had happened.

He returned to the nursery, and half an hour later she appeared with two tins of ice cold diet cola. He moved a large old steamer travel trunk to the window, and sitting looking out over the garden, Kay explained what had happened. He couldn't believe what he was hearing, and sat staring out of the window shaking his head with his mouth open. 'He needs a bloody good slap,' he suggested. Kay, managed to laugh at the comment, but declined the offer.

When Dave had finished working for the day, he stopped off at the Green Man on the way home. Kay Beswick's rage had unsettled him. He was no stranger to seeing comrades-in-arms display immense anger and frustration when pinned down by enemy fire. It often produced acts of immense courage. What he had seen at the manor house, however, was so unexpected, and it had upset him. I still think he needs a slap thought the ex-soldier as he sat down with a pint of cider. What he couldn't fathom out was why Jeremy had verbally attacked Kay so ferociously. It had been so out of character and unnecessary.

'Looks like you're billy-no-mates tonight, Dave.' The decorator looked up at a smiling Edward Broadhurst.

'Evening, Edward. I don't want to be rude, but I've had a terrible day, and I'd like to be on my own for a bit.'

'Fully understand, Dave. Not a problem. Ah, there's Jeremy Hughes. I'll go and bother him.' The ex-soldier watched Jeremy standing at the bar, chatting and laughing. Geriatric Trotskyite he thought. The longer he sat there listening to Jeremy's laughter, the more frustrated he became. He heard a woman's raised voice behind him, and out of curiosity turned around to see who it was. A woman and a man were sitting at a table in the bay window having an argument. He didn't recognise them. Out-of-towners he thought. He looked at his phone. It was nine o'clock. I'd better get home; early start in the morning. He downed the rest of his drink, and was about to leave when Jeremy bid Sue Cooper goodnight, and left the pub. The decorator sat for a moment looking at his empty glass. I will not let him get away with today's behaviour. He has to be taught a lesson.

On leaving the pub, Dave stopped to light a cigarette. He took a long draw, and looked up and down the high street. The nights were starting to draw in, and there was nobody about.

CHAPTER 31

Dave Wright burst into the pub.

'Sue. Quickly. I don't have any signal on my phone. Phone for an ambulance. Jeremy Hughes has been hurt. He's outside in the road.' The pub fell silent.

'There's a first aid kit in the kitchen,' informed the landlady as she dialled 999. Dave with the kit under his arm dashed out of the pub, with the punters close behind him.

Jeremy was lying on his back on the pavement with his head in a large pool of blood. Dave knelt down next to him, and could hear shouting in his head; man down, man down, we need a medic. He put on a pair of latex gloves, and gently turned Jeremy's head looking for the source of the bleeding. He had obviously fallen backwards, and hit the back of his head on the pavement.

'He's unconscious, but still alive,' said Dave looking up at the onlookers. 'We need to stop the bleeding. Edward is there a wound dressing in the bag?' Edward Broadhurst rummaged around in the first aid kit, found a wrapped sterile dressing and handed it to the ex-soldier. Dave expertly applied the dressing to the wound and winding the bandage around Jeremy's head, secured the pad by tying the ends of the bandage directly over the pad to keep it in place.

'We'll have to apply another dressing over that one if the blood seeps through,' commented the decorator as he stood up. 'I hope the ambulance arrives soon. Still being unconscious is not good. Can somebody go back to the pub, and get a couple of blankets. We need to keep him warm,' he added looking down at the injured man. The blankets arrived, and once Jeremy had been made comfortable, there was nothing else to do, except wait for the ambulance.

'How did it happen, Dave?' asked Sue Cooper.

'Have no idea. I had a couple of puffs of my cigarette before getting into the van, drove up the road, and found him here,' replied the ex-marine.

'Anyone around?' asked Edward.

'No, not a soul,' replied Dave, running his hand through his hair.

The sound of sirens could be heard in the distance, and a few moments later the blue flashing lights of an ambulance accompanied by a police car turned at the church into the high street, and approached the silent group of bystanders.

It did not take long for the paramedics to transfer Jeremy to the ambulance, and thanking Dave for his prompt action drove off. The police asked everyone to return to the pub, and two constables spent a couple hours taking personal details and statements.

When the police left, Sue poured everyone a shot of Cointreau and the punters raised their glasses to Jeremy and a swift recovery.

Tia Hughes suddenly opened her eyes. She was fully clothed and half lying in a chair covered by a blanket. She sat up in bewilderment and looked around the darkened room. In front of her was what looked like a shroud covering someone lying in a raised bed.

'Jeremy,' she whispered as she realised where she was, and slowly got up from the chair and approached the bed. She was feeling awful; a raging thirst and a pounding headache. She looked at the bank of machines plugged into her husband, but had no idea what they were monitoring. She stood looking vacantly at the screens.

She stopped staring at the monitors, and looked at Jeremy lying motionless in bed. Last night was a complete haze. She remembered getting home after work, and not feeling like cooking, she had sat down at the kitchen table and poured a glass of wine. I wonder how many bottles I drank she thought. She remembered being very drunk when the police arrived at the house. Tia heard voices in the corridor, and opening the door saw two nurses sitting at the nurses station. One of them looked up.

'Mrs Hughes. Good morning,' greeted the nurse getting up and coming around from behind the work station. 'You were in quite a state when the police brought you in last night.'

'Yes, I think I might have been. I can't really remember arriving. I hope I didn't cause any trouble,' Tia replied sheepishly. 'Is it possible for me to call my daughter and tell her about her Dad?'

'Help yourself,' replied the nurse placing the telephone on top of the workstation. 'I'll let the consultant know that you're awake. He wants to update you on your husband's condition.'

Tia opened the front door of the house, and leaving her shoes at the door, went through to the kitchen. There were three empty claret bottles on the table. She sat down and stared at them. The house seemed unusually quiet. Taking her phone out of her handbag, she opened *#weatherford*. My God, she gasped when she saw the number of new postings.

Just herd Jeremy Hughes was murdered last night.
Probably them east european foreigners.
Stop being such a xenophobic git!
No he wasn't you idiot. He was knocked down by a car.
Yous guys no nuffing. Wright punched him.
Where there's smoke, there's fire.
Shut up Aristotle!
Ignore the village gossip. Dave saved Jeremy's life. I was there.

A video attached to this last posting showed Jeremy on a stretcher being lifted into an ambulance. Tia played it a couple of times before adding her own post.

Stop the gossip! It's not helpful! Jeremy fell and hit his head on the pavement in the high street last night. We do not know how it happened. He has a fractured scull, swelling of the brain, and is still unconscious. The doctors cannot say whether he has any permanent brain damage. The next 24 hours are critical.

Tia was in the back room, or as Jeremy called it 'the music suite', trying to find her husband's work number. She never ventured into the cluttered, untidy mess that the musician had accumulated over the years. She wasn't particularly interested in what he did with his abundance of time. Hours of self-pity, and navel gazing whilst hiding away in the back room, had not provided the family with anything creative nor financial.

The musician's wife didn't know where to start. She sifted through the piles of paper on the desk. Opened the drawers, and quickly closed them as more paper jumped out. She tried to remember where Jeremy had said the music studios were based. Was it Folkestone or Ashford? No neither of those. I seem to remember him saying something about south of the M3. After a brief search, she went back to the kitchen, and poured herself a glass of wine. I think it was Chertsey. A search on her tablet produced *The Proscenium Music Studio,* a tv and film music library company. Yes that's it, I remember thinking at the time the name was a bit presumptuous.

The musician's wife phoned the studio, and was initially passed from one person to another, until she finally ended up talking to someone in Human Resources.

'Good morning, my name is Tia Hughes. My husband Jeremy has been working for you for a few months. I'm just phoning to let you know that he has been seriously injured. He's in hospital, and will be off for a while.'

'Sorry, I didn't catch the name.'

'Hughes, Jeremy Hughes,' repeated Tia.

'Ok thanks. Just hang on a minute.' Tia waited. 'Hello Mrs Hughes. Thanks for waiting. In what capacity was your husband working for us?'

'A musician,' replied Tia.

'And when did he start?'

'About six months ago,' responded Tia.

'I'm really sorry, but I cannot find any record of a Jeremy Hughes working for us.'

Dave Wright slowed down as he approached the tail end of a queue of cars. The police had set up a road block on both sides of the Weatherford high street. He sat patiently, listening to *Radio 2*, while watching the police officer wave the cars to come forward, bend down to talk to the occupants, and appearing satisfied, allowing the driver to continue.

'Evening Constable,' greeted Dave as he switched off the radio.

'Evening Sir. There was an incident here last Thursday evening between 9 and 10 o'clock. A local man, Mr Jeremy Hughes, appears to have been attacked by an unknown person and badly injured. We're doing a routine stop in the hope that someone saw something that night,' explained the police constable.

'Constable, I was the person who found Jeremy.'

'Your name Sir?' asked the surprised policeman.

'Wright, Dave Wright. I gave your lot a statement last Thursday after Jeremy was taken off to hospital.'

'Mr Wright, please will you pull forward, and stop over there on the left. My colleague will take the necessary details. Thank you for your help.'

Details written down and the colleague's questions answered, the decorator was allowed to continue his journey. I hope they find the culprit soon thought Dave as he pulled into the filling station.

The village rumour mill had gone into overdrive on social media, and he was being singled out as the perpetrator. He had nothing to hide. He had found Jeremy. He had given the injured man first aid, for God sake. Kay Beswick had suggested he close his online accounts. He was not sure what to do. Is it better to see what the ill-informed are saying about you, or deny them the opportunity to spread false accusations? He filled his van up with petrol and joined the queue to pay. He felt that everyone was either staring at him, and those who were not, were deliberately ignoring him.

CHAPTER 32

KS finished reading the short article in *The Counties Herald* reporting the alleged attack on Jeremy Hughes, and the standard media comment about the lack of police progress with the investigation. Poor sod he thought as he tossed the newspaper onto the oak desk. Elsa Nel knocked on the office door, and opened it.

'Two gentlemen here to see you KS,' she announced. The chairman of the charity looked towards reception. He didn't recognise them.

'Tell them I'm busy. They must make an appointment.' He watched Elsa walk back to the reception desk. They were obviously not pleased with the message that she conveyed to them. She returned to the office.

'They say bollocks to your appointment idea, and insist on seeing you now.'

'Not bloody interested. Who do they think they are? Tell them to leave the premises,' replied the chairman, ever the diplomat.

'They gave their names as Steve and Michael Pollock. Two of Charlie's uncles,' replied Elsa. The blood drained from KS's face. 'Are you alright KS?' asked Elsa.

'Yes, yes. I'm fine,' replied the ashen face. 'Um, um, yes, show them in.'

'What's going on there?' asked Tia as Elsa returned to her desk.

'Not sure, but the vibes are not good.'

The women sat watching the three men. Michael Pollock, the bigger of the two uncles, was leaning forward in his chair, and tapped his right forefinger on the desk to emphasise each word he was saying. KS kept holding his hands up and shaking his head, as if to say what Michael was saying was incorrect. When it was the second uncle's turn to speak, he stood up, and lent forward across the desk in an attempt to intimidate the estate agent. Tia and Elsa couldn't hear what the men were saying; only angry muffled voices. When Steve Pollock finished saying his piece, KS leant back in his chair and laughed. This resulted in Michael Pollock angrily pushing back his chair and standing up. Both Pollock uncles were now leaning forward to get as close as they could to the pale face looking up at them.

'I think they're going to kill him,' whispered Elsa.

'About time,' replied Tia.

'Get out of my office. I will not be threatened by anyone,' shouted KS, getting up from his desk, and opening the office door.

'You WILL pay the money back,' said Michael pausing at the open door, and looking the trembling chairman in the eye.

'And you WILL do it this afternoon,' hissed Steve, poking KS in the chest with his finger. The uncles stormed out, leaving a visibly shocked KS grinning sheepishly at his bemused staff.

'Now that went well,' commented Tia. Elsa laughed which set off sniggers and giggles from the rest of the staff.

'Get back to work. The lot of you,' shouted KS as he slammed his office door shut.

KS decided he was not going to let the Pollock family bully him. He had done nothing illegal. Charlie Pollock had given him the money as a gift. As he drove home, he went over the sequence of events since the chance meeting with the stable hand in the Green Man. He hadn't made any mistakes. The scam was watertight. I've done this all before he thought as he pulled into his driveway at home.

Dinner was waiting for him. Eve's attempts at small talk were met with customary indifference, and the couple ended up eating in silence. In any case, KS was preoccupied with the Pollocks, and anything his wife had to say was of no consequence. While Eve cleared the table, KS switched on the tv and had no sooner sat down when the phone rang.

'Kettering-Smythe.'

'Hi KS. Sorry to bother you at home. I need some help,' said a distraught sounding Tia.

'You sound upset. What's the matter,' replied KS.

'The hospital's phoned. Jeremy's condition has apparently worsened, and they have asked me to go in,' she sobbed.

'I'm sorry to hear that, Tia. Do you need a lift to the hospital?' offered KS. She's probably had a few drinks already he thought.

'No. I'm ok thanks. My daughter Jane's staying with me at the moment. She'll take me in. I'm not sure if I'll be at work tomorrow,' sniffed Tia.

'Don't worry about work, Jeremy is far more important. Come back when you're ready.'

'Thanks KS. That's very kind of you. I'll keep you updated.'

'That was Tia. Sounds like Jeremy has taken a turn for the worse,' commented KS as he sat down in his fireside chair.

'Poor girl. Such bad luck,' replied the wife. 'Do you mind if we watch the news?'

'Whatever.' replied the husband. He stared at the screen, preoccupied with his thoughts. If I return Charlie's money, I'm back where I began. I'll still have to find money to pay the blackmailers. He was not taking any notice of the news items; Brexit, retail job losses, racism in football.

A 36 year old builder from Cambridge has been jailed for 6 years for defrauding a number of elderly and vulnerable people in the Cambridgeshire and Lincolnshire areas. KS sat up and took notice. *The incidents took place over a period of five years, and involved a total of £600,000. Scott Sleaward targeted vulnerable people and pressurised them into paying thousands of pounds for work he had no intention of carrying out. A police spokeswoman told the press outside the court that the police would relentlessly pursue and prosecute those few who prey on the vulnerable.*

The next morning, as soon as the bank opened, KS arranged to meet Charlie Pollock at the bank and transferred the money back into Charlie's account.

Tia took the first left at the now familiar roundabout at the entrance to the hospital grounds. Her daughter had, under the guise of offering her mother much needed support, come to stay with Tia when Jeremy had first been injured. This had turned into a full board and lodging vacation, including laundry, for the daughter and grandson with very little reciprocating support for the grieving grandmother. Story of my life she thought as she navigated the narrow road system that weaved itself around the hospital buildings.

She parked in Zone F on the fourth floor of Car Park J. I didn't expect so many cars to be here at this late hour she thought as she searched in her handbag for a pen. Switching on the map light she wrote Car Park J/4th floor/Zone F on the parking ticket. A multi-storey car park ritual she had started years ago after she had fetched Jeremy from Heathrow Airport. She had been late, was in a hurry, and didn't pay attention to where she had parked. This resulted in pushing Jeremy's luggage and saxophone case up and down rows of parked cars, and at the same time trying not to be run over by car owners who had actually found their vehicles.

With the parking ticket formality completed, she sat for a moment wishing that she was not in a hospital car park. Most people have a fear of the dentist, Tia's dread was having to visit the surgery or landing up in hospital. Years of listening to the negative media coverage about the health service had resulted in Tia wondering whether they could be trusted. If she could avoid going to the surgery, not that Weatherford had one, she did. She put her trust in the internet for medical advice, and the chemist six miles away in Wolburn Market.

Taking a deep breath, she got out of the car and followed the signs to the lift. The concrete wall on either side of the lift doors was decorated with a huge diagonal purple stripe proclaiming on the left hand side *Welcome to Car Park J* and on the right hand side *The Pay Station is on the Ground Floor*. There were a number of people waiting for the lift; she decided to take the stairs.

Descending the flight of stairs, she recalled the first visit she made on her own to see Jeremy. She had been in a state of shock, and the sheer size of the hospital had been overwhelming. The first challenge was navigating the one-way road system. Having eventually found the entrance to one of the numerous multi-storey car parks, she then had a long walk in semi-darkness courtesy of European Union compliant lighting, passed unfamiliar dark and joyless buildings, pedestrian detours around fenced off building works, and started to panic because she thought she was lost.

It was not much better once she was inside the correct building. Long institutionalised corridors without windows, gloss painted walls and clinically shining floors. Signs placed at intervals along the length of the corridor, announcing more unfamiliar departments. Eventually she asked someone in a uniform for directions. She could hardly understand what the friendly smile was saying because of the heavy foreign accent. Luckily the hands and fingers were able to translate the mystery. You've missed it, go back that way, up lift to next floor.

Regular visits breed familiarity, and Tia confidently stepped out into the warm night air, and walked along the long covered walkway towards the building that housed the neurology department. It was almost eleven o'clock and the usually busy hospital felt eerily calm without the throng of the daytime visitors.

The lights had been dimmed in the wards, and Tia headed towards the lighthouse that was the nurses station. She was asked to take a seat. I really don't want to be here she thought, I'll probably get MRSA if I stay too long. After a couple of minutes a dark form came walking slowly down the unlit corridor towards her. As the shape got nearer it changed into a doctor in scrubs. Too old to be a junior doctor worrying about his contract she thought.

'Mrs Hughes, I'm Marshall Griffiths, neurosurgeon. Your husband's condition deteriorated late this afternoon, and a scan showed he was experiencing a subdural hematoma. That's when the tiny veins between the surface of the brain and its outer covering known as the dura start to stretch and tear. We rushed him into surgery and tried to stop the bleeding. There was a lot of blood. Unfortunately we were unable to stop the bleed, and we lost him. I am so very, very sorry for your loss.'

Tia thanked the doctor and declining the offer of a cup of tea from the nurse headed back along the dimly lit corridor. Well I wasn't expecting that she thought. Jeremy's dead. How did that happen? She stopped at the food court near the entrance and bought a black coffee at McDonalds. The restaurant was empty except for a small group of twenty-somethings. She sat down amongst the upturned chairs balancing on the tables and looked across at the group of young friends eating and drinking.

They're about the same age as Jeremy and I were when we met. How we were going to change the world. Replace the old order, and put the workers in charge. So what happened? LSD and pot that's what happened. Christ, these days a burger and a few fries are considered bad for your health; what we consumed and inhaled during our twenties destroyed us. Who would have thought that almost forty years later I would be sitting in a restaurant belonging to one of the world's largest multi-national corporations. Tia looked down at her wedding ring. What a waste of life she thought, and burst into tears.

CHAPTER 33

Every year members of the Wolburn Market Golf Club select a charity of choice, and by sheer coincidence, the County Air Ambulance had been chosen for 2018. Although raising money for charities is an all year round club activity, the annual charity golf day is the high point of the fund raising effort, and was now only a few weeks away.

Alistair Burns had joined Wolburn soon after the family moved to Weatherford. The isolated existence and, for the most part, the solitary life as a farmer meant social interaction was limited, and the club gave him the opportunity to meet people. Back then the landlords of smoke filled pubs actively discouraged children, and with restaurants all but non-existent, the golf club provided a family friendly restaurant type alternative to Sunday lunch.

Like many club golfers, Alistair has a love-hate relationship with the game. He had not played much sport at school, and even if he had displayed sporting talent, he grew up in an age when competition and striving to be a winner was considered vulgar. So at the age of thirty with very little hand, eye and ball coordination experience he started to play golf. He soon discovered that it was almost impossible to hit the tiny white ball in the desired direction. The more he tried, the worse it got until eventually his visits to Wolburn did not involve the game at all, but weekly visits for Sunday lunch with the family.

Moz Nel has not played much golf, but is always willing to give it a go. He is no stranger to sport, competition and the desire to win at all costs. There were family stories of him as a toddler diving onto the sofa with a rugby ball while watching tries being scored during provincial matches on tv. He is happy to try his hand at anything that involves a bat and ball.

He does, however, find golf a difficult game to master. He has always felt golf was a reflection of life. You start off with great expectations, quickly land up in trouble, and having found a way out of the difficulty, you then continue a journey of great joy and happiness followed by periods of despair and misery. If you end the round without having thrown your clubs into a water hole, you have successfully survived to fight another day.

Alistair drove his Land Rover Discovery slowly between the sandstone uprights and the open cast-iron gates of the unassuming Victorian entrance to the golf club. The drive was not quite wide enough for two cars to pass each other, and yellow and black speed bumps forced drivers to reduce speed to below 10 mph. The drive was lined with a healthy looking hedge; something that only a farmer would find interesting.

'Very neat hedge,' remarked Moz. Alistair glanced across at this passenger, and smiled.

'Called Green Beech. It has always been the club's policy to plant native species,' Alistair replied, stopping in a passing place to allow an oncoming car to squeeze past.

'A very commendable thing to do,' replied Moz.

'I think so. It certainly contributes to the ecosystem in the area. Native plants adapt well to local soil and climate, and tend to need less water than introduced plants.'

'Not to mention food and shelter for local insects, birds and animals,' added Moz.

'I saw a red squirrel sitting on the 9th tee box a couple of summers ago,' continued Alistair. 'Golf's critics are right when they say it's a pastime for the privileged. Over 80% of the population live in urban areas, and very few of them will have the privilege, as golfers do, of seeing nature at such close quarters. Those long shadows during the autumn, walking through the thick winter frost, and the summer arrival of the ducks, swans, crows and geese. Not to mention the squirrels and the insects.'

'It's also fascinating to see the young being reared and protected from predators. The wonder of God's creation, we should rejoice and thank him for sharing it with us,' added Moz. This ecclesiastic summation interrupted Alistair's train of thought, and he turned his attention to finding a parking space.

'Oh dear, someone's taken the Lady Captain's parking,' commented Alistair, pointing towards a man and a woman engaged in a heated discussion.

'Obviously the man is not the Lady Captain,' smiled Moz.

'Could be, you never know these days. Just goes to show, give someone a title, male or female, and they become all territorial and officious,' added Alistair as he parked between a Porsche Cheyenne and a Maserati Levante.

'Nice wheels,' commented Moz. 'Keeps the elite golf image alive and well.'

'Things are not what they seem, Moz. The Porsche belongs to a local electrician, and the Maserati is owned by a plumber. I know both of them. They each have a property at one of those Spanish golf resorts. Always jetting off for a golf break.' The men took their golf bags out of the back of the Land Rover, and headed towards the club house; a converted Victorian coach house.

'I always look at the workmen's white vans parked here, and make a mental note not to give them a call if I need something doing on the farm. It's bad enough trying to get someone to come and give you a quote, but nigh impossible if they spend the whole summer on the golf course,' lamented Alistair.

'There are quite a few of them here,' replied Moz surveying the car park. The farmers followed the finger post to the pro shop with the clubs on their backs clunking loudly against each other as they walked along.

They were greeted by Patrick the pro golfer, a sun tanned athletic looking man, in his mid-thirties, sporting a short hair beard. He politely booked the players' tee time on the system, handed each of them a scorecard, and wishing them a good round, Alistair and Moz left him sitting in the semi-dark, surrounded by golf clothes, equipment and logos. His dream of winning the Open extinguished. The tedium of taking tee time bookings day in and day out had convinced him that in his next life he was going to manufacturer golf balls and make a fortune.

Alistair suggested that they warm up at the range before having breakfast. The farmers made their way towards the driving range, both of them knowing that hitting a few balls to warm up was not going to improve the outcome of their game. They were the only people there, and in the early morning light there was an eerie feeling of desolation and abandonment.

'You know Moz. Five years ago, it was so busy here, you had to wait for a bay.'

'Ya, I read an online article recently about declining golf membership in the US of A and the UK. It had a photo of three guys in plus fours,' commented Moz.

'I've never seen anyone playing club golf in plus fours,' replied Alistair as he pitched a ball towards one of the coloured flags. 'The reality is there's a whole cross-section of men and women playing golf, and they all just wear plain ordinary casual clothes,' he added with an irritated edge to his voice.

'Thank goodness golfers don't wear lycra,' Moz added as he paused for a moment before hitting his next ball. Alistair laughed and shook his head.

For the next thirty minutes, Alistair and Moz hit balls in silence except for the occasional grumble of 'shit', 'rubbish', and 'not again'. Warm up over, and with two hours until their tee off time, the farmers headed off for the long awaited breakfast. They weaved their way through the obstacle course of people, golf bags and trolleys assembling outside the pro shop, and headed down the wide corridor that lead from the old coach house towards the restaurant.

The width of the passage-way made it an ideal place to exhibit the club's golfing history dating back to its inception. There is an imposing glass-fronted solid oak display showcase that runs half way down the one side of the passage. It displays various cups, bowls, plaques, trays and crystal that have been won by the club or its members down the years. This showpiece is finished off with an ornate oak honours board surround, recording the Club Captains since 1892.

On the opposite side and mounted at regular intervals along the corridor's length are matching oak boards listing, in gold letters, past club, senior, junior and ladies champions. Standing between each honour board, and completing the exhibition, are small display cabinets containing a variety of golfing memorabilia belonging to members who had excelled at golf.

'An impressive collection,' commented Moz stopping to take a look at the display of trophies. 'Club Captains,' he read looking up at the oak surround. '1892 – 1899 Major Robert Kettering.'

'Why does fried bacon smell so good?' said Moz as the golfers entered the restaurant.

'It does doesn't it. I also like the smell of toast in the morning. The breakfast is always good here,' replied Alistair. Walking slowly down the length of the buffet, the farmers contemplated what they were going to order.

'Morning, Alistair,' greeted the teenager standing behind the buffet wearing a white Nehru jacket.

'Hello Steve, looking smart this morning.'

'I don't really have an option,' smiled the young man, shrugging his shoulders.

'This is Moz Nel, a research farmer visiting us from South Africa.'

'I spent six months playing golf in South Africa,' replied the teenager as he shook Moz's hand.

'Where in SA?' asked Moz.

'Cape Town and the Wilderness. Best time of my life,' replied the young golfer, his eyes lighting up.

'Bloody windy,' laughed Moz.

'Need a bit more hair gel that's for sure,' smiled the youngster. 'What can I get you, gentlemen?'

'Full English please,' responded Alistair.

'Make it two,' replied Moz as he dished up a large bowl of Coco Pops for himself.

'Young Steve is a club protégé,' explained Alistair as he took the plates off the tray and placed them on the table. 'The club has never had a youngster with such natural talent. Wins everything, which annoys the older members a bit,' smiled Alistair. 'He's taking up a golf sponsorship in America. Leaves sometime next month.'

'A great opportunity,' commented Moz.

'The general feeling is there's a benefactor. His Dad died some years ago. It is just his Mum and a younger brother,' continued Alistair.

'That's a very generous thing to do. I'm sure everyone wishes him Godspeed.' added Moz.

The two men tucked into their breakfast of bacon, fried eggs, sausages, baked beans, grilled tomatoes, and fried mushrooms. The food was freshly cooked, the portions generous and if it was at all possible, the sunny green summer view out of the bay window overlooking the 18th green, made it taste even more delicious.

'Did you see that anti-food story on tv the other night about bacon. All doom-and-gloom about getting bowel cancer if you eat too much of it.'

'Trouble is the naysayers sit in front of computers, and only need a handful of berries to get them through the day. We can't do a physical job like ours on a few bloody nuts and an orange juice,' replied Alistair.

'The chances of being murdered back home in SA are probably a lot higher than getting bowel cancer,' answered Moz in such a matter-of-fact way that

Alistair stopped eating and looked across the table at his companion. Murdering the man opposite him was not really a subject he wanted to discuss at the breakfast table. He decided to ignore the comment and change the subject.

'Looking on the bright side, the wheat results could have been much worse. I think we were fortunate that production was only 5% lower than last year. The price of flour shouldn't be affected by the lower yield. A heavy spring rain followed by such a long, dry summer is so rare in this part of the country, Moz. To be quite honest I had many sleepless nights thinking we were going to lose the harvest. This year's Harvest Festival will be special.'

'It's unfortunate we lost the test harvest,' responded Moz.

'I still think it was an opportunity to collect data outside of the laboratory in weather that we might only get once or twice in a lifetime. The white coats have some unique data. Maybe it will contribute towards developing an even more efficient seed; something that needs even less water.'

'I can't help feeling that I'm responsible for the failure. Maybe I should have worked harder. Maybe we should have irrigated the test area. We're going home early with nothing to show for it,' lamented Moz.

'Moz, I think you are being very hard on yourself. There is every chance that the test will be repeated next summer, and we will have normal weather conditions. I've been assured by head office that you will be asked to return if the trial continues. Elsa's mum is not well. Go home and enjoy the time with the family. We'll still be here next summer.'

It took Alistair and Moz two hours and fifteen minutes to complete the front nine holes. Things had started off quite well until they caught up with a four ball. A steady pace of play turned into long periods of waiting behind four elderly players; two in a golf cart, and two who looked as if a buggy should have been mandatory.

'Players behind us, slow play ahead of us, it's like being kettled in by riot police,' commented Alistair.

'They haven't once looked back to see if there's anyone behind them.'

'They don't have to, they know they are holding everyone up. Selfish gits,' responded a frustrated Alistair as they walked off the 9th green. They waved 'thanks for waiting' to three players halfway down the 9th fairway, and headed for the 10th tee.

'Hopefully they can only manage nine holes,' commented Moz. The farmers were soon to be disappointed. The four seniors were soldiering on down the 10th fairway; 20 yards at a time.

'I'll go and get us a drink. What would you like, Alistair?

'A couple of cold cokes will do nicely, Moz. Thanks. You can get them from the bar. Opposite the restaurant.'

Moz was pleased to be out of the blazing sun for a few minutes while he looked for the bar, which he found without any difficulty. The bar had recently been refurbished. The terracotta and green tones of the 1970s, the subject of many a committee meeting, had been replaced by modern purple and off-white hues. The old hardwood walnut bar counter, which had given service for close on fifty years, had been moved from its place in the middle of the room and superseded by a counter made from light oak veneer running down the length of the sizeable room. There were no matching tables and chairs, but an eclectic mix that clashed slightly with the neat, dull, clean lines of the bar counter. No doubt a potential subject for upcoming committee meetings. Not all of the old had been discarded. The collection of golf memorabilia and bric-a-brac had been spared, and if it was not displayed in cabinets, it was mounted on the walls. The end result of the refurbishment was a cross between a corporate hotel reception area and a pawn shop.

There were three men waiting to be served when Moz entered the room. He was in no hurry to get back to standing in the sun behind a bunch of slow players. He looked around the room, and a photograph hanging above a small display cabinet caught his eye. It was of a man in a military uniform. Wanting a closer look, he walked over to it. There was a large leather bound bible in the cabinet. The display card read

The South African War 1899 – 1902
ON LOAN FROM THE KETTERING FAMILY

Moz's pulse started to race. He looked up at the black and white photo hanging on the wall, and read the caption on the brass plate attached to the bottom of the frame

Inaugural Club Captain, Major Robert Kettering 1892 -1899

Buying a cold drink was no longer a priority for Moz. His pulse was racing, and he could feel his heart pumping furiously in his chest. The research farmer was very seldom fazed by anything, but he stood staring at the British Officer, acutely aware of the ramifications for Elsa that this extraordinary discovery was going to have on her and her family. He closed his eyes for a moment, desperately trying to calm down and slow his racing pulse. While they were closed he also took the liberty to ask his Maker for guidance. Guidance provided, he left the bar and walked briskly back to the 10th tee.

'For heaven sake Moz, where the hell have you been?' asked a hot and grumpy Alistair. 'At least four pairs have gone through. Where are the drinks?'

'Alistair, I'm really sorry but something has come up, and I need Elsa's help. Would you mind finishing the round on your own? Elsa will take me home.'

'Moz, what's wrong. Can I help?' asked his now puzzled and concerned golf partner.

'Alistair, everything is fine. It's just a personal matter,' replied Moz. 'Please excuse me, I must call Elsa. I'll fill you in, later.'

'Moz, what's the problem?' asked a confused and worried Elsa as she got out of the car.

'I've got something to show you,' he replied. He took his wife's hand and lead her towards the bar. At the entrance, he stopped and cupped Elsa's face in his hands and looked her in the eyes.

'Els, you are not going to believe what I have discovered. It is a coincidence beyond all comprehension. I just pray to God that it will give your family some sort of closure.'

'Mozzie, I love you very much, but you overdo the praying sometimes. Come on, show me.'

The Nels walked hand-in-hand across the bar, and stopped in front of the photograph hanging above the small Kettering display cabinet. Moz didn't say a word. Elsa looked at the bible, and then raised her head to look at the British army officer. Moz felt her tighten her grip.

'So, Major Robert Kettering, this is what you looked like,' she said quietly.

CHAPTER 34

Since Jeremy's funeral, Tia had gone through a whole range of emotions; sadness, anger, guilt, relief.

His death had been so sudden and unexpected. She had despised him for so long. Now that he was gone, there was a void where the old habit of chastising him at every turn had once been. She had a first from the University of Hard Knocks, and her late husband had certainly handed out some tough assignments.

Her lowest points were fuelled by alcohol, and brought on periods of extreme sadness and anger. Great sadness that she had wasted her life on him. Intense angry at how useless he had been. When she sobered up, she felt liberated, hopeful about the future. There were even short periods of guilt; could she have done more to understand and support his artistic temperament. The guilt did not last long and a few more plates were angrily thrown against the kitchen wall every time she finished a bottle of claret.

Two weeks passed by and Tia managed to stay sober long enough to return to work. Keeping busy proved to be a healing panacea. She started to have fewer and less intensive mood swings, was able to think more clearly, and started to consider the future.

One Saturday morning, she woke up thinking about Jeremy and the mystery of the music studio. She finished her breakfast of scrambled egg and bacon, made another coffee, and headed down the corridor towards the closed door to Jeremy's music suite. The door that had excluded her from his life. She paused, hesitated for a moment, and with a trembling hand opened it.

Walking slowly over to the desk, she carefully avoided the piles of sheet music on the floor, sat down, and looked around the room. Sheet music everywhere, music cases leaning up against the walls, abandoned musical instruments gathering dust, a few leather briefcases scattered around the room. She looked at a brown wax jacket hanging on a wooden coat stand and hesitated for a moment. Not sure that's Jeremy's she thought. She got up and walked over to it. She opened both lapels and looked at the checked olive lining, and felt inside the large pockets. They were empty.

She returned to the desk, and angrily rummaged through the heap of papers in front of her in the hope of discovering the answer to the music studio question. Finding nothing, she turned her attention to the desk drawers which resulted in her emptying the contents of each one of them onto the floor. The last one contained a number of mobile phones.

She threw handfuls of sheet music across the room, and opened the music cases leaning up against the walls. Most were empty. She found a violin and smashed it down on top of the desk. Wood splinters and violin strings flying everywhere. There was a dusty clarinet on one of the window sills, and picking it up, hurled it across the room. She picked up a couple of briefcases and flung them in the general direction of the wind-bourne clarinet.

As quickly as it had started, Jeremy's widow stopped her rampage, and bending over with her hands on her knees, breathed heavily in short deep gasps with her eyes closed. Catching her breath, she stood up and opened her eyes. She was standing in front of Jeremy's steel grey gun cabinet. Such a bloody hypocrite she thought. When I met him he was a violent anti-animal cruelty protestor, and then ended up at weekend shoots with the landed gentry. Tia was not a fan of the shoot, and smiled at the thought of selling the guns. Actually I cannot wait to get rid of everything in this room. Wipe out every last memory of him she thought.

She opened the cupboard. Jeremy's guns were secure, and there were boxes of cartridges on the top shelf. As she closed the door, she glanced down at the bottom of the cupboard. No it's not possible. She closed her eyes, and shook her head to try and clear the image of what she had just seen. She opened her eyes slowly; it was still there.

Kneeling down she picked up a bundle of twenty pound notes held together with an elastic band. There were bundles of 10, 20 and 50 pound notes stacked up in neat piles. She sat down on the floor and stared at the money. There must be thousands of pounds here. Where did it all come from? What was Jeremy doing with so much money?

A yellow envelope that had been pushed down the side of one of the piles of money caught her eye. She pulled it out, and lifting the flap saw there was a letter inside. Her hands were shaking as she removed the single sheet of paper. It was an invoice addressed to Brian Townsend. Something had been written on the back, Tia turned it over.

My Dear Hanna
By the time you read this note, the despair, sadness and disappointment I feel for having failed you and your mother will be over…… Christ this is Brian's suicide note thought Tia……*The failing crops and the never ending spiral of debt have finally beaten me……*Tears started to well up in her eyes……*There*

is no fight left in me. ...... She could hardly see through her tears...... I watched Kettering-Smythe visit his new house at Fields View almost every day last summer while it was being built. The reason for our demise lies in that house. Corrupt officials and crop saboteurs....... That bloody dodgy KS sniffed Tia wiping away the tears with the back of her hand *.......please find out the truth, but most importantly of all, please forgive me. I'm so ashamed. Love Dad. XX.*

The freedom that Jeremy's death had given Tia was short lived with the discovery of the suicide note and the money. She raged against him for returning from the grave to continue messing up her life. She started to drink heavily again, showed signs of agoraphobia, and her absence from work was putting her job at risk.

Elsa had, on a number of occasions, taken her work colleague much needed meals, stayed to tidy up the house, and take away dirty washing that was piling up. Despite Elsa's attempts to get Tia to talk, she refused saying it was a family matter and nobody else's business. Elsa's kindness irritated Tia, especially when her visitor kept on proclaiming that God would provide the answer, and that she would pray for Tia in this, her time of need.

Despite the alcoholic haze, Tia started to piece together what her husband had been up to. He had somehow come into the possession of Brian Townsend's suicide note. Although she was not entirely sure, the mysterious wax jacket had something to do with it. Then there was the desk drawer full of mobile phones. Blackmailers on tv call them burners.

The unemployed musician, having been given an ultimatum from her about getting a job, had obviously seized on the opportunity to blackmail KS. If the money was anything to go by, it had worked. KS was obviously hiding something. Then the musician covered up the extortion by creating the bogus job at the music studio. He would get up early so that he and his saxophone could warm up before breakfast. Then, with a cheery wave, head off to a non-existent job, whistling to himself like one of the seven dwarfs, and return eight hours later still whistling and smiling.

Night after night, she lay awake with questions swirling around her throbbing head. How did Jeremy get hold of the suicide note? Why did he not hand it in to the police? Did he at any stage consider Hanna? What made him think he would get away with it? Does his death have something to do with the blackmail? Did KS have him murdered?
Don't care she thought. Come to think of it, what am I going to do with the suicide note and the money? Tia switched on the bedside light and sat up in bed. What am I going to do she thought.

CHAPTER 35

Bella and Paul Nel ran ahead of their parents, through the open wooden lych-gate of All Saints, and along the gravel path leading up to the church. Father Aldridge was standing at the church door looking suitably liturgical in his vestments.

'Hello Father Aldridge,' greeted Paul.

'Welcome to both of you. Second harvest festival celebration in one week,' smiled the vicar, his hands appearing from beneath his robes as he unfolded his arms.

'We walked from the farm. Mom and Dad are slow coaches, so we ran ahead,' added Bella gasping for breath from the exertion.

'I'm sure they won't be long. Go inside and have a look at the harvest decorations. The church is looking very beautiful.'

The children disappeared into the church, and a few minutes later their parents arrived.

'Good afternoon, Father. I hope the kids haven't been a nuisance,' greeted Moz.

'Not at all. I wish all my young parishioners were as enthusiastic about the church as your two,' replied Father Aldridge, his hands disappearing again as he folded his arms.

'Father Aldridge,' greeted Elsa shaking the vicar's hand. 'The children enjoyed the harvest assembly at school on Wednesday. You have quite a fan in Paul,' she added. 'He finds our minister back home very solemn and morose.'

'Ah, one of the brimstone and fire crowd,' smiled Father Aldridge. 'Not good PR for the church. Anyway, each to his own. Moz, while I've got you here, I read an article in *The Counties Herald* about the warm weather adversely affecting the wheat trials. Is it true or was it just fake news?'

'Ya, I read it as well. It was partially correct. True, the hot weather didn't produce the results we were expecting, but the bit about the trials being abandoned indefinitely was just thumb-sucking. Some of the technical detail in the article was also incorrect, which was irritating,' replied the research farmer.

'We're going home for a couple of months. My mother has dementia, and isn't very well. The plan is to spend Christmas at home, and return in the New Year when the trials start again,' added Elsa.

'I'm sorry to hear about your mother, I'll add her to our prayers,' responded the vicar. 'I'm pleased you will be returning. You've all been a refreshing and delightful addition to my congregation.'

'That's very kind of you to say so,' replied a beaming Moz. 'Actually Father, we've come a bit earlier than necessary, we have a favour to ask of you.' Moz glanced at his wife. She nodded her head slightly giving him permission to continue. 'Would it be possible for Elsa and I to have a chat with you after the service? It's a personal matter, but it shouldn't take long.'

'By all means Moz. The vestry will probably be the best place to talk. A bit more private,' replied the vicar. 'Right, back to the here and now, enjoy the evening. There's tea, coffee and cake in the south aisle. Please help yourself.'

The harvest festival display was laid out along the length of the narthex against the railings which separated it from the nave. Picture perfect would best describe the array of foods that cascaded from the north aisle side of the church to the south aisle. Neatly tied sheaves of wheat, large wicker baskets filled with barley, borrige, echium and rape. Pyramids of sugar beet. Peas, beans and apples. Potatoes, eggs and honey roast hams. Tantalising ingredients for a tea of ham, egg and chips. Contributions made by local residents added to the pageantry; autumn flowers from the gardens; carrots, onions, lettuces, pumpkins and courgettes from the allotments. A display of thanks for a successful summer harvest.

A harvest assembly had been held at the primary school during the week, and the tins of food that the children had brought to that gathering were now exhibited in the church along with the food that had been collected from the land. The children's contribution will be donated to the food bank at Blacktree Crossing once the festival is over.

The stone font standing near the entrance to the west tower was seconded for use as a large vase. It had been filled with unconsecrated water; its deep bowl supporting a huge peacock tail shaped flower display; hydrangeas with their white, blue and pink florets, single and double flowered dahlias, roses, and orange, red, and yellow daisy-like cosmos; ivy and blackberries entwined between the stems.

A large leather bound bible lay open on the altar in front of a brass cross. The three stained glass windows behind the altar sparkled in the afternoon sunshine, their coloured patterns moving slowly across the floor. The tall altar candles on either side of the bible pointed resolutely towards the heavens and appeared uncomfortable with having to share their normally minimalistic surroundings with flowers and ivy that appeared to have been flung onto the altar.

Father Aldridge joined All Saints as the priest-in-charge at a time when the parish was in the doldrums, and the church was under threat of closing. As an ex-army chaplain, he has the touch of the common people and from the outset he immersed himself in the ways of rural life. Married with two sons, he was able to relate to the lives of the people of his parish. He is a straight talker, a characteristic that often has him at odds with the church leadership. Despite these sporadic disagreements, his greatest asset, the ability to get a large number of people to attend his church, was recognised, and he was appointed the vicar of All Saints six years after arriving in Weatherford. Running a bit behind schedule due to people arriving late, Father Aldridge climbed the pulpit's short flight of steps. The church fell silent as the vicar, looking out at the sea of faces below him smiled, and started his twelfth harvest festival service at All Saints.

Throughout the service, Father Aldridge had tried to think of a reason why the Nels wanted to talk to him. Parishioners usually came to him for advice and guidance if they had marital, money, wayward children or any one of a multitude of family problems. Apart from Elsa's mother being poorly,

Moz and Elsa never struck him as having personal problems that needed airing, let alone consultation.

When the service was over, Alistair and Jessica Burns offered to take Bella and Paul home and give them their tea. With the children safely on their way home, and the vicar having bid the last parishioner goodnight, Moz and Elsa followed Father Aldridge to the vestry.

Sitting at the large vestry table, surrounded by clerical robes, old pews and rusty filing cabinets, Elsa nervously told the vicar about the discovery of the family bible at the golf club. A very surprised vicar found himself staring at Elsa with his mouth open.

Without showing any emotion, she explained how the bible had ended up 6,000 miles away from their family home. Elsa paused for a moment, and Moz asked Father Aldridge if there was a family connection between Major Kettering and Richard Kettering-Smythe. The vicar said he was not absolutely sure if there was, but if his memory served him correctly, Richard had taken on his wife's name Smythe when they got married. It was something that could be checked very easily.

Father Aldridge then turned to Elsa, and asked her what it was that they wanted him to do. She said that they were facing a huge dilemma. They're able to prove that the bible belongs to their family, and want to take it home with them when they returned to SA. What they didn't want to do was make a fuss nor upset anyone. She went on to say that despite preconceived ideas about living in England they had been made to feel so welcome, and the whole family loved the farm, the countryside, the people, and most importantly of all, they felt that they were safe.

Father Aldridge sat looking across the table at the farmer and his wife, and knew what they wanted him to do. He was not sure however, whether his remit included retrieving plundered family heirlooms. He broke the silence and suggested a plan of action which required the cooperation of the golf club and the Kettering family. He would approach both parties with a view to persuading the club to return the bible to the Ketterings, and the Kettering family, in turn, would allow it to return to South Africa with the Nels. The vicar finished off by saying that although he felt this problem could be easily resolved, the two parties involved might have other ideas.

Father Aldridge was not one for spontaneous action, and when faced with an important decision, he liked to wait 24 hours before doing anything. A cooling-off period he called it, and always used the time to calmly consider the best course of action. A life mantra that had served him well.

Despite his reservations as to his ability to convince KS and the golf club to return the Nel's bible, he had, on reflection, come to the conclusion that it should be given back. To his surprise, the vicar discovered that he was having far more success than the government's Brexit negotiating team.

KS did not hesitate to invite the vicar around to his house to discuss the extraordinary coincidence. In the time that it took to drink a cup of tea, the parish councillor requested a few days to discuss the matter with the rest of his family, and   agreed that Father Aldridge should go ahead and arrange a meeting with the golf club management committee.

Setting up the meeting with the golf club proved to be a little more difficult. The vicar's initial attempt to get hold of the committee chairman proved to be problematic. He left numerous messages, but got the distinct feeling that either they were not being passed on or the chairman was just not returning his calls.

Undeterred he resorted to a Google search and discovered that the President of the golf club was Sir Lionel Grail, a very successful city businessman. He called Sir Lionel, explained the reason for the call, mentioned the press, and by mid-afternoon the vicar received a call from the chairman of the golf committee. A meeting with the full committee had been arranged for Monday week.

KS waited at the main entrance to the golf club for Moz and Elsa to arrive. Walking ahead of them, he escorted them through the administration office housed in the original wattle and darb part of the building, and up the stairs to the boardroom.

'Isn't it strange to think that Robert Kettering probably walked up and down these very stairs,' commented KS struggling to come up with appropriate small talk. Neither Moz nor Elsa replied.

KS opened one of the oak double doors at the top of the flight of stairs, and ushered the Nels into the boardroom. A group of men and women were standing around a table laid with cups and saucers, plates of biscuits and a boiling urn. They broke off their conversation about the cooler weather and the Northern Ireland backstop, and looked up as their three visitors entered the room. KS introduced Moz and Elsa to the group, and with cups of coffee and tea poured, the committee members took their seats on either side of the chairman who sat at the head of the large oak table.

Unlike those parts of the club house that overlook the beautifully manicured golf course, the boardroom is at the back of the building, and looks out over the roofs of the greenkeepers' sheds. The view consists of green corrugated iron, sit on lawnmowers, in various stages of disrepair, a couple of golf carts that have been robbed for spares, and a pile of metal that nobody ever bothers to cart away. Unfortunately, the small lead and glass windows of the boardroom are unable to keep the noise of machinery, and the occasional colourful banter between the greenkeepers from interrupting agenda items.

'I would like to open this meeting by welcoming Mr and Mrs Nel, and of course KS a very familiar face here at the club and around town,' smiled the chairman Matthew Davies, a retired carpenter. 'I have to confess today's business is so unusual I was not entirely sure which members of the committee should attend. In consultation with Mrs Debbie Gardiner, our General Manager here on my right, it was decided that it would be prudent if we called the whole committee together rather than make arbitrary assumptions as to who should or who should not be here.' The treasurer Richard Walters started to fidget in his seat. The chairman glared at the restless treasurer as if he was one of his former wayward apprentices. 'As mentioned in the email to all attendees, this meeting was requested by Sir Lionel, and this morning he text me to say that he expects the office bearers make decisions that uphold the good name and reputation of our club.' Richard Walters a habitual pen clicker started to click his pen with impatience. 'Well, there are obviously some of us that need to get on,' commented the chairman, giving the secretary a filthy look. 'It's cooled down considerably, but if anyone wishes to put the fans on, be my guest. Right, let's get on with today's business,' announced the chairman after a brief pause to allow a lawnmower to start up and drive away. 'I trust you have all read my email outlining the subject matter of today's meeting which involved Major Kettering during the Anglo-Boer War.' The committee members nodded their heads in unison. 'Mr Nel would you like to begin?'

'Um, Mr Davies, as this is my wife's family business I think she would like to give you the background to the bible.' replied Moz, taking Elsa's hand and squeezing it.

'By all means, please continue Mrs Nel.'

'You can call me Elsa,' smiled the farmer's wife. She paused to pour water into a glass and take a small sip. 'I would like to start by saying that we are not here to cause any trouble. I think the discovery of the bible has been as much of a shock to you as it has been for my family. I'm able to prove that it does belong to us, and I can tell you the story, that has been passed down by my family through the generations, as to how it was removed from the family farm.' Elsa stopped for a moment, as a lawnmower skidded to a halt on the gravel outside. 'Here is a photograph,' continued Elsa handing copies to the Ladies Captain, Linda Edwards who took one and passed the rest on to the other members. 'It shows my great-grandparents sitting at their kitchen table with the bible between them. The little boy is my grandfather Paul, and the girl is his sister.' Elsa's voice did not waver. 'One morning just after breakfast, the British arrived at the farm. An officer and 10 soldiers. The officer was Major Kettering and he told my great-grandmother that the railway line had been blown up a mile from Kempdale during the night. He told her that as her husband was part the Kempdale Commando, he was under orders to move the family. They had a horse and cart with them, and he ordered his men to remove furniture that was worth taking, and to destroy the rest. One the soldiers brought the bible out of the house to show the officer, this bible,' Elsa said pointing at the photograph. 'The Major told the soldier to wrap it up in a blanket, and to make sure it did not get damaged on the cart.' Elsa stopped and took a long sip of water. There was a deathly silence in the room. 'The soldiers found bags of corn, stockpiled for the winter. They were told to pour it out onto the ground and set it alight. Our family still refer to the destruction of the food as the lost harvest. The family were given ten minutes to gather their belongings. Once the furniture had been loaded onto the cart, the soldiers turned their attention to the farmworkers. Their meagre dwellings were set alight. A soldier found a stone-walled pen full of sheep. He was ordered to shoot them. Eventually, everyone was herded into the cart, and the farmhouse torched. The soldiers waited until the roof had collapsed before the order to move out was given.' The Ladies Captain wiped tears from her eyes with a tissue, while the rest of the committee members sat in shocked silence. 'I've taken up too much of your time,' apologised Elsa. 'I just want to finish off by saying that my great-grandmother and the children were taken to a concentration camp near Bloemfontein. Only Paul survived. Their farmworkers were taken to a separate concentration camp were they all died. Long after the war ended, we heard that Major Kettering became the Acting-Superintendent of the Bloemfontein Concentration Camp, for a short period, before being transferred to Irene, another concentration camp, just outside Pretoria.' Sitting perfectly still and upright, Elsa had described the incident without showing any emotion. She was not going to show any sign of weakness in front of the strangers sitting in front of her. She was there to retrieve the bible, and she would not leave without it. 'I'm here today Mr Davies, to respectfully request that the bible be returned to our family. It does not belong here in England.'

'Mrs Nel, Elsa, whilst the sheer coincidence of you being reunited with the bible is remarkable and what happened to your family is very sad, I'm not, however, in a position to pass comment about the behaviour of nor the actions of my countrymen 120 years ago. You have asked us to return the family possession, and under normal circumstances we as a committee would put the motion to a vote. Before we proceed I would like to ask Mr Kettering-Smythe for his comment.

'Thank you Mr Chairman. It goes without saying that this discovery has been discussed at length by the Kettering family. We are of the opinion that the bible should be returned to Elsa and Moz. On behalf of my family, I am advising the committee that we wish to withdraw our loan of the bible to the golf club. Our family would like to return it to the Nels.'

'Thank you, KS. I think it's time for a vote. All in favour of the bible being returned to the Kettering family, please raise a hand.' To Elsa and Moz's joy, the vote was unanimous.

'I guess we'll have to find out the best way to get the bible transported back home,' commented Elsa as she and Moz got into their car.

'Might be an idea to ask Kay Beswick. She sends things all over the world.'

'Good idea, Mozzie.' Husband and wife sat in silence while they slowly made their way through the grid-locked town. 'Phew, I'm exhausted from the tension,' said Elsa looking across at Moz.

'Ya, I guess we both are.'

'We really need not have worried about it. It was pretty straight forward. Asking Father Aldridge to be our go-between certainly helped,' smiled Elsa.

'You were very brave in there, Els. You did us proud. I don't know how you got through it without breaking down.'

'It was something that I had to do for the family. Coming out of that meeting without the bible was not an option. Actually, I can't wait to tell the kids.'

When the bible was first discovered at the golf club, Elsa had told the children the story surrounding its origin and significance to their family. Paul had sat quietly and sensing the importance of the story listened carefully to his mother. Unlike her brother, Bella had been far more inquisitive and asked a number of questions. She wanted to know why the farmhouse had been burnt down; what had happened to the people living in the house, and how did the bible get to England.

Chloe Burns had child-minded Bella and Paul while their parents were at the meeting. When she left, Elsa told the children that the bible was going to be returned to the family. To Elsa's surprise the children showed very little interest in the retrieval of the family heirloom. Their priority was nutella toast, and another half an hour watching CBBC before going off to bed. Elsa's parents made up for her children's indifference. She skyped them, told them the news, and then thought they were both going to drop down dead with excitement.

The golf club meeting had been stressful, and although Elsa was very pleased with the outcome, she was exhausted from having spent the day coiled up like a spring. When she finally did go to bed, she was unable to sleep; tossing and turning until it was time to get up.

CHAPTER 36

Elsa had already been at her desk an hour, when the *Swarm International UK* office started to come to life as people began arriving for work. She sat at her desk and listened to the sound of her colleagues muffled conversations; she watched Sally, one of the PR staff, opening the windows along the west side of the open plan office. The heat wave was relentless, and getting cool air to circulate was a priority. It even replaced the sacrosanct number one daily ritual of first switching on the kettle before doing any work. The telephones woke up from their overnight slumber, and it was not long before printers could be heard churning out pages of the rain forest's finest.

KS was on leave, and although it was still early, the atmosphere in the office already felt more relaxed in his absence. The edgy silence that usually prevailed was replaced by a comfortable level of chatter and noise. There was even a bit of laughter.

The chairman was not a people-person. His rudeness, bad temper and confrontational behaviour were certainly not the best attributes one would expect from the head of a charity. He was, however, an exception administrator, and despite his crassness, he had the ability to move in social circles that offered the charity plenty of opportunities and supporters. He also had an uncanny appreciation of the complexity of the logistics involved in getting the mosquito nets from the suppliers to anywhere in the world. No mean feat, considering many of the destinations were remote and often in war zones.

Tia Hughes arrived half an hour late, and Elsa was very pleased to see her.

'Welcome back Tia. You're looking well. I've missed you.'

'Hi Elsa. Was bloody dreading coming back. Didn't really have a choice,' replied Tia slinging her handbag onto the desk. She slumped down in the chair, and kicked off her sandals.

'When you came in yesterday, we thought KS was going to fire you.'

'Final warning,' replied Tia shrugging her shoulders in a matter-of-fact way.

'Well, we'll all have a break from him for a fortnight. He's on leave,' smiled Elsa. 'While you've been away, I've kept an eye on things for you. Cleared your mail, done your filing, and passed things that I thought might need action onto PR and Marketing. I hope you don't mind.'

'No not at all. Very kind of you. Thanks.' Tia turned on her computer. 'Shall we get a sandwich and catch up at lunchtime?'

'Sure,' replied Elsa.

'It's lovely and relaxed with KS away,' remarked Tia as she and Elsa sat down at a table in the shade of a large oak tree in the court yard behind the office building.

'Very different,' answered Elsa. 'Forget KS, I want to hear how you are,' she added unwrapping a smoked salmon and cream cheese sandwich.

'Where do I start? I think I'm coping better. I must just stay off the booze. It isn't the answer.' Her friend nodded in agreement.

'Do the police know how Jeremy was injured?' asked Elsa taking a sip of orange juice.

'They have pieced together a sequence of events, and think Jeremy had an altercation with someone, a person or persons unknown, as they call it. They have plenty of DNA, but no match apart from the people who tried to help him that night. We just have to be patient. What have you and that lovely family of yours been up to in my absence?' Tia asked as she took a bite of the vegan mock tuna sandwich she had bought out of curiosity.

'We're all fine. Unfortunately the unusually warm weather has thrown a spanner in the works with the wheat trials. The results are not useable.'

'Yugh!' exclaimed Tia with a painful expression on her face. 'This is awful,' she added, throwing her sandwich into the bin. 'Would rather eat the packaging with a bit of ketchup on it.'

'Here have half of mine,' laughed Elsa. 'Can I ask you a question about work?' she added.

'Shoot,' replied Tia.

'Who is responsible for the *Africa Wide Haulage* account?'

'They're the transport people we use in Africa. That's one of KS's suppliers. He deals with them himself. Always has done. Why?'

'No reason. I had to deal with a query the other day. KS and you were not here so I dealt with it myself.'

'Not surprised Elsa, you're very capable. Talking about the wheat trials, I hear on the village grapevine, they're stopping them,' continued Tia as she gleefully bit into Elsa's remaining half a sandwich.

'No, not entirely. There is talk of giving it another go next summer,' replied the farmer's wife. 'Moz has already been asked to come back in the New Year if they go ahead.'

'How do you feel about it?'

'Mixed really. On the one hand it will be nice to see my parents again. My mum is not very well. She has dementia, and I feel it's my duty to return home. On the other hand, living here is so easy and relaxed. Everything is so organised. The one thing I haven't missed about home is waking up every morning and asking God to protect our family, friends and farmworkers from the violence around us. I wake up here knowing that my husband and children will be safe.'

'Didn't really work out like that for Jeremy,' Tia commented looking Elsa in the eye.

'Tia, I'm so sorry. I didn't mean it like that. What happened to Jeremy was terrible.'

'Elsa, I know you didn't mean it. Don't apologise. I understand where you're coming from and in any case I'm better off without him.'

Elsa's gaffe dried up the conversation. She felt terrible about what she had unintentionally said to Tia. I wonder if I should tell her about the bible. Take too long. Anyway it's only a family story of no interest to anyone else. Should I mention my discovery about KS she pondered.

'Elsa can you keep a secret? You are not to tell anyone. Not even Moz. Promise me. It's about KS.' Elsa turned white. 'Are you ok? You look like you're going to faint.'

'No, no. I'm fine. I was miles away,' replied Elsa.

'Well?'

'I promise.'

Elsa's promise opened a floodgate. Tia told her colleague what she had found in Jeremy's music room. How she had pieced together the mystery about her late husband. The non-existent job, the money, Brian Townsend's suicide note and what it said, the mobile phones, the mysterious wax jacket, and finally coming to the conclusion that Jeremy had been blackmailing KS. The only thing that she could not work out was why he had been blackmailing the parish councillor.

'Do you think KS murdered Jeremy because of the blackmail,' asked an astonished Elsa.

'I don't know, but it all points to that conclusion,' replied the widow. 'There's something else.'

'What?' There surely cannot be more thought the dumbfounded Elsa.

'I really, really want to keep the money,' exclaimed Tia.

'Tia you can't do that. You need to go to the police. If you don't you will end up in jail. They need that suicide note. Hanna Townsend needs to see the note. More importantly if KS murdered Jeremy he has to be arrested. You have to get justice for your late husband regardless of how you feel about him.'

'After all I've been through, I think I'm entitled to keep the money,' replied Tia getting up from the table. 'Lunch break is over. Let's get back.' she added rather bluntly.

'Ya, we've been here awhile,' agreed Elsa.

'Mozzie, pour us a glass of wine. I want to run something passed you? It involves work.'

'Sounds a bit ominous,' replied the research farmer taking a bottle of white wine out of the fridge. 'OK, go-ahead.'

'Well, as you know Tia Hughes has been off sick. Came back to work a couple of days ago,' began Elsa taking a sip of wine. 'While she was away, I kept an eye on her post and anything else that landed up on her desk. The other day, Rosemary from Accounts gave me an invoice for *Africa Wide Haulage.* She said it was a duplicate invoice, and asked me to put it aside for Tia to follow-up when she returned. With Tia away and KS on leave I decided to contact the transport company myself. The thing is, I couldn't get through to them. The telephone number was not in service and the emails bounced back as undeliverable.'

'Where are they based?' asked Moz topping up the glasses.

'Place called Spalding,' replied the farmer's wife. 'I did a google search and couldn't find anything. Google map showed the address belonging to a second-hand car dealership on an industrial estate.'

'Have you mentioned it to anyone in the office?' asked Moz.

'No. I did ask Tia when she came back to work. She knew about the invoices, but said KS had always dealt with them,' replied Elsa. 'I've been through the invoices on file, and the strange thing is there are no orders, only invoices. None of them have order numbers and all of them were approved by KS for payment.'

Moz raised his eyebrows. 'It sounds very similar to the fraud at that charity you worked for when we were first married.'

'Certainly does.'

'How much money are we talking about?'

'Thousands of pounds,' replied Elsa.

'So what are you going do?'

'It's a dilemma Mozzie. If it's what we think it is, exposing the fraud will get KS into serious trouble. He was magnanimous in returning the bible to us. Can we really do this to him? I've only been at the charity a few months, and after all the kindness that has been shown to us, can we really do such a thing. I'm not sure I have the courage to do it. I'm also worried that the offer to come back next year to carry on with the trials might be withdrawn if the villagers turn against us.'

'Els, I wouldn't worry about the trials. When we get back home, we might decide that we cannot leave your mum. She is not well. It might also be too disruptive for the kids. We've had a wonderful time here, and maybe it would be better to quit while we're ahead.'

'True, Moz. We really can't second guess the future, can we?' replied Elsa. The couple sat in silence, holding hands. Elsa felt disappointed that they might not return to England. She desperately wanted to keep her family safe. She let out a long sigh of surrender.

'Defrauding a charity is wicked,' commented Moz. 'Of course, there's more than one way to skin a cat.'

'How do you mean, Mozzie?'

'Give the information to someone who would like to see KS behind bars,' he replied smiling.

'Anyone in mind?'

'Hanna. She's got an axe to grind, and she's a solicitor. She'll know what to do with the information. Give her copies of the invoices, and ask her not to tell anyone how they came into her possession.'

CHAPTER 37

'Morning ma'am.' greeted Chris Brown, as his boss DI Veronica James entered the open plan office.

'Morning, Sergeant. Are you ready?'

'Yes, ma'am. Here's the file. I'll get the coffees.' He returned a few minutes later with the drinks, and politely hesitated at the DI's office door.

'Come in, Chris. Close the door.' Pushing the door shut with his right foot, he put the mugs of coffee on the desk and sat down opposite his boss. 'Ok let's start at the beginning, and go through the sequence of events,' began the DI opening the file her sergeant had given her a few minutes earlier. 'The couple in question, Richard Waters 34 years of age and Holly Pilkington 32 years old, currently living at 30 Mount Hall Lane, Otley were in the Green Man in Weatherford the night that Jeremy Hughes was found injured on the pavement. They were on holiday travelling around Essex.'

'Proof of their itinerary is all there in the file, ma'am, and it matches up with their statements.'

'Good. We have several witnesses who heard and saw them arguing in the pub,' continued the DI.

'Yes, and I've re-checked the statements and there are no discrepancies,' replied the DS.

'Do we know what they were arguing about?'

'One of the pub witnesses mentioned it was about an engagement party. There is no record as to what was actually said,' replied the sergeant.

'Probably a bog-standard family squabble about a wedding. So, moving on, they were seen leaving together. According to Mr Waters, the couple got into their car and drove away from the pub towards the church. They were a few hundred yards down the road when they saw Jeremy Hughes waiting to cross the road. For some unknown reason, he stepped out from between two parked cars into the path of the oncoming vehicle. They couldn't stop in time. Both Mr Waters and Miss Pilkington got out of the car. Jeremy was getting up off the ground, and they helped him to the kerb. He was on his feet and told them that he was fine and his house was only a couple of doors away. When the couple left him he was walking along the pavement towards his home.

According to them he seemed fine, possibly a bit groggy.'

'The problem is we have no witnesses from the time they left the pub until Mr Wright found Jeremy lying on the pavement,' commented the DS.

'Which is unfortunate. However, forensics have evidence that the car was in the high street, and estimate it was travelling at 30 mph when Jeremy stepped out into the road. His injuries match this hypothesis,' continued the DI.

'Are we sure about his head injury,' asked the DS.

'We have to trust the post mortem and forensics on this one. They are of the opinion that when the couple stopped to help Mr Hughes he might have felt battered and bruised, but there is a strong possibility that he actually did feel fine. It was only later, after they left, that the hematoma began which caused him to collapse and hit his head on the pavement. The injury is consistent with this type of fall. There were a few other bruises and grazes on his body which are consistent with contact with a moving vehicle the size and weight of Waters' car. There is no evidence to suggest he was attacked. It's just an unfortunate accident.'

'Are we absolutely sure Dave Wright didn't attack him, ma'am.'

'There's no evidence, Chris,' answered the DI shaking her head. 'You've gone over his statement with a fine toothcomb.'

'A dozen times,' replied the DS.

'And?'

'There are no irregularities.'

'I think Waters, as the owner of the vehicle should have left his details with Mr Hughes and reported the accident to the police. I can understand not doing it at the time, all the confusion, the shock, etcetera, but surely after a couple of days you would come to realise that the accident should be reported to the police.'

'They were probably too excited about their trip to the States ma'am, and didn't give the accident another thought,' suggested the sergeant.

'Probably. Unfortunately I think they will land up in court.'

'In all fairness, they did come forward as soon as they got back and heard that Mr Hughes had died,' replied the DS.

'You're right. They did cooperate fully with us. Should help, if they're charged. We have checked all the details of their American itinerary?'

'Yes, ma'am. Miss Pilkington's relatives confirmed that they were visiting them in Albuquerque, and we've received booking details from all of the hotels and airlines they used. We can account for every single day that they were away,' replied the sergeant.

'Good. I think we've finished. We need to let Mrs Hughes know the results of our investigation. It'll probably be best if we visit her in person. I'll sort out a date.' The DI closed the file and handed it to her sergeant. 'Well done, Chris. Send the file upstairs, and let them decide the next step.'

'Thank you ma'am,' replied the DS.

'Everything ready for the big day?' asked the DI with a smile.

'Just about, ma'am. I think my family, especially my aunts, are all on speed.' he whispered. 'Planning the wedding has been fun, but enough is enough. I just want it to be over now.'

Tia had spent so many nights agonising about the suicide note, the blackmail and the money. When DI James phoned her, it proved to be a godsend. On hearing the detective's voice, Tia knew what she had to do.

Two days later, the DI accompanied by DS Kate Hope, were sitting in Tia's lounge. The Detective Inspector went through the details of the investigation, and after answering a few questions from the widow, she ended up by saying that all of the evidence pointed to Jeremy's death having been an unfortunate accident.

With no further questions, it was now Tia's turn. She had forewarned the DI that she had information that might have some bearing on Brian Townsend's suicide. Tia told them about the bogus job, and how after years of having no money, it had suddenly become plentiful. The DI wanted to see Jeremy's music room. She showed the police the suicide note, the money, the mobile phones and the mystery wax jacket. The Inspector didn't say much. Just looked and listened. Eventually, she told Tia that the blackmail would be investigated, and she would make arrangements for Jeremy's music room to be searched, and items of interest to be removed. Tia said she would cooperate fully with the police. The police eventually left, and Tia stood at the front door waiting for them to leave. The DI made a couple of telephone calls before driving off.

The widow waved goodbye, and slowly closed the door. She went through to the kitchen, sat down, and stared at a half full cafetiere that had recently replaced the claret. For the first time in years, she felt liberated. *Jeremy can no longer make my life a misery. I have finally got rid of him.*

DI James opened the file in front of her, and picked up an invoice for two rear tractor tyres. A purchase Brian Townsend had made a year ago in September. She turned it over, and looked at the unsteady hand writing. She managed to keep her feelings under control, as she started to read Brian Townsend's last letter to his only daughter.

My Dear Hanna
By the time you read this note, the despair, sadness and disappointment I feel for having failed you and your mother will be over. Since your mother died, I have carried on the daily drudge of life, but without the joy of having her here beside me. I know she would have been bitterly disappointed with me for not having looked after your inheritance. The failing crops and the never ending spiral of debt have finally beaten me. I have tried my best to save something of the farm for you, but I am now exhausted. There is no fight left in me. I followed the correct procedures when I submitted the planning permission to build

new houses on part of our land. I did everything that was asked of me, and ignored the 'off-the-record' conversations outside of official meetings. I firmly believe that we could have saved the farm if we had been granted permission to build the houses. I have been left homeless, penniless and defeated. I watched Kettering-Smythe visit his new house at Fields View almost every day last summer while it was being built. The reason for our demise lies in that house. Corrupt officials and crop saboteurs. My Darling Hanna, I have one last wish, please find out the truth, but most importantly of all, please forgive me. I'm so ashamed. Love Dad. XX.

The detective put the letter down, took a deep breath, and closed her eyes.

It was a huge shock for Hanna when DI James contacted her and informed her that her father's suicide note had come to light. She had quickly composed herself, and agreed to meet the Inspector at the South Essex Police Headquarters the following morning.

With the passage of time, the farmer's daughter had come to terms with the fact that KS had not been involved in the contamination of the fields, and together with the demise of Pasternak Construction she had accepted the fact that the truth as to why her father killed himself might never be known. She had, until receiving the telephone call from the police, accepted the impasse. On seeing her father's familiar hand-writing, the dormant feelings resurfaced. She read the letter twice without showing any emotion. She's reacting exactly as she did at the farm when I told her about her father's death thought the Inspector.

'It does look as if Kettering-Smythe and the developer were up to something after all,' remarked Hanna looking the Inspector in the eye.

'Taken at face value, it would appear so, Hanna,' replied the police officer. 'We are going to reopen the case, and just to keep you in the loop, I've assigned DS Kate Hope to take over from Chris.'

After the meeting Hanna met up with Chris for lunch. His boss had briefed him the day before about the new development, and she had suggested he take the day off so as not to make the visit too uncomfortable for Hanna.

'You kept that quiet,' she said taking comfort in her fiancé's arms.

'It was very difficult not to tell you last night when you phoned.'

'It's not a problem. I understand,' replied Hanna linking arms with her policeman. 'I don't suppose you can come back to London with me? I could do with the company.'

'Sure. Let's skip lunch. I just need to pick up a change of clothes.'

CHAPTER 38

Lady Kay's online business had got off to a good start. The month on month sales were increasing, and it was not long before she realised that the expanding business would outgrow the converted garages. With Sir Michael's encouragement, she decided to refurbish an old barn adjacent to the garages to make space for the expansion. Once the renovation began, the use of the sound bite 'it turned into an absolute nightmare' soon became appropriate.

The restorer's original time estimate was six months. Kay soon discovered that not all workmen were as reliable as Dave Wright, and having to deal with the council planning department, her mood changed from joyful expectation to endless frustration. What she could not understand was why the saving of an old barn, that would eventually fall down anyway, should generate so much red tape and sucking of teeth.

The delayed completion of the barn, however, worked out in Chris and Hanna's favour. It was Father Aldridge who suggested to Hanna that Lady Kay's new barn might be a perfect venue for the wedding reception. Kay, who had been considering a roof wetting party for the new barn, was thrilled with the idea.

With three weeks to go, the wedding arrangements were progressing well. Liz Turner was arranging the flowers, tables and chairs, cutlery and glassware, and a photographer. The food was agreed and menus printed. There were a couple of outstanding issues;

the table seating plan needed to be finalised, and the band was yet to agree a fee.

During the bank holiday weekend in Weatherford, Hanna and Cassie had found Hanna's mum's wedding dress. It had been carefully stored for almost thirty years, and as Hanna took it out of its wrapping, it unfolded like a glistening rose made of satin. To her surprise it fitted perfectly. At the time, the bride-to-be was not sure about the lace sleeves. She had tried it on a number of times since, and with a final stamp of approval from Cassie, she decided not to make any alterations to the dress.

Paul Nel was pleased with his page boy outfit. Bella Nel's flower girl dress was ready as was Chloe Burns' bridesmaid outfit. Chris and his brother Jo had their suits, and very shiny new leather shoes. Much to Hanna's amusement, Cassie, her maid of honour, was not at all comfortable having to wear a chiffon dress AND high heels.

Hanna took out her to do list and ticked off 'corsages'. Who said you couldn't arrange a wedding in less than twelve months she thought. The phone rang.

'Kramer and Partners, Hanna Townsend, good morning.'

'Hanna, it's Lizzie Turner. Do you have a minute, Babes?' Lizzie sounded a bit more flustered than normal.

'Of course I do. What's the matter?'

'Babes, I've decided to close down my wedding business.'

'Why Lizzie? I thought you were doing well.'

'Business is good, Babes, but I've been freaked out by the allergen regulations. I don't want to land up in prison,' replied Lizzie.

'Tell me more, Lizzie,' asked Hanna in surprise.

'Babes, I give my customers probably one of the happiest days of their lives. It's that simple. The problem is if someone with an allergy comes to the wedding and eats something that disagrees with them and they die, I go to prison.' explained the wedding planner.

'But don't you protect yourself by having a list of the allergens that are in the food?' asked the solicitor.

'That's the theory, Babes. If you have a serious allergy surely it's your responsibility not to eat anything other than food that you have prepared for yourself at home? Why would you risk your own life like that? Why must I take on that responsibility? It's daft, Babes. If I step out into the road in front of a car, and get knocked over, it's my fault, not the driver's.'

'Lizzie, I don't really have enough knowledge of the subject to comment. When are you planning to stop?'

'Your wedding is the last one. I will do everything I can to help, but I'm not doing the catering. I'm very sorry for the short notice, Babes.'

'Wow, everything was going so well. Are you sure you won't change your mind?' asked Hanna trying not to sound as if she was begging.

'I've been spooked by this, Babes. I don't want to take the risk.'

'OK, Lizzie. Not to worry. I'm sure we can sort something out. Thanks for letting me know. See you soon.' Hanna put down the phone, sat back in her chair, and let out a long sigh of disbelief. Spoke too soon, she thought. Now what?

Although Hanna tried her best not to think about catering, Lizzie's news was totally unexpected. Teach me a lesson for being so full of myself she thought. It was all going so well, and although I'm not going to tell anyone, I've actually enjoyed organising the wedding.

Hanna phoned Chris and shared the bad news with him. He didn't sound too bothered, and in his usual calm and unemotional way he reassured her that she needn't worry, and they would somehow find another caterer. She was not entirely convinced, and went out for a walk to clear her head. When she returned there was a message to phone Sue Brown, one of Chris' aunts. I wonder how she got hold of my number.

'Sweetheart, Chris has told me about your catering problem. There's no need to worry girl,' the aunt cheerfully told Hanna. 'I'll round up all the aunts, and we'll come over and do the cooking. Forget about the authorities, honey, our cooking has never killed any of our relatives,' laughed Aunty Sue. 'The only thing we need is a big kitchen. Three aunts in a kitchen need a lot of space.' More loud laughter. The problem was solved. They hired the community centre kitchen from Pat Pollock, and a couple of days before the wedding, the aunts arrived and checked into the Green Man.

Hanna had not slept very well, and woke up early. It was her wedding day. She made a cup of tea, and it wasn't long before Cassie joined her in the farmhouse kitchen.

'The big day's arrived,' announced the agronomist, hugging the bride.

'It feels a bit surreal. You spend so much time talking about it, and then it's suddenly here,' replied Hanna.

'Excited?'

'I actually woke up feeling a bit sad, Cas,' replied Hanna feeling slightly guilty about being sad on her wedding day.

'What about?'

'Mum and Dad,' replied Hanna looking down at her cup of tea. 'I'm ok, really. I'm good.'

'Good morning, ladies. Doing anything special today?' smiled Dudley Baines as he burst into the kitchen.

'Oh, for God's sake Dudley, don't you ever give it a rest?' scowled the agronomist.

'Not very often, my love. Hanna have you got an iron? This shirt is more crease than cloth.'

'The ironing board is in the broom cupboard over there in the corner. The iron should be in there as well.'

'Do you know how to use it?' quipped Cassie.

'Nasty, nasty,' replied Dudley giving Cassie a kiss on the forehead.

Preparations continued throughout the morning. The smell of cooking wafted across the valley from the community centre. Two hours before the wedding ceremony was due to start, Lizzie decided there was insufficient room between the tables. She rearranged all of them with the help of Jo who came to her rescue when she called out 'I need some muscle.'

The band 'Marital Bliss' arrived with a van load of equipment. There was an awkward moment when the lead guitarist had a strop because there were not enough plug sockets. He was quickly placated by his fellow band members, before he had the opportunity to revert to his default behaviour of breaking furniture. That was the quiet bit. The noisy bit was 'testing, testing, 1, 2, 3, and incessant blowing into the microphone, before subjecting everyone to 110 decibels in a confined space.

Eventually, everything was ready for the reception. The frantic activity of the morning ended, and attention turned to the church. Tom Burns, in his role as usher, did a superb job. He knew many of the guests. The lanky and at times sullen teenager was replaced by a competent mature young man who, as his mates would say 'owned the space'.

There was great excitement, and amusement, when Chris' family and friends arrived in two 50 seater luxury coaches. Plenty of parking space in the road outside the church masked the problems the bus drivers would have later that afternoon trying to get down the narrow lane to the manor house.

Father Aldridge, suitably attired in his robes, waited patiently for the key players to arrive. *Here Comes the Bride* heralded their arrival, and heads turned to see a smiling Hanna in her perfectly fitting white satin and lace dress walking down the aisle on the arm of Alistair Burns. The Burns family were lifelong friends of the Townsend's, and Hanna had asked Alistair to give her away. They were followed down the aisle by a maid of honour, a bridesmaid, a flower girl, and a page boy.

'This is when you ask me if I have the ring,' whispered Jo.

'Very funny,' replied Chris as he turned to look at Hanna. He caught his mother's eye, and she winked at him. His father looked pleased as punch, as did the aunts who looked as if they were going to start singing and dancing at any moment.

'Just ten more minutes,' pleaded Jessica Burns as she pulled the duvet up over her head. Alistair sat up, turned on the bedside lamp, and reaching over switched off the radio clock alarm.

'I'll come back later for breakfast. You have a lie-in,' he said turning to look at his wife's dormant shape.

'No, no. You're not going out there without having breakfast,' replied Jessica throwing back the bed clothes, and sitting up.

Alistair and Jessica had reluctantly left the wedding just before midnight. The winter wheat drilling was about to start, and as luck would have it, the seed drill that a number of the farmers in the area co-owned, had been allocated to Alistair the day after Hanna's wedding. Jessica would not allow her husband to start a long and arduous day without having a proper breakfast. It was something she had always done.

'What a great party,' commented Jessica as she put a tray of smoked back bacon and pork sausages into the oven. 'Hanna looked beautiful, don't you think?'

'Yeh, she looked ok,' replied Alistair as he handed his wife a cup of tea.

'Oh, Alistair. She looked better than ok. That was Sarah's wedding dress, you know.'

'I must say it was good to see her happy. Isn't it bizarre how life works out. There's Hanna without any family, and the next minute she has more relations than any of us.'

'God, weren't the aunts a hoot. The food was absolutely delicious. Makes me so jealous. Actually everyone had a great time,' smiled Jessica opening the oven door and standing back as a wave of heat made its escape. 'Bacons done, sausages need a couple of minutes. Scrambled or fried?'

'Fried, please. Another tea?' asked the farmer.

'Coffee, please.' A few minutes later the breakfasts were ready. 'This should keep you going till lunchtime,' remarked the farmer's wife as she put the plates of food on the table. 'Coffee and toast at half ten?'

'Sure,' replied Alistair liberally sprinkling salt and pepper on his fried eggs.

'Tom seemed to be enjoying himself. He was quite animated, and looked so grown-up all of a sudden,' remarked Jessica.

'A whole afternoon away from his video games. There's hope for him yet.' smiled Alistair.

'Well, your favourite child certainly looked very pretty in her dress. Didn't Paul and Bella look cute. They are such well-behaved children. It's scary.'

'I'll be sorry to see Moz and Elsa go. I hope they do return.' Alistair swallowed the last of his coffee and kissed Jessica on the forehead. 'Thanks a lot for the lovely breakfast. It was delicious. See you later.'

'It's my pleasure. Take care out there. Love you,' replied Jessica. The farmer stopped momentarily and looked at his wife.

'Love you too.'

CHAPTER 39

Grant Watt, the ultralight pilot, who crashed at Oak Tree Farm had arranged, with the help of the Air Ambulance Charity, a function to thank those who had rescued him.

The drive to Earlsfield Aerodrome was a bitter sweet journey for Moz and Elsa. They were looking forward to meeting the pilot, but sad that it was their last night in England. This time tomorrow they would be at Heathrow about to board an Airbus for Johannesburg.

'Do you think the pilot will let me sit in the helicopter,' asked Paul.

'If you ask nicely, I'm sure he will,' replied Elsa.

'Well he won't let you fly it, you're too small,' quipped Bella.

'OK you two, stop it,' interrupted Moz. 'We're here.' The children got out of the car, and to their surprise and joy, Lucas Galkeviciene and Dominic Babickas were there talking to Alistair and Jessica.

'You kept this a surprise, Alistair' smiled Moz shaking hands with the Lithuanians.

'I thought it was only right for them to be here. Got them a flight into Stansted. Moz, I don't know if you remember James Walsh, the helicopter pilot?'

'Of course I do. Good to see you again, Mr Walsh,' replied Moz shaking the pilot's hand. 'This is my wife, Elsa.'

'Pleased to meet you Elsa.' They shook hands and for a brief moment their eyes met. Elsa felt herself starting to blush, and quickly let go of the pilot's hand. 'Let's go inside, everyone's waiting,' suggested the pilot.

Grant, in a wheelchair, was still recovering from his injuries, and gave a short speech thanking everyone for saving his life. There was a bit of gentle heckling from Alistair about the wisdom of saving a GM crop protestor. Dr Emily Jones and Paramedic Kamal Khan explained what their roles were as part of the helicopter response team, and when asked by the children, were happy to show them what was in their medical bags. Paul got the opportunity to sit in the red and yellow helicopter which was parked on the hardstand in front of the hangar. Not surprisingly, he announced to his parents that he wanted to be a helicopter pilot when he grew up.

'Mum, ask Mr Walsh if he'll let you sit in his helicopter. It's awesome,' suggested Paul.

'It's getting a bit late, and we have a busy day tomorrow,' Elsa replied.

Two weeks had passed since Moz, Elsa and the children had returned home to Kempdale. It had been a joyous home-coming. Their respective parents were overjoyed to see the grandchildren, and were amazed at how much they had grown. The school year was coming to an end, but both Bella and Paul were keen to see their friends, and had decided to go back to school for the remaining two weeks. It only took a couple of days, and they were back in their old school routine.

Invitations from the neighbouring farmers to come over and have a braai were plentiful. The first few nights were spent sitting in the shade of farmhouse patios, drinking Cape wine, and watching the searing sun set on a scorched earth.

The winter wheat had been harvested the week before Moz's return, and the farm workers all clambered onto a tractor and trailer, drove down to the silos and proudly showed the farmer the fruit of their summer labour. This was followed by a rowdy welcome home party of lamb chops, pap, gravy and sorghum beer.

When the home-coming euphoria passed, Moz and Elsa were left feeling empty. They were finding it difficult to settle down. Their stay in England had changed them. Their families and friends were not interested in what they had experienced over the past year. Their lives had stood still while they were away. Moz and Elsa had changed. They had a severe dose of wanderlust, and wanted the adventure to carry on.

One Saturday afternoon in early December, the Nels were returning from having had lunch with Elsa's parents. It was a typical Kalahari day; cloudless, sweltering heat, and a hot wind that lifted the dry red soil and carried it along in small crimson dust clouds. Moz turned into the brick-paved driveway and stopped the 4x4 in front of the double garage doors. The family got out, and two men appeared from around the corner of the house. Each were armed with an AK-47 assault rifle.

'Hey, what are you doing here?' shouted Elsa.

'Give us your keys,' answered the thinner of the two men pointing his rifle at Moz who was standing in front of the 4x4.

'Bella, Paul, run to granny and grandpa, quick, don't stop.'

'But ....'

'No buts Paul. Go. Run,' replied Elsa. 'For God sake do as you're told.' The children turned and ran down the driveway, across the road and into the maize field opposite the house. One of the gunmen raised his rifle and aimed it at the fleeing children.

'Leave the children, Jonas, leave the children. Let them go,' shouted the thin gunman. Jonas lowered his rifle, and turning pointed it at Moz.

'You will have to kill me. I won't give you my keys. Get off my land,' hissed Moz moving towards the thin gunman. There was a short burst of gunfire, followed by the hollow ping of 7.92mm cartridges bouncing off the brick driveway. Elsa looked across at Moz as he fell forward clutching his chest. She intuitively dived on top of her husband and covered him with her body. She lay there with her eyes closed, waiting for the inevitable.

After what felt like an eternity, the farmer's wife heard the 4x4 being started, reverse and then drive off down the dirt road in a plume of dust. She waited a couple of minutes before moving. All was quiet. She stood up, and took her mobile out of her dress pocket. Kneeling down next to Moz, she called the emergency services. To her surprise her call was answered. It's highly unlikely that an ambulance will arrive she thought as she dialled her parents. Her father answered, and said he was on his way with the first aid kit. She then phoned her parents-in-law, and told Moz's mother about the children.

She held her husband's hand and looked down at his perspiring ashen face. He was drifting in and out of consciousness. He was bleeding profusely. His breathing was laboured.

'Mozzie, look at me,' Elsa pleaded. He opened his eyes, and looked at her. 'Remember the snow, Mozzie, remember the snow.'

Jessica Burns turned on her tablet and sat waiting for it to boot. It was Wednesday evening, and she wanted to book her regular Friday morning online grocery delivery slot. As the boot completed, an audio alert announced that there was an unopened email. She tapped the icon, and was surprised to see that it was a message from Elsa Nel.

To: Jessica Burns
From: Elsa Nel
Subject: Moz
Hi Jessica.
I'm sorry to be the bearer of very sad news. A terrible thing happened to us on Saturday. We were car hijacked by two gunmen at our home. We had been visiting my parents. Thankfully, the children were not harmed. They escaped and ran to safety. Moz tried to stop the gunmen taking the 4x4, but was shot in the chest and stomach. He died on Sunday morning in hospital. His funeral is next week on Wednesday. We are devastated. My only comfort is that the children are unhurt, and thankfully I was not raped. I've been spared so that I can look after my children. I will write again once things settle down.
Please send my love to the family.
Love.
Elsa.

Jessica was shocked at the news. She picked up the tablet, and took it through to the lounge were Alistair was watching the weather.

'Terrible news from Elsa.'

'Why what's happened?' Alistair muted the tv and took the laptop from Jessica's trembling hands. The farmer read the email and seeing the tears running down Jessica's cheeks, put the tablet down on the coffee table, and held her tightly in his arms.

'Moz and Elsa often mentioned how safe they felt here in England,' sniffed Jessica.

'Murdered for a poxy 4X4. The world has gone bloody mad,' exclaimed Alistair.

CHAPTER 40

DI James entered the interview room followed closely by her sergeant.

'Good afternoon, Mr Kettering-Smythe. This is DS Kate Hope.' The two police officers sat down opposite a dejected looking KS. Placing a purple file on the table, the Inspector opened it, and slowly read the top document. 'I sincerely hope you will be more forthcoming with the truth than you were back in February,' commented the Inspector raising her head, and looking the parish councillor in the eye. 'I would strongly suggest you co-operate with us,' she said tapping the file. KS looked down at his folded hands, avoided the Inspector's stare, and forlornly nodded his head. 'Ok. Let's start right at the beginning with Potts Lane. What exactly happened that Saturday morning?' KS glanced at the sergeant as she opened a wire-bound A5 notebook and started to write.

'I was on my way back from the gym in Great Dunsford, driving down Potts Lane towards London Road, when I came across Brian Townsend's Land Rover parked opposite a gap in the hedgerow. I stopped.'

'Why did you stop?' asked the Inspector.

'I'm not sure. It's not unusual to see local farmer's vehicles parked up. The sun had not yet come up, and I suppose it being so early and still quite dark, I thought Brian might have broken down or something. I looked out across the fields through the gap in the hedgerow, but couldn't see anything. He was nowhere to be seen. I went back to the 4x4 and opened the front passenger door. There was an invoice lying on the seat. I picked it up, saw it was for tractor tyres, and then realised that there was handwriting on the back of it. It was a suicide note from Brian to his daughter Hanna.'

'With Mr Townsend nowhere to be seen, an abandoned vehicle and a suicide letter, did it not cross your mind that he might be close by?' asked the DI.

'Inspector, it is easy to sit here in this air-conditioned room and think these things out logically. The truth is I panicked. I was holding a piece of paper in which Brian was telling Hanna that I was the reason for his actions. There was my name, in black and white.' Despite the air-conditioning, KS was perspiring.

'Would you like a break, Mr Kettering-Smythe?' asked the Inspector.

'No, I'm fine. I want to get this over and done with as quickly as possible. I wouldn't mind a glass of water though.' The DI nodded to the sergeant who dutifully left the room in search of water.

'So what happened next?'

'I quickly folded the note, and put it in one of the inside pockets of my wax jacket. I then went home to shower before heading back to the shoot at Oak Tree Farm. Before you ask Inspector, you are correct, taking the note was a stupid thing to do. I simply panicked. In hindsight, I should have left it in the Land Rover, and tried to find Brian.' DI James paused to allow her sergeant to give KS his glass of water.

'So what happened to the note?' continued the DI.

'When you eventually allowed us to go home, I left without my jacket, and only realised my mistake when I got home. I returned to Oak Tree Farm, and Jessica and Alistair Burns helped me look for it. It was nowhere to be seen. Somebody else had obviously taken it.'

'Well, Mr Kettering-Smythe I have some news for you. We have recently received information relating to Mr Townsend's suicide note. In actual fact we are in possession of the letter, and from what you have just told us, I'm of the opinion that we have also found your missing jacket.'

'Who had it?' asked the surprised estate agent.

'Jeremy Hughes,' replied the DI.

'What was he doing with it?' KS blurted out in frustration.

'Let me hand over to DS Hope. She'll fill you in.'

'Thank you ma'am. Mr Kettering-Smythe, not only do we have the letter, and the jacket, but there is strong evidence to suggest that Mr Hughes was blackmailing somebody. Was it you?'

'Um, um. No.'

'Are you sure?'

'If I was being blackmailed, surely I'm the victim. Why are you treating me as if I'm guilty?' KS was starting to feel like a trapped animal.

'What interested us, was the fact that Mr Townsend's letter clearly implicated you in some underhand deal with the developer who built your current house. This was the reason why Mr Hughes was blackmailing you, wasn't it?'

'All lies. Absolute rubbish,' insisted KS.

'We think differently, Mr Kettering-Smythe. A careful forensic look at the accounts of the now defunct Pasternak Construction shows an endemic practice of selling new houses, at prices below the market rate, to key people who are in a position to influence the planning approval process.'

'That's preposterous. I want to call my lawyer now,' shouted KS getting up from his seat.

'Sit down, Mr Kettering-Smythe,' warned DI James. 'We'll take a break while we wait for your lawyer to arrive.'

When John Harber arrived, the police officers provided the lawyer with the details of the allegations against his client. KS and the lawyer where given time to discuss the allegations in private, and the interview resumed, under caution, five hours after having been adjourned.

'Mr Kettering-Smythe I would like to return to the subject of the blackmail. The thing that intrigues me is the fact that you paid the blackmailer. It is behaviour that tells me you have something to hide. What is it that you are hiding?' asked the Inspector.

'My client is not obliged to answer that question, Inspector. It has no relevance to the allegations being made against him,' responded the lawyer.

'You're absolutely correct Mr Harber, but I would have thought with your client in so much trouble, he would like to make life easier for himself. We have the evidence, all he has to do is tell us what he has been up to,' replied the DI. She paused for a moment while she paged through the documents in the purple file. 'Very well, let's move on. Mr Kettering-Smythe you appear to have a number of people out there with an axe to grind. Firstly, we're given information about the blackmail, and then a few weeks later copies of invoices pertaining to the charity of which you are the chairman land up on my desk. Who said a policeman's lot is not a happy one?' smiled the Inspector. 'I'll spare you the denial. It would appear that you have been defrauding the charity using false invoices for a number of years.' KS turned, and looking at his lawyer shrugged his shoulders.

'Inspector may I have a few minutes with my client please?'

When the two police officers returned to the interview room half an hour later, a defeated Parish Councillor told the Inspector that he was ready to make a full statement. Statement completed, he was bailed pending further enquiries, and two weeks later the estate agent was asked to return to the police station. He was charged with criminal fraud, accepting a bribe while in office, and attempting to pervert the course of justice.

THE END

NICK HAYTER

THE DIAMOND RUN

look out for this new title

CHAPTER 1
December 2019

Max Clarke drove slowly through the open wooden gate leading to the St Giles' car park. There were already two rows of parked cars; Maddy would have been touched by the turnout, he thought. Avoiding the uneven ground and the large puddles, he manoeuvred his car into a gap between a mud-splashed SUV and the stone-wall to his left.

He got out of the car, stretched his stiff back, and side-stepping what looked like the deepest of the puddles, headed towards a small group of people standing near the church door. He relaxed slightly when he realised he knew most of the group. He stopped and greeted everyone; handshakes, accompanied by words of condolence. The cloudless sky and sunshine was mentioned, as was the countryside covered in an inch of frost and the temperature of -8C.

'Dad, thank God you are here,' exclaimed Max's son Josh as he appeared at the church door.

'What's the problem?'

'She's here,' exclaimed the son.

'She?'

'Lauren.'

'You've got to be fucking joking,' exclaimed the father. 'Where?'

'She's in the church already.'

'Go and get her. I want a word.' Josh dashed back into the church, and Max could hear his wife remonstrating that she was not going anywhere, and had no wish to talk to his father.

Max paced up and down outside the church, and was about to go in and fetch his wife when she appeared accompanied by his son. The small group of the congregation had not moved. They stood in silence, and watched the family drama unfolding before them. It was like watching a three-star Netflix Original. Max motioned to Lauren and Josh to follow him around the side of the church in search of a bit of privacy.

'Lauren, what do you think you are doing? How dare you,' riled the husband.

'Max, I have every right to be here. I have endured years and years of playing second fiddle to that woman.'

'Maddy, her name is Maddy. You could have at least had the decency to discuss attending the funeral with me. Where did you stay last night?'

'I stayed at some pub in Haddington.'

'Josh, did you know about his?'

'I had absolutely no idea that this was going to happen.'

'And what are you wearing. This is not a cocktail party.'

'Dad, that's enough,' interjected Josh.

'I'm sorry to interrupt, but the hearse will be here in a couple of minutes. A modicum of decorum would be appreciated,' requested the priest as he appeared from around the corner of the church. Nobody ever dared to reprimand Max for his behaviour, embarrassed he apologised to the vicar.

'You can stay for the church service, and then you leave. I don't want you there when we bury Maddy.

Do you understand?' Max whispered to his wife as they entered the church.

This is the BBC News at two o'clock. The Met Office has, in the past hour, issued a further ten flood warnings for western parts of the country stretching from Cheshire to Cumbria, and as far north as Ayrshire and Edinburgh. Prestwick Airport has been closed since mid-morning due to torrential rain. North Yorkshire and other eastern counties are bracing themselves for more rain later this afternoon. Almost 10 centimetres or 4 inches of rain fell yesterday in the Yorkshire area resulting in local flooding.

Max pressed the audio button on the steering wheel, and the radio faded away. He had been driving for a just over three hours, and much of it had been in heavy rain since crossing the English/Scottish Border. The rain was not a problem per se. The challenge was the spray on the A1 single-carriageway from the other traffic, especially the lorries; it required concentration, added to the journey time, and was quite exhausting.

Max knew the road like the back of his hand. He had done the journey from home to East Lothian and back so many times. He knew the distances off the top of his head, the time it took to travel between the various places along the route, every comfort break as well as the best places to stop for food. I wonder if this is the last time I'll be doing this journey he thought to himself as he approached the turn-off for Thirsk.

It was time for a break. Thirsk was one of Maddy's favourite stops. When they had done the journey together, and were not in a hurry, they would stop at the little Yorkshire town with its picturesque market square for a meal. The phone rang.

'Hi Josh.'

'Hi Dad. Just seen the new weather warnings. Phoning to find out if you are ok.'

'Everything is fine this end. The rain started just this side of the border. Haven't seen any flooding though. I've turned off the A1 and heading for Thirsk.'

'I don't think that's a good idea, Dad?'

'It'll be fine. Don't worry. Prestwick has been closed. Is Edinburgh ok?'

'Yeh. The rain has eased off quite considerably. Dad, I know it is none of my business, but please go easy on Lauren. I don't think she meant any harm.' Max shook his head and smiled, so much for the Josh's concern about the weather.

'I've already text her and apologised for my outburst. I only wish she had discussed it with me first.'

'I can understand that. OK I must go. The flight's been called. Talk later. Love ya.'

'Thanks for your concern. You take care out there.'

The low grey rain clouds hung heavily in the skies as Max drove towards a place that held so many memories. He hadn't realised how stressful the past couple of days had been; Maddy's funeral had emotionally drained him, and he was tired. His tiredness made the familiar countryside look uninspiring; wet flat farmland with low hedgerow, and the buildings dotted along the roadside damp and drab. He drove slowly over the single lane bridge that crossed the River Swale. The level of the water was much higher than normal, and it was starting to spread out over the adjoining fields. Yorkshire in the sunshine was a special place, but not today; it looked gloomy.

Max's back was starting to ache. Josh was right he thought, this was not a good idea. He decided to abandon Thirsk, and five miles from the market town he pulled into the car park of the The Golden Coach. Although they had driven passed this pub on many occasions, he and Maddy had never stopped there. Getting slowly out of the car, it was a relief to stand up, and before going into the pub, he walked slowly up and down the length of the car park a couple of times to stretch out his stiff back.

'Good afternoon, Sir. Welcome,' greeted a smiling bartender in his mid-twenties sporting a peaky blinder haircut.

'Afternoon. Am I too late for something to eat,' replied Max.

'Not at all,' replied the young man passing a menu over the counter. Max's phone started to ring again. He put the menu down, and went outside.

'Amy.'

'Max I'm so sorry to disturb you. Can you talk?'

'Yes. I've stopped for a bite to eat.'

'How was the service?'

'All fine. There were quite a lot of people there. I was pleasantly surprised. What's the problem?'

'Garlick Agricultural want to bring the demonstration forward to tomorrow.'

'I'll be there,' replied Max without hesitating.

'Are you sure? Don't you want a couple of days off?'

'Definitely not. I need to keep busy. While my phone was off this morning, I received eight voicemail messages. I'll deal with them when I get home. In the meantime, if anyone is looking for me, tell them I'll be back in the office tomorrow. I'm sure things can wait until then.'

'Of course they can. Enjoy your lunch. See you tomorrow. Safe journey.'

It was starting to rain again, and Max dashed back inside the pub. He picked up the menu he had left on the bar counter, ordered a pint of Yorkshire Gold and made his way to a window table looking out at a wet and muddy beer garden with waterlogged wooden tables and benches. He was not feeling very hungry, and skimmed through the menu. He ordered fish and chips, with mushy peas and sat back stretching out his back and legs.

Apart from the youngster behind the bar, he was the only person in the pub. He looked around at his surroundings. The pub was adequate, if a bit tired. It had lost much of its traditional pub feel when it was upgraded to a gastro pub; most probably in the early 1990s. Obligatory Lowry prints adorned the walls. Its overdue its next makeover thought the weary traveller.

Max stared out of the window at the drowning garden furniture, and his thoughts turned to Maddy. I can remember the first day I met her. It's as if it were yesterday, and yet our time together on the diamond mine feels like two, three lifetimes ago.

ABOUT THE AUTHOR

Nick has had a long and successful career in aviation. He flew for 20 years, retrained as an accountant, and three degrees later, embarked on an aviation management career. For the last eight years he has assisted his wife Kerry run her high street business in the small rural English town in which they live. 3 years ago Nick had a stroke which resulted in him having to, excuse the pun, throttle back. He has no recollection of the first year following the stroke. His memory function began to improve slowly, logical thought started to return, and although he was still confused, he found he was able to write coherently. A couple of sentences became paragraphs; a few paragraphs became pages; pages became chapters. The result being his first book *The Lost Harvest*. Last year Nick returned to work, albeit part-time, and continues to write. He has started writing his second novel *The Diamond Run*. All profits from his books will be donated to help fund stroke research.